# Praise for Barbara Claypole White's debut novel, *The Unfinished Garden*

"I learned so much about myself from this story—
that fear doesn't have to hold me back, but rather, it can move me forward.
*The Unfinished Garden* is a touching and accomplished debut."
—Diane Chamberlain, bestselling author of *The Secret Life of CeeCee Wilkes*

"White…conveys the condition of OCD, and how it creates havoc
in one's life and the lives of loved ones, with style and grace,
never underplaying the seriousness of the disorder."
—*RT Book Reviews*

"A powerful story of friendship and courage in the midst of frightening
circumstances….I highly recommend this wonderful love story."
—*Bergers' Book Reviews*

"A mesmerizing tale of fear, loss, and love.
Tilly and James are richly drawn and wonderfully flawed characters
who embody the contradictions and imperfections that exist in all of us.
Barbara Claypole White has created a novel as beautiful and complex,
dark and light, sweet and sensuous as Tilly's beloved garden."
—Joanne Rendell, author of *The Professors' Wives' Club*

"Barbara Claypole White has created such a likable, adorable, entertaining
main character that I never wanted this book to end."
—Lydia Netzer, author of *Shine Shine Shine*

"I found the writing style in *The Unfinished Garden* reminiscent of
Rosamunde and Robin Pilcher. As a fan of both, I truly enjoyed this book
and look forward to many more from Barbara Claypole White."
—Julie Kibler, author of *Calling Me Home*

Also by Barbara Claypole White

THE UNFINISHED GARDEN

# BARBARA CLAYPOLE WHITE

# THE

# *In-Between*

# HOUR

**HARLEQUIN® MIRA®**

Recycling programs
for this product may
not exist in your area.

ISBN-13: 978-0-7783-1475-2

THE IN-BETWEEN HOUR

For questions and comments about the quality of this book, please contact us at CustomerService@Harlequin.com.

**Printed in U.S.A.**

First printing: January 2014
10 9 8 7 6 5 4 3 2 1

For my sister, Susan Rose
And for my friend Leslie Gildersleeve

Do you know me in the gloaming,
Gaunt and dusty gray with roaming?
—From "Flower-Gathering" by Robert Frost


Alone we can do so little; together we can do so much
—Helen Keller

# THE

# *In-Between*

# HOUR

# AUTHOR'S NOTE

**O**cconeechee Mountain became a North Carolina State Natural Area in 1999. Rising above the Eno River, the summit is the highest point between the town of Hillsborough, Orange County, and the Atlantic Ocean. Rare plants growing on the mountain and the presence of the brown elfin butterfly suggest the habitat has changed little since the last Ice Age.

**The Occaneechi Band of the Saponi Nation** is a small Native American community located primarily in Pleasant Grove, Alamance County. In 2002, it won state recognition as North Carolina's eighth official Indian tribe.

**The seventeenth-century Occaneechi village** in Hillsborough was excavated between 1983 and 1995. The Occaneechi Band of the Saponi Nation held its first powwow there in 1995, and John Blackfeather blessed the ground in 1997. Reconstruction of the village began shortly afterward and was completed in 2004. The village has been moved to the ancestral lands in Pleasant Grove.

For information on the **Occaneechi Homeland Preservation Project,** please visit www.obsn.org.

For information on the **Occaneechi Path,** also called the **Indian Trading Path,** please visit tradingpath.org.

# ONE

Will imagined silence. The silence of snowfall in the forest. The silence at the top of a crag. But eighty floors below his roof garden, another siren screeched along Central Park West.

Nausea nibbled—a hungry goldfish gumming him to death. Maybe this week's diet of Zantac and PBR beer was to blame. Or maybe grief was a degenerative disease, destroying him from the inside out. Dissolving his organs. One. By. One.

The screensaver on his MacBook Air, a rainbow of tentacles that had once reminded him to watch for shooting stars, mutated into a kraken: an ancient monster dragging his life beneath the waves. How long since he'd missed his deadline? His agent had been supportive, his editor generous, but patience—even for clients who churned out global bestsellers—expired.

Another day when he'd failed to resuscitate his crap work-in-progress; another day when Agent Dodds continued to dangle from the helicopter; another day without a strategy for his hero of ten years that wasn't a fatal "Let go, dude. Just let go."

The old-fashioned ring tone of his iPhone burst into the night as expected. Almost on cue. His dad's memory might be jouncing around too much for either of them to follow, but it continued to hold both their lives hostage.

*Answer, aim for the end of the call, get there.*

"Hey, Dad."

"Fucking bastards. They're—"

"Fucking bastards. You told me earlier." *Fifty-seven minutes earlier.*

Finally, this vacuous loop of repetition had given them conversation, and always it started with the same two words: *fucking bastards.*

"Fucking bastards won't let me sit out and talk to the crows. Took away my bird call. Said I were disturbin' folks."

"We talked about this last time you called, Dad." Will kept his voice flat, even. Calm. Defusing anger was an old skill—the lone positive side effect of his batshit-insane childhood. And emotional distance? He had that honed before he'd turned eighteen. "I told you I'd look at the contract in the morning. And you promised to take a temazepam and go to bed."

There had to be some way to persuade the old man to meet with a psychologist, some way to unpick the damage of Jack Nicholson's performance in *One Flew Over the Cuckoo's Nest.*

"Fucking bastards. Want to steal my Wild Turkey, too."

His dad veered off on the usual rant: *trash the staff of Hawk's Ridge Retirement Community—check; pause to exclude the new art teacher with the cute smile—check; ask Will when he last noticed a woman's smile—check; hurl expletives at ol' possum face, the director—check.* Strange, how the old man failed to drop his *g*'s with the *f* word.

A retired grave digger who'd dropped out of school at sixteen to work in the cotton mill—*third shift*—Jacob Shepard might refer to himself as dumber than a rock, but he'd read every history book in the Orange County Library before retirement. The old man was an underachiever by choice, devoting himself to the only thing that mattered: loving his Angeline.

His dad was cussing again. *One obscenity, two obscenities, three obscenities...four.*

All those years in the family shack, neither of them had sworn. Wouldn't have dared. Four foot ten, magical and mad, Angeline Shepard had ruled the house with more mood swings than a teenage despot. There had been no room for anyone else to flex temper muscles. Raising a voice in his mother's domain would have been akin to standing in front of the biggest fucking bonfire and pouring on enough gasoline to fuel an Airbus. Great, now *he* was swearing. Will never swore (*batshit* didn't count). But since his dad had started calling to unleash rage ten, fifteen times a day, Will's psyche had slipped into battle-fatigue mode.

Will sighed. "There are rules about drinking in your room. You know that."

"I'm eighty years old, son. I reckon I'm old enough to partake, if I so choose."

"But you're a loud drunk, Dad."

"So I pick my banjo—"

"And tell people they're dickheads."

"That's why I don't talk to no one 'cept you. Half them folks in here is dickheads, son. Half them is."

"And the other half?" Will didn't mean to smile.

"Old-timers who get to complainin' about bladder control. At least I don't need no adult diapers, and my health is still good, pretty good. Why you at home of an evenin', son? You need to be out dancin' with an angel like your mama."

"I write at night. You know that, Dad."

*Darkness keeps me alive, keeps me on the edge. Keeps me sharp.* There was always a moment, in the middle of the night, when the world hardly breathed. When he could write safe in the knowledge that no one would intrude, that he had nothing to fear. But *New York Times* bestselling author Will Shepard wasn't writing. Wasn't sleeping in his institutional white bedroom, either. These days he catnapped fully clothed on his leather sofa—as if he were a millionaire hobo.

Even when he managed to close his eyes, there was no peace. His favorite dream in which he glided like an owl above the forest had contorted into a nightmare. In his subconscious state, Will didn't drift on air currents anymore— he stumbled through the woods on Occoneechee Mountain. Searching for, but never finding, escape.

"So when you goin' to start livin' that dream of yours, son? Find a woodland property with a driveway that's impassable after a real heavy snowfall?"

"That was a kid's fantasy. I'm never moving back to North Carolina, you know that."

*You know that.* Why keep bashing his dad over the head with all that he'd forgotten?

A gust of wind whipped through the chocolate mimosa in the huge glazed pot. Buffeted, the delicate leaflets held on and bounced back. *You can do this, Will. You can do this.*

"The new guy, Bernie, who just moved in down the hall, his grandkids took him to that fancy diner on Main Street last Sunday. You know how long it's been since I've had blueberry pancakes?"

When did the old man start caring about pancakes?

"You know what they give us for breakfast? Little boxes of cereal fit for kids. You know how long it's been since I've eaten anywhere real nice? I want blueberry pancakes. And I want to see my grandbaby, goddamn it. When you bringin' Freddie to visit?"

Time slowed or maybe stopped. Will was at the end of a tunnel, his dad's voice muffled as it said, over and over, "Willie?"

Will's arm shot across the wrought-iron table, smashing an empty water glass to the concrete. A spill of shards spread.

Unwanted memories multiplied, images tumbled: Frederick and Cassandra in the car moments before it crashed; Will driving through the night to Hawk's Ridge with news no grandfather should ever have to hear; his dad flailing and screaming before the security men pinned him down, before a nurse sedated him. And in the months that followed, a never-ending cycle of short-term memory loss and anger. The old man vented, forgot, repeated. Alcohol didn't help.

"Freddie with his mama this week?"

Will ground his knuckle into his temple. "Yeah. He's with his *mama*." A half-truth that kicked him in the chest like a full lie.

Was this his dad's new reality—living with a mind so broken that it found fault with the breakfast menu and yet erased family trauma? Would Will have to constantly torture his dad with the news that had felled them both? Certain sentences, no matter how brief, should never be repeated. Never. If his dad could forget the crash, could he, one day, forget Freddie?

"You tell Freddie's mama to have him call his granddaddy."

"I can't!" Will didn't mean to yell, really, *really* didn't mean to yell, but he could hear Cassandra taunting him: *So, William. You're a father.* She always called him William, pronouncing it Willi-*amm,* treating his name the way she treated life—with a wild exaggeration that had led only to tragedy. A scene flashed—an illusion. A little boy and his mother caught between realms of life and death. Traveling from the plane of existence to a blank page of nothing. "I can't because… they're traveling."

Shallow, jagged breaths stabbed his throat. Blood thundered around his skull; a frenzy of lights exploded across his vision. Airway closing; heart fluttering; pulse yo-yoing.

Will sucked in oxygen with a whooshing sound, then exhaled quietly. He would reduce everything to the skills that enabled him to scale a rock face with his hands and his feet and his mind. He would focus on nothing but finding balance in this moment in time, on finding a good, solid hold.

"I…I don't remember, Willie. I…I can't remember stuff."

This, too, was part of the daily roller coaster. The realization that his grizzly bear of a dad had become a featherless fledgling fallen from the nest. Will could end the conversation right now. Make some excuse and get off the phone. But what was the chance his dad would remember any of this? Zero. Tomorrow would bring a fresh memory wipe. Tomorrow, Will's computer screen would still swirl with patterns, not words. Tomorrow, his five-year-old son would still be dead.

"Where, Willie? Where they travelin'?"

Will stared up at the blinking lights of a jet floating across the black sky, carrying families toward new memories. He'd never taken Freddie on a plane, but he'd planned their first trip in his mind. Europe, they were going to Europe as soon as Freddie was old enough to appreciate the art, the architecture, the history.

"Europe." Will swallowed hard. "Listen, I've gotta go. Get some sleep and we'll talk tomorrow."

"Okay, son. Okay."

Will whispered, "Good night, old man."

But the line was dead.

Will scooped up his laptop and walked back into his empty apartment. Out in the hallway, the elevator dinged. A couple passed his front door, stabbing each other with words. The woman would win the fight. She was the one setting the tempo, as Cassandra had done. He'd never figured out why, eighteen months after their affair fizzled, Cass contacted him to suggest he meet the son he hadn't known existed until that very moment. As an heiress she didn't need child support, and the ground rules were set from the beginning: Freddie's my son; you're not listed on the birth certificate; you see him if and when I decide.

He should have fought for his son.

"Munchkin, I'm sorry," Will said.

*Sorry for not keeping you safe. Sorry for being a coward.*

His cowardice slid out as easily as the fast and furious plots that had made him a thirty-four-year-old literary powerhouse. Corporation Will Shepard careened from success to success, despite the fact that its CEO had been writing-by-numbers for years. When fans looked at him, they saw nothing but the glitter of achievement, which was the way his staff tweeted and scripted his life. Everything was about creating the cardboard cutout.

Only fatherhood was real.

He'd been a good dad—patient, fun, firm. Although there had been a few too many online purchases from FAO Schwarz. Not that he was trying to buy Freddie's love. He'd just wanted Freddie to have everything Will himself had never had. But not in the material sense. A young kid should believe that he was the center of his dad's universe. Because once you realized your happiness mattered to no one but you, life was a slalom ride through loblolly pines—until you crashed into the revelation that all your relationships were severely messed up. Except for fatherhood. From day one, he'd cleared out space physically and psychologically for his son.

Freddie looked at Will—all five feet seven inches of him—

and saw a dragon slayer! The invincible hero! A storyteller who could answer the only question that mattered: "What happened next, Daddy?"

Will placed his laptop in the middle of his desk and stared at the drawing on the wall. Two colorful stickmen—one big, one small—were holding hands and celebrating the day they met. March 30. "Happy Our Day," Freddie had said, jumping up and down. "Mommy helped me pick out the frame in a huge store. *Huuuuuge!*"

Not so long ago, Will had believed that if his apartment were on fire, he would risk everything to save his laptop. But now it contained nothing more than a stalled-out, unnamed manuscript, and his only possession worth saving was Freddie's drawing.

Will flopped onto his leather sofa and covered his eyes with his right arm. Storytelling had always been his escape and his shield. His last line of defense against the truth. And for the first time in his life, he was without a story.

Jacob twisted his hands around the phone. Some thought—just out of reach.

*Where you hidin', thought?*

It were warm in his room, too warm. All summer, it been too cold. Most non-Carolina folk didn't understand how to live, wanted to be sealed up all nice and tight with air-conditionin'. He and Angeline never had no air-conditionin'. No sir. And now it were too hot. Couldn't even manage his own goddamn heat. But them dickheads, they couldn't control him. They could take away his bird call and try to take away his Wild Turkey—if they could find it. But they didn't know what they was in for, 'cos Jacob Shepard, Jr., eighty years old with a mind shot to shit, were gonna fight.

"Ha," he said, liked the way it sounded and repeated it. "Ha!"

If only he were outside sittin' by a fire, punchin' it with a stick. He'd use hickory on that thing, make it nice and toasty. That were his kind of heat.

Jacob threw the phone on his bed, his narrow only-for-one bed, and heaved open his window. No moonlight tonight, no stars. No owl to call to. No trains. When Angeline disappeared into one of her spells, he would listen for the rumblin' and the whistlin' of the trains—sounds as soothin' as real heavy rain on a tin roof.

He inhaled the night. Couldn't see the forest, but it were out there, waitin'. He could smell cedar. Sweetest smell in the world. You burn that stuff and *mmm-hmm, fannnntastic.* He made a smudge once that were just plum cedar dust. Willie used to love that. Said it were like Christmas all over again.

A man could suffocate in this shithole of a hotel. Stank of bleach and death. 'Course that could be part of the plan to hurry the inmates along their journey to the spirit world. Death were comin' faster than it should, thanks to them dickheads.

Freddie were on his mind. Freddie.

Freddie loved all them stories about his grave-diggin' granddaddy. Like the time at the cemetery he'd...what? What had he done? What! He circled his room and concentrated real hard, but that trickster memory kept on hidin' from him.

He slapped the table. White, round, new, Will had bought it without permission. Why'd he keep buyin' furniture and payin' bills as if his daddy couldn't afford to?

He'd been happy in the shack with his memories of Angeline. The good memories, only the good memories. Why couldn't he stay in the shack? He reached for the pen next to the phone and gouged a nice scar into the tabletop. There.

Now the table was all scratched up, like him. Like his shack, like…

Freddie were travelin'! Lucky little scamp.

He'd wanted to travel, take Angeline places, but they couldn't afford the gas to cross the state line. Heck of a woman, his Angeline. Loved a good adventure, yes sir. Best smile in Orange County. Woo-wee! Sweet sixteen and she'd had her pick of the menfolk. Day she stood by his side and spoke her marriage vows, he had to pinch hisself into believin'. But no, he weren't thinkin' about his Angeline, his angel… Freddie! That's right, Freddie.

Freddie were travelin', going places his granddaddy couldn't imagine.

Jacob grabbed an unopened envelope and scrawled "Ask Will about Freddie's trip" across the back. *Look at that.* Goddamn hand had the shakes. Better have another drink to stop them tremors. But first he was gonna stick his note on the fridge. Get to his age and you'd forget half your life if you didn't write it down.

*C.R.S., can't remember stuff.* But this, *this,* he wanted to remember.

He'd write another note, and another and another. Tape one to the phone on his nightstand, so he could see it at sunrise. And he'd buy a map. Heck, a big world map! Take the shuttle to the Walmart and buy a map. Nail it to the wall! That would annoy them dickheads. And he'd label it My Grandson's Great European Adventure.

*Ha! Take that, Bernie down the hall!*

Maybe he'd follow Willie's advice and get some sleep. Tomorrow were gonna be a real fine day. He had a project and it didn't involve sittin' on his ass in the arts and crafts room with tissue paper and a pair of safety scissors.

# TWO

An owl hooted in the forest, a mournful farewell to the night. Yanking the scrunchie from her wrist, Hannah wrestled her hair into a ponytail. Early-morning air—Saponi Mountain air—expanded her lungs and forced out the pollutants of LAX and the flights. Made her clean. Made her whole. Welcomed her home where everything was familiar and nothing was the same.

The crispness of fall carried the silent threat of forest fires. All summer, with Orange County cycling through murderous heat and once-in-a-century drought, she'd prepared for brush fires like a general perfecting frontline strategy. Even her contingency plans had backups. But while she was busy figuring out how to rescue her animals, the real threat in her life had built. Silently. Unobserved. Until her firstborn staggered into the nearest E.R. and told the receptionist, "I want to open my veins and bleed out." Less than ten words that allowed the state of California to lock up her son for seventy-two hours under an involuntary psychiatric hold—section 5150. A number she would never forget.

Hannah flattened her hands across her chest. Her thoughts would not turn maudlin. For Galen's sake, she needed to be strong and well rested, a mother at peace with her mind and her body. A mother who could heal herself and her son; a mother who could paste her shattered family back together.

Top of her list? Good sleep hygiene. In the two and a half weeks she'd been in California, she'd slept only in snatches, jolting awake as anxiety marched through her chest and what-ifs scratched at her brain. Images of Galen strapped to a gurney. Screaming and struggling. He hadn't been in restraints—at least, she didn't think he had. It was hardly something she could ask. *By the way, honey, did they restrain you during those three and a half days you were in the locked psych ward?* And Galen wasn't sharing.

Parenthood started with such optimism: your child would achieve his baby milestones, collect gold stars, maintain a good grade point average, hang out with the crowd that didn't drink and drive. And then, when you weren't paying attention, it all stripped down to one horrifying truth: you just wanted your son to find the will to live.

Behind her, a hundred acres of tangled forest waited to reach out and protect her, to pull her back into its bosom. Sunrise over Saponi Mountain with the blended light of day and night always lifted her spirits, but the clocks wouldn't change for another month. In the meantime, she and the dogs were trapped in dark mornings. Once dawn came, however, they would hike up to the Occaneechi Path, the historic Native American trading route on the crest of the hill. A well-marked trail, nothing grew there. Soft-soled moccasins had packed the soil tightly day after day, month after month, decade after decade, treading memories into the land. Sealing them in forever. And after the leaves were down, the track would remain hidden until spring.

Jink, the newest member of the household, wheezed her asthmatic cough and wound around Hannah's ankles. Hannah reached down and combed her fingers through satin fur. If only everything in life were as simple as adopting a stray cat.

"Go scavenge," Hannah said. "Catch a vole for breakfast."

The voles had inflicted more damage than the drought. Two months earlier the loss of her scarlet ruellias—a gift from an aging client who couldn't afford her vet bill—would have caused genuine pain. But now she had real context for the themes of life and death.

Hannah's right foot nudged a pile of broken acorn shells—a squirrel's last supper—and she stared down at the decking. Boards long overdue for pressure washing and weatherproofing, she and the ex had nailed them together fifteen years before with dreams of withstanding hurricanes and ice storms and poundings from little boys and big dogs. Dreams came, dreams left, and she would do what she always did: adapt.

In the distance, a car spluttered and clonked as it began the torturous journey down her driveway. A predawn pet emergency, no doubt. Containing work between the hours of eight in the morning and ten at night was a pipe dream. Clients knew she was available 24/7, and how could she not be? A holistic vet specializing in peaceful euthanasia could hardly keep office hours. Not that she had an office, other than her duct-taped Ford truck.

The dogs rose one by one to close around her in a circle. Mush for brains, all five of her rescue babies. Introduce people to their world, and they could flee. An eternity ago she had juggled the demands of work, laundry, motherhood and cooking as if she would never surface for air. These days she was responsible only for herself and a pack of strays. Turn around, and everything changed.

Rosie, her blind German shepherd, whimpered.

"It's okay, baby." Hannah kneaded Rosie's head, and the dog trembled against her leg.

Hannah didn't mean to have favorites, but she and Rosie were conjoined at the heart. Some woman had found Rosie four years earlier, scavenging for food in the Occoneechee Mountain parking lot and bleeding from a gash on her paw. The woman flew in with kinetic desperation, wanting to adopt Rosie *now,* wanting Hannah to fix Rosie *now.* But Rosie had needed stitches and a quiet, warm place to sleep. Hannah insisted on keeping the dog overnight; the woman begrudgingly agreed. Older, but still beautiful, she had a gray pallor and yellow patches around her eyelids that suggested heart disease. Hannah had planned to inquire gently about her health the next day. But the woman hadn't returned as arranged, and for that, Hannah was grateful. Her mother had encouraged her to believe in fate. And Hannah and Rosie-girl? They were meant to be.

The car lurched around a bend and stopped, the beam of its lights illuminating a lumbering opossum. Only one person she knew braked for opossum. And thank goodness, because she couldn't face anyone else's high-voltage chatter.

There would be comfort food in the back of that turquoise Honda Civic, too. High in carbs, sickly sweet and much appreciated. Dropping a jean size had been the only welcome side effect of her son's breakdown; dropping two jean sizes had been a warning.

Poppy's car spluttered through a mechanical imitation of Jink's asthmatic cough. Time to remind her friend, yet again, about the importance of oil changes. Guided by instincts—some good, most not—Poppy's monkey mind never settled on the mundane, unless it involved sugar or sex, horses or art.

The Honda chugged around the final curve. Hannah's ex had insisted on this ridiculous gravel drive despite the acres of pasture that lay between the house and the road. He'd pronounced it authentic and likely to deter bikers from joyriding up to their house after spilling out of the redneck bar opposite. Of course, that could have been Inigo's secret wish all along, since he'd upped and left six years earlier for a gay ménage à trois in rural Chatham County. A midlife crisis with not one younger lover but two. Both guys.

Hannah searched the top of her head for her reading glasses and had a flashback to stuffing them into the seat pocket of the airplane. Oh well, another pair lost.

Poppy parked and flung open the door decorated with a prancing mare. She painted horses on every surface except paper. Take the norm, turn it inside out and flip it backward—that was Poppy's thought process.

"Hey, girl." Poppy emerged, bottom-first. "Thought you might need a sugar fix."

"At seven in the morning?" Hannah and the dogs walked down the steps.

Poppy jiggled a Whole Foods bag, and her silver horse earrings danced a rhumba. Then she took out her gum and dumped it in the car's trash can. "Never too early for chocolate."

"Come here. You've earned a hug." Silly move caused, no doubt, by sleep deprivation. Even drunk, Poppy wasn't a hugger.

Poppy stiffened, and Hannah tried to cover her mistake with a pat on the shoulder blade.

"Thank you. For looking after the animals, the house and—" Hannah pulled back and chewed the corner of her lip. She hadn't cried in two and a half weeks. Why now? She sniffed. "But *you* should not be shopping at Whole Foods, not on your budget."

"I know, I know, but I figured you needed first-rate treats.

Chocolate croissants, still warm." Poppy sniffed the bag. "*Mmm-hmm*. And extra chocolate supplies. Had no idea Brits understood chocolate, but this, girlfriend, is the real deal."

Poppy reached inside the bag and waved two long, thin sticks of chocolate wrapped in twisted yellow foil. They resembled emaciated Christmas crackers, the kind Inigo had introduced to Christmas dinner when the boys were little. Such a fraud, the ex, flooding their lives with all things British—or rather Celtic—when he'd left Wales as a two-month-old. A Christmas memory snuck out: Inigo, Galen and Liam popping crackers and giggling. Her guys, the three people she thought she'd known best in the world. Turned out she hadn't known them at all. If her mother were still alive, how would she label this bottomless emotion Hannah refused to name? Was it grief? Was she mourning her *before* life?

*Think better, Hannah.*

"Cadbury Flakes, they're called," Poppy continued. "The Brit section in Whole Foods is opposite the dog food, but don't let that put you off. What time d'y'all get back last night?"

"Late. Or early, depending on your definition. And it's just me."

"Our boy?"

"Couldn't spring him from the post-hospitalized program. Another twelve days and then he can come home." Hannah paused. "I need to find him a therapist here. And an A.A. group."

"On it, babe. I know a shitload of drunks."

"Somehow, I never doubted that."

Poppy disappeared into her car, muttering about a lost cell phone. She bobbed back out. "Sleep on the plane?"

"I rested."

"The answer's no, then."

"Welcome to my brave, new world."

Poppy took a bite out of one of the chocolate croissants, then shoved it back into the bag. Her eyes flicked toward the house; clearly she was thinking, *Coffee*. But talking about Galen was easier in the dark surrounded by sounds of the waking forest rather than under the glare and hum of kitchen halogens.

"I just need to get him home," Hannah said. "Out of California, away from the ex-girlfriend and the mental hospital. Home to the cottage, so I can help him heal."

"Think that's a good idea—leaving him unsupervised in the cottage?"

Acorns splattered the cottage porch in a series of pops as if fired from a muzzled BB gun, and the Crayola-colored spinners she'd hung for her father the week before his death swirled in a sudden breeze, whirring softly.

"He'll be home," Hannah said. "And he won't be unsupervised. I'll be watching over him, which is better than right now. His therapy ends at four and then he returns to an empty apartment for the rest of the day. He spends every evening and every night alone."

Poppy sucked chocolate off her fingers. "And the whole heavy-duty meds thing isn't freaking out your inner holisticness?"

"Sometimes medication is the cure."

"And sometimes it makes things worse. People in pain do painful things, Han."

The downside of exposing secrets to a friend: she knew how to hurt you.

"So." Poppy rustled the bag closed. "You figure out what happened? I mean, the whole sequence of events?"

"Not entirely, since Galen didn't want us in any of the therapy sessions. It still makes no sense to me. How can you return to grad school, drop out of classes and decide to die in a matter of weeks? I was hoping, when he came home, he might talk to you."

Poppy broke eye contact. "Sure."

In the forest, a pair of coonhounds bayed, a nasty reminder that at least one of the fancy new homes on the ridge was now occupied.

"On to happier things. Fill me in on your life," Hannah said. "What have I missed?"

"I met this guy."

"*Poppyyyyy*. Not again."

"Eighty-year-old guy. You'd approve."

Hannah slapped the side of her head. "Argh, sorry. Completely forgot about Hawk's Ridge. How's it working out?"

"You were right about the whole art therapy thing. Love hanging out with the old folks. Don't think it's going to turn into a paying gig, but the director and the staff stay clear. Let me do my own thing. There's this sweet guy, Jacob. You, missy, would love him. Knows a shit-ton about plants and trees. A real woodsman. Such a shame to see him cooped up in that place. Has this grandson who's on an amazing European adventure. I took Jacob to Walmart the other day and we bought a huge map and colored Sharpies so we could plot the kid's route. They're not supposed to tape stuff to the walls." Poppy grinned. "So we stuck it up with half a roll of packing tape. *Bwah-hah-hah*."

"You think that's a good idea?"

"Rules, Han, are for breaking. Especially when you're eighty. Can I borrow the truck today? I found a kiln for sale. Thought I'd check it out."

Poppy already had two kilns but barely used one. The recession was strangling her ceramics business.

"And where are you going to put another kiln?"

"Lordy, a girl can never have too many kilns!"

"Okay, sure." Hannah meant *no. No,* it's horribly inconvenient; *no,* I need the truck for work. But *no* was such a difficult word. It always gummed up her mouth like sticky toffee. Still, good to know your greatest weakness, even if, at forty-five, it was more of a fluorescent tattoo inked on your forehead.

Hannah stretched her right arm, then her left. Fanning out her hands, she released the tension needling at her fingertips and imagined it floating up into the sky. Disintegrating into the earth's atmosphere.

"Galen's going to be fine." Was she reassuring herself or Poppy? "It won't be easy; it won't happen overnight, but I can fix him." Her words condensed into a tiny cloud, the only water vapor in what would, no doubt, be another beautiful, dangerously dry day. "And I've promised he'll never have to return to another mental hospital."

"I know, girl. We'll keep him safe. So. We standing out here till the next millennium, or are you offering me coffee?" Poppy brushed past Hannah and jogged up the front steps. The dogs, except for Rosie, followed.

The screen door slammed, but Hannah stood still in the dark and listened for the sound of falling leaves. A reminder that cooler weather was on the way, that eventually the oppressive heat would break.

Ghosts stepped out of the shadows—memories of Galen and Liam riding bikes and falling out of trees. Well, Liam was the one who fell out of the tree, while he was grounded and attempting an escape. Galen, always the big brother, had tried to cover up the misdemeanor with a lie. Not a very good one, either.

Hannah smiled.

*Lie to me and your asses are mine,* she'd told the boys when they were old enough to understand. She had never elaborated, preferring to let their imaginations construct a suitable punishment. Liam had decided this meant Mommy would smack him with a wooden spoon—a threat she had issued once. But Galen's mind had drawn an elaborate scenario that involved Mom locking him in the crawl space where he would be bitten by a brown recluse spider and die in excruciating pain.

Honest to God, she used to believe Liam would end up in Sing Sing. Constantly seeking to be high on life, his wild streak far exceeded hers, and she'd lost her virginity at fourteen. But Galen? The worst thing he ever did was stay up till 3:00 a.m. on a school night writing poetry.

Through the darkness, a flush of blooms hovered over her mutabilis rose like brightly colored butterflies. How wrong she had been to assume all roses were high maintenance. This old-fashioned plant had thrived in her parched garden, and now it burst open with a second round of buds and flowers the color of apricot, baby pink and crimson. As petals unfurled in drought and sometimes opened at dusk, hope grew in unexpected places.

Hannah shoved her hands into the front pocket of her UNC hoodie and stared toward the tree line, wishing on miracles and ignoring the whisper of concern that told her wind in a bone-dry forest was never a good sign.

# THREE

Needles of rain softened to a drizzle as Will slipped on his Ray-Bans and became another B-list celebrity walking through Central Park. A bag lady ranted about the Apocalypse, and a beautiful young woman pushing a double stroller smiled at him. Or maybe she was appreciating the ridiculously large bouquet of flowers he had bought for his overworked publicist.

The path climbed steeply toward Dene Rock, and Will followed. He would perch on the outcrop and find the solution to unraveling this mess with his dad. Lying once about Freddie's death had been an unforgivable lapse of judgment, and yet Will was now stuck in the middle of that lie—a spider caught in its own web. The old man had hooked up with the substitute art teacher, and the two of them were tracking Freddie's trip with an energy previously reserved for circumventing the rules at Hawk's Ridge Retirement Community. The first time Will had lacked the patience to deal with his dad's memory loss, the first time he'd thrown out some comment that was meant—*meant*—to be forgotten, and his dad had glommed on to it. How could the old man recall a brief, late-night phone conversation but erase the evening Will had told him about Freddie's death? Some cruel cosmic joke that wasn't funny. And it had spun out of control. Time to bring the charade to a close.

Tucking the bouquet under his arm, Will scrambled up the slick rock behind the rustic summerhouse. As he sat, his iPhone vibrated in his pocket.

"Hey, Dad. How did you sleep?"

"Good, good. Had a great day, son. Had a great day."

"Had? It's only nine o'clock."

"Been to Walmart and bought a map." The old man chuckled. *Chuckle* was a verb Will hated, a word he would never use in his writing. His dad, however, was definitely chuckling. "Bought me a huge world map, son. To track Freddie's trip."

"I know, Dad. You told me yesterday."

"I plan on showin' it to that new guy, Bernie, down the hall. His grandsons visit every Sunday. Take him to that fancy diner on Main Street for blueberry pancakes. Wait till I tell him the whole cotton-pickin' story about Freddie. Hell. Five years old and he has a passport. I never owned one, son. Never been outside the state."

Will flopped onto his back. Droplets of mist fluttered to his sunglass lenses, but in his mind a slab of grief was falling from heaven, crushing him into dust. Three months and nine days, and each hour the grief took on a more solid form.

"Willie? You still there?"

Will positioned the bouquet across his chest like an arrangement of funeral lilies. "Dad, Freddie isn't—"

"Able to contact us. Yes, yes, you told me yesterday. Shame on you, son. Just 'cos Freddie's out of reach don't mean we should give up on him, do it?"

"Dad—"

"Sorry, son. Poppy's here with some more of them colored markers. Got to go."

For real? His dad had hung up on him? Will stared at a flock of gray pigeons moving silently through a gray sky. Always he forced himself to look up, never down, forward never backward, and yet these days his mind lingered in places he didn't want to visit: the last game of tickle monster; Freddie pumping his legs on a swing and singing "The Wheels on the Bus"; Freddie standing alone on a crowded street because the woman who should have been holding his hand had wandered off to look at a pair of five-hundred-dollar shoes in a boutique window.

If only he'd paid as much attention to Cass's personality as he had to her ass, then maybe he would have figured out that she was a total psycho and self-medicating with alcohol. You'd have thought, given his childhood, he'd be able to spot crazy—despite the disguise of a well-cared-for body poured into sexy, couture clothes. Unlike his mom, Cass could've afforded the best treatment. When Will was sixteen, he'd found a psychiatrist who would take Medicaid patients, but always his dad had the same answer: "I've seen *One Flew Over the Cuckoo's Nest,* son. Besides, your mama's just high-strung. That's the price we pay for her beauty." As if his dad were really that shallow.

Will breathed through his nostrils, panting like a beast.

He'd spent three decades praying he didn't have a dark side, since that concept came with seriously twisted DNA. Retreat was his strategy for relationships; anger was a soul-sucking distraction he had learned to push aside...and yet. And yet. If he allowed himself to think of Cassandra, the person who had murdered his son, who had turned his baby into a statistic, another kid killed by a drunk driver with a blood alcohol level of point two-six, Will would have to admit that he was capable of violence. How could he wish two people were still alive for such different reasons—Freddie so he could hold him and never let go; Cassandra so he could kill her himself?

Will jumped up and scrambled down the rock. There was only one thing left to do.

The light would be fading and the temperature dropping as he down-climbed, but he wanted to feel air on his back, on his exposed skin; he wanted to strip away his layers. If he could climb naked, he would. Will tugged his T-shirt over his head and tossed it into the trunk of the Prius along with his iPhone.

He pulled back his shoulders and stretched into a swan dive without leaving the ground. The clutter in his brain floated away, disappeared into the blue sky above the Shawangunk Mountains like a handful of balloons set free.

Nothing existed beyond the challenge ahead: the mastery it would take to scale Shockley's Ceiling; the choreography of his body moving across the horizontal cracks; the euphoria of standing above the world and looking into the face of God.

He was going unroped.

He would ride doubt and push aside fear, and trust in nothing but his own judgment. And the payoff would come as his mind and body lapsed into harmony. When everything reconciled. When he found clarity. When he knew what to do next.

He grabbed his chalk bag and his nylon shoes. The rest of his rack was still in the car from his last climb. He would sort it out when he returned to the city.

Will began walking. He followed the connector trail to a twenty-foot-wide toe of rock and ignored the small group of tourist spectators. A woman with a pair of binoculars giggled.

*Loss of concentration leads to poor self-control and frantic climbing.*

Already, he was reading the route, decoding the puzzle,

figuring out individual moves. He could climb left of the roof, but no, he would not avoid the crux. He would face the obstacle and crank it. A deceptive 5.6, pitch three demanded more skill than less-experienced climbers realized.

He strode past the large flake to the right and arrived at the base of the climb. He cracked his knuckles and stared up at the rock. No doubt, no thought except for one: *I can do this.*

An easy mantel would get him over. *Don't think, don't hesitate, don't stop.*

Will pushed down on the ledge with his hands, swung his feet up, balanced and stood. Hard not to feel a little gripped. He had cleared the roof; he had nailed the crux. But he had to keep going. Momentum would take him the last sixty feet to the top. Soon he would rest but now wasn't the time. His mind was often ready to quit before his body. He was not going to flame out.

He stepped around the corner to the second roof and eyeballed his next hold, trusting his left hand for balance.

He dipped into his chalk bag, blew on his fingertips, reached up with his right hand, found a roundish hold, gripped with his finger pads. The muscles in his shoulder stretched out. Taut. For a moment he hung, suspended in air. Time grew still, stripped down to a single camera shot, a study in absolute control. The world stopped breathing. There was nothing beyond the rhythm of the climb flowing through his limbs, through his muscles, through his breath.

He pictured his next move—a heel hook—held it in his mind, executed it. He was over the second roof.

Grabbing, pulling, swinging, Will kept moving upward into the sky.

When he topped out, he threw back his head and let his spirit soar toward the heavens. He released his voice into the air: a scream of triumph, a scream of existence, a commitment to life issued in his own private chapel. The echo floated down to the forest below, to the vast seascape of green speckled with advancing fall. Green, the color of rejuvenation, the color of life. His mind was clear; he knew his way forward. His work-in-progress may have grown cold, but Freddie's adventure had a heartbeat. So what if it was fiction with an audience of two? He was crafting a better version of the truth, crafting a story worth living for, a story to remember. Giving his dad the gift of untainted memories when he had so few left.

Will flung his arms wide. Standing above the world, he got it. He finally got it.

In the four years since his mom's death, his dad had been a mess of binge drinking and misfiring brain signals. Only a few weeks ago the old man had said, "People tell you it gets easier, son. But that ain't the truth. Every day I miss your mama more." Despite the mashed-up memory, his dad never forgot how much he still loved that one person who'd meant everything.

Just as his dad had never let go of his mom, he would never let go of Freddie.

He would never stop missing Freddie, and he shouldn't have tried. He shouldn't stomp down the memories. He should bust them open. He should celebrate Freddie's life.

As soon as he got back to his apartment, he would start re-searching Freddie's adventure. His last, great adventure. And for as long as it took, he would hold Freddie in the present tense.

The second he picked up his phone, Will knew he'd screwed up. Four text messages from Ally, all variations on a theme: "Where the hell are you, and why are you not answering your phone?" Then one message that said, "Have you lost your freakin' mind?"

As he tugged his T-shirt over his neck, he glimpsed the tiny scar Ally's teeth had left on his bicep. Thanks to his mother's stories, he'd grown up believing that true love was a narrow path with room for only one. What a masochistic legacy to hand a commitment-phobe.

They were five years old with his-'n'-hers scraped knees when Ally bit him. It was the first time he'd tried to kiss her. He tried again at seventeen, adding a declaration of love, and she slapped him. There hadn't been a third time. When her husband lost his Wall Street job five years ago and Will hired her, even he hadn't been sure of his motivation. But the moment Freddie entered his life, that whimsical decision to put Ally on his payroll proved to be the wisest move he'd ever made. After all, Ally had been guarding his secrets since grade school. She'd always had his back.

He hit speed dial one and pictured five feet two inches of brown-eyed female indignation.

"You went soloing?" she yelled.

"How did you know?"

"I wouldn't be a very effective P.A. if I couldn't weasel information out of your publicist, would I?"

Damn. That was a silly mistake. Why had he felt the need to explain his absence from the weekly spin session?

"So, what's up?" he said.

"A journalist from the *National Enquirer.* She was prowling around outside the apartment when I stopped in to check messages. She wanted to know if you were the father of Cass's little boy."

Will ground his teeth. "What did you tell her?"

"To move or I'd call the cops, you dolt."

"She's just fishing, eliminating former lovers by the math

of dates. No one's buying the story that the poor loser who died in the crash with them was Freddie's father." Will and Cass had only agreed on one thing outside of the bedroom: keeping Freddie's life private and his paternity secret. Will had expected everything to change once Freddie entered the school system, but Cass, who loved to travel on a whim, kept insisting on private tutoring. No preschool, no kindergarten, but Will had been gearing up to fight for first grade. A kid needed friends. How else could he survive his parents?

"No one knows the truth except you and Seth."

"Not strictly true. Your entire P.R. office knows. And so does Cass's publicity machine—"

"Ally, I just worked hard to clean Cass out of my mind. Can we not talk about her?"

Ally sighed heavily. "You scared me. I thought you'd do something stupid."

Will fiddled with the beads wound around his wrist. A one-of-a-kind gift of mini skulls strung together like shrunken heads, the friendship bracelet had been Ally's idea of a joke the first time he hit the *New York Times* bestseller list: *In case you get bigheaded.* The one person who knew him better than anyone, and even she didn't understand. He hadn't driven to the Gunks that morning to end his life. He'd been trying to save it.

"Come on, darling. You know me better than that."

"Will, you've barely left the apartment in three months, and suddenly you want to shimmy up a rock face alone and unroped?"

"I picked a climb I've done many times before."

"When you had good reasons to live."

"I still do."

"Not that I don't agree with you, but since you refuse to talk with a therapist about any of this, it's my job to make sure you're thinking straight. What, exactly, do you have to live for? And if you answer the Agent Dodds movie deal, I'll bite your other bicep."

"You. Your poor, long-suffering husband. The chocolate mimosa you guys gave me for my thirtieth birthday. My dad. All good reasons to live. Happy?"

"If you'd told me you were going, I would have come along. Kept my eye on you."

There was a time when the thought of Ally watching him climb would have floated his boat for all eternity. Loving her had saved him many times, but like the healed scar, it was no longer a mark of anything more than his past.

"I wanted to be alone. I came here to work the piss out of a route and get my head together."

"Be one with the rock?"

"If you want to put it that simplistically, yeah. Look, I didn't mean to cause worry. Why don't you take Seth out for dinner on the corporate credit card? A pre-Halloween bonus."

"What the hell is a pre-Halloween bonus?"

"A gift from a grateful boss. Listen, I'm going to find somewhere to stay overnight. I'll be back in the city tomorrow."

"You want us to come join you?"

"No. It's ninety miles—a colossal waste of time and money."

"Promise me you're okay, Will. No bull. Just you and me and the truth."

Will looked back at the mountains. "I'm good."

"Okay, but do me a favor. Please take an hour to check your email, answer some messages. Act like a guy who cares about his business."

"I don't need to care about my business. That's why I have you."

"Will—"

He knew that tone.

"Let it go, Ally. I'm doing all I can right now."

"I know. Love you."

"Ditto."

"And, Will? Don't forget you have a hair appointment tomorrow at four. Please don't make me reschedule again. You look like a surfer dude with a really bad dye job."

Will ducked down and glanced in his wing mirror. She had a point. He inspected a clump of dirty-blond hair. The tip was platinum—discolored by the sun during his last climb. He stood and tried to run his hand through what used to be his bangs, but his fingers snagged on a huge knot.

"Go henpeck your husband."

She gave a laugh. "Bye, you."

Will stared at his phone. Might as well take ten minutes to dump emails. Trashing unread messages was strangely liberating. Grief had either desensitized him or revealed that ninety percent of his life was disposable. He clicked on the email icon and began deleting. He stopped, finding one he should read—one from Hawk's Ridge. What was his dad's latest infraction? Will huffed out a sigh. Had the old man demanded pancakes? Circulated another petition for a fall dance?

Dear Mr. Shepard, the director had written, I trust this email will solicit prompt action on your part.

Pinching his thumb and forefinger together, Will touched the scene and then spread his fingers apart to zoom in on the type.

His dad had been right all along. *Fucking bastards.*

# FOUR

Blinding October sunlight burst through the trees, jolting Will's attention to his speedometer. Eighty-five, he was clocking eighty-five. Flying, rather than driving. He slammed his foot on the brake pedal, and the tailgating idiot behind blasted his horn.

Will pulled into the inside lane and waved. *Dickhead.*

One state away and already he was thinking like his dad. Will hit Pause on his iPod. Bad enough to be heading back to Orange County, North Carolina. He didn't need to mess with his head by listening to the drumbeat of a Boxer Rebellion song that summoned up the ghost of powwows past.

Why hadn't he waited for sunup and dealt with this latest crisis by phone? Why had he driven back to New York, packed an overnight bag and jumped into the Prius at two in the morning like Batman on an ecofriendly mission? Will Shepard planned and orchestrated, didn't *do* spontaneity, never released anger, but here he was, acting like a caped avenger. Rushing to defend what remained of his dad's honor. Trying to save someone who likely as not could no longer be saved.

The state border zipped past; the forest, a sleeping ogre with the strength to tear him to pieces, stretched toward the Carolina blue sky.

A bloated deer lay on the grassy verge, its flesh ripped open to expose bone, and unidentifiable chunks of roadkill littered the painted lines dividing the lanes. To his right, a barn—roofless and caving in on itself—struggled to rise out of the undergrowth only to be tugged back by wild vines. To his left, a regiment of transmission towers flattened everything in their path as they marched over the horizon like metal warriors.

Will clutched the steering wheel. Two days max and he could do this trip in reverse. But first, figure out how to take down the director of Hawk's Ridge.

*Precision and balance, Will.*

A climber who rushed, who didn't strategize, was a dead climber.

He would book into a motel, crash for a few hours, meet with the director, placate him, spend an afternoon with his dad, get knee-walking drunk, sleep it off, drive home. But how to placate the director? Be nice, but firm: *You can't kick my dad out. Where else will he go?* Will shook his head. *Lame, totally lame.* Begging might be involved. Or maybe he could offer to do a book signing. Yeah, right. Like that would make a difference.

"How about I organize a book signing with local authors?" Will said five hours later in a face-off across a cherry desk. Beautifully crafted, it was too big for the room, too grand for the doofus opposite.

"I don't think so." The director of Hawk's Ridge craned his neck—not that he really had one, just a gelatinous mound of fat—and peered into the mirror on the far wall. He adjusted his tie slowly.

Will flipped over his hand and rubbed the calluses. If he could tackle cliffs of rock, he could handle this groundhog of a man who lumbered through the leftovers of people's lives.

*Thud.* Will jumped as a bird crashed into the sparkling windowpane. "A bluebird just—"

"Mr. Shepard, please."

Will stared beyond the splatter of feathers to Occoneechee Mountain. *My blood's all over that mountain,* the old man used to say. Unfortunately, so was Will's.

"Your father is loud, abusive and, half the time, drunk."

*I would be, too, if I had to live here.*

"Last week he hounded poor Mrs. Wilson into signing his petition for a Friday-night social. Chased her down the hall."

*Mrs. Wilson's in a wheelchair. How much chasing could be involved?*

"She was terrified."

Why could Will think of nothing to say other than *fucking bastard?*

"Alcohol was involved."

"I appreciate everything you're saying. But I want to assure you that my father is not an alcoholic. My moth— I grew up with someone who abused alcohol. I know the signs. As I'm sure you do. I don't mean to question your judgment." Will's left eye began to twitch. "My father's always been a heavy drinker, but he's not a drunk. And right now, seems he has little to enjoy but his Wild Turkey. Where's the harm in that?"

*Stupid, Will. Never ask a question if you're not prepared to hear the answer.*

"With all due respect, Mr. Shepard, I don't think you realize how the situation has deteriorated since your last visit. Many of our residents are heavily medicated. They cannot drink. And, to be honest, I think your father has emotional issues. We've had great success with Risperdal in some of our more aggressive residents."

"Seriously? You want to give my dad an antipsychotic used to treat schizophrenia?"

"And, finally—there's this business with your son."

Will sat up, senses alert.

"When he told one of the staff his grandson was on some big trip, we let it go. We thought it might be his way of dealing with grief. But then he started bragging to other residents, and...well. This incident last night. Brawling, Mr. Shepard." As the director shook his head, his entire upper body waddled.

"We've never had a violent episode in our community before. Not one. I don't need to tell you how upset the female staff was to see two grown men rolling around on the floor like boys. The security guard who separated them has a black eye. A. Black. Eye."

Will heard it just fine the first time.

"According to witnesses, your father entered into some silly game of my-grandson's-better-than-yours with one of our new residents."

"Bernie down the hall?"

"Mr. Fields, yes. I have already spoken with his family. They have generously agreed not to press charges."

"Oh, come on. They wanted to prosecute an eighty-year-old granddad for bragging?"

"Mr. Shepard. I cannot allow your father to stay here if he's going to incite violence. Your father is an alcoholic. He has psychotic breaks with reality. He has problems with anger management."

Really, the guy didn't have to speak at half-speed. Will got it, totally got it.

"These are serious issues," the director said. "I need you to treat them as such."

"I do, honestly. And I'm not questioning your experience." Will picked up a glass paperweight and put it back in the same place. "But have you considered that he's still mourning my mother? Could we bring in a grief counselor?"

The door that Will had deliberately left ajar crashed open, and a woman carrying a Kit Kat and wearing jeans that clung in all the right places marched into the room. Oranges, she smelled of oranges. And chocolate chip cookies.

The director's face turned puce. "Poppy, I'm in a meeting with—"

"You cannot be serious about kicking Jacob Shepard to the curb," she said. "Where will he go?"

*My point exactly.* Then Will couldn't help himself, he looked at her butt, which was hard to miss, since it was rather large and she was now bending over the cherry desk. How many hours had he wasted staring at women's asses and where had it led? Back to the one thing he'd spent his life running from: craziness. Will cleared his throat and focused on the bookshelf, empty except for a set of Agent Dodds novels in hardback—signed and donated on moving-in day.

"Mr. Shepard." The director's voice was tight like a slingshot. "I don't believe you've met our *temporary* art teacher, Poppy Breen. She's filling in for a few weeks."

"Jacob's a sweet, lonely guy." Poppy spoke to the director and ignored Will.

Sweet might be taking it a bit too far. Stubborn, ornery...

"Short-term memory in the shitter," she continued. "But he just needs a buddy. When I took him to Walmart to buy his map, he chatted away like a kid. Told me about his days in a bluegrass band with his baby brother."

Really? His dad had talked about Uncle Darren? The old

man hadn't mentioned another family member in decades. There'd been some falling-out when Will was little. He didn't remember the details but the cause was the same as always: his mom.

"What about music therapy?" Poppy said.

"I'm in a private meeting, Poppy. With Jacob's son."

"Excellent." She hurled herself into the chair next to Will. "Then I arrived just in time."

"Poppy, I'd like you to—"

"Stay." Will turned to his new ally. "I'd like you to stay."

She looked at him for the first time and her eyes—not quite amber, not quite green, not quite brown—slowly appraised his face. Will waited for her to finish. It wasn't that he was some egomaniacal dick, but women often looked at him and liked what they saw, which proved you shouldn't judge a book by its cover. Fantastic, exhaustion was dragging him down the primrose path to overused clichés.

Will sighed. "We were talking about grief counseling for my dad. I think he's still grieving for my mom."

"Yup. Agreed."

"If you're going to stay, Poppy—" the director's eyes, which were too small for his face, flicked sideways in an oddly reptilian gesture "—at least close the door."

Will tugged on the neck of his T-shirt. Closed doors, trapped in a confrontation with two other people. Not good. So much of his life wasted hoping his mom would be incarcerated, and yet shove him in a room and shut the door, and he could blow. Claustrophobia—yet another legacy of his childhood, and the one thing he could blame on his dad. He used to beg—*please, Daddy, don't lock me in my room*—but his dad always had the same response, "It's for your own good, son. I need to deal with your mama." What was that supposed to mean? That Will could look after himself even as a tyke?

Will stood and grabbed the back of the chair. He had an appalling desire to shove the director and make a run for it.

The director's index finger tapped the open folder on his desk. "It says here your mother died four years ago."

"You think there's an expiration on grief?" Will glanced at the now-shut door. His mouth was dry; the words tasted stale. Palpitations, definitely had heart palpitations. "You want my dad to be complacent, easier to handle, right?" Firing dumb questions again. *Stupid.* Might as well be tumbling off a rock face in an uncontrolled fall.

The art teacher with the cute butt gave a smug laugh.

"Mr. Shepard, this meeting is over." The director closed the folder. "You have two options: you take your father to a geriatric psychiatrist and get medication, or you find alternative accommodation for him."

Reason snapped. Will would not be cornered like a dog. He was done listening; he was done following other people's ultimatums. Cass's voice seemed to trill in his head—*He's my son, William, and you will see him when I say.* This small-minded stranger had no understanding of a private family matter and no right, none, to make decisions about the old man's mental health.

"You know what? Forget it. He's leaving today."

Relief—the relief in the room was palpable. But was it his or the director's? Didn't know, didn't care. Needed out.

Will tugged his books free from the bookshelf—a self-destructive act that deleted a fan from his Facebook page. Team Shepard would not be happy.

"I donated these to the library," Will said, "not to you personally."

"We don't have a library, Mr. Shepard."

"Exactly. Which makes this place hell."

★ ★ ★

Will tossed open the door and slammed into his father's chest.

"Aren't you a little beyond listening at keyholes, Dad?"

The old man's shirt was untucked on one side, and he was carrying an armload of empty cardboard boxes. He was smiling, too—his grin as fat as Freddie's had been after he'd unwrapped the two huge Playmobil sets on his fifth birthday. Will had been unable to decide which castle to buy, so he'd settled on both. Plus the catapult. And the battering ram. And the dragon.

"Where you been, son? Got some boxes off Poppy."

"Boxes?" Will bit his lip.

"For packin', son. For packin'. Ol' possum face kick me out, did he? And look!" His dad held up a cardboard mailing tube. "Look what Poppy found me. I said I reckon it's the perfect thing to protect our Freddie's map."

Behind him, Poppy shouted, "You can't fire me, asshole, I'm a volunteer."

"Hi, Poppy," his dad said. "Have you met my son? Poppy's a firecracker. Only spark of life around here. You leavin', too, Poppy? You leavin', too?"

His dad repeated himself when he was excited, which, admittedly, wasn't often these days.

*Great.* Will had just hit the self-destruct button, and the old man was behaving as if they were embarking on a fishing trip.

"Yup, we're both moving on to greener pastures, Jacob. Can I borrow your cute son for a sec?" Poppy beamed at his dad, who beamed back.

"Sure thing, Poppy. I'll wait right here."

His dad used the cardboard tube to point at the red carpet that appeared to be the evil twin of the hall carpet in *The Shining.* Will looked up at the empty bulletin board with the smiling employee-of-the-month photo, and along the silent hallway of closed doors with the handrail that ran only on one side. Somewhere a door slammed. This was a place inhabited by nothing but echoes. Why had he never noticed before?

"Come with?" Poppy stroked Will's arm, and the edge of a jagged scar poked out from under her cuff.

Will jolted back. He was so done with crazy. "Nasty scar."

"No, I didn't try and off myself," Poppy said in a bored tone that suggested she was used to this comment. "I rescued an abused horse, a Thoroughbred chestnut mare. In other words, the triple whammy of high-strung. Miss Prissy's as spirited at they come. Bucked me off into some barbed wire during the breakout. Love that mare, hate her former owner—my turd of an ex. Asshole wanted to make her another tame possession, like his trophy wife, who wasn't me in case you're wondering. Best guess? He abused them both."

A story Will would normally consider harvesting for his writing notebook—despite the undercurrent of betrayal. As a kid, he'd collected stories the way most boys collected live critters or plastic dinosaurs. Right now, weighed down with a full set of Agent Dodds hardbacks, he lacked the energy to care.

Poppy opened the second door on the right, and they entered a small bedroom with a walnut dresser and a rocking chair. The bed was too neatly made, the colors in the framed print of Jesus too sunny.

"I'm sorry about your job," Will said.

"Bah. I've been fired before. Being dumped from a volunteer job might be a first, though." She bounced onto the bed, grabbed a needlepoint cushion that had been placed in middle of the pillows and hugged it to her chest. "Where're you taking Jacob? Any thoughts?"

"I have a motel room in town. Guess we'll stay there while I search for a new place."

"You make crap decisions."

"This wasn't exactly something I planned." He scowled at her.

"Yeah, whatever. I have this friend, a holistic vet, with a secluded place in the country. Ten acres of pasture in front, one hundred acres of forest behind. And a guest cottage with beautiful views. She's looking for a tenant." Poppy grabbed a copy of *Triangle Gardener* magazine from the nightstand. She ripped off a piece, then tugged a pencil from behind her ear and scrawled a phone number. "Hannah. Give her a call."

"Thanks, but I'm not looking to rent. I have to be back in the city by—" When? He'd thrown his deadline away. For the first time in his adult life, he didn't have to be anywhere.

"Wait lists around here are a nightmare. Could take a while." She wrote an address under the phone number. "Drive by, have a look. You'll love Hannah. She projects calming vibes."

Right, the last thing he needed—some new-age hippy-dippy chick projecting anything at him.

"She'll adore Jacob. Her own father—" Poppy waved the rest of the sentence away. "Jacob can catch his breath, detox from this place. You really think he'd cope with the bustle of a motel?"

*I don't think I can cope with the bustle of a motel.*

"Want directions?"

"No," Will said, but she kept writing.

A decade younger and she'd be just his type: great curves, shiny chestnut curls fighting to escape from a barrette. He had only one dating rule—no woman old enough to hear her biological clock, and this art teacher with the great butt was definitely over twenty-five. Closer to forty, if he had to guess.

By sixteen, he'd known he never wanted kids, which was a no-brainer for anyone with his family background. Birth control was something he established at the get-go of a sexual relationship, and Cass had told him she was on the pill. A lie, of course, since she'd hand-selected him to be a sperm donor. But the instant he drew his son close and smelled that powdery baby scent, Will had known their relationship was forever. And yet forever had turned out to be less than five years.

The fist of grief grabbed his throat, cutting off his air supply.

"Hey," Poppy said. "You okay?"

"Fine." Will forced himself to breathe. "I'm fine."

"Here. Directions. Take them."

She placed the scrap of paper on the quilt, hopped off the bed and disappeared before Will could say, "I have a GPS."

The odor of bleach in the room was thick, thick enough to mask the lingering fumes of death. It transported him back to a summer evening fishing on the oxbow behind the ghost field, the year after the excavation of the Occaneechi village started. He and his dad had just caught a bucket of bream when Will snared himself on a hook. Bled all over his new shorts—thrift-store new, but his mom had bought them for his first day of kindergarten. "Your mama's gonna be real upset," his dad said, and young Will was terrified. Mama being upset could mean anything from her dragging Will by his hair to screaming that he was worthless. But his dad told him not to fret, told him bleach was the magic cure. Possibly, but not in the quantity the old man had used. Will never wore the shorts again, and his mom never noticed.

"Willie?"

Will jumped. In the five minutes he'd been responsible for his dad, he'd forgotten him. The old man was standing in the doorjamb, trailing empty boxes with one hand and clasping the roll of cardboard to his chest as if it were the family Bible.

"Had me a real bad thought while you were talking to Poppy. Heck of a bad thought, son."

"Hey, it's okay. Come here, sit." Will guided his dad onto the rocking chair. "Want to tell me what happened?"

"Nope."

"The gist of it?" Will crouched down.

"Somethin' real bad happened to Freddie. He were in a car with his mama...."

Strange, how moments of heartbreak didn't announce themselves, they just ambushed you. Shouldn't there be an earthquake measuring nine point five on the Richter scale when the plates of your life shifted? But outside this room with the cheap print of Jesus and the bed with hospital corners, traffic continued to speed through the forty-five-miles-per-hour zone. And in the time it took to inhale, the cycle of grief regenerated. The wound tore open.

Will would never know what happened in the minutes after the crash, sometime around sunset. The sudden loss of light had added to the confusion. One witness had heard screams but couldn't determine if they'd come from a child or a woman. True or false, Will's brain had latched on to that snippet of information and created a scenario he could never escape: his son dying in pain and terror.

The chair clicked as his dad rocked back and forth, back and forth. "But I ain't listenin' to my no-good brain, son. My brain, it's a trickster from one of your mama's fairy tales. And I choose not to listen. Freddie's the only good thing we got in our lives, ain't that true? You didn't tell me where he and his mama were headin' this week."

Will fell to his knees. Relief swamped him—ridiculous,

selfish relief. He could still hide behind his story, one that wasn't finished.

"They're leaving for Florence," Will said, "so Freddie can see Michelangelo's David."

"Woo-wee. Who would have thought? My grandson, seein' a real live *Mickel*-angelo. Remember how you wanted to see that statue when you was a boy? Darren thought it meant you was, you know." His dad's right hand flopped as if his wrist were broken.

"You remember?"

"My mind ain't gone, son. Full of holes, but some things I remember just clear as sunlight. Just clear as sunlight."

Will stood and shifted the books to his hip. "Here. Let me take the boxes."

Jacob handed over everything except the cardboard tube. "Heck, my memory's just fine. Ask me about how your uncle and me went fishin' down in the Eno this past summer with cedar poles we cut ourselves. Caught a lot of suckers down there."

The window opened a crack, then slammed shut. *Oh, Dad. You haven't left this place in two years. And Uncle Darren died right before Mom. I know, because I paid for both funerals.*

"If you throw liquid in the Eno, it'll end up in the Atlantic Ocean." His dad creaked up to standing. "It joins the Neuse River down in Durham."

"I know, Dad."

"And those rivers, they was trade routes and a source of food 'cos animals like bison got to have water. After the Europeans came they killed all the bison. One of the presidents, I forget which one..."

"Dad?"

The old man glanced around as if trying to orient himself. "When we was kids, Mother only let us play on the rivers and creeks. And on Occoneechee Mountain. It ain't now like it was then. We was labeled colored and segregated in church, in school and in the movies, but they couldn't segregate us in the woods. That's how I met your mama. 'Course, she were only a little bitty thing first time I spied her."

"Come on, old man." He took his father's arm. "Let's get you packed."

"Packed? We joinin' Freddie?"

"I wish, Dad. I wish."

Will stared up at the ceiling covered in bobbly plaster. Thirty-four years of practice at smothering his emotions, but how could he talk about Freddie with his dad person-to-person, lie-upon-lie, and not mentally disintegrate?

# FIVE

Poppy smacked her cell phone on the steering wheel. *Stupid cheap piece of shit.* Best she could afford, but still... *Aha!* A ring tone.

"Han, it's me. Where are you?"

"About to leave Saxapahaw. I had to put a Siamese cat to sleep."

The line crackled.

"And how was that?"

"Peaceful. You're not driving and talking on the phone, are you?"

Poppy laughed. Her friend had her pegged years ago, even before she'd liberated Miss Prissy and accused Asshole of felony animal abuse. He'd tried to bully her out of the lawsuit, since he hadn't wanted his rich friends to know about the banging of the hired help, but it was Hannah who'd persuaded her to walk away. And offered up her pasture for Miss Pris. That was Han, the world's biggest fan of lost causes and underdogs. *Underdogs, ha!* Besides, if she hadn't done the dirty with Asshole, she might never have been fired from the interior design company for sleeping with a client, might never have branched out on her own, might never have met Will Shepard.

Will was definitely no asshole. Plus he was the cutest guy she'd met since dumping the last putz. But dating was like baking. Pie crust didn't always turn out right the first time, either.

"Poppy, honey? You called for a reason?"

"Sorry, girl. Miles away." Poppy swerved around a black snake. *Dang. Car nearly off the road.* "Guess what? I just met this total hottie. Looks kinda young, but didn't Demi Moore prove age is irrelevant? Isn't whatshisname fifteen years her junior?"

"What are you talking about?" Hannah said.

"Wait, forget that. They're divorced. Still. Age doesn't matter these days, does it? This guy looks like a young Daniel Craig. With more hair." Poppy fanned her T-shirt against her boobs. "Lots of hair you want to run your fingers through. Bone structure says Johnny Depp, but his abs are definitely Brad Pitt in *Troy*. You know what? Picture the love child of Johnny Depp and Daniel Craig. He's mighty purty." She slathered on the sassy Southern accent that had cost her parents a small fortune to erase.

"Daniel who?" Hannah's voice echoed.

"Girl, I'm going to pretend you didn't ask that."

Poppy pulled down her visor, grabbed the Green Day CD she'd burned with a continuous loop of "Horseshoes and Handgrenades" and shoved it into the slot.

"When d'you last go to the movies?" Silly question since all Han did was work and sleep. Sleep was so not Poppy's thing. Lucky if she could crash for five hours a night. "You still there?"

The line had gone dead.

*Piece of shit phone—oh. Out of juice. Must've forgotten to charge it again. Imagine that.*

Poppy hummed along to Green Day and tossed the cell phone onto the passenger seat where it bounced off the boxed-up set of mugs destined for some Duke professor. She really had meant to deliver the order before 2:00 p.m. Package was C.O.D. and that grocery money could be mighty useful. Nah. She'd make up some excuse and take it over bright and early Monday. Painting Thoroughbreds on mugs for her parents' country club friends sucked, but she loved the stock pieces. Always rearing up, her prancing mares reminded her to keep spinning just as she'd done since she was a little girl skipping in circles, earning her nickname of Poppy Bean. "Goodness gracious, child," her grandmama always said, "you're full of beans."

But once in a while, when she looked at her painted mares, Poppy saw fear in their eyes, self-defense in their raised hooves. Not one for overanalyzing, she'd never followed that thought—until today. And it led to Hannah.

She was creepy calm. Did she not realize that her son was in a heap of trouble? Depression had been grabbing at him for years, and yet he'd always managed to stumble free. 'Course, Poppy didn't know too much about these things, but Galen had confided plenty when he was a teen trying not to worry his mom. Should she have told Han how far back this crap went? Nah, Hannah would only have worried twice as much. And Galen? He would've been spooked worse than Miss Pris during a tornado warning. One thing about her godson, he was more locked down than Fort Knox.

Even as a kid, Galen had tried to protect his baby brother and his mom. But now *he* needed protecting, and Poppy could do that just fine without betraying any secrets. Steer things in a better direction. Interfere a bit.

Yes, Han told her frequently she should stop sticking her nose where it didn't belong. *Blah, blah, blah.* But this idea about putting Galen in the cottage was beyond catastrophic. Give him too much personal space and who knew what could happen.

Han had always been the one to look out for Poppy. Now it was role reversal time. And her cunning plan had nothing to do with that stud-muffin, Will Shepard. Although, technically, he was more of a twelve-pack of Krispy Kreme original glazed donuts.

Poppy licked her lips and went back to singing.

The forest were his real home: his daddy and his mama, his ancestors and his past, his present and his future. 'Course, he didn't have much future. His flame were goin' out. But to finish his days in the forest? Now that might give him some peace of mind. There were trees all around. Not forest he recognized but didn't much matter. If Willie stopped the car, he'd take hisself off for a walk so he could hear leaves rustlin' under his boots.

Maybe Darren would be there, when they got home. Him and Darren were real tight as kids. Big fight, though, over the record deal. Darren wanted to go on the road, but how could he do that and leave Willie alone with his mama?

Be good to hear the clackety-clack and the whistlin' of the trains again. Couldn't hear no trains from Hawk's Ridge. Missed home-style Southern cookin', too. Institutional food weren't no better than cardboard. Freddie, though, he were eatin' real fancy food.

"C.R.S., son."

"C.R.S.?" Will said.

"Can't remember stuff. What's the name of that ice cream Freddie's bin eatin'?"

"Gelato."

"Gel-*aaaa*-to." His grandbaby were eatin' things he couldn't pronounce! "Think we can get some, for when Freddie comes home? Heck, son. You need me to drive? You plum near went off the road."

He didn't look so hot these days, his Will. Must be workin' too hard. Needed a haircut and a good woman. A man his age should have a wife. Heck, he were married at Willie's age. How old was he now? Couldn't keep track of time. Lost August and September altogether. Now it were October. He could tell from the dogwoods.

"Dad?" Will said. "We're taking a detour."

"You're not drivin' to the cemetery, are you?" Jacob glanced down at the cardboard pipe in his lap. Looked like a giant bullet casin'. Freddie's map were tucked up inside. Well protected. Good, good; good, good. "I won't go."

"No, Dad. I don't want to go to the cemetery any more than you do."

How many years since she'd crossed over? Three? Four? Didn't want to know. Some memories was best left to rot. Never wanted Angeline buried. Wanted her ashes spread in the wind, but Will, he needed a grave. Needed to go visit her, make amends. Things been real bad between them when his Angeline crossed over. The boy wouldn't even come to the funeral. It should have been him under that pile of dirt, not his angel. Ten years older. Should've been him.

Woo-wee, she were somethin', his Angeline. Flitted around like a butterfly. Filled him with awe. Put him through hell during her black spells, but did he regret a single day? No siree, not one. Tough on Willie, though, real tough. She could be a real handful. The temper on her! Been hard on young Willie, that temper. Sometimes he'd had to lock Willie in his room. The boy resented it, of course, but how else could he keep his son safe?

Will swung the car around and put out an arm. Sort of thing he used to do when Willie were little, to keep him from shootin' forward into the dashboard. Willie better not start treatin' his old man like a kid. Where was they goin'? To the cemetery? He hoped not. He never visited. Couldn't. Couldn't think of his dear sweet Angeline under that red clay.

"I thought we was goin' home, Willie. This ain't home. Goddamn it. Take me home!"

"We can't, Dad. We sold the old place two years ago. You had that fall, ended up at the rehabilitation center and we sold the shack. I tried to get you to come to New York, but you wouldn't consider it."

"I ain't movin' to New York. I been followin' the trail of my people all my life. I ain't livin' anywhere but in the footprints of my ancestors."

"I know, Dad. You made that pretty clear after your fall."

Fall? What fall? But he remembered Will leavin' him in that shithole, all right. Some things he remembered clear as day.

The car bounced around a curve. And that bubble of anger, it vanished. *Pop! Gone.*

Jacob sat up straight. Real straight. Ahead were a big pasture with snake-rail fencin' and a horse skitterin' around. And behind? A mighty fine view. So fine it could've been Occoneechee Mountain. His blood were all over that mountain. Heck, his skin, too. One time he banged up his right knee real bad sleddin' down on the back of an old rockin' chair. Woowee. Flew like the wind and ended up in the Eno. Still had the scar to prove it. Willie, he got scarred on Occoneechee Mountain, too. His mama, she felt real bad about that, but the boy never would let her apologize.

Them dogwoods, they were crimson, but the rest of the

forest were still shades of green. Best color in the world. Color that made his heart sing. Didn't he write a song about that once?

Well, he never. And an owl at the edge of the forest! Lots of Lumbee Elders, they said the owl were a bad omen, that if he hooted four times in a row, death were comin'. But he respected the all-seein' night owl. Could set a man to thinkin'. No matter how great you thought you was, that ol' rascal could look down and say, *"Whoo, whoo,* who are you?"

# SIX

Hannah followed half-buried signposts of time: a wagon wheel and two rusty mule shoes. There was living, breathing history in this forest, history that was tangible, history that endured. Protective spirits.

Saponi Mountain had spoken to her from the first day: *You belong here.* So much in life was transitory, but not the connection she felt to this piece of land. If she believed in reincarnation—and maybe she did, because her mother had been a psychic healer who taught her to discount nothing—she had lived here before, in another lifetime. And after everything that had happened with her father, well. Leaving wasn't an option.

Weaving around wild blueberry bushes, Hannah turned into a shaft of dying sunlight, the orange glow of the magical hour her mother had called the gloaming. These days the gloaming descended too quickly into evening. Nothing beat the thrill of hearing coyotes and owls on her land, but nights alone were a bitter reminder that loved ones could leave and never return.

Crispy leaves crackled under her old hiking boots, and Hannah shivered despite the late-afternoon warmth. Dry wind rattled through the leaves of the hardwoods and, for a moment, she thought she heard a car. No, she did. There was a car on her driveway. Rising up on tiptoe, Hannah found a peephole through the sweetgums.

The back of her neck tingled.

Trusting people was her strength and, according to the boys, her weakness. Still, she was a woman without neighbors to hear her scream. She shook her head. How ridiculous, to think like Poppy and second-guess everyone's motives, when honestly, who ever heard of a serial killer driving a Prius? Pretty pale green one, too.

Daisy whined, and Rosie flopped onto Hannah's feet, rooting her to the forest floor.

The engine died and a young man got out. His hair said Californian surfer, but his clothes of tonal greens and browns suggested urban chic. Despite his tangle of blond hair, he blended in with the forest. He was slight but not skinny. Well-toned if she had to guess from this distance. He seemed oddly familiar. Was he one of Galen's friends? Unlikely, since Galen hadn't brought anyone home in a while. This guy didn't look much older than either of her sons, but he moved with the stiffness of an old man. Maybe he needed some pokeweed. Always good for arthritic pain.

The stranger stared at her, or rather at the spot where she was standing. No way could he see her through the foliage and the shadows, but she huddled back against a white oak. A wave of light-headedness hit her. Another warning, maybe, that it was time to end the granola-bars-on-the-go diet.

A second man emerged from the car, much taller than the first. With the long, white ponytail and black leather vest, he had to be Native American. His head bobbed in agitation.

The younger man moved quickly, circling the older man's waist with an arm and guiding him back into the car. It was a filial gesture, and yet the two men couldn't be related. They looked nothing alike.

The air tightened as if sealed in an invisible container, and the squirrels and the birds fell silent. Hannah closed her eyes through another wave of dizziness, her hands digging into the bark of the oak. A door slammed, the car drove off and a crow cawed.

When she opened her eyes, she was alone with the dogs. And in the bough above, there was an owl.

# SEVEN

Will circled the bathroom. How were two grown men expected to share a space this small? How long would they have to stay here like a pair of shipwrecked refugees?

Dinner sat in the middle of his stomach—a coagulated mush of hushpuppies, the only thing he'd dare eat in the diner where everything was drowning in grease and nothing was organic.

He should find a hotel with a suite. No, find somewhere with a kitchen, a real kitchen, so he could prepare real food for his now-homeless dad. If nothing else, he could at least feed the old man. Will had learned to cook through observation at corn shuckings, wheat thrashings, canning parties and hog killings. The Shepard clan was huge. You only had to clock reactions when you answered the question "Who's your people?" to realize the reach of his family. And yet it all boiled down to him and his dad and a cardboard tube in a Best Western. With a tiny bathroom.

On the other side of the paper-thin wall, a handful of kids screamed and giggled. A parental voice shushed them, and

Will's heart raced like a souped-up engine. No way could he stay here another night. He needed out; he needed to ditch this feeling of running barefoot through briars. He yanked the scrap of paper from his back pocket and stared at it. A cottage would come with a kitchen. Maybe Poppy's friend would even consider a short-term lease. Really, at this point, what did he have to lose by asking? Will took a deep breath and punched in the phone number.

"Hello?" a quiet, warm voice answered immediately.

Was it too late to call? Had he woken her? He breathed through his mouth as he tried to block the smell of his dad's shaving cream. A memory tackled him: his mother, breasts exposed, drunk in the family bathtub. His dad lifting her out. *Now, son. You don't need to see this. Go to your room and shut the door.* Most of his family life had happened on the other side of his bedroom door.

"Who are you trying to reach?" the voice said.

Jesus, he'd forgotten to talk. "Sorry. Hannah Linden."

"I can barely hear you. Can you speak up, please?"

"The art teacher from Hawk's Ridge gave me your number. You have a cottage for rent?"

"Yes, Poppy stopped by earlier this evening, mentioned she'd given you my number." Hannah paused but something had shifted. Wary, she had become wary. "I'm afraid she made a mistake. I'm not renting the cottage right now."

In the next room, his dad snored.

"I'll pay double whatever you're asking."

"That bad?"

"Have you ever shared a motel room with an aging parent?"

"I'd like to say yes, but both my parents are dead."

Her honesty slapped him; pain settled in his temple. He was losing this conversation before it had begun. "Sorry. About your parents, I mean." Apologizing, retreating. Time for his ace, the one that never failed. A lousy trick or a sign of desperation? "I haven't introduced myself. I'm Will Shepard, the writer. Maybe you've heard of me?"

"*The* Will Shepard? The one and only?"

"Poppy didn't mention it? She saw me lugging a full set of Agent Dodds novels out of the director's office."

"When Poppy's on a mission she doesn't notice much. You could run past her buck-naked and she wouldn't clock your ass."

He smiled and caught his reflection in the bathroom mirror. The smile, a nod to pleasure and happiness, felt like a betrayal to Freddie. He contorted his face back into its customary mask. Blank, expressionless.

"Plus, Poppy only reads glossy magazines," Hannah said. "Ones filled with celebrity gossip."

"But *you've* heard of me?"

"I'm a fan. Your plots suck me in and don't let go."

"And my characters?" Damn, his ego had to ask.

"You seem to enjoy exploring broken minds."

*Not so much enjoyment as an inability to escape total psychos.*

Hannah started talking again. "Poppy hasn't been at Hawk's Ridge for long, but I've heard a great deal about your father. I gather he loves to brag about his grandson." She paused. "Such a special bond between young boys and their grandfathers."

*A bond that transcends even death.* Grief stirred in his stomach, moved up through his esophagus, threatened to spew out of his mouth in a macabre chant of *He's dead, my son is dead.*

"Yes," Will said quietly. He wanted to say more, but just breathing was a struggle. This bond, this special bond between young boys and their grandfathers, also led to fiction. To a lie, even though Poppy clearly thought it was the truth. He'd assumed all the staff knew about Freddie's death. Or at least the night staff who'd had to restrain his dad one hundred and two days earlier when Will had driven down with the news of the accident. Maybe the director hadn't briefed Poppy because she was a volunteer.

Will took a deep breath. Now he really, *really* wanted that cottage. It offered a clean chalkboard. No explanations necessary. What the hell, he'd go for some honesty. Not his normal strategy with women, but it was the only play he had left.

"My dad's had a few rough years since my mom died. She was his life. His world collapsed and he's...he's not bouncing out of his grief." The hitch in his voice was surprising. Unnerving. "We drove by your place earlier and it seemed peaceful. I think it would be good for him—the quiet, the forest. He's always loved the forest. It would only be temporary, until I figure out what to do long-term."

Silence. Was she digesting what she knew about his dad and Hawk's Ridge? How much had Poppy told her? How much should he tell her?

Hannah sighed. "Okay, then."

"He's suffering some short-term memory loss. Is that a problem?"

"I don't know. Should it be?"

Wait, she'd totally agreed. Why was he risking more information than necessary? He held the phone tight against his cheek. "My dad can be difficult."

"And you can't be?"

Was she teasing him?

"When he gets confused he gets upset," Will said. "I think the lack of control scares him."

"Lack of control scares most people."

"Did Poppy tell you what happened at Hawk's Ridge?"

"In some detail, yes."

"I know how it looks, but he's not violent." Although the old man had just been kicked out of a retirement home for

brawling. "Dad doesn't even squish bugs. I had this patho-
logical fear of spiders as a kid. He taught me how to catch
and release them." Did he just reveal personal details to a fan?
"But I'll be with him the whole time."

"It's fine." He could hear her smile. "A senescent grandfather doesn't bother me in the least."

How perfect, she had used the word *senescent*. Will loved
to be surprised by people's word choices. Words held such
power and such beauty. And such escape. As a young boy, he
chose *magical* not *mad* to describe his mother. As an adult, he
chose *alive,* not *dead,* to describe his son.

"You said this was temporary, but I prefer a six-month
lease." She gave a soft laugh, an easy laugh. No drama. "Is
that a problem?"

Yeah, because if he thought he'd still be in Orange County
in six days let alone six months, he'd kill himself and his dad.
But he could easily pay out the lease. It was just money. The
one thing he had plenty of.

"It's not a problem if we can move in tomorrow."

They discussed a price—or rather she suggested a figure
and he agreed. Then Will hung up and cracked open the bathroom door. The old man snuffled from one of the twin beds
with the psychedelic comforters. The giant map, stored away
in its thick casing, lay on the floor next to him. Memories-to-
go rolled up safe and sound. At some point they would have
to return to Hawk's Ridge—box up the rest of his mother's
knickknacks and arrange for a mover to haul the furniture,
even though his dad had said it could stay for all he cared.
Wasn't his goddamn furniture, was it?

The old man had a point. Will had purchased it while his
dad was at the rehabilitation center. New furniture for a fresh
start, that had been the plan, but Will had given no thought
to his dad's taste. Problem was, he didn't know if the old

man had any taste. Always his mom set the tone; always his dad followed.

Even when his mom was going whacko and smashing crockery, his parents had a bond that excluded everyone. One of the reasons he'd been such a self-reliant kid. That and the fact of being a midlife oops baby, a bear cub—*Little Moondi*—according to his dad. But bear cubs were meant to follow and learn from their mothers, not run from them. When they were teenagers, Ally had pronounced him to be a coyote, and he'd believed her. Until he'd found out that coyotes often mated for life.

# EIGHT

The pale green Prius from the day before crawled to the end of her driveway, and Will Shepard turned neatly to one side in a considerate act of parking.

His author photo had revealed nothing. Black-and-white, it was taken from a distance as he glanced over his shoulder. Headshots didn't seem to be to his liking. Hannah had seen a partial of his face years ago in an out-of-date *People* magazine picked up in the dentist's waiting room. At the time, she'd just finished the third Agent Dodds adventure, and her radar had been tuned to all things Will Shepard. If she remembered correctly, the photo had shown him escorting a young heiress to a gala.

Hannah fingered the key, and the dogs cowered around her. She could lavish ten more lifetimes of unconditional love on her babies, and still fear would stalk them. Daisy's abuse had gone beyond neglect. The dog had been forced to fight. So many damaged creatures had passed through Hannah's life in the past twenty years and most of them had come from Poppy.

Now her friend had brought her a bestselling author and his grieving dad. A small happening that felt huge.

Hannah read Will's bumper stickers: "I'd Rather Be Writing," and "Love a Climber, They Use Protection." Climbing—that made sense since Agent Dodds was an extreme sports freak. Was his creator an adrenaline junkie, too? Or a nocturnal reveler who dated beautiful socialites? The two of them hadn't signed anything. If she had even a twinge of doubt, she would renege.

Will turned to talk with his father, and Hannah drummed her fingers on the porch railing. Impatience didn't come often, but she had an appointment in… Unbelievable, she was wearing both her watch and her dad's, and yet she had no memory of putting on either one. Focusing on life's details was becoming impossible. She sighed.

Would it be inappropriate to ask Will to sign his books? Or would he be offended that she didn't own anything beyond volume five? Galen was scathing about commercial fiction, especially the kind of thrillers Will had produced in recent years. Her MFA poet preferred incomprehensible allegories written by alcoholics and drug addicts who'd been dead for at least a century. And he would not be happy when he discovered she was renting out the cottage. Privacy was everything to Galen, and since the age of thirteen, he had proved himself worthy of trust, not surveillance. But during the previous night's phone conversation with Will, she had realized it was time, once again, to adapt.

Coincidence spoke of connection, and renting the cottage to an aging widower was nothing short of symmetry. Her father would approve. No, he would applaud. After all, the cottage had been built as his refuge. And what if it went deeper than that? Her father's last selfless act had been to protect Galen and Liam, to spare them from the moment of his death, to wander into the woods to die alone. What if some echo of that love reverberated across Saponi Mountain, telling her to contain Galen in his childhood room where she could keep him safe? Her mother had believed that the dead often remained tethered to the living—trapped either in their desire to right wrongs or in their refusal to leave loved ones. Hannah, too, was drawn to the idea that the dead never really moved on, although often it was the living who refused to let them go.

Kookiness aside, renting the cottage was a sound financial move. Galen had become a dropout in need of aid. Her father's money was gone and she barely made a living, but Will hadn't quibbled at her inflated price. Overcharging, not undercharging, was oddly liberating.

Will pulled himself from the car. She'd been right: he was small for a guy. His taupe knit shirt, however, revealed a muscular torso, and his thick, straight hair was only slightly less tousled than the day before. Obviously, he didn't own a comb. He walked toward her, not with the swagger of someone whose name was a long internet search of awards, but as if he were a kid dragging his body to a reprimand. An unexpected blend of curiosity and recognition tightened in her gut. He was so familiar she almost said, "Oh. It's you."

His eyes were concealed behind funky green-tinted sunglasses, which wasn't helpful. You could learn a great deal from a person by the way he held—or avoided—your gaze. He was also beautiful. A pretty boy young enough to be her son, if she'd gotten pregnant that first time.

Will paused in front of the cottage, squatted and waited. Rosie and Daisy sidled down the steps, their claws clacking on the wooden boards. He held out both hands, offering his palms, and a chunky silver sports watch slid down his wrist. He cooed something at the dogs, words Hannah couldn't make sense of, but her girls clearly understood. Daisy flopped to the ground and exposed her belly; Rosie actually whimpered. Animal behavior rarely surprised her, but her dogs had just told Hannah all she needed to know about this man. Even if he hadn't been polite enough to remove his sunglasses.

Hannah joined Will and the dogs. Up close, his face was a little too perfect, its bone structure a little too predictable. She preferred faces with wrinkles and scars, faces that spoke of struggles and triumphs. This guy looked no more than thirty.

"Will Shepard." He rose slowly.

"Hannah Linden. I imagined you to be older."

"I write fast." Will extended his hand but flinched.

Now the sunglasses made sense. "Want something for that headache?"

"I thought Poppy said you were a vet."

"A holistic vet. Treating pets often means treating owners. You'd be surprised how many clients ask for help with minor ailments. But if it makes you feel better, my father was a rural doctor. When I was a teenager, he let me help out with patients."

"Is that legal?"

"Would it bother you if it wasn't?"

He winced.

"Bad one?"

"Killer."

"I have to visit a couple of clients this afternoon, but I'll be back by early evening. I can pop over then with my acupuncture needles and a feverfew tincture. Should help you sleep, too."

Will turned as his dad clambered out of the passenger seat. "I don't sleep much."

"Well, there's your problem. Good sleep habits are the key to a healthy mind."

"Really."

She would excuse his snide tone, since her girls had given their approval. "By the way, we're in a drought, so please be mindful of water usage." Hannah handed over the key. "Short showers, minimal toilet flushing. And any water you'd like to recycle, please toss over there, for the garden."

As she pointed at the huge galvanized tub under the outside shower, Jacob Shepard shuffled over. Hannah covered her mouth and swallowed. Jacob's expression was identical to the one her father had worn in those final months of unbearable grief—his eyes, his mouth, even the skin on his cheeks appeared to be dragged down by sadness. The lines grooved between his eyebrows, the faint scowl, seemed to say, "I no longer understand the world in which I live."

"Are we home, Willie?" Jacob said.

For a moment, she considered kissing Jacob's cheek, whispering, *You can be happy here.* Instead, she strode to meet him with a smile.

"I certainly hope this will feel like home. You must be Jacob. I'm Hannah, a friend of Poppy's. She's promised to swing by this evening and see how you're settling in."

"Poppy?"

"My friend Poppy. The art teacher at Hawk's Ridge."

"Firecracker, that Poppy." Jacob grinned, showing yellowed, higgledy-piggledy teeth. He was taller than Will—over six feet—and broad shouldered, despite a slight stoop. If she had to guess, she'd put him around eighty. Once again, Hannah glanced from father to son. These two couldn't possibly share a gene pool.

"I—I'm not good with names, little lady," Jacob said.

"That's okay. I answer to anything. Call me Hey You if it's easier."

"Hannah," Will said, his voice sluggish. "Her name is Hannah."

"That's a pretty name, name for an angel, but I like Hey You better."

"Hey You, it is. I love your necklace." Hannah nodded at the string of bear claws that hung on his chest. "Occaneechi?"

Jacob's eyes crinkled.

"Yes," Will answered. "My dad is Occaneechi."

Will Shepard was Native American? Although, something about his square jaw and thick eyebrows... Yes, she could believe he had native ancestry.

"My mother—" Will pushed his sunglasses up into his hair, and Hannah gasped "—was not."

"What do you mean you've seen his eyes before? Haunting as they are. Huge and icy blue." Poppy swirled wine around her goblet and then drained the glass.

The sun disappeared behind the treetops, and Hannah brushed an oak leaf from one of the cushions under her arm. Dry and brittle, the leaf crumbled to ashes, then scattered into the air.

"I don't know," Hannah said. "They're so distinctive, so familiar."

Jacob was napping when Poppy had arrived, but she'd insisted on staying for a girls' night. A feeble excuse, no doubt, to keep Will in her sights. And the overnight bag and large screw-top bottle of wine suggested Poppy intended to get snookered in the process.

Poppy had a proclivity for dating guys who were either married or inherently messed up, and Will Shepard clearly fell into at least one of those categories. The absence of a wedding ring meant nothing, but Will didn't act like someone who was married. He did, however, act like a person in pain,

pain that went beyond a mere headache. You didn't have to be a holistic practitioner to understand that physical symptoms often hinted at emotional distress. Hannah chose not to think about the study she'd read that morning, the one linking depression with heart disease.

She and Poppy slid back and forth on the retro metal rocker, both of them watching Will retrieve a brown bag of groceries from the trunk of the Prius.

*"Hubba-hubba,"* Poppy said. "Look at the muscles on those forearms. Girl, I bet he gives new meaning to the term *sexual endurance.*"

"Maybe he spends his nights hanging from the rafters."

"Think he's dating right now?" Poppy fiddled with the array of elastic bands on her left wrist, none of which represented anything other than her love of bright colors.

"He has a son, Poppy. Kids tend to come with mothers."

"It's weird, there's so little about his personal life on the web. It's all work, work, work. Wikipedia doesn't even mention that he's a dad."

So, they'd both checked him out.

"At one time he was linked briefly with that New York socialite who died a few months back," Poppy continued.

"No idea what you're talking about."

"You should read the gossip mags, Han. She killed herself, her lover and their son. Smashed their car into a wall. Theory is her brakes went, which is pretty suspect. Smacks of a cover-up if you ask me. But nothing I found says he's married. Used to be a player, these days he seems to be a monk. What a waste of that body."

"I'm changing the subject. Tell me what you know about Jacob."

"Not much to tell. Sundays were skeleton staff days at Hawk's Ridge—the director told me sweet-shit-nothing about the residents. Jacob has short-term memory loss, adored his wife, worships his grandson. Figured all that out by myself."

"And Will?"

"Didn't know Jacob had a son until I butted into Will's meeting. Bad blood between them, if I had to guess. What's the Galen update?"

"He's coming home next week. Inigo's promised to pay for his ticket and give us a two-week pass before he visits. Until he can check his melodrama at the door, Inigo's a problem I can't handle. He was completely hysterical in California. It was like having a third child." Hannah sighed. "Sometimes I wonder what my parents were thinking, allowing me to marry at nineteen."

"Could they have stopped you?"

"No." Hannah smiled. "He was hard to resist in those days—the exotic name, the Celtic heritage, that sexy smile." Her in-laws had scheduled Inigo for greatness from inception, hoping he would become a famous architect like his namesake, Inigo Jones. And Inigo carried himself with a confidence that suggested he believed the family propaganda. But he alienated his parents in three easy steps: he married a high school classmate who wanted only to be a country vet, then he became an English professor, and for his *pièce de résistance,* he changed his sexual orientation.

"Of course, now my ex is a dick."

Poppy snorted out a laugh. "Finally, after six years she trashes her ex. Proud of you, girl. So, it all worked out, then. With the cottage."

Will balanced the bag on his hip as he tugged open the screen door.

"I guess," Hannah replied, chewing the inside of her cheek.

★ ★ ★

The screen door slammed and Will turned to watch the two women on the porch drinking red wine.

Hannah and Poppy were clearly plotting, leaning toward each other in a female conspiracy. Maybe they were discussing him and his dad, trying to figure out their relationship. Good luck on that one. Thirty-four years of living the relationship and *he* couldn't figure it out.

Will placed the last bag of groceries on the kitchen table and headed upstairs to check on the old man. Exhausted from the stress of food shopping, his dad had gone upstairs to lie down the moment they'd returned. Wise move. Normally, grocery shopping was heaven on earth: the smells, the tastes—grazing around the free samples, concocting recipes in his head. Before Freddie's death, buying fresh produce was the closest Will came to a hobby. Today, with his dad, it had ranked on par with drug-free wisdom teeth removal. Next time, he'd hire a dad-sitter.

The stairs creaked as Will dragged himself up by the banister. The ceiling of the stairwell was midnight blue and covered with plastic glow-in-the-dark stars, the same ones he'd stuck all over Freddie's bedroom. When the interior decorator had finished, Will had balanced on a stepladder for hours, creating a perfect constellation for his two-year-old. After the accident, he'd destroyed it in minutes—ripping down stars, paint and drywall. When he returned to New York, he would hire another decorator, a cheaper one, to erase the evidence of grief.

The upstairs hallway in the cottage was empty except for a large black-and-white photo framed and hung at the far end. The photographer had captured the woods at sunrise in early April. Dogwoods, in full bloom, rose like ghosts through a veil of early-morning fog.

Everything else in the hall was white like the edges of a dream. Interesting how different white could be. White in Hannah's hands seemed to be warm and calming. White in his apartment was cold and sterile. And since all his furniture was crafted out of pale wood, the only color came from his lime leather sofa. One of his ex-lovers had referred to it as the bilious margarita.

Will ran his hand over the hall railing, reading the grain. Wood could reveal a thousand stories. He'd done some carving as a kid, inspired by his dad's garden sculptures of downed tree limbs. He and Ally had once imagined them to be fantastical creatures. By the time he was a teenager, Will saw them for what they really were—talismans.

He pinched the bridge of his nose, pushing against the crouching headache, the throbbing pain. Nothing about this trip was turning out the way he'd planned. Not that he'd had a plan other than get in, get drunk, get out. He would never start a climb without a strategy for descent, and yet in this situation he was behaving like a frantic novice about to bomb.

His dad used to have a horde of cousins in the area. They'd spent their adolescent years together, toe-to-toe, as Uncle Darren used to say. Were they still alive? Should he reestablish contact with the tribe? Maybe his dad just needed to be part of a community again. *Yeah, right.* Whatever his dad needed went way beyond socializing and probably involved a retirement home upgrade from independent to assisted living. From stage one to stage two.

Will eased open the door to the larger of the two bedrooms. A twenty-four-hour crash course in the care of the elderly had taught him that the old man's balance was seriously off-kilter when he woke up. The shortest possible distance to the nearest toilet had been the deciding factor in the bedroom allocation—unless he wanted to start cleaning up his dad's shit. Literally.

The old man had collapsed onto the bed like a battery-operated toy run out of juice. A very large, very broken toy. Jacob Shepard used to have such presence—his height, his ability to say a great deal with a handful of words, his snippets of self-made philosophy.

Even now, Will could hear his dad's voice teaching him to hunt rabbit. *Got your bow, Willie? Don't get excited now. That rabbit, he's under the wheat straw, but he's gonna zig and zag.* Will didn't believe him, and when the rabbit performed as predicted, Will fell on his butt. His dad had howled with laughter.

Will slid down the wall to the pale gray carpet and watched the man with his white hair tugged half out of its ponytail. The man who had taught him to hunt and fish, to whittle wood and identify animal bones. The man who had been a devoted husband and yet had failed to teach his son how to love a woman so she loved him back.

Uncle Darren had said, "Your daddy, he loved your mama his whole life. Like she cursed him. He waited for her to grow up. He waited through her mistakes with other men. He waited with nothing more than the faith that, one day, Angeline would love him. And one day she did."

Once upon a time, Will had applied that philosophy to his feelings for Ally. For so many years, she was the only good part of his life. Such a fierce friend, Ally was the one person he trusted, the one person who—until the lie about Freddie's Great European Adventure—knew Will's every secret. But somewhere along the way he'd found hard cynicism. Or maybe he'd just been smart enough to realize she would never love him as more than her best friend. He'd dated other women, never seriously, but then Freddie had entered his life and filled the hole Ally had left in his heart. And now? Now it was as if he were slowly bleeding to death.

A small thought escaped: he should have brought Freddie's ashes. Death had finally granted Will full parental rights, and he didn't need a headstone. He carried Freddie in his heart. Maybe Freddie's spirit could be happy here. The few times they'd visited, he'd loved the forest.

Will glanced around the sparsely decorated room that ran the width of the cottage. Two smaller windows on one wall looked directly into the main house; a huge pinnacle-shaped window at the back held a perfect view of Saponi Mountain. Through it, a wall of dark green was splattered with bursts of foliage the color of dried blood. The dogwoods were turning, which meant every morning his dad would wake to what was about to become a symphony of fall.

The headache tightened. Now that he'd brought the old man back to the forest, how would he ever persuade him to leave?

A small glass vase of horribly familiar greenery sat on the dresser. Hauling himself to his feet, Will reached out and ran his fingers up one of the stalks. Hesitating, he raised his palm to his nose and sniffed. Freshly cut sage and the memory that reeked of madness.

A herb renowned for its healing properties, sage had become a popular bedding plant. Will had seen beautiful sage flowers of red and purple in private gardens—had even admired them from a distance. But get too close, and sage could blister his mind the way poison ivy blistered his skin. Sage was the smell of powwows; sage was the barbed remembrance of his mother dancing half-naked and disgracing them all; sage was the symbol of Uncle Darren warding off evil.

Will staggered downstairs and out onto the porch swing. The headache was waiting to roar, waiting to tear him apart.

Even the fading daylight burned his retinas. He closed his eyes and let his head droop to his chest. Blood pounded; pain pulsed through his brain in leaden waves.

The smell of sage clung to his nostrils, leached his brain with the slow-moving film playing in his head. It must have been winter, since he was in his footed pj's, similar to the ones Freddie had owned. Will was supposed to be asleep, locked in his tiny bedroom off the porch. Uncle Darren was outside yelling, waving his bundle of dried sage, demanding to come in and smudge the shack to banish diabolical spirits. The old man refused and there was another blowup about his mom. Had she been laughing outside the bedroom door, or had Will invented that last part?

Pressure on his knees. Soft and gentle. Human touch.

"Will?"

Where had Hannah come from? He didn't hear her approach. She smelled of hay and lavender. Mild country scents warped into sensory overload by his exploding brain.

He opened his eyes and tried to look at her, but he couldn't raise his head. She had beautiful hands with long, healthy fingernails—surprising for a vet. No nail polish. One ring on her right index finger—silver, engraved. Native American.

"The headache still bad?" Hannah said.

He moaned.

"Give me your hands." Her voice was low, soothing, the voice on the phone from the night before. "This won't hurt."

He obeyed, ignoring the intuition that murmured, *Of course it's going to hurt. You're a woman.*

"Do you trust me?"

"Why not?" What did he care if she stuck a thousand needles in his hand when ten times that many pierced his heart every minute of every day?

"Give me your right hand. Good, now splay your fingers."

She ripped open a small packet and took out a long, thin nail partially covered in copper coils. "I'm going to slide one needle into the webbing between your thumb and index finger," she said, "into the LI4."

"LI4?"

"Large Intestine 4. An acupuncture point for the head and the face."

"In my hand?"

"In your hand."

Will closed his eyes. This, he preferred not to watch. He felt a small amount of pressure but no pain.

She stroked his left hand, her fingers lingering.

"How did you get this scar?"

"Which one?"

"Oh," she said. "You have several. Some nasty accident?"

"Ripped flesh. From rock climbing."

"Interesting sport."

"More like a religion." He swallowed through the pain. "Are you going to do that hand, too?"

"Already done." She placed both his hands in his lap. "Now sit for an hour, try to relax, then remove the needles. I'm leaving a bag of dried feverfew. Pour boiling water over it and drink it."

"If I get blood poisoning, I'm suing for medical malpractice."

Was that a laugh?

Everything went quiet, except for the tree frogs croaking through their nightly social. He didn't hear Hannah leave, but he couldn't sense her anymore. A random act of kindness. Wow, that was the stuff of folklore.

Will kept his eyes shut to avoid confronting the fact that his hands had become pincushions. They felt a little odd, a little tight, but there was no pain from the needles. Maybe, just maybe, if a stranger could pierce his skin with foreign objects and he could feel nothing, then a five-year-old could die by lethal impact and feel no pain.

His mind darted through unmoored thoughts, disjointed waking dreams he could remember only the essence of. Freddie died strapped into his five-point harness. Safest car seat according to Consumer Reports, unless, of course, your mother hurtled into a wall at seventy miles per hour. Why did Will's mind have to sketch every detail, re-create an entire scene he had never witnessed and play it over and over again? Screeching tires, the crunch of metal buckling, screams, the smell of gasoline, the whoosh of flames. The explosion.

A tsunami of grief swamped him, dragged him down to the depths. He would never break through to the surface. He would never come up for air.

Eyes tightly closed, Will started to cry the only way he knew how. Silently.

# NINE

Will woke to bright moonlight and the howling of coyotes. And a pair of delicate nails poking out of his skin. So, Hannah hadn't been some ghostly mirage created by his burned-out mind. He felt—Will concentrated—okay. The headache had retreated into an echo of pain. Staring up at a full moon, he eased out the first needle, then the second.

How long had he been asleep? *Jesus.*

Will jumped up and tugged open the front door, gagging on the smell. The old man was stretched out on the futon, asleep and drooling. The new bottle of Wild Turkey, a quarter empty, pinned a note to the coffee table. "Dinner in—" *indecipherable scribble.* Oven? *Oven!*

Running into the kitchen, Will stopped to glance around for a fire extinguisher. As expected, Hannah was a woman with her shit together, a woman who placed a small fire extinguisher on the wall and a smoke detector on the ceiling. The green, blinking light suggested it was fully operational.

Will made a quick check through the glass door of the oven. *Good, no flames.* And the knob was turned only to two hundred degrees, probably because the old man couldn't see without his glasses. Who knew what had happened to those.

What other details had Will missed? On a rock face, he never doubted his ability to protect lives, and yet here he was—spectacularly inept at looking after one octogenarian. Was he supposed to remind his dad to change his underwear, brush his teeth, wipe his ass—Will eased open the oven door—take the plastic wrapping off the lasagna before heating it?

No wonder Hawk's Ridge charged exorbitant rates. The staff earned every cent.

A large mug of black coffee and an internet search later, Will had compiled a list of local assisted-living facilities and researched another leg of Freddie's trip. Will laced his hands behind his neck and stretched. Rediscovering the joy of in-depth location research was invigorating. As with every aspect of his writing, he'd grown lazy, choreographing action around backdrops rather than exploring the psychological impact of setting on character. After all, a patch of forest could brand you for life.

The scar on his knee itched; he ignored it.

Freddie and Cassandra were in Vienna. They'd spent the evening before at the Prater, riding the Giant Ferris Wheel, and the morning at the Augarten Park. Fortunately, they'd avoided Hitler's anti-aircraft flak tower, a concrete monument to evil.

If only Will could figure out how to use that Nazi behemoth in his work, incorporate it into a hate crime Agent Dodds could stumble into while on vacation. Except his hero was still suspended from the helicopter. Besides, Agent Dodds didn't do vacations. Didn't do downtime. Sex was rushed, desperate and usually with someone's wife; A.A. meetings were an excuse for Dodds to check email. The only time Dodds unplugged was when he visited his paranoid schizophrenic mother in the nursing home surrounded by razor wire.

Will pushed back from the kitchen table and wandered into the main room. He should try and get his dad upstairs to bed. Or maybe not. Life was so peaceful when the old man was out cold. It was the relief of watching a sleeping toddler after a crazy-ass day of playground supervision. It was also the writing hour—or would be, if he had a story worth telling. Something other than the Great European Adventure.

He eased the cotton throw off the back of the futon and tucked it around the old man. A walk in the moonlight might unlock a little inspiration. Will refused to think the word *muse,* which resonated with literary pretension and angst. Of course, he'd always dissed the phrase *writer's block,* too. Cosmic payback was one sick bitch.

Five minutes—Will tiptoed onto the porch—he'd only be gone five minutes. Long enough to take a look at the mare that was always tearing up grass with her teeth. Didn't want the old man waking to an empty house.

A large buck with a trophy rack appeared on the edge of his vision, then glided back toward Saponi Mountain. Will turned his head away from the siren song of the forest. With any luck, he wouldn't have to set foot in there before returning to New York.

Tree frogs croaked a concerto, and snuffling came from the compost pile. The raccoons were out in force. Above, an expanse of night sky shimmered with stars. Man, he'd forgotten the glory of Southern nights—how he was drawn to the stillness, the raw energy. As a kid, he'd loved reading or writing in the middle of the night. Unless there was a storm to whip up her craziness, terror tended to come with the light, when his mom was awake.

On the ground floor of the main house, a figure moved behind closed curtains. His temporary landlady was still awake. *Temporary* was such a wonderful word. It didn't hold you to a thing.

And was that running water? Curious, Will changed direction and headed toward the beam of artificial light illuminating the far side of the main house. Too late he remembered what Hannah had said about an outside shower. He swallowed a huge, painful gulp.

Poppy was standing under a jet of water, and she was full rearview naked.

If she were ten years younger—and he hadn't stopped dating when Freddie was old enough for sleepovers—Poppy would have been a classic Will Shepard babe. Curvaceous, wild, outspoken, she was fire inside and out, a woman who dazzled with a good-time guarantee and the knowledge that she could lose interest and vanish. Great sex, no future. But thinking with his dick had only ever led to disaster, and dealing with his dad was enough of a calamity.

He should turn away. Really. Because to stay meant crossing the line into being a sicko, a total perv. He should look away, but like a twelve-year-old with a stack of porn magazines, he couldn't.

Poppy rinsed her hair, tilting her head from side to side. *Eyes up, Will, eyes up.*

But his eyes, unable to heed the message from his brain, trawled lower. What was it about women's butts that made him behave like a kid confronted with a wall of jelly beans in every flavor you could imagine and some you couldn't? *Grab and eat your fill.*

Then a door opened, and Will sprinted for the camouflage of the forest.

Had anything ever felt quite so divine? The buzz from a bottle of wine—minus Hannah's one teeny-weeny glass—and the cool water caressing Poppy's body. No wonder Hannah liked to shower in the moonlight. This was bliss. At least, it was until Hannah started cawing like trailer trash.

"Poppy!"

Poppy hummed loudly.

"Poppy!"

She should have plied Hannah with more wine, but her friend had stopped drinking after droning on and on about being on call. 'Course Hannah didn't do drunk, didn't do mad, and she hadn't had sex in forever. What *was* her problem?

Stupid, stupid, *s-t-u-p-i-d* for a woman in her prime to say she wouldn't date because of her sons—neither of whom even lived at home anymore. If she put in the smallest effort, Hannah would be a red-hot babe. And the boys *wanted* their mom to get it on with someone so they didn't have to worry about her being home alone in the middle of nowhere. Well, that was Galen's take. Liam's motivation was more along the lines of "So she'll, like, stay out of my business."

Poppy had only kept one secret her whole life: that when Liam was sixteen and wasted, he'd asked Poppy to be his mom. Well, maybe she'd kept more than just that one secret.

The water stopped, and Poppy shivered.

"What?" She swallowed a belch. "I'm recycling water for your plants."

She was thrust into a warm, fluffy white towel.

"You mean you're hoping Will Shepard notices you recycling water for my plants while you're standing out here naked." Hannah raised her eyebrows.

"That, too."

"Making goo-goo eyes at my new tenant is the worst idea you've had in a series of worst ideas. He's got issues. It's written all over his face."

"I'm more interested in his body...."

"Which is barely out of diapers."

"*Yummy*. Everything all firm." Poppy snorted a laugh. "Dang, girl, you don't have a hankering for him, do you?"

Hannah sighed. "I'm old enough to be his mother."

"Bull crap, he's older than he looks. Only a few years younger than me." Eight. She'd done the math.

"Suppose it had been Jacob? You could've given him a heart attack. Although—" Hannah's mouth did that cute little twitchy thing it did when she was thinking "—he would've died happy."

"Ah. Didn't consider that."

"Exactly. No more outside showers while I have tenants."

"Yes, mama dearest." Poppy hiccupped.

"Are you drunk?"

"Yup."

There was definitely movement by the tree line. Man-size movement. Poppy sashayed her hips as she followed Hannah and the dogs back inside. The trap was set and sprung. Now all she had to do was reel in that hunk of an author. *Game on.*

Branches snapped all around him, and Will glanced over his shoulder, half expecting a pack of saber-toothed tigers to leap from behind the oaks and shred him with six-inch razor fangs. Reduce him to gristle and bone.

Less than two days in Orange County, and he was back in the forest. It was nothing more than a Pandora's box of the past, and unlike his dad, Will wanted that part of his life to remain in storage.

The memory assaulted him, anyway: his mother grabbing him by the hand after his first day of kindergarten, shrieking, "Let's celebrate with an adventure! Slay the beast of Oc-coneechee Mountain!"

There had been a time when her grandiose schemes had

sucked him in. Even after they'd imploded in a flurry of ex-
cess or fizzled as her attention darted to something else, he'd
allowed himself to believe that next time, next time, things
would be different. But by then he'd learned better. Five years
old and already he was skeptical. As she pulled him deeper into
the woods that day, he had cried to go home, and he never
cried as a kid. Will rubbed his arms. The memory crawled
under his skin, wormed into his cells, returned in stereo surround sound.

All morning in school, he'd been anxious, waiting for the
other kids to tease him for being a runt, for not having a lunch
box, for wearing secondhand clothes. His fears were realized at recess, until the little girl in a hot-pink tutu knocked
down the bully who'd stolen his swing. Ally got in trouble
for that, but she didn't care. And he was smitten. No one had
ever stood up for him before. No one had ever put him first.
He jumped off the bus, eager to invite his new friend over
to share his stash of library books. But his mom had other
plans, and she wouldn't let go. She held tighter and tighter
until she dragged him over the rusty animal trap that sliced
open his knee. It was the first time—maybe the only time—
his dad got angry with his mom; it was the first time Will
fantasized about escape.

He touched the scar through his jeans. The itchiness from
earlier had gone. Once again, it was numb.

Waiting until the outside lights on the main house switched
off, Will crept back to the cottage and picked up the plastic
bag Hannah had left on the porch swing. What did she say?
*It should help you sleep.*

Better pilfer one of those orange capsules from his dad—
add a temazepam chaser on the off-chance dried feverfew
wasn't strong enough for total blackout.

# TEN

Jacob smoothed out Freddie's map on the table. Been another rough night. All them nightmares about Freddie. His grandson were on the trip of a lifetime. And his granddaddy's no-good-for-nothin' brain weren't gonna say otherwise. 'Bout time he crafted a dream catcher, hung it above his bed and then took it outside so all them bad dreams could perish in the sunlight. Plenty of sunlight this morning. And warm in the front room. Shouldn't be this warm when the dogwoods were firin' up. Wouldn't be much color this fall, not with the heat and the drought. Drought were a real serious business. Weakened trees fell, wells ran dry and that phantom of forest fires didn't never go away. October could be a real dry month, too. Mighty fine month for travelin', though. One time he took Angeline to Asheville—special trip for their weddin' anniversary. They even stayed over! Spent a night in a motel! And they drove up and down the Blue Ridge Parkway drinkin' in the wonder of fall in the mountains.

Where was Freddie and his mama travelin' today?

He wanted to stick the map on the wall, but Willie said

no. And he could argue the heck out of it, but seemed like a protest not worth makin'. Besides, with this sturdy cardboard casin', he could take the map out whenever and wherever he chose.

It were real nice in the main room of this house. Big house, too. Had two bathrooms! And a separate toilet downstairs! Never lived in a house with more than one toilet.

Mornin' sun hit them front windows just right. Whoever built this place sure knew what he was doin'. And all that glass at the back framed the forest real nice, like a paintin'. This weren't his shack, and it weren't Occoneechee Mountain. Didn't rightfully know where he'd woken up this mornin', but he reckoned he'd got it good this time. Real good. Bless Willie for bringin' him here.

Now—Jacob rolled up the sleeves of his denim shirt—where was Freddie and his mama today? He squinted at the map.

"I'd offer to lend you my reading glasses," a pretty gal with blazing blue eyes said. "But I have no idea where they are. Sorry to just walk in. I did knock but you didn't hear me."

He scratched his head. Had they met before?

"I'm Hannah. Or Hey You."

Hannah, a name to keep, a name to treasure.

"How are you doing today?"

"Fair ta middlin', I reckon."

She held out her hand—delicate like china, but calloused. A little lady who grabbed life and held on. He smiled. Been a while since he met anyone who made him want to smile. Other than that firecracker of an art teacher. He wanted to smile—little enough to smile about since his Angeline crossed over. People told him death got easier, but he knew otherwise.

*Once death finds you, he ain't leavin'.*

Could say the same about grief.

A big dog, a shepherd, pushed its nose against the screen door.

"I'm right here, baby," the gal said.

Now he remembered where he'd seen her—at daybreak, takin' them dogs into the forest.

"Reckon they can come in, too." He nodded as a mutt joined the shepherd. Real jumpy, them two. Just about broke his heart to imagine what made them so.

Hey You smiled. *Damn pretty smile.* Smile like redbud blossom welcoming spring. Had Willie noticed her smile? He worked too hard, that boy. Needed to notice the pretty women more, especially this one letting in a whole pack of dogs.

One of the dogs had such mean-lookin' scars, he had to turn his head. What kind of a monster hurt an innocent creature? Dogs and kids—he always said they just wanted to love and be loved. Didn't hold true for his Willie. He were so shut down when he were little, hard to even hug him. And in high school, he moved through the world like he were a spirit. Were that before or after his gal got herself a boyfriend that weren't Willie? Weren't no one's fault she didn't love him right, but when you gave your heart and didn't get it back, there weren't nowhere to hide. He'd been so worried about Willie that summer when…what? What had happened that summer?

The pretty gal said, "I just thought I'd check in, see if you needed anything. Will not around?"

Plum forgot her name. But then she smiled. Hard to forget that smile. Had Willie noticed her smile? He could ask if Willie put her up to this, but he didn't want to sound ungrateful. Besides, he wouldn't mind a bit of company.

"He went into town visitin' some retirement *hotel*." Damned if he would use the word *home*. "Thinks I don't know where he's at. But I know. He told me to stay here and not move. Thinks I'll wander off into them woods and get lost."

"And would you?"

"Well, now, I might decide to take a stroll up that hillside. Looks real invitin' to me. But get lost? Heck, no. I been trackin' through the forest since before either of you was born. Should have disappeared off into the Appalachians when I had me the chance."

He'd always planned to live up in the mountains and the caves. Be self-sufficient. That were his dream after his dear, sweet Angeline crossed over. But what kind of a daddy and a granddaddy would he be if no one could ever find him?

"Poppy tells me you're one helluva banjo player," the pretty gal said. "I expected to hear you picking away over here."

"Bah, them days are long gone." And they weren't comin' back. Just like his Angeline. "Don't play much these days." Only ever played for his Angeline—and to annoy ol' possum-face at Hawk's Ridge.

"I'd love to hear you play sometime," she said.

"I weren't ever that good, little lady."

She knew things about him, this gal. Had she been talkin' to the art teacher? Art teacher were the only person he'd told half them things to. He'd been braggin'. Embarrassin' for a guy his age, but she was one pretty gal, that art teacher. Hard not to want to be a bit of a peacock. Angeline wouldn't mind. Not his dear, sweet Angeline. Now *she'd* known how to move. At fifteen she swung her hips like a woman twice her age. She had every man for three counties beggin' at her door. Never did figure out why she chose him. No siree. He used to play for her, when she came to listen to the band in all them bars, just for her. When they got that record deal, though, she were in a dark place. Demons took her bad that winter. Always worse in the winter.

So he quit the band. Had to stay home with Angeline. She needed him, his dear, sweet Angeline, and so did Willie. Motherin' were hard for her. Sometimes he had to be the daddy and the mama.

"What's that?" The pretty gal nodded at the map.

"My grandson, he's on this trip. Woo-wee. Trip of a lifetime and he's only five years old. I'm trackin' him and his mama."

Her cheeks flushed a pretty shade of pink. "Your son's married?"

"Nah. Never been married. Near broke his mama's heart. Want me to show you where my grandbaby's been?"

"I'd like that," the gal said, and pulled up a chair to sit real close. Two of the dogs came and sat beside her.

"You know where Cardiff, Wales, is?" he said.

"Actually, I do."

"Here." He handed her one them colored markers. "Could you circle it for me? Poppy and me, we're havin' a sweepstakes to figure out where my grandbaby's goin' next. You want to join in?"

"What's the prize?" She smiled that pretty smile. Shame Willie weren't here to notice.

"Well, I reckon Poppy's still workin' on that. You ever travel to Europe, little lady?"

"Once, when I was a kid." She looked a bit sad, like she needed one of his special hugs. He patted her knee. "It was the last trip my family took together." She paused. "You know, you can tape this to the wall if you like—until you find a new home."

A new home? Heck, he reckoned he'd found it. And this time, he weren't leavin'—with or without a fight.

# ELEVEN

Puddles of light from the midday sun decorated the forest floor as Hannah crunched through tinderbox leaves. A turtle lumbered past, and the dogs startled a murder of crows. Eyes down, she watched for poison ivy and venomous snakes. Both were easily hidden to anyone not paying attention. Copperheads were especially well concealed at this time of year.

Was that whistling? Looking up, she smiled at the tall, white-haired man waiting on the edge of the forest. For once, the prospect of leaving her woodland cocoon came without the wrench of transition, the sinking knowledge that she was stepping back into real life.

In the past three days, she and Jacob had fallen into a lunchtime routine. After she came back with the dogs, he would follow her into the house, sit down at the kitchen table and eat whatever she offered. Never did he ask what she was serving; never did he leave a crumb.

Her lunch breaks were stretching out, forcing her to slow down and eat. There were even moments when she caught herself thinking like a normal mother wanting to celebrate her son's homecoming. But then the truth would body-slam her, and after Jacob left she would, once again, grieve for the sensitive little boy who had grown into an unknown man. Depression was a monster she knew well, but she'd spent many years praying that they would never meet again.

The dogs rushed forward, tails wagging. Her girls were turning into such Shepard groupies. When confusion wasn't spawning anxiety, Jacob had a calm way with animals. Will had the same gift.

"Hey You!" Jacob raised his hand.

"Hey you, yourself."

He nodded at her fistful of wild ginger. "You got an earache to cure, little lady?"

"Not today." The ginger was for an emmenagogue, but she wasn't about to discuss her menses or recent lack of. Stress had been quietly taking its toll on more than her sleep cycle.

"I saw some pokeweed over there." Jacob pointed to where Miss Prissy was yanking up grass as if she hadn't eaten in a month.

"You, Mr. Shepard, are a walking, talking encyclopedia of local plant life." Hannah slipped her arm through Jacob's.

The human mind was so cruel. Jacob could recall the smallest detail from his childhood on Occoneechee Mountain and sometimes not remember an action he had taken minutes earlier. Retreating into old memories was reassuring at any age, but without the reliable creation of new memories, how did you keep moving forward?

They wove past the cottage, pausing to wave at Will. This, too, was part of their new daily ritual. Will would watch Hannah and Jacob establish contact, then disappear into the cottage. The first day it happened, she was concerned Will was either taking advantage or being irresponsible. Turned out he was simply avoiding contact.

Will never left them alone for long. As if he'd set a timer, he would knock on the front door after thirty minutes, but he never crossed the threshold. "Come on, Dad," he would call out, eyes lowered. "Hannah has work to do, and I need to give you the Freddie update."

Jacob's face always lit up at the mention of his grandson, just as her father's had done every time Galen walked into a room. She wasn't sure anyone else noticed her father had a favorite, and he treated the boys fairly. But Galen and his granddad had a connection no one could penetrate.

Today Will was pacing on the porch, his iPhone clamped to his ear. He looked a little rumpled. In fact, he seemed to be wearing clothes from the day before. But then everything he owned was so similar. All those muted tones—even his jeans. The kind of jeans money could buy. Did that sound snide? Hannah replayed the comment in her mind. Yes, it did.

*Think better, Hannah.*

Her new tenant spent a great deal of time on his cell phone. With his agent? His publisher? His cheerleaders? You couldn't be that successful and not have an entire retinue of staff. And yet he seemed oddly adrift, as if he were barely able to manage his own life, let alone his dad's.

Will gave a clipped nod and bolted into the cottage. It was strange how he kept his distance, but people did what they needed to do. Will chose merely not to interact with her. Where was the harm in that?

An idea began to form. A rough sketch but something to work through later with a glass of Irish. And she would have to talk with Poppy....

"How about you join me on my lunchtime walk tomorrow?" she asked Jacob.

"I'd like that, Hey You. I reckon the exercise'd be real good for me. Do a lot of sittin' nowadays."

"Are you managing to read? I'd be happy to pick up some books for you at the library."

"My Angeline, she were always stoppin' by the library for me. Don't read like I used to. Get muddled and forget who's who." Sadness flickered on his face, then vanished. "Did I tell you where my grandson is today? London, England! Willie says they're gonna see the crown jewels." Jacob shook his head. "And last night Freddie ate fish and chips out of newspaper! I were still sleepin' when he called, but he told his daddy all about it."

But fish and chips weren't sold in newspaper anymore. Health was a topic that always caught her attention, and just the other night she'd been reading about European health and safety regulations on the web. Either Jacob had misunderstood or Will was telling tales. And why would anyone choose to lie about something so insignificant?

Or maybe exaggeration was part of the author psyche. Inigo was a natural storyteller, and he could re-create an entire event that had never actually happened. Amazing what you could project with a little research and a lot of fancy. Was Will Shepard full of B.S., too?

Her phone buzzed with a text. Hannah pulled it from her jean pocket. Galen.

Dad booked ticket. Land @ 4 Tues. Can U pick up?

Last week Galen had been like a bulimic—binging on anger, then vomiting despair. This new emptiness manifested as emotional evisceration. Three clipped sentences revealed nothing, told her nothing. To understand people's mind-set, she needed to hear, to see, to touch. She could always tell when a pet owner was ready to let go from the way he or she responded to a pat on the arm or a soft sentence.

Was Galen holding back, not wanting to cause worry? Or did he not care enough to share? Or did he not care, period?

Once, conversations with Galen had been thought-provoking exchanges, and the ordinary became spectacular when Galen transcribed it into a poem. He could ignite hope, laughter, sadness. Now his words were flat, and she couldn't read them.

Hannah had always believed that what happened in life was less important than how you handled it. Every action, every reaction, was a chance to grow. But Galen's depression had destroyed her safety net, annihilated her ability to interpret his world. Or hers.

"Something wrong, Angel?" Jacob said.

"My son's coming home."

"There's good and there's bad in that." Jacob turned toward the cottage where Will was pacing behind the floor-to-ceiling windows of the front room, still on his iPhone. "Don't get easier, the parentin'. My boy, he wants to put me back in some institution. That last one were real bad. You know why they kicked me out?"

"For brawling, I believe. But I have a hard time picturing you baring your fists."

"Yeah, I feel bad 'bout that. Security kid got caught in the middle. Never been one for violence, but it were necessary. Knew they'd have to kick me out. There were this new guy, see, loved to tell the world about his amazin' grandsons. So I says, well, I reckon goin' out for pancakes ain't worth mentionin' when I got a grandson that's travelin' all over Europe with his own passport. It were real easy to get Bernie riled up." Jacob winked. "Didn't want Freddie comin' to some institution. Were hard on him the last time. Some of the residents, they was old and mean. Didn't want a young'un bringin' noise and life. You know where he is today, my grandbaby?"

It was the longest speech Jacob had made.

Hannah squeezed his arm. "London, isn't it? Did he see the crown jewels yet?"

"He sure did, Angel. And he's been eatin' fish and chips out of newspaper."

"Jacob, are you happy in the cottage?"

"I reckon so."

"That's what I thought."

He bent down and kissed the back of her hand. A sweet, gentle kiss that reminded her of her dad. If he were still alive, her dad would have just turned eighty. She would have thrown the biggest party—to hell with the cost—and persuaded her brothers and their families to come down from Vermont. Her dad would have liked Jacob. Her mom, too. Jacob may have been a grave digger and a high school dropout, but he was just as smart as her parents had been. Jacob's doctrine of everyday life was pure gold; his nuggets of wisdom, polished gems.

"You do know," she said, "that you can stay in the cottage as long as you like."

Jacob grinned. "Why, thank you, Hannah."

# TWELVE

Trapped. Will was trapped in the role of good son without a dress rehearsal. Worse, he was establishing routines. Bad, very bad. Routines stank of permanence. For the first time in ten years, he was also living like the rest of the adult population, forcing himself to get up at eight and work during the day instead of falling asleep around four and setting his alarm for noon—unless, of course, he was heading out to the Thursday 10:00 a.m. P.R. session.

Writing in the afternoon had never been more than a warm-up exercise, but with his dad's long naps, it made sense to try. Although, yet again, he had failed to transcribe even the smallest amount of crap. Not one fragment of a thought.

How was a parent meant to bury his child and resume his daily word count?

Will closed his laptop with a snap, and stood. At least the old man seemed calmer, less muddled, and nothing his dad said or did fazed Hannah. That eased one worry. When his dad called her Angeline, Hannah merely laughed and grabbed his arm, which would have broken Will's heart had there been anything left to break.

The dogs appeared around the side of the main house, followed by Hannah. Except for that first day when she'd doctored him, he'd stayed clear of their landlady. He'd smelled lavender a few times and known she was close. And he'd watched her from a safe distance. People-watching was an old instinct. Hard to buck.

Hannah disappeared from view, and Will leaned over the deck railing to track her with his eyes. As usual, she moved quietly—a woman who didn't announce herself with loud behavior or shower naked in public. Impossible, though, to ignore those breasts straining under the white T-shirts she favored. White—an unexpected choice given her profession.

Always busy but never harried, Hannah seemed to live heart wide-open. How could anyone be so at ease in the world, so trusting, so friendly? If she was in the middle of something and another person appeared—even the UPS guy—Hannah stopped whatever she was doing to chat. If he knew how to ask for help, Will might sound her out about dad-sitting. Clearly, she had the caregiver gene he lacked.

*Intriguing.* She was clutching a clump of sweet flag. Despite staring down thirty-five, his eyesight was still twenty-twenty. He could recognize calamus root from any distance. The old man had always chewed it after a performance, swearing it was the best remedy for sore throats. When they were twelve, Will and Ally discovered the bitter taste also cured smoker's breath.

Using the back of her hand, Hannah pushed blond curls from her face. "Have you seen a trowel anywhere?" she called out.

Nothing in her body language had suggested she was aware of him. So, someone else around here understood pretense.

"It's about so big." Hannah gestured. "An implement used for digging."

"I know what a trowel is," he said.

"Aha, he speaks." She tugged a dead marigold from a pot. "The trowel is sticking in the pot to your left."

"Thanks."

Pulling himself up to retreat, Will turned toward Saponi Mountain. The porch on the front of the cottage might be small and functional, but the back deck extended down two levels and out into the forest like a tree house. Breathtaking—for anyone with a glass prison fetish.

"I guess you don't get to garden much in New York." Her voice seemed to echo behind him—soft but strong.

"I have a large roof garden."

"Good for you."

Did she misunderstand, think he was bragging when, really, he was just stating fact? He turned back to face her and wished he hadn't. She was reaching over the plant pot, inadvertently displaying cleavage. Lots of cleavage with perfectly rounded, medium-size breasts spilling over a white, lacy bra. And a vining tattoo that curled from her shoulder down to her right breast.

Now that was enthralling: the fact of a tattoo and its placement. Art designed to be hidden, exposed only to a lover. He swallowed the words, *Nice ink.*

"I'm glad I caught you," Hannah said.

His eyes jerked up. *Caught me?*

"I've been meaning to talk to you about the other night. I saw you—when Poppy was in the shower."

A red-tailed hawk swooped low through the space between them, something dangling from its beak. Behind him, dead leaves snapped and popped as squirrels darted through the trees. No one who'd lived in the forest could forget the sound of squirrels. And no red-blooded male could forget the sight of Poppy's unclothed Marilyn Monroe curves.

Despite the blush, he stood his ground. "I'm sorry about that. I never expected—"

"Oh, no. I wanted to apologize on her behalf."

Hannah didn't think he was a creepy, oversexed Peeping Tom?

"We're so used to being alone out here. She just didn't think."

Will stared at the shower. *Yeah, right.*

"I want to assure you that no one will use the outside shower again while you're here. I would hate for anything to upset your dad."

"I don't count?" he said.

"I'm assuming you can look after yourself."

"You, too, I imagine." That should have been an end, but while he picked at the green mold snaking along the wooden railing, his mouth kept moving. Words kept forming. "I've been having some problems writing since—since this business with my dad. I was looking for my muse," he said, with more than a touch of irony.

"Did you find her?"

"Not even close."

The chip of a cardinal's song filled the air.

"Since it's Friday, I thought I'd be a wild woman and have a cocktail before supper," she said. "You're welcome to join me. I'm not well stocked with alcohol, but Poppy left some red wine here, and I keep gin and tonic for my ex. Otherwise, it's Bushmills."

Irish whiskey? He would have pegged her for vodka tonic. And she kept gin *for her ex.* How very mature. She looked to be around his age, and yet she wore the confidence of someone much older. Someone who, unlike him, was all grown up.

She pushed the sweet flag into the pot and pressed soil around it, working as if time were elastic and could expand to her whim. Then she wiped her hands down her jeans and headed inside the house.

Will raised his face into the long shadows that crept from the forest. Vapor trails slashed the sky, and the tops of the trees blazed molten gold. He used to love this hour, when the light connoted hope. Hope that his mom would seek help, and when he abandoned that fantasy, hope that he could escape. Now the gloaming was simply a reminder of his son dying at the close of day.

Yes, he wanted a drink. It was the only thing he wanted right now. Tucking his laptop under his arm, Will walked down the back steps and followed in Hannah's wake.

Her screen door creaked as he eased it open and entered a white hall filled with light.

"I'm in here," Hannah said.

Several dogs appeared through a doorway ahead; the small, ratty-looking one bounded up and slobbered over his hand. Will pushed his way through the animals and into a long, thin kitchen and breakfast area.

Her kitchen appliances weren't top of the line—labels *did* matter when you were talking ovens and refrigerators—but everything was orderly and functional. Lots of bleached wood and stainless steel and a large butcher's block, its shelves clogged with a hodgepodge of cookbooks, their spines cracked. No dishwasher.

At the far end of the room there was a fig tree strung with white Christmas tree lights, a round pine table with matching chairs and a window seat piled with pale cushions. A tabby cat sat upright in the middle of the cushions, giving the dogs the evil eye.

"You don't like cats?" she said.

"How did you know?"

"Your expression." She smiled her easy smile. "Bad childhood experience?"

Was that a lucky guess or was she really that perceptive? Either way, she didn't seem to miss much.

"Our family home was feral cat central." Will cleared his throat and laid his laptop on the counter.

Hannah moved to the sink filled with several dirty plates, a teapot for one and a mug of what appeared to be leftover tea—ginger, according to the label hanging over the side. She washed her hands—shutting off the water with her elbow as she lathered the soap, then flicking the tap back on to rinse. Sensible water-saving gestures. Exactly what he would have expected of Hannah. Everything about her was expected. Although…there was the white T-shirt thing. And the tattoo he wouldn't mind seeing again.

"We should sit out on the porch." Hannah dried her hands. "That way your dad will know where we are when he wakes up."

*Jesus.* Why hadn't he thought of that?

She stepped forward; he stepped back. She crossed one foot over the other and moved to the left; he moved to the right. Then she circled ninety degrees around him to open the fridge.

"Bushmills okay?" She pulled a wedge of Brie from the deli drawer.

"Sure."

"With ice?"

"Please."

Hannah took two tumblers from an overhead cabinet and then stuck one of them under the ice maker. "I've had some wonderful conversations with your dad about your son. What an adventure he's on."

Ice cubes fell slowly. *Clonk. Clonk. Clonk.*

"I believe he's five?"

Will clawed at his thigh, nodded. Didn't answer.

"Only child?"

Will nodded again.

"Off-limits?" she said.

Will exhaled. "Sorry, I'm very private."

"I imagine you have to be when you're famous."

"I'm not that famous."

"I think your fans would disagree. But it's okay, we can chat about the weather until your dad wakes up, and then he'll talk enough for both of us."

"He never used to be social. You bring out his inner chatterer."

"Listening's part of my job. But with your father, it's the joy of hearing him reminisce. His knowledge of plants and herbs is a bonus."

She poured a small amount of whiskey into his glass, then checked the level and added a splash. Should he have offered to fix drinks? He'd never been good at sexual stereotypes, acting all hunter-gatherer-ish. His dad had always been more of the mom; his best friend, Ally, more of the alpha-male. He wasn't sure where that left him.

"How long since you've had rain?" he said.

"About ten weeks. I've been a bit distracted recently. Sort of lost track of the days."

"Yeah, funny how that happens."

She gave him a quizzical look. Her eyes—how had he not noticed before?—were such a deep blue they were almost violet.

"There you go." She handed him a glass, and he smiled his thanks.

Then she turned on her heel and filled her own glass. Neat,

no ice, and again, a conservative amount. His dad's voice intruded into his thoughts: *Fill 'er up please, Angel.*

"Do me a favor. Don't offer my dad a drink." Now he was being flat-out indiscreet. Did vets have to follow the same code of ethics as doctors?

"He's an alcoholic?" She reached up into a cabinet, pulled out a plate and then turned to open the breadbox.

"Borderline. Possibly. I don't know. I should have told you when I signed the lease."

"And yet you didn't."

"I was worried you'd say no."

Cellophane crinkled as Hannah opened a box of crackers and arranged them in a firework burst around the Brie. "Thank you, for being honest. But it wouldn't have made a difference. I'm a pushover for people who are lost. Metaphorically speaking."

Did she mean him or his dad? A whisper in his subconscious said, *Tell her about Freddie. She'll understand.* But if he did that, he'd be expanding the parameters of his lie. And even lies needed boundaries. Besides, Hannah would figure out he'd used her and her best friend to perpetuate said lie, which made him a total shithead. A soulless slug. And he could tell himself he didn't care what Hannah thought, but that would be another lie.

"Does your dad drink to drown his sorrows?"

*No, I'm the one who does that.* "He drinks because he likes alcohol."

"Then I don't see the problem. He's what—late seventies, eighty? He lost the woman he loves, his memory is failing. And moving is a known trigger for stress. If alcohol allows him an hour or so of escape, where's the harm?" She handed him the plate. "Could you carry that out for me?"

"Wow, thanks."

"For what?"

"Making me feel less incompetent. I feel as if I should set ground rules for him. I feel as if—"

"You should be the parent?"

"Totally."

They walked back outside, onto the porch with a view of the cottage and his dad's bedroom window.

He inhaled and held the breath for an impossibly long moment. The air shimmered with dry heat, and a warm wind had picked up. Will shivered. He didn't like wind any more than he liked cats. Maybe it was growing up listening to the wrath of hurricanes rattling the bones of the forest. Or maybe it was the dread that came whenever his dad was at a gig, and his mom dragged him outside in his pajamas to dance in the lightning. He no longer wore pajamas, and he no longer danced. He'd seen firsthand what happened when you released such energy, such passion.

Hannah curled up on an old metal rocker that had clearly been refurbished. Will placed the cheese next to her, away from the dogs, and sat on the top of the steps. Away from Hannah.

"How's the search coming," she said, "for a retirement community?"

"Badly."

They had visited only three retirement homes in four days, and the old man had sabotaged the last tour by pinching a nurse's butt. His dad had never done anything so demeaning before. And now what? He no longer dared leave the old man alone, not since returning from a quick toiletries-purchasing trip to discover the electric kettle warming up on the gas stove. Needed to add buying a replacement kettle to his growing to-do list.

"Don't think I'm interfering," Hannah said, "but can I make a suggestion?"

Will tugged on his lower lip. A conversation that started with *don't think I'm interfering* couldn't end well. The dog called Daisy joined him, even though she was shaking.

"Your dad likes Poppy. Poppy likes your dad. And her business, well, it's not doing so well. And no offense, but you look pretty stressed out while you're pacing on the porch. I was wondering if you would like some help? If you were willing to hire her, just for a few hours each day, you could get some writing done, visit retirement homes, whatever, and it could work out to everyone's advantage. I've been trying to encourage Poppy to develop an art therapy program—that's why she was volunteering at Hawk's Ridge. Maybe your dad could be her guinea pig. What do you think?"

*What did he think?* It was as if he'd reached a solid hold on a rock face, a place where he could pause and compose himself.

"I think you're amazing," he said. Then he did something so out of character that he was more surprised than the dogs. He leaped up to hug her. And as he veered toward Hannah, Rosie nipped him in the butt.

# THIRTEEN

Hawk's Ridge was off his radar. Will was done with that place. Done! His dad's old room was empty except for a bottle of Wild Turkey abandoned, with care, in the middle of the carpet. A small act of rebellion that had given Will real pleasure. The furniture was in storage; his mother's knick-knacks were in his trunk.

He glanced at the bottle of Bushmills on the passenger seat. Maybe Hannah would stop apologizing once he gave her the gift. Rosie had administered little more than a warning shot. Abused creature she may be, but there was nothing damaged about her canines. He'd felt them up close and personal. If Rosie had wanted to maul his sorry ass to pieces, she would have done so. And if Hannah wanted to invite him over to share the Bushmills, he'd accept. Within less than twenty-four hours, the tightness in his throat—a hybrid of heartburn and slow asphyxiation—had vanished.

Climbing out of the Prius, Will retrieved the mail. The sales flyer from some chichi lingerie boutique was unexpected, the flyer from Southern States Cooperative about birdseed wasn't. What a relief to find zip addressed to Will Shepard. On the other hand, no one knew where he was. Even Ally didn't have the full details. It was as if he was hiding. Maybe he was.

Poppy had to leave by five, and it was ten till. *Perfect.* He could give her the money with a passing *hi and bye* and avoid a second conversation littered with double entendre. This morning's encounter had been awkward enough.

Putting Poppy on the Will Shepard payroll would've been ideal, but she'd demanded off-the-books cash. Will peered into his wallet. *No cash, for real?* He never ran out of cash. Ever. Growing up poor meant he always carried at least a hundred dollars in small bills. If nothing else, he kept twenty-five dollars in singles for the homeless guys and the buskers.

The details of everyday life had been sliding through the cracks. But not anymore. Now that Hannah had given him room to breathe, he was going to pull back and apply the problem-solving skills of climbing to the business of resettling his dad. Tackle a rock face without a strategy and you could drift onto hazardous rocks. Rush, and you could face calamity that proved fatal. And he had been rushing.

Will looked around, taking his time. The leaves couldn't be far off their peak, and yet they shriveled and fell without a blaze of color. Only the dogwoods were putting on a display this year. Across the road, a large hand-painted sign dripping fake blood advertised a haunted forest—Two Nights Only! A scarecrow hung nearby like a decapitated body on the gallows. Its pumpkin head lay splattered on the ground.

The sound of tinkling glass came from his back jean pocket. Had his agent resorted to texting? Will yanked free his iPhone and stared at the screen.

"At powwow in Pleasant Grove," he read aloud. "Home @ 6. Dad and Hey You. X"

Mail scattered to the ground. Somewhere a leaf blower

whirred like an oversize dentist's drill, a harsh, grating screech that made Will grind his teeth.

Why had he been so cavalier and handed over the care of his dad to strangers? Why had he trusted Hannah? She had no idea what she was getting into, none. He and his father had removed themselves from tribal life for good reason. And this wasn't a family hoedown. It was a powwow. On tribal lands. *Jesus.*

As he bent down to pick up the mail, his left knuckle grazed gravel splattered with fallen dogwood berries—berries the color of fresh blood. He flexed his fingers, itching with the need to restrain someone. Itching with the need to restrain Hannah. And what the hell had happened to Poppy?

Jumping back into the Prius, he threw the mail aside and snatched at his seat belt.

The tightness in his throat returned. This was what happened when you reached out to others. You dropped your guard and they blindsided you with do-gooder intentions. Maybe that had been his dad's philosophy all along with his mom: close ranks against other people's interference. Will shook back his hair. God save him from the good intentions of others. In fact—the car squealed onto the road—God save him from others.

Stuck doing twenty miles per hour behind a peloton of cyclists pedaling frantically as they hogged the road, Will streamlined his irritation into a plan. Enough hiding out in a rented cottage with his brain-addled father, a pretty holistic vet and a motley bunch of dysfunctional dogs. He was done with this screwed-up version of happy families. And his dad had forfeited the right to call the shots the moment his delinquent behavior had hurled both of their lives into chaos.

Will passed the tribal sign to the right and pulled into the car park.

Weren't the powwows normally in June? And why hold one all the way out here, on the tribal lands? The living village was closer to the interstate—a more logical location. Will was sixteen when the Occaneechi Band of the Saponi Nation had held its first powwow on the old ghost field—before it became the site of the living village. Dancers cooling off in the Eno in buckskins, the crush of people, drums beating—the event had bewitched him with his first taste of family pride. But by the time construction of the village had been finished, and the Occaneechi had won state recognition as North Carolina's eighth official Indian tribe, his mom had managed to poison even that part of his life.

He needed to get back to the city, back to deadlines, back to forcing himself to write—write faster, write better, write more. He had become a writer to forget, not to enjoy a lifestyle of bright, shiny things, but his success was the Siamese twin of Agent Dodds's success. Every Dodds adventure upped Will's personal stakes, gave him more to lose. And right now, he stood to lose a career ten years in the making. A career that funded two grown men plus a defunct college account.

Tomorrow he would start preparing for the reality of moving his dad to New York, even if that involved doping him with tranquilizers, strapping him into the Prius and making a getaway across state lines. Because really—Will slammed the car door and stomped across the field—enough was enough.

*See Will run. All the way back to New York.*

Drums. He slowed his pace. The beat of drums pounded up through the earth, through the flattened grass, through the soles of his Converse and into his calf muscles. The drums tugged at him, calling him to dance.

*No.* He wasn't being pulled back to a life of poverty and

mental illness, a life of being trapped between two worlds and not belonging to either. Not belonging to the tribe because he looked so all-white American. Not belonging at school because he wasn't a jock: he was a writer. The small kid in kindergarten whose only friend was a girl; the high schooler with the crazy parent. The first-year college student with the white-trash mom who made a spectacle of herself at his last powwow, throwing it around like a whore.

She should have been watching from her lawn chair, tapping her foot, keeping company with all the other nonnative spectators. But his mom? Sit on the sidelines when she could have been kicking up her heels like a middle-aged Rockette? No, his mom had jumped up, burst into the circle of dancers and decided to strip.

Who would have blamed his dad for throwing her out after that? But the old man had calmly wrapped a blanket around her shoulders, and guided her, as if she were an invalid, back to the truck. His mom had fought to begin with, ensuring the Shepard family held center stage among the tourists out for an afternoon of entertainment: normal families who wanted to admire the costumes and the dancing, peruse the stalls and buy trinkets. Instead, they got to participate in the theater that was his nuclear family. But it wasn't only strangers who'd witnessed her behavior—it was also a bunch of students Will had corralled into volunteering on the construction of the Occaneechi village. New friends from his new, untarnished college life.

That was the final blow, the one that made forgiveness impossible. His dad had chosen to stay with her; Will had chosen not to.

Memories stacked up here like unopened parcels marked Return to Sender: his mom ripping off her shirt; the bra—old, graying, since everything that started out white ended up gray in their house; her pale stomach and protruding ribs. Her diet was liquid by then and she was borderline anorexic. Maybe she *was* anorexic—something else that went undiagnosed.

They had to get away from this place before the old man confronted the same memory and recalled his wife acting like a pole dancer in a strip joint.

Legs shaking, Will pushed through the crowds gathered around the stalls, through the heavy smell of fried food and sage, through the master of ceremonies's voice, the singing, the jingling of bells and the drumming. Always the drumming. *Who's your people, boy? Who's your people?*

"Willie! Is that you? It is! How've you been?" His father's second cousin once removed tugged Will into a hug.

"Good, sir." Lying really did improve with practice.

"Look at you! You gonna come dance? Your daddy, he's been having a fine old time. He got to see my grandson, Little Wolf. He's fourteen now. Reminds me of you the way he can dance! I'll never forget our first powwow with you in your regalia. All the girls, they were fainting at the sight of you with that long blond hair. Cut your hair, I see. How old were you back then? Sixteen, seventeen?"

"About that, sir." Will didn't remember any girls except for the one he'd failed to impress.

"Your mama, she was something that day. Your mama, she was—"

*Crazy.* Will waited for him to say *crazy*.

"Such a beauty. Voice like honey."

Seriously? That was what Uncle Stephen remembered about his mom, or was he going senile, too? Granted, the tribe's first powwow was not the one where she'd flaunted her lap-dancing skills and her total disrespect for the ceremony. No, that had come three years later, but even so it was a memory to erase all others.

"Why didn't you tell us you'd come home?"

The drums continued to echo through his skin, through his muscles, through his blood. Calling him to dance.

Uncle Stephen smiled the enigmatic smile he'd always had, the one that said, *Boy, I know where you're coming from.* Then he brushed back his hair and pushed on his marine corps baseball cap. "I reckon it's time for the Veterans' Song. Your daddy, he's over on the other side with the purtiest young lady I've seen in years. Can't decide if he's keeping his eye on the fry bread in the food trailer or on her. She your lady friend? Mighty fetchin'. Almost as fine as your mama."

Could people not forget that he was related to his mother? He'd certainly tried hard enough.

"No, sir. She's our landlady."

"She have anywhere else to rent?" Uncle Stephen guffawed. "Don't be a stranger, you hear me, Willie?"

"I hear you, sir."

The drumbeat grew stronger, and the smell of sage was thicker now, making Will's head swirl. A white hawk screeched and dipped down into the middle of the dance circle. Color and sound swirled. The bells on the Head Lady's dress jingled. Her long black hair was braided to her waist, just as his mom's had been. His mom's hair was dirty blond, same as his, but she always wore it braided. She had no family history of her own, so she'd co-opted his dad's. Stolen it and wrecked it.

Half of him screamed to leave; half of him—the half he'd long denied—pleaded to stay. And nowhere could he see Hannah or his dad. How hard could it be to find a tall man with a shock of white hair pulled back in a leather thong?

"Willie!" His dad spotted him first. "You got our text, then?"

His dad was with Poppy. Where was Hannah?

Poppy walked toward him with a broad smile. She didn't even have the decency to blush. "I'm teaching your dad to text," she said.

"I'm amazed he can see anything as small as a phone keyboard since he isn't wearing his glasses again."

"Oh, Hannah lent him her reading glasses," Poppy said.

"I thought you had to be home by five-thirty."

"Plans change." Poppy gave Will a blatant once-over.

"And where's Hannah, other than avoiding my wrath?"

Poppy laughed. Yeah, he had that effect on people when he tried out anger. Like an invisible member of the chorus line, he wasn't cut out for front-row emotions.

"Let me get this right—you're pissed because we're giving you a break and enjoying an afternoon out with your dad? And by the way, this was my idea. Not Hannah's."

"Really." Will crossed his arms. He always felt emboldened when he protected his chest. "You should have asked."

He'd been right about Poppy. She was as irresponsible as Cass.

"It's fine, Will. Look at your dad. He's having fun."

She had no idea. No idea.

His dad wandered toward the circle, his feet tapping through a straight dance. "Dad—"

"And he's been remembering things, about your mama."

No. Poppy was not going to talk about his mother. His mom was off-limits except to people who had their own memories of her.

"Suppose he'd had an accident," Will said. "Dad! We're leaving!"

"You don't think Hannah and I could manage one sweet, old guy with mashed-up memories?"

"Suppose he'd had a *bad* accident?" Okay, so now he just sounded stupid.

"Jeez, do you take everything so seriously, Mr. Bestselling Author? Is that how you approach life, by playing suppose-bad-shit-happens? Each day is a gift. Open the box." She widened her eyes, offering an invitation. "Enjoy what's inside."

"If I wanted advice, I'd hire a therapist."

"Dancing's cheaper." Poppy reached for him. "Wanna try?"

Will jerked back and slammed sideways into someone, into Hannah. She stumbled and grabbed his shoulder; he ground down with his left leg to stop them from toppling. He knew better. As a climber he knew not to hang on to the bitter end. He knew when to let go, and yet here he was, hanging on to the beautiful woman who was straddling his leg. His thigh was buried in her crotch, and he had grabbed her hip. Somehow, in that bungled move, he had pinned Hannah's body against his. He inhaled lavender and vanilla, and his breathing slowed to the steady heartbeat of drums. His arm moved up to curve around the dip of her waist. To pull her closer.

A thought, pure and simple: he didn't want to let go.

The shoulder of her T-shirt had tugged down to expose part of the tattoo. Grow up in the South, and any idiot could recognize wild wisteria. What was more intriguing was that she had chosen to mark her body with the symbol of love lost and the ability to endure.

"Beautiful ink," he said, and looked up into eyes that met his at the exact same level.

Unharnessed energy traveled between them, and he shivered. Or was the smell of sage making him light-headed? Air roared in his ears as if he were listening to a rogue wave through a conch shell.

*No.* How long since he'd touched a woman? *No.* He was getting hard. Could she feel him? They were pressed up against each other. Surely she could feel him.

But she didn't flinch and neither did he. His pulse raced

into overdrive as if he'd been shot with a defibrillator. He wanted to rip off her T-shirt and press the warmth of her body into his skin. He wanted to hold her knee-to-knee, thigh-to-thigh, chest-to-chest, while the outside world stormed. He wanted her in his bed.

And yet she was *so* not his type. She wasn't crazy and she wasn't under twenty-five. Hard to tell how old Hannah was, but probably around his age, which would put her biological clock in overdrive.

Their foreheads weren't touching, but they were close enough that he sensed the pressure of her face against his. And once again, the rhythm of his body slowed.

He dipped closer and forced himself to speak. "Why are you here?"

"To have fun," Hannah said.

"I'm not having fun."

"Then maybe you shouldn't have come."

She broke free, and Will felt a spark of loss.

Then the moment shattered.

# FOURTEEN

Drums were beating and she was dancing with Will. They were twirling around and around and she was giddy with the promise of what would come. Desire sparked and he laughed. She hadn't heard him laugh before. It was a fragile sound, like a hand-blown Christmas tree ornament shattering on a wooden floor. But then the drums stopped, and Will fell silent. He held her at arm's length and stared hard with those eyes that seemed to pull her in, then shut her out.

"Where do we go from here?" she said.

"Nowhere," he replied, and let go.

Hannah shot up, heart racing, and punched the alarm clock. She fell back into her pillows and breathed slowly, releasing the residue of the dream, forcing Will from her mind.

Galen was coming home today. Nothing else mattered; nothing else would steal her focus.

Hannah searched her bedding for the hair tie that had fallen out overnight. No hair tie, but she found a pair of reading glasses and a Will Shepard novel—one that had been at the bottom of her reading stack for several years. She flipped to the back cover and stared at the black-and-white photo that told readers nothing about the man who had created Agent Dodds.

In the three days since the powwow, she had seen Will only from a distance. But the thoughts wouldn't stop. They pounced during sleep and snuck up on her when she was feeding the dogs or idling at a stop sign. Why now? Why after six years was she finally distracted by a guy and he happened to be a celebrity—eleven years her junior—with a kindergarten-age son?

Hannah raked her fingernails across her scalp. Whenever Will was in her sight line, the breath sucked out of her lungs. It was childish; it was maddening; and it was wrong.

She didn't want to be this person who wasted precious minutes applying mascara before going to work. She didn't want to be this person who had turned out her underwear drawer to find her one and only push-up bra. She didn't want to be this person whose chest fluttered at the sight of Will's car.

Beyond her bedroom window, a Carolina wren whistled with such energy, such beauty. She had neglected the birds over the past few months. When Will and Jacob left, she would put up more birdfeeders, and she would keep them filled. She would even find new ways to outwit the squirrels. Projects, no matter how small, kept a person moving. Once Will had gone, that would be her quest: keep moving.

According to Poppy, Jacob was on the wait list for a place in New York and Will had visited two retirement communities near the Virginia border. What bookends of mistakes. Take Jacob out of Orange County and you might as well lock him in a cell with a loaded handgun. But Will wanted everything settled by the weekend, or so Poppy had said. Today was Tuesday.

Hannah eased aside her muslin curtain and there he was—

wearing his running clothes and pacing on the gravel between the two houses. Normally, he paced on the cottage porch. Had he chosen to move closer to her territory? *Ridiculous.* Now she was finding meaning where there was none.

Sideways there wasn't much of Will. Hannah swallowed. Her waist had never been as skinny, her stomach never as flat. But his forearms were surprisingly buff and his shorts revealed plenty of muscle and sinew in his calves. This was not a man who spent his life sitting behind a desk.

Will scuffed up a haze of dirt and glanced toward her bedroom, and Hannah dove for the floor. How could he possibly know which room was hers? And why, when he looked at her with those eyes, did every nerve fiber scream?

# FIFTEEN

The wheel of his rolling duffel caught on the aluminum step of the escalator, and Galen almost let go. It contained only possessions. But a missing bag would be one more problem for Mom. He tugged it free.

The line of people behind him all wore traveling faces: trapped in transit, happiness checked along with their luggage. There was a poem in that thought, if words could break through the brume in his brain. Words had become empty vessels no longer infused with affect.

A jerk, and the escalator spat him out on the main level. Regurgitated him back into the world. The prodigal failure had come home.

*Thump, thump, thump* went the wheel secured with duct tape. The duffel had been a present from Dad. Galen had never liked it.

Eyes on the floor, he shuffled down the walkway.

Such a hike to the greeting area. Dead man walking.

He raised his head. As expected, Mom was standing off to the side, surrounded by silence, her battered messenger bag slung across her torso. Galen tried to smile. Counterfeit emotions he could do, but gestures involved effort. Hard to send messages of movement to a body weighted down by invisible, wet sandbags.

Mom's voice—comforting, reassuring. The voice from his childhood. "That's all you brought, sweetheart?"

He wavered and fell into her. *Make it go away, Mom. Make it go away.*

People hurried past, but he clung to his mother. With just the two of them, there would be no one to say, *Perk up,* as if depression were a jacket he could slip off and stow in the overhead bin of an airplane. Dad didn't understand that he couldn't perk up, he couldn't aim that high. Galen just wanted one day when he didn't wake up crying.

Mom pulled back and tucked his hair behind his ear. "Have you eaten?"

"Not hungry. I just want to get to the cottage and sleep."

She fiddled with the strap of her bag.

"Something wrong?" he said.

"Come on—" She grabbed the duffel. "Let's get you home."

"You didn't answer me."

"I'll tell you in the car."

He reclaimed his bag. Did she think he was an invalid? "Tell me now, Mom. I don't have the stamina for guessing games."

"It's the cottage. I've—"

"Please don't tell me you've rented it to some destitute client." That would be so like her, taking on someone else's hard-luck story when she should be worrying about her own.

"Poppy found us a temporary tenant." Mom smiled but her lips quavered. "A six-month lease with the rent money going into a special bank account for you. But please don't share that information with your brother."

For years the cottage stood empty, and now she rented it out.

"I'm not a charity case, Mom."

"You need money, sweetheart. For food if nothing else."

"I don't eat much these days."

"I can tell."

The automatic doors slid open and they stepped from the vacuum of the terminal into air too warm for late October. Cars pulled to and away from the curb, and a plane roared overhead. The sky was steel blue. Behind the barricades and across the labyrinth of runways, the forest. The first poem he wrote was about the magic of fall on Saponi Mountain. Today the forest was just a stand of trees on the other side of the tarmac. The colors were unimpressive.

"Besides—" Mom was already in the crosswalk. She turned and waited for him. "Our tenant's a writer. You two have something in common."

"I'm not a writer. Not anymore."

"Don't say that." She sounded tired. "You have a gift for poetry. Nothing can take that away from you."

*Not even heavy-duty meds that make me feel as if I'm crawling across the ocean floor?*

"I'm being honest, Mom."

"No, you're not. You're letting depression speak for you. You're a poet, you're a brother, you're a wonderful human being and you're my son. I love you. And before you attempt another apology, I forgive you. For everything."

Galen stared at the rows of parked cars. All waiting, all empty.

*Don't make it easier, Mom.*

Will sat on the porch pretending to type, much as Freddie used to do when he exclaimed, "Look, Daddy! I'm working, too!" He hit keys randomly, and gibberish leaped from his fingertips. At least he wasn't hunched over his keyboard like Jack Nicholson in *The Shining,* typing "all work and no play."

His mom had raised him on R-rated horror. People in her twisted fairy tales didn't die easy deaths. They were sliced and diced, disemboweled or dragged behind stampeding bulls. Keep your audience scared, she'd always told him. Great lesson for a five-year-old. Even then, she'd been plotting his life-path. He couldn't stomach violence, and yet his storytelling mind circled psychopathic behavior like a hummingbird hovering over a red hibiscus flower. Most mothers showed their kids how to fold laundry. His mom schooled him in the darkness of the human psyche.

Terror had always infused his writing, and yet real fear hadn't found him until he was a dad. Fatherhood had filled every day with paralyzing anxiety: the fear of his son falling off the climbing frame; the fear of a stranger snatching Freddie away while Cass was distracted; the fear that Freddie died in agony.

Will slammed the laptop closed and ran down the steps toward Hannah's house. He yanked his hands through his hair. Her truck wasn't here, but he hadn't noticed her leave. Where was she, and why should he care? Before a nine-month-old baby upended his universe, he wouldn't have cared. Sixteen years ago he left for college with a small bag and a short list of positive negatives—things he knew, with absolute certainty, he never wanted in his life: love, mental illness, a family. He needed to hit rewind, to rediscover that set of beliefs, because he could no longer live this way—emotionally raw. Stripped as bare as the trees would be in another month. Winter, he'd always hated winter. A forest should be impenetrable and overgrown. A place to hide, not a place to see through.

Hannah's truck lumbered down the ridiculous driveway

and stopped next to the Prius. Maybe the positioning of her truck was a subliminal message. Or maybe sleep deprivation was turning him into a demented romantic. No doubt she was as confused as he was about what had—or hadn't—happened at the powwow. Why else would she have stayed out of his way for the past three days?

And who the hell was the bearded man in her passenger seat?

One of the dogs barked inside the house. Those mutts never barked.

Hannah climbed out and it was obvious, even to a guy accused—many times—of being insensitive to a woman's needs, that she was upset. She also looked worn thin with exhaustion, which wasn't surprising given that she'd returned home at 2:10 last night, or rather, this morning. Not that he'd been watching for her.

"You okay?" he asked.

Eyes locked on his, her head gave the slightest twitch. It was almost a nod.

A tall, emaciated guy appeared by her side. His skin was gray, his cheeks sunken—as if he'd been sick, really sick. Maybe even endured a little hospital living. There was no physical resemblance between the stranger and Hannah, and yet something spoke of family connection. A younger brother, maybe? He moved closer to Hannah. Too close.

"Galen, this is Will Shepard." Hannah wrapped her arm around Galen's waist. "Will, I'd like you to meet my son, Galen. He's a writer, too. A poet, doing an MFA at UC Irvine."

Her *son?* Hannah was a mother, and this bearded young man was her *son?*

Galen scowled at him. "Did you give a talk on campus this spring?"

*Campus?* Jesus, she had a son in grad school. Will shook his head. "UC Irvine? Yeah. Yeah, I was there. Favor for a friend during my west coast tour. Were you in the audience?" *That would be too weird.*

"No." Galen's upper lip quivered as if he'd just caught a whiff of raw sewage. "I don't classify genre fiction as literature."

*Really.*

"Galen!" Hannah removed her arm from her son.

"Sorry." Galen didn't sound like he meant it. He inhaled. "Sorry. I didn't mean to be a jerk." Okay, so the second apology was genuine.

"It's cool." Will had never understood the whole commercial versus literary debate. He wrote stories, people liked them, the end. Although, truth be told, he had cranked out the last two. Possibly three.

"You're Mom's new tenant?"

"Afraid so, dude." Will forced out a smile that made his cheek muscles ache. "But don't worry, I won't be around long enough to corrupt you with my evil genre ways. I have to get my dad settled in a retirement home, and then I'll be heading back to New York. Hopefully sooner rather than later."

Will glanced at Hannah; she ignored him.

"Stop by sometime and I'll tell you how I sold my literary soul to the devil."

Galen shrugged as if he didn't much care whether he saw Will again or not. "Thanks." And then he turned and walked toward the now-yipping dogs.

"You have a grown son?" Will watched Galen disappear.

"No." Hannah heaved a duffel from inside the cab. "I have two, either side of twenty-one."

*Two?* She was a mother twice over? And how could someone his age have a son in grad school? Had she been one of those kids-having-kids moms? Sure, a few girls in his high school had been pregnant in sophomore year, but she must have been—

"Here—" Will stepped forward and placed a hand on the bag. "Let me help."

"It's fine. I've got it."

But it wasn't fine, because they were as close as they'd been at the powwow. He had a bizarre urge to smell her hair. And feel up her butt.

Will shoved his hands in his pockets. "You totally don't look old enough."

"Haven't we had this conversation in reverse?"

"But seriously. Did you start having babies when you were twelve?"

"I was married at nineteen. Pregnant by the time I was Galen's age. Divorced before my fortieth birthday." Hannah chewed on the corner of her lip. It was kind of cute, for an older woman.

"So you're…"

"Forty-five," Hannah said. "You can close your mouth, you know. It's not as if you're staring at a member of an endangered species."

Will scratched his head. "No, it's just—wow, you look great for your age. I mean, you don't look old enough—for the grown-kid thing."

Hannah sighed. "Technically I'm old enough to be your mother."

Okay. That was the end of the conversation.

"Not even close," Will said, and walked away.

# SIXTEEN

Hannah continued to scrub Galen's plate, but the flake of salmon skin on the edge of the rim refused to dislodge. *Stupid plate.* She dumped it in the trash can, on top of the dinner Galen had barely touched.

Normal people threw out perfectly good plates all the time, right? Besides, one less plate in her cabinet meant nothing. She owned a dinner service for twelve yet lived a cater-for-one lifestyle. Hannah dried her hands with the yellow towel. Too cheerful, too soft, it made her think of daffodils and the rejuvenation of spring. Maybe she should dump the towel, too.

Reading people had always come easily, but tonight she'd offended her celebrity tenant with a simple reference to his mother, and had prepared a dinner her son was unable to eat. Apparently Galen had told her out in California that he was a vegan. What else had she forgotten? Had Will warned her off his mother, too?

The interaction with Will was a blessing—really, a blessing. One more reason to have even less to do with him. But this thing with Galen… She'd welcomed him home with a fridge full of fish and his once-favorite cheese.

When Galen was little, she knew he was going to cry before he did. And wasn't that the definition of a good mother—to anticipate your child's agony? How could she do that if she no longer understood his most basic needs? Gone were the days when she could find jeans on clearance for her son and drive home to a hug and "Awesome, Mom. You're the best." She couldn't even feed him.

She stared through the uncovered window into the black wall of trees. The forest had inspired and terrified Galen since he was little. His best poems contained imagery of light through the trees; his worst nightmares played out in the forest. They both believed Saponi Mountain to be haunted, but the ghosts he encountered came straight from hell.

Hannah kicked the trash can back into its cubbyhole.

She should have answers; she should know how to reach her son. When life fell backward into a repeating pattern, the way forward should be obvious. Or maybe the second time was worse because you understood the price of failure.

Galen had chosen to stay with the therapist in California, which didn't sit right. Surely he needed a mental health care professional in the same time zone, one he could talk with face-to-face. The nuances of depression were easily missed over the phone. She knew better than anyone. But they'd reached a compromise: Galen could keep the out-of-town therapist provided she drove him to and from A.A. meetings. When Galen was a teenager, car journeys were a time for confidences, especially given the way her job could intrude on their lives. Starting tomorrow, once a day for two twenty-minute car rides, he would have her undivided attention, and she would have his.

If she could just find the starting point, then maybe she

could help Galen rebuild his life. She knew only the bare facts that made up the iceberg of her son's mental collapse: his growing uncertainty about the future; his belief that he would never get a job—*You should have talked me out of poetry, Mom;* his girlfriend dumping him.

Until they'd met a month earlier, while Galen was in the hospital, she'd cast the girl as the villain. Hannah had watched a young woman walk into the trendy Californian coffee shop and had known, without doubt, that she was staring at Galen's former lover. *Soul mate* was not a term Hannah liked—it was reserved for people who believed in true love—but she hoped the future would bring these two back together. They seemed to be a fit.

The girlfriend had explained, stopping to cry, that she still loved Galen, but that she, too, struggled with depression. She had tried to persuade him to seek help, to stop drinking. But when she'd finally told him she could no longer cope with the toxicity of the apartment, he'd acted blindsided. But then again, the girlfriend had said, he could have been drunk. Drunk Galen and sober Galen were one and the same. Hannah had been unable to comment, since she didn't recognize the person they were discussing. He certainly wasn't the little boy who had once created whole worlds out of Legos.

Hannah sighed, retrieved the plate from the trash and left it in the sink. Tomorrow she would try harder.

She tiptoed into the living room where Galen was curled up in the fetal position on the edge of the sofa, a cushion clasped to his chest. As a baby, Liam slept sprawled out as if to say, *I can't walk or talk, but I own this world.* Galen, however, always slept in a self-protective huddle. Much as she did.

When did she stop thinking as a mother and start settling for throwaway conversations? *Sure, first day of classes were great.* Translation: *I had a monster hangover.* How's life? *Oh, you know.*

How're your courses? *Fine.* What happened to that girl you liked? *Which one?* After twenty-two years of worry for her boys, she had allowed empty-nest syndrome to trump everything, to torpedo maternal instincts.

One tear escaped, followed by a second. She had told herself she wouldn't cry, but she was moving through a world where there was no correlation between what she wanted and what happened. And she had never been this scared in her life.

When had Galen decided to give up on himself? Did self-loathing just slam into him one day like a piece of space junk falling from the sky, or had it always been there, festering in his DNA, and she'd been too busy to notice? If he were bleeding, she could fix it. If he were a client seeking answers, she could give them. But he was dying inside, and she was lost.

Rosie licked her hand, and Hannah sank to her knees for a hug.

"Stay with him, baby," she whispered.

Then she stood and switched off all the lamps except one—to guide Galen back upstairs to his childhood bed. Rosie padded across the wood floor and flopped down by the sofa. Daisy and the other dogs followed. Nothing bad would happen tonight, not with her girls on watch. But what about the next night and the one after that?

# SEVENTEEN

Hannah wasn't sure about this, but then again, she wasn't sure about anything right now. She fastened her thumbs through the belt loops of her jeans as Will opened the door. He looked neither pleased nor surprised—merely sweaty. Thank God he favored baggy shorts and a muscle shirt for his workout. Lycra would have been far too distracting.

Will leaned against the doorjamb, blocking her entrance to the cottage.

She shivered. Yet another sultry afternoon in the longest, most dangerous month of her life. It was as if she and Galen were snared in a time loop with the thermometer stuck in the red zone. And now Jacob and Will were stuck with them.

"Cold?" Will said, frowning.

"Bad mojo in the air."

He nodded in silent agreement; the frown stayed in place. She almost inquired about his sleep, but the answer was obvious.

"Things seemed a little out of whack between us last night," she said, "and I can't help but feel I touched a nerve when I mentioned your mother. I'm sorry if I offended. It wasn't my intention."

"It's cool." He stared at the deck floorboards.

"Is your mother off-limits, like your son?"

He glanced up, and she wished he hadn't. "Yeah."

*Good to know.* "How's your dad doing?"

"Great." Will crossed his arms over his chest, accentuating his biceps. "Poppy's great with him. That all worked out...great."

Stunning articulation from a world-class author. "I was hoping to catch her, before she left for the day."

"She's gone."

"But her car—"

"Some guy picked her up."

"Right. The possible stalker. I thought that was tomorrow." Hannah paused. "It's hard keeping track of other people's lives."

Will stood up straight. "Poppy's on a date with a nutjob?"

"Oh, I'm sure he's perfectly nice. But they met online and he seems rather intense. I'll catch her tomorrow."

Hannah started to walk down the cottage steps.

"Wait. Can I help?"

She glanced backward and her body, unbidden, turned.

"I owe you," he said, and gave an uncertain smile.

How much had it cost to make that offer?

Instinct told her Will would be a good confessor, if she ever needed one, and maybe she did. When Galen was stronger, she planned to share the family medical history with him. But the timing had to be right, since the truth came with potentially devastating consequences. She would have to orchestrate the perfect, wrinkle-free moment, and Will might be a good test subject. He lived a private life without melodrama and, parent-to-parent, he might understand. Besides, he would soon be gone, which gave her nothing to lose. Tentative thoughts worth considering. But right now she needed help on a smaller level.

"I was going to ask Poppy if she could keep an eye on Galen. Not that he needs looking after, and I won't be gone more than an hour. I have to run to the store, do a food shop."

"You're feeding him up?" Will said.

"Trying."

Will hesitated. "Has he been sick?"

Sick sounded so much better than *recovering from a major depressive episode.* "Yes, that's why he's home."

"Would you like me to walk over in a bit, see how he's doing?"

How curious, that he hadn't asked for an explanation. She'd been right, then. Will was someone who understood discretion.

Hannah gave a long sigh. "Thank you, but no. He'll think I'm fussing. I feel better, though, knowing there's a responsible adult around."

"Between me and Dad, you've just about got one of those," Will said. "Give me your cell number, and I'll call if I see any delinquent student activity—drugs, rock 'n' roll, hookers. Sorry. That was totally…"

She almost laughed. What she wouldn't give to have a problem as simple as catching Galen with a prostitute.

"I should be quiet now." Will snagged his bottom lip with his teeth.

Hannah wasn't sure she'd seen a grown man, even a young one, blush quite so impressively. She smiled.

"I doubt he'll do anything but sleep, but call me if your parenting hackles rise. You can use the number from the powwow text."

And once again, Will focused on the floorboards.

★ ★ ★

Hannah wandered the aisles at Trader Joe's with a shopping list of vegan delights and a basket so laden it felt as if her arm were about to rip out of its socket. Her current mind-set—*if in doubt, buy it*—was not her usual shopping mode. She was trying too hard, and Galen would realize.

The store's cinnamon-spiced air spoke of seasonal comforts, and the cheerful calls of the staff—*three bells!*—jolted her into the world of ordinary people living ordinary lives.

She moved to the front of the store and picked out six green bananas.

A little boy, probably around the age of Will's son, pointed at the huge carton full of pumpkins and squealed. "Please can I have my own pumpkin, Mommy? *Pleazzzzzze!*"

The mother snapped out a reprimand and dragged him away. As the boy's wails disappeared down the dried-fruits aisle, Hannah tightened her grip on the basket. She wanted to rush after them, tell the mother to buy the blasted pumpkin, tell her to make her son smile and treasure a moment that would never come again.

Hannah pulled out her phone, then slid it back. She'd checked on Galen four times in the past twenty minutes, using his new eating habits as the excuse. By the second conversation, he'd figured out that she was, in his words, "Treating me like a suicidal son left home alone."

Did he have to use the word *suicidal?*

Maybe she should ban all big-picture thinking, shrink her world into one small, obtainable goal—cook a meal Galen could eat.

Her phone vibrated, and tucking the basket next to a display of decorative gourds, she walked outside into the dying light of the gloaming. Life always seemed brighter, more auspicious, at this time of the day. Something to do with the quality of the light, she supposed—so soft, so gentle—and the way it illuminated the treetops with gold. But right now the gloaming spoke of lives suspended, of an endless sense of waiting. But waiting for what—for things to get better or worse?

Part of her dreaded, but also hoped, her caller would be Will. She remembered his voice on the phone—quiet and heavy with pauses. Had they moved beyond pauses?

"Hello?"

The person on the other end of the phone sucked in his breath and released a sob. Not Will, then, but a call Hannah had been expecting for days. It was time to euthanize Lucky, the hundred-pound shepherd who hadn't walked in a year. Until his disc surgery, Clay, a Vietnam vet, had carried his dog into the yard several times a day to pee. In the past few months, Lucky had peed on pads placed beneath him.

"I'll be there in half an hour," she said.

She tried calling Galen, but his phone went to voice mail; she tried the landline—the same. Concern prodded her, but she refused to listen. Galen was probably asleep. She would rush back into the store, check out and, with any luck, dinner would only be an hour late. He might not even realize she wasn't there.

She slipped on her reading glasses, which, for once, were where they should be—on top of her head.

Pet emergency, she typed with one finger, home bit late. Mom. xox

Galen woke up crying. He wanted to feel something—anything—but anxiety. Anxiety wasn't even a true emotion. It was the space between emotions. And it was feasting on him like a parasite.

He wiped his nose on the back of his hand and looked at

his bedside clock. Eight. As a kid, he had resisted sleep. Now it was his drug of choice.

He heaved himself up, walked to the bathroom, pissed.

The house responded with silence. No banging in the kitchen; no cooking smells. His stomach rumbled. He hadn't eaten since a piece of burned toast at 11:00 a.m. He never used to eat burned anything, but scraping toast involved effort. Besides, he couldn't taste.

He tugged on the sleeves of his T-shirt and rocked. Mom should be home by now. He needed a hug; she gave good hugs. She'd promised him a gourmet vegan dinner, too. Not that he cared about the gourmet distinction, but she was trying, even though her optimism dragged him down. Everything he tossed at her, she batted back dressed up in the finery of positive thinking. Was she capable of understanding what he was going through? Did dogs and cats suffer from depression?

Buzzing in the distance. His phone. Must have left it in the living room.

Galen schlepped down the stairs.

He removed pillows from the sofa, one by one, then shoved his hand between the seat cushions. His fingers hit something solid. His phone. He pulled it up close. Thanks to the crap of genetic inheritance, he had Dad's eyesight. Couldn't read unless his nose was touching the paper. He should have his contacts in, but he hadn't worn them since he arrived. Remembering to brush his teeth was hard enough. No energy reserved for contact lens care.

He shook back his hair, which Poppy had offered to trim—after she'd teased him for looking like a caveman. He hadn't taken her up on the offer, although he had shaved off the beard. He trusted Poppy's opinion. She had no parental agenda. Besides, the beard itched.

Poppy treated him and Liam as men. Mom still saw them as kids. Not that she'd ever treated them like kids, but she'd typecast them, adhered labels that stuck: Liam was her little imp; Galen was her little thinker. Liam was wild; Galen was sensible. Trying to kill himself hadn't prompted a role reversal in her mind.

He squinted at his phone.

Pet emergency taking longer than expected. Fix yourself some toast. Home later. Mom. xox

From gourmet dinner to toast. Why could his mother never say no to others? Yet again, she was putting clients before family.

His grandfather's clock ticked on the mantel.

People didn't want to be around him, which he understood. Hell, *he* didn't want to be around himself. But he couldn't be alone in this empty house, in the middle of nowhere. Reaching out to others meant dragging them into his contamination, but he wanted to talk to someone; he wanted someone to listen. The staff on the psych ward never left the crazies alone. He'd found that comforting.

Will had told him to stop by. If he talked to Will, maybe he would care enough to write again. He'd been too smashed to attend Will's lecture in the spring, even though he'd planned to go and heckle.

Galen dropped the phone back onto the sofa. Then he went into the kitchen, dragged a chair across the floor and positioned it in front of the fridge. The liquor had vanished from the pantry—cleared out and dumped before he came home, no doubt. But his mother should have placed a little less trust in her son, because he knew about her hiding places. There were only two—under her bed and at the back of the cabinet above the fridge.

He stood on the chair and started pulling out relics of failed family life: a waffle maker, a deep-fat fryer, an ice-cream maker. Why did she keep this stuff? It belonged in the salvage shed at the dump where another parent could claim it for a fake family montage. He reached up on the balls of his feet. Hands gripping the neck, he yanked free a bottle of red wine. Thirty-two days sober, that was his life's achievement. And he was about to wash it down the drain.

He stared at the bottle. If his parents had brought him home so they could find the old Galen, they'd blown it. He was either gone or hiding so deep that no one could find him. Just how deep, they were about to find out.

# EIGHTEEN

Will was washing up the dinner things when he heard a hesitant knock, one that almost said, *Don't answer me*. Hannah, no doubt, to tell him she'd returned. Longest trip to the store ever. By seven o'clock, he'd been worried enough to consider firing off a text, but if he expected her to honor his privacy, he owed her the same respect. Anyway, doing nothing was preferable to a go-round with female anger. Why did some men find the pissed-off-woman thing a turn-on? To him it yelled, *Hide!* through a bullhorn.

He dried his hands on the dish towel and opened the back door.

Galen stood on the deck, looking a little out of whack: messed-up hair, bloodshot eyes, stale smell. Smudged fingerprints on the lenses of his Coke-bottle glasses. Will had his own crazy-gauge—a scale of one to ten—and Galen was peaking around a five. The guy had the appearance of someone off his meds, but then again, he could have just woken up. And forgotten to shower in the past twenty-four hours. Or maybe the convalescing had taken a turn for the worse.

Should he have asked Hannah if Galen's illness was contagious? The old man was in good health but he was also eighty. Sniffles and sneezes weren't quite so benign at that age. Damn, he should have pressed Hannah for an explanation, but thinking as a caregiver had never come naturally. It was at least a year before he'd felt confident enough to be the parent-in-charge anywhere but FAO Schwarz.

"Can I take you up on that offer?" Galen held out a bottle of wine.

"Sure, man." Will opened the door wide. His universe was shrinking, more people crowding into his space with each passing day. But this time, he'd extended an invitation.

"I didn't hear your mom's truck." For reasons he chose not to explore, Will found the sound of Hannah's truck coming down the driveway oddly reassuring. "She working late tonight?"

Galen gave a sneer. "She's always working late."

Ah. A mother/son spat. The one thing Will had no experience with. Well, he did, just not within the realms of normal. And Hannah, surely, did normal mother all the way. He should probably avoid the subject of Hannah.

"How about we sit in comfort." Will glanced into the living room, where his dad was asleep in an armchair, mouth open. The old man gave a snort. Nice. "Or maybe not."

The crazy look in Galen's eyes dropped a notch. "What are you going to do, about your father?"

Will had never been one for confidences, but pussyfooting around just increased his heart rate. He hated subtext and innuendo: *Sorry my mom missed the parent meeting. She was indisposed. Yeah, my dad, too. We were all indisposed.* Sometimes honesty *was* the answer.

"I'm trying to find the right assisted-living facility. Trouble is, they're so depressing. And he has days when he's fine.

I don't want him locked away with the psychos. Know what I mean?"

"I always worry that'll be my future. Looking after Mom." Galen scraped around a chair and straddled it. He draped himself over the back with the insouciance of an English major who believed genre fiction belonged in the ninth circle of hell.

"You think she'll need looking after?"

"She may." Galen stared for a moment, and Will sensed a meaningful exchange pass between them, even though he didn't understand the meaningful part.

"Mom's alone. She's going to stay alone, and my brother isn't responsible. Sucks being the eldest."

"Sucks being an only child."

"You haven't met my brother."

Will smiled. He liked this guy a lot better when he wasn't being a complete tool.

"Where's your dad?"

"Split six years ago. And Mom hasn't been on a single date since. You know my dad's gay, right?"

*Holy shit.* That could put you off dating for six years. "I don't really know your mom. She's been kind to my dad, though. Adopted him."

"Yeah, well, she would. She likes to take in strays—whether they're pets or people. And half the time she doesn't charge. At best, she undercharges." Galen sniffed. "She's good at what she does, but she doesn't know where to draw the line, when to put family first. She can drop everything for a client, even if it's during Christmas dinner."

Will raised his eyebrows. Ruined Christmas dinners? That was his territory.

"She's a people pleaser with really shitty boundaries," Galen said.

Interesting. Will had pegged Hannah for someone who

was generous, not someone who was incapable of saying no. But Galen's version was more appealing. It painted her as flawed...vulnerable. A people pleaser—that made sense given how she'd allowed his dad to slot into her daily routine. Never once had she accused Will of taking advantage, but the thing is, he had. And he hadn't been aware of it until now.

"Must have been tough when your dad left." Although Will's secret fantasy had always been for at least one of his parents to leave.

"Not really. Dad excels at pimped-out emotions so it was easier without him around. He performs everyday life as if backlit with floodlights, but Mom sucked the drama out of divorce." Galen sighed. "She and Dad are still friends, so it never really affected us. Although my grandparents cut us off as if we were unclean. Can't say I miss them. Dad's parents are jerks. Mom's parents, though? They were awesome. Especially her dad."

"He died?"

"When I was ten. My grandmother was killed in some freak boating accident while they were on vacation in Florida, and he never recovered. Papa moved in with us after that. Mom and Dad had this cottage built for him, but he never lived here. Died the week it was finished—of a broken heart. How sad is that?" Galen's head sank to his arms. "You know, when I came out this morning and saw your father standing on the deck staring into the forest, I thought of Papa. They're nothing alike, but memory follows its own piper."

So, that explained why Hannah took them in, why she'd changed her mind. The bestselling-author bit had never been part of the equation. Good for her. And the no parents/gay husband was enough to bring any woman to her knees. Not Hannah, though.

Will rummaged through kitchen drawers, searching for

a corkscrew. He wasn't much of a wine drinker, but Galen looked like he needed a drink. And drinking alone never solved anything. Just gave you a worse hangover. As he well knew.

"Not sure if we have any wineglasses," Will said.

"Upper left cabinet by the window. I normally stay here, when I come home."

"We displaced you? Sorry, man."

Galen shrugged and retreated from his family history dump into silence. Silence in solitude was good; silence in company was bad.

"So," Will said. "Not a fan of genre fiction, then?"

"I guess I would be if I were making the kind of money you must make." Galen turned even paler. "Shit. That was unbelievably crass."

"Forget it." It was Will's turn to shrug. "My earnings are pretty much a matter of public record. But it's not a conscious decision, you know—to write commercial fiction. I write what I want to write. I grew up with characters and stories in my head. At some point, I had to release them onto the page. My hero, Agent Dodds, has been keeping me company for many years." *Until I bailed on him three months ago.*

"Don't you ever want to write something serious?" Galen said.

"Entertaining people is serious." Even though he was treating his business with all the aplomb of a retarded rookie. Will winced. He never, ever used the word *retarded,* even in thought. Grief was clearly desensitizing him, thought by thought, word by word.

"But when you read a novel like *The Road,* don't you wish you'd written it?"

"I'm not reading much fiction these days. But, for the

record, I loved *The Road* just as much as I love every Jack Reacher novel. Now he's a fabulous hero."

"Who's Jack Reacher?"

"Dude! You were an English major and you've never read Lee Child?"

Galen gave a shrug that seemed hardly worth the effort. He shrugged a lot, this guy. Will found the corkscrew. How quaint, an old-fashioned twist and turn model. He put the wine bottle between his legs for better leverage, and then nearly let it smash to the floor when Hannah burst in.

She grabbed the bottle and tugged it free, and Will staggered back. Was this an extension of the mother/son spat? Galen slumped forward again and buried his face in his arms.

"What do you think you're doing?" Hannah's voice hit like a bullet fired through a silencer.

Will considered asking the same question, but he kept his eyes on the bottle of wine. If only these two people would take their argument away from his kitchen, away from him.

"Galen, sweetheart?"

Galen said nothing. Hannah held up the wine, and Will ducked. In his experience, a woman who raised a bottle often did so to make it a projectile.

"How did you find it, Galen?"

"You need better hiding places, Mom." Galen spoke into his arms.

She turned, slowly, to Will. "My son isn't supposed to drink."

"Don't," Galen groaned.

"No," Hannah said. "If you're going to spend time with Will, he needs to hear this."

"Mom—" Galen raised his head.

"Hear what?" Will fought the urge to run out into the night and keep running.

"My son is in A.A., Mr. Shepard."

He'd become Mr. Shepard?

"Mom, please. Enough."

"You don't have to explain," Will said. *Really, neither of you need to take this any further.*

"You know what?" Galen kicked back his chair and stood in one swift movement. "It doesn't matter. Nothing fucking matters. What my mother wants to tell you, but she's too polite and God forbid she offend someone, is that I just spent three and a half days in a locked psych ward. After I tried to kill myself. Biggest regret of my life is that I failed."

*Jesus.* Will took a step back and hit the fridge.

"Sweetheart, you didn't actually—" Hannah reached for her son, but he shied away, raising his elbow in a protective gesture.

"Does it matter what I did or didn't do, Mom? I wanted to end my life. I wanted to die."

Galen blundered across the kitchen like a fatally wounded warrior. The front door smacked into the edge of a cabinet, feet shuffled down the back steps and he was gone.

A memory crystallized inside Will's brain, forcing him to hear, to see, to reexperience the horror of Freddie's first temper tantrum. Will hadn't cared that his son was behaving like a brat in public; he'd seen worse from rich kids in New York restaurants. But the sudden breakdown in mood had reawakened Will's long-suppressed terror of messed-up family DNA. If Freddie had lived, would the shadow of madness have manifested in him, too?

Will raised his chin, grew tall in the face of public panic. Keeping his eyes on Hannah, he concentrated on presenting his blank face, the face that had served him well since grade school.

"I'm sorry," Hannah said. "I didn't mean to drag you into my family drama."

"Because I have enough of my own?" He should probably smile, but it wasn't possible to multitask through the adrenaline rush turned sour.

Two moths drifted in, and Hannah closed the open door. "Something like that. Here." She handed him back the bottle. "You keep it."

"I'm not sure that's a good idea."

"Sorry, I forgot about your dad."

His heart rate began to slow, and then instinct kicked in. He wasn't wired for physical contact unless it came with sex, but he stepped forward and touched her. A light touch on the arm. All that he was capable of. Should he attempt a hug?

Hannah stared at the bottle. "My favorite. I was so excited when I found it on sale. I threw out all the liquor yesterday, but I kept this in case Poppy needed cheering up after her date. It's so hard to make good decisions, so easy to make bad ones."

She had him on that.

He took the wine from her. "How about we hide this somewhere neither my dad nor Galen would think to go? Then you can come over and have a glass whenever you want one. What about my bedroom?" That was *so* not what he meant to say. Had he just given her an open invitation to his bedroom?

"I can't believe I was so stupid. What kind of a mother leaves her alcoholic son alone with a bottle of wine?"

"You did hide it."

"Not well enough."

"At some point he's going to have to learn to desensitize himself. Galen's a grad student—he's going to be around alcohol. No parent can protect his child 24/7. No parent." Will clenched his teeth. "What happens when he goes back to college and his friends have a keg party or invite him to a poetry slam in a bar?"

"I'm not sure he is…going back to school." Hannah glanced at the closed door.

"Maybe we should open the wine, anyway."

She shook her head. "I'm sorry—for asking you to keep an eye on Galen without giving you the facts. I'm not normally so irresponsible, but this—" she rubbed at her mouth "—this is unknown territory for me. I really don't know what I'm doing anymore."

*Me, neither,* he wanted to say.

"We're both sorry?" He wasn't sure why he was apologizing, since he'd acted out of ignorance with the wine. Then he gave his public smile, the one he used for sold-out author readings because it made his gut knot a little less.

"I should go after him. Good night, Will."

And she left. Quietly.

Will slid down the fridge and sat in a heap on the cool tiled floor. A suicidal writer. A young guy who had the gift of life—a gift his son no longer had—and wanted to throw it away.

He had to speed things up; he had to get out of here; he had to get back to New York.

What were Willie doin' on the floor? And why'd he have a bottle of wine between his legs?

"Son, we got our choice of chairs, you know."

But Willie just sat there, all curled up like he did when he were a boy tryin' to make hisself real small so his mama wouldn't notice. 'Course, she always did. You couldn't hide from your mama, now, could you?

"Dad, we need to talk. About where you go from here."

"Don't reckon I want to go nowhere, son. Feel like I'm home."

"I know, but we can't stay. I'm only renting the cottage."

"So buy it." He patted Will's knee. "New memories to make, and I have a mind to do it here with Poppy and Hey You."

"Hannah. Her name's Hannah," Will said, and got a real distant look. "We have to find you somewhere to live permanently, Dad. And I have to get home."

But that made no sense. Willie were home.

"I have to get back to New York, Dad."

"So you been tellin' me all week, son. But you're still here."

Will pushed hisself up to standin'. He looked tired, his boy.

"C.R.S., son. Can't remember stuff, but that don't make me a baby. I don't need lookin' after, but if you need to go, those two little ladies will keep an eye out."

"Hannah and Poppy have to work. They can't look after you."

"You're not listenin' so good, son. I don't need lookin' after. But if it makes you feel better, you can stay, too. Hell, you can bring Freddie."

"Dad, Freddie—"

"Where is he today, anyways? He and his mama still travelin'?"

He didn't like the look on Will's face, like he was figurin' out how to say somethin' real bad.

"When you talk about Freddie, you come back to me, son. So many years, you were distant. Your mama, now, she didn't make it easy for you, but we did all right, didn't we?"

Will nodded, but he wasn't in agreement. A father could read his son's eyes.

"Tomorrow we have to talk, Dad. You have to look at some

of the pamphlets for these retirement communities. We have to start making decisions."

A plan came to him, just like that! He needed to write it down real quick, before he forgot. He started tappin' on his palm. *Poppy plan, Poppy plan.*

"You go on up to bed now, Willie. You look done in."

"Dad, it's only nine o'clock. I haven't been to bed before midnight since I was in diapers."

"Sleep when you're tired, son."

And Willie obeyed. Got up and took that wine with him. Good kid, his Willie. Always done what he were told. Knew how to be quiet, too, so as not to upset his mama. And knew when to go to his room. One time, had to lock the boy in for a whole night while he went searchin' for Angeline. Came home and found Willie curled up asleep in the corner of his room. Felt real bad about that, but couldn't hire no babysitter. Family secrets, they weren't for sharin'.

Now. He had somethin' to do. What was it? Go to bed hisself? Nah. He just woke up. He had a mind to sit out on the porch, look at the stars and listen to the katydids. Might even hear that rascal owl again. He was one active bird, that owl. Always out in the evenin', sometimes in the mornin', too.

He tapped his palm. *Poppy plan.* But first, he had to write hisself a note.

# NINETEEN

How could you avoid someone on a mission to apologize? Damn A.A. and their steps of forgiveness. Will jogged past the main house and glanced at the porch cluttered with coziness. Galen was curled up asleep on the metal rocker, submerged in a mound of brightly colored cushions. Behind him, a mass of mature houseplants in huge, glazed pots—all of them shades of midnight blue. A twinge of longing jabbed at Will, longing for his jungle of a roof garden. He'd fire off a text to Ally after his shower, remind her to give the pots a good soaking.

Using his T-shirt, Will wiped sweat from his face and then paced until his body slowed. Not the most relaxing run after a second day spent either hiding from Galen or trying to figure out what was going on with Poppy and his dad. A subplot was developing right under his nose; he could smell it. And it had nothing to do with art, although the painting they were working on wasn't half-bad in a primitive way. Very Gauguin.

His mom had been the creative parent—enough creativity to fill several city nuthouses. Despite his music and his wood carving, the old man had been the practical parent, the one who took care of the bills, the house, the car, the yard, even the vegetable patch. Of course, his mom tore down the deer fence whenever she veered off on an alcohol-fueled rant—some weird reasoning about caged wildlife that made no sense to anyone except her. And every time she ripped it down, his dad replaced it.

The front door opened, and Will jumped.

"Nice run?" Poppy's eyes went straight to his groin. She wasn't even subtle.

"No." Will flopped onto the front steps and started unlacing his sneakers. "You about ready to leave for the day?"

"Close. I've been slow-pokin' it around. Waiting for you to come back. Mind if I join you?"

A redundant question since she was already in motion to do just that. Some indignant squirrel kicked up a ruckus in the forest, and Will scooched over.

"Thought we should chat while your dad's asleep," Poppy said.

His stomach did some bizarre little backflip. She wasn't going to quit on him, was she? Will leaned forward and collapsed his arms onto his knees.

"You know Hannah told your dad he could stay in the cottage as long as he likes?" Poppy said.

"She shouldn't have, because he can't."

"Yeah, whatever. Gum?"

What were they, like, twelve? "No. Thanks."

"Thing is—" she unwrapped two sticks of Juicy Fruit and shoved them both in her mouth at once "—your dad *really* doesn't want to leave."

"I know. But he's not thinking about what's best for anyone but himself."

"Not strictly true. I may have to leave my duplex soon. Had a few rough years, financially. The recession's been hard on the custom ceramics business. Paying rent's getting to be, you know, problematic. And the horse isn't cheap." Poppy looked toward the paddock where Miss Prissy was prancing around, mane flying. "Shouldn't have stolen her, but no regrets."

"I thought you rescued her."

"Rescued, stole. Same thing."

*Hardly.* Will watched a black snake at the edge of his vision. It slithered out from under the Carolina jessamine by the side of Hannah's house, hesitated, then made a mad dash for the forest. He had half a mind to follow.

"Look. You want to go back to New York to be near your work and your kid. I get that."

He closed his eyes briefly, but it didn't help. Freddie's giggle surrounded him, bled through his pores, speared his heart.

"But your dad wants to stay here, and I need somewhere to crash before I end up living out of a rusty Honda Civic."

Will sat up straight. "You don't mean what I think you mean. Do you?"

"You always cryptic?"

"Okay," Will said slowly. "How's this—do you have any experience living with an old and possibly senile man?"

"Jacob's not senile."

"Not yet, but his memory's failing faster than the *Titanic*."

"I can beg." She butted her hip into his. Will jerked back. "Because if you say no, I'll have to return to the parental home in Raleigh, and I might not recover. Mama will put me on a carb-free diet and force me to watch beauty pageants, and Daddy will make me relive his glory days as a TV weatherman."

"Fascinating family."

"We all have our crosses to bear. Mama's a former beauty queen who hasn't forgiven me for not entering Miss Magnolia. After three boys, I was her last great hope for a tiara."

Will couldn't help it, he smiled. "So, you're local? You don't sound very Southern."

"Fucking elocution lessons. And two voice coaches before I turned fourteen. I can sing the Star-Spangled Banner like a damn Yankee." She paused. "You'll think about my offer?"

Will nodded, even though he had no intention of following through. Hers was a half-assed solution at best. No way was he going to settle for a Band-Aid when his dad was a step away from full-time nursing care.

The repetitive laugh of an Indian hen woodpecker—loud, harsh, more of a cackle—came from behind the cottage.

"You've met our boy, then." Poppy bobbed her head toward Galen.

"Is it true that he tried to kill himself? There seemed to be some discrepancy between Hannah's and Galen's views of the event."

"He stumbled into an E.R. shit-faced and talked about slitting his wrists. Hannah prefers to focus on the positive—that he sought help before actually trying it."

The long, brightly colored twists of plastic that hung from the porch ceiling swirled above them.

"And what do you think?"

Poppy stared at Will until he looked away. "I think Galen needs a friend."

The footsteps stopped outside Galen's room.

"Dinner's ready," Mom said, and walked away.

In the past forty-eight hours, there had been no reprimand for dragging their celebrity tenant into the family debacle, no harsh words concerning the bottle of wine. Mom had offered understanding and acceptance. Neither of which Galen deserved; neither of which he wanted.

*Spiritual* was the word people attached to Mom, but therapy had taught him to be honest and *repressed* was more ac-curate. Thinking in adjectives—empirical proof of how low he had sunk.

Had she really not expected him to search for booze? He used to admire the way she allowed people to be themselves, but her inability to question his flaws was a burden he no lon-ger wanted. Trust was a dangerous disease. He'd hated him-self since he was ten years old. Why could his mother not see that? Why could she not see that the steadfast, dependable guy of the family no longer existed? Had he ever?

Yes, he shared the blame. He'd wanted to protect her from the horror inside his head. And now he lacked the persuasive energy to show her the truth: that depression was his life force.

Galen stood and walked down the stairs, barefoot. Poppy was meant to join them, but her social life was like quicksil-ver. Mom was often Poppy's insurance against a quiet Satur-day night, but it never seemed to bother her. "Poppy likes to party," she'd once explained. "I don't."

He entered the kitchen and Mom offered him a smile and a warm plate of ratatouille. He mumbled his thanks.

They ate without conversation. The food tasted of nothing.

He scraped his fork around the plate, until Mom leaned over and stopped him.

"What do you think of our new tenant?" She gave a shaky smile.

He shrugged; his mind had become an empty plastic bucket. The cheap kind kids used for building sandcastles on cold beaches.

"Why don't you go over tomorrow with some of your poems?" she said.

"I doubt he's going to renew his invitation."

"I could talk with him, ask him for you."

"No." Galen positioned his fork diagonally across the plate.

He'd never before appreciated the power of such a simple gesture. It screamed, *I'm done.*

"I think—" she picked up his plate and stood "—that you'd be surprised by Will. I'm sure he could help you get back to writing, offer some useful tips."

"He produces genre fiction, Mom. That's one up from boxes of frozen vegetables. He's not Hemingway."

"His debut novel is outstanding. One of my top ten books of all time. I have a copy upstairs if you're interested." Mom cleared the table while he sat. No tongue-lashing for being a sloth. "He portrays mental illness really well."

How could she say that and not link her own situation to those two words: *mental illness.* "You mean I might be fodder for one of Will's stories."

"Galen, you need to ease up on yourself. Let the meds work, let your body and your mind recuperate, but please, climb off the pity pot."

"Nice attitude."

"It's the best I can do, given how little you communicate with me."

Galen stared at a slice of zucchini on the floor. Daisy snapped it up before the rest of the pack noticed.

"I'm sorry, Mom. No one wants to be around me right now, and I know I'm making it worse. But my mind is a dead weight. I can't lift it up."

"Why don't you try some positive thinking? Find one happy thought right before you go to sleep and then remind yourself of it first thing when you wake up."

But he couldn't tidy up his thoughts, categorize them into happy or unhappy. The medication blurred every line.

"Healing takes time and patience, but if you set yourself small goals every day, you can work toward bigger and brighter things."

He rested an elbow on the table and leaned into his palm. "Do you have answers for everything?"

"No. I just refuse to give up."

Words of a holistic warrior, when all he wanted was to crawl back into bed and wave the white flag.

"Yeah, like you understand failure. Name one thing you've failed at."

"My marriage," she said, without bitterness. "Sometimes I feel as if I've failed at being a parent, too."

"It's not your fault I'm this way, Mom."

"Possibly, but that doesn't explain your brother, does it?" She grinned.

Sex and drugs had filled Liam's life since he was fourteen. Mom didn't know the half of it, because Galen had worked hard at being an efficient big brother. Since kindergarten, Liam had flown on charm and bad behavior. Even the high school teachers who spent their lives disciplining Liam loved him. And there had always been girls. Liam's current girl-friend was a fox. Unlike Mom, unlike him, Liam would not end up alone.

Galen's elbow slid across the table, no longer able to support his head. "Why am I sick, Mom? Why do I have messed-up brain chemistry?"

She brushed her fingers through his hair: slow, calm strokes that caused his eyelids to flutter with the promise of more sleep.

"I don't know, baby. But we will figure this out. I promise."

"It doesn't feel that way to me. I don't see an end, and I've lost the beginning. Sometimes I wonder if there's a genetic component."

Her hand retreated. He turned to face her, but she had moved to the sink and was rinsing off plates.

"Have you ever suffered from depression, Mom?"

"No." She slotted his plate into the drying rack. "I haven't."

"What about after Dad's betrayal?"

"I thought we all agreed that worked out for the best."

"How can you be so clinical, so detached?"

She turned, her face a complex chart of creases and worry lines. "Is that what you think?"

Their conversation was a mind-suck. Galen pushed back his chair.

"Thanks for dinner," he remembered to say.

His foot was on the bottom stair when he heard Mom's voice—alone in the empty room. "That went well."

When someone tapped on the back door at 11:00 p.m., Will knew who it was. And he briefly considered not answering. But Hannah had rescued him when he was desperate; the least he could do was open the door for her son's apology. Besides, he wasn't game for another day of hide-and-seek with a tenacious, possibly suicidal poet.

Galen glowered. A definite six on the crazy-gauge. "I'm not carrying tonight." He held out empty hands. "Can I come in?"

"Sure."

But Galen stayed rooted to the porch, surrounded by a halo of bugs and moths. The night air vibrated with crickets and katydids. Maybe a few tree frogs mixed in.

"I've noticed your lights on, late at night," Galen said. "Figured this might be a good time."

Will tightened his grip on the doorknob. Could they just do this and move on? He wasn't accustomed to apologies, had never gotten them growing up.

"I'm sorry about the other night. It was unfair to drag you into my shit." Galen fiddled with his thick glasses. The guy must be one step away from total blindness.

"You don't have to apologize, dude. Really—you don't. Suicidal, huh? Are you still?" Might as well be up front. It was surprisingly easy to be blunt with a screw-up who ranked your work on the same level as that of a hot dog vendor.

Galen shrugged with the effort of a centenarian on his deathbed.

"Sorry." Will swallowed through a hot rush of guilt. "That was a tough question."

"I've got a tougher one."

"Shoot."

"Do you know what it's like to wake up crying?"

"Yeah. I do." *I know what it's like to cry through the day, through the night, through my dreams.*

"You have depression?"

"Not exactly. Nothing personal, man, but I don't talk about it."

"That's cool. I don't have the energy for other people's context."

*Finally, we can agree on something.*

"Why don't you come inside before we invite the entire insect population of Orange County to join us? You drink coffee?" Coffee had to be safe for an addict, although, if he remembered his research from novel five, caffeine was bad for anxiety, and anxiety fed off depression. "Or I have orange soda. Generic crap that my dad likes."

"Coffee, please." Galen walked into the kitchen and pulled back a chair—déjà vu.

Will almost said, *Does your mother know where you are?* Which was a dumb question to ask a twenty-two-year-old. He stuck the electric kettle under the tap and the sound of water hitting metal filled the room. He wasn't too fond of company who stayed past ten o'clock. How should he feel about company who arrived after eleven?

"You work at night?" Galen nodded at the open laptop.

"Used to."

"Writer's block?"

"First time." Will switched on the kettle, then dug around in the freezer, pushing aside the Maple View Farm pints of Carolina crunch, pumpkin pie and black walnut. Had he been trying to buy his dad's compliance with ice cream? He grabbed the bag of coffee beans, slammed the freezer door and took the top off the grinder. Another new possession along with the French press he was about to use. Gradually he was acquiring objects down here, hoarding worse than a blue jay.

"I can't write, either," Galen said.

"Poetry?"

"Used to be."

The grinder whirred, pulverizing the beans.

"How long," Will said. "Since you wrote?"

"Anything worth reading?"

"Anything."

"July."

Will braced himself against the counter.

"You?"

"Same." Although he'd lost more than his talent in July. "If you want to write something, even crap, I'll read it."

"I can't write crap." Galen exhaled.

"Well, there's your problem, right there. You've got to dig through trash to find gems."

"That might be true of fiction, but in poetry every word counts."

"In the final draft, yes, but don't you edit?"

"Some, but it percolates in my head first. Comes out close to perfect." Galen winced. "God, that sounded egotistical. I mean—"

"I've got it. We're good."

"This is the most guarded conversation I've ever had," Galen said.

To his horror, Will laughed. Laughter didn't belong in a conversation concerning the month of July. "It's a sort of macho pissing match, isn't it? Except you don't strike me as a testosterone-driven guy." *Wild guess, could be wrong.* "I'm not much of one, either."

"My best friend in high school was a girl."

The kettle clicked off and Will poured water into the French press. Steam belched toward his face like a mushroom cloud. "Mine, too. You guys still friends?"

"Not since she went all corporate America and picked up a fiancé with monogrammed shirts. How about you?"

"Yeah, we're still best friends. She's married, but to a good guy. She works for me."

"Were you ever in love with her?" Galen said.

"You're not undercover with the *National Enquirer,* are you?"

"You don't have to answer." Galen sighed. "I'm trying to think like my mother and find stories of hope. How anyone survives a broken heart is a mystery."

For a moment, Galen's expression was the perfect reflection of Hannah, although they looked nothing alike. Hannah was a blonde; Galen had black hair and dark, stormy eyes. If he ditched the glasses and did something with his lanky hair, he'd be cute. For a guy.

"Yeah, I was in love with her," Will said. "But only for a decade or two. I've always been a one-woman guy."

"You still in love with her?"

The freezer made a weird sparking noise, then fell silent.

"No. Cream? Sugar?"

"Black, please." Galen played with a piece of braided string wrapped tightly around his wrist. "I tried to kill myself over a woman."

"I doubt it was that straightforward."

Somewhere in the forest behind the cottage, a coyote howled. When Will was a kid, coyotes were mostly mythical, misunderstood creatures from his mom's stories. But once he'd left Orange County, the coyotes had moved in. Now they were as common as crows.

"I'm sorry, too," Galen said in little more than a whisper, "about being an asshole when we met."

"We're good on the whole apology thing." Will forced the plunger down with the flat of his hand and poured two cups of black coffee. A little weaker than usual, just in case.

"Mom told me to read your first novel."

"Did she? Good choice, that's the best one." He'd forgotten Hannah was a fan. The thought warmed his ego, which proved how shallow he was.

"She said the same thing."

Okay, that little ping of pleasure had nothing to do with ego. "You want me to get you a copy?"

"You travel with a stash?"

"Nah. Free shipping on Amazon."

"I only shop indies."

"I shop everywhere. I'm a big book shopper. So. Want a signed copy?"

"I can't read right now," Galen said. "I can't write. I can't read. Time creeps by, and I'm unable to fill it. It's like losing my sight. If I can't write, I can't process the world. I can't engage with anything or anyone."

"You're engaging with me."

"But you're not writing, either."

"Thanks for reminding me." Will sipped his ridiculously weak coffee, then joined Galen at the kitchen table. He hit the return key on his laptop. "Before you came in, I was pretending that posting on Facebook was writing." He scrolled down on his touchpad. "You go by the same last name as your mom?"

"No. Galen Jones."

Will typed and then peered at the screen. "Yup, that looks like you. I've sent you a friend request. You better accept it."

"Really?" Hard to tell, but that could have been pleasure in Galen's voice. "I'm not on Facebook much these days. There seems little point. Can't take an interest in myself, can't take an interest in anyone else. Besides, I get nauseated hearing how great everyone's lives are."

"People don't always post happy things," Will said. "Maybe you should log on sometimes, to get out from under your own shadow."

"Is that why you do it?"

"Hell, no. My marketing person makes me. If you met her, you'd understand. She's a total ball-breaker."

Galen didn't smile. "You do Facebook every day, then?"

"Yeah. I try and do an hour about this time every night. My messages pile up if I ignore them for too long."

"You tweet, too?"

"One of my assistants does it for me."

"Blog?"

"Gave up. Felt too personal."

"And yet you're on Facebook."

"Because you can stay connected without really saying anything." Will leaned in. "Don't believe anything I post on Facebook. I use it as a promotional tool, nothing else."

"You make stuff up?"

"I perpetuate an image."

On Saponi Mountain, an owl hooted twice.

"My writer friends will be stunned when you pop up on my wall."

"Use it to add to the mystique of your breakdown. Pretend I seduced you to the dark side."

And then Galen did something totally unexpected. He laughed.

# TWENTY

The ceiling fan hummed, and outside the katydids rubbed their forewings together in song. Hannah stood by her open bedroom window as darkness filtered through the screen. The local forecast had promised temperatures in the low sixties once night fell, but the house continued to creak and groan through another evening of record-breaking dry heat.

If only she could lie awake listening for rain gushing through the downspout, not the sound of the Chubb lock snapping into place on the front door. Last night Galen had stayed over at the cottage for two hours. And she'd been awake for another hour after that, trying to reassure herself he was home to stay, that he hadn't taken the truck and run away as Liam had done when he was sixteen. Or—she shuddered—that he hadn't wandered into the forest with a stash of pills.

Tonight Galen had gone to see Will the moment she'd come back to her room. Her son was reaching out to someone, which was good, more than good. It was fantastic. Really, fantastic. But he hadn't chosen her or Poppy; he'd chosen a stranger.

She was in uncharted territory with her eldest, stumbling through a desert and searching for a large neon signpost that flashed This Way to Being a Good Mother.

When the boys were little, she'd moved through motherhood with such confidence: play dough was homemade, not store-bought; her boys collected leaves and downed birds' nests, not G.I. Joes; they constructed ride-in rocket ships out of cardboard boxes and caves out of ripped sheets. How she longed to return to simpler days of worrying about nutritious lunches, sharpening colored pencils and making sure letters to Santa were mailed up the chimney.

She moved away from the window, tugged off her T-shirt, unsnapped her bra, stepped out of her jeans and threw herself facedown on her white bed. Fan-circulated air tickled her spine.

She twisted her hair away from her neck, then let it spring free.

*Why Will Shepard?*

Galen picked friends with caution, and yet Will had made the grade.

If not for the playground bravado of his younger brother, Galen would have been bullied mercilessly throughout middle school. There was little room in a county school of jocks and science nerds for a published poet. The incidents, however, stopped during Liam's first week. No need to ask why. Liam and his posse of hangers-on had, undoubtedly, taken revenge. Liam had been a pack leader since kindergarten; Galen was a loner, drawn to kids ostracized as freaks.

Hannah reached under her pillow, grabbed her camisole and wiggled it over her head. No sleeping naked when the boys visited.

She chewed on her bottom lip. What did Will and her son talk about for hours? Galen had always been a secret keeper.

Interrogation was pointless. She had, however, extracted one fact on the drive back from A.A.: they discussed writer's block. Then, at dinner, Galen had slipped up and made reference to Ally, someone Jacob had mentioned, too. If Hannah had known this Ally was the love of Will's life, she would never have pressed for details. Galen had sworn her to secrecy, but it was too late. Will was earning her respect in pieces, and she hated him for it. Physical attraction could be dismissed, but love that stretched over two decades—or was it three?—could break her heart. If only Will would hurry up and leave. But she couldn't let him, could she? Not if he'd become the only person Galen trusted.

Please, God, don't let Will have figured out that she was infatuated.

The light beating on his eyelids was too bright, too damn serene. This was not the half-light of his Manhattan bedroom that never saw the sun. And the chirpy thrush was definitely not a New York cabbie riding his horn. The context may have changed, but the memory Will woke to never varied: Freddie waving over his shoulder, saying, *Bye-bye, Daddy. See you next weekend.*

But this morning there was a second memory hiding behind the first: the memory of touching a woman and being ambushed by the consciousness of belonging. Which was crazy enough to have stepped from one of his mom's fairy stories. Everything about Hannah was unexpected—her age, her sons, the side of her Galen revealed—so why not the emotions that her touch evoked? But that didn't mean he belonged here, with Hannah, in Nowhereville, North Carolina. Not that he belonged anywhere without Freddie.

Pushing up onto his elbows, Will let his head flop back. He opened one eye, then the other, and stared upside down through the window above his bed. A cheerful Carolina morning exploded, white-hot, around the edges of the pale blind. A sign that the Indian summer was set to continue for at least another day. If he checked online he would know for sure, but paying attention to the five-day forecast smacked of permanency.

He sat up and massaged his shoulders, working a tension knot. At the corner of his sight, clothes sprawled over the empty dresser and dirty laundry spewed from the open duffel.

Never a neat freak, he liked a minimal sense of order. Piles that made sense. This Will-made mess was more of a statement or possibly a pledge: I may sleep here—when I'm not up half the night with a suicidal grad student—but I'm not staying.

He leaned over the edge of the bed, picked up the new Dennis Lehane and placed it on the nightstand. Talking with Galen had encouraged him to start reading again—although trying to concentrate on anything except Freddie's journey was like running across sheet ice.

Ten o'clock? He glanced at the alarm clock a second time. *For real?* He was slipping back into New York habits, behaving—once again—as if the world had to function around him and his schedule.

His dad would be up and waiting. Possibly even cooking his own breakfast again. It was hard to tell now that the old man had dismantled the smoke detector.

Had Hannah left already? He pulled up the corner of the blind and peered down into the yard. The truck was gone, but then she'd probably done several hours of work by now, as had most people. Everyone except him and Galen.

Throwing the blanket aside, Will swung his legs around, pausing to scrunch up his toes on sun-warmed carpet.

"Dad?"

He grabbed his jeans from where he'd abandoned them

in the middle of the floor. Tugging them on, he hopped to the door.

"Dad?" he called into the hallway. "You down there, Dad?"

Will leaned over the banister and listened to an empty cottage. Nothing moved, except for the creeping dread in his gut.

"Dad?"

Will dashed through the main bedroom, past the bed made with perfect hospital corners and into the bathroom. The counter was wiped clean; a folded hand towel was laid out next to the sink; the toilet seat was down. Unlike the small bathroom he'd claimed, this space had the air of a hotel room waiting for its next guest.

Will turned and ran downstairs. Now he was officially freaking out.

# TWENTY-ONE

Hannah was feeling the tumor on Scarlet's leg when her cell phone rang. Reaching across her stomach with her left hand, she unclipped the phone from her jeans and stared at the screen.

Which was more ridiculous—the thrill at seeing Will's name pop up on her phone or the sudden wave of motion sickness when she was standing still? Her heart rate had definitely increased, her palms were sweaty and she had tinnitus in her ears. It was as if she were floating.

"Did you take my dad somewhere?" Will said.

The lack of greeting provided an instant cure. Anger was not an emotion she wanted to own, but yes, she was ever so slightly pissed. Pissed that she had developed a ridiculous crush; more pissed that her crush hadn't said hello.

"Good morning to you, too."

Will blew into the phone.

Hannah mouthed, *Excuse me,* to Andrew, Scarlet's owner, and walked out onto the screened-in porch.

"Have you lost Jacob?" she said to Will.

"Maybe. Yes. Should I call 9-1-1?"

"No. I can be home in half an hour. We'll find him together." Hannah grabbed her wrist and pinched. *Together* was a loaded word.

"Don't you think I should issue a silver alert or something?"

"You're overreacting and he'll resent you for it." As thirteen-year-old Liam had done when she hadn't been able to find him and had called the cops. Afterward he insisted she knew he'd been sleeping over at a friend's and blamed her amnesia on the latest pet emergency.

"Suppose he's in trouble?" Will said.

"I think it's more likely he's gone for a wander in the forest."

"Exactly. Where he could get hurt. The forest is a place of a thousand and one dangers."

"Not my forest. If he's on the mountain, he's safe."

"Can you come home any quicker?"

"Sure," she said, and hung up.

In the small backyard, submerged beneath drifts of leaves, crows cawed. A squirrel practiced acrobatics on the plastic bird feeder; a robin flitted in and out of a large pot containing deer-mutilated pansies; and her secret crush burst wide-open. The boys had always criticized her inclination to trust people, but this need to be needed was far more dangerous. It could turn fantasy into love.

Andrew opened the door. "Is everything okay out here?"

"Fine. Just fine. Sorry for the interruption."

Hannah walked back into the living room cluttered with mementos: china cats, stuffed cats, pictures of cats, needlepoint cushions of cats. In the two years since his wife's death, Andrew had devoted himself to the care of her seventeen-year-old cat. Now Scarlet had cancer.

The tragedy of a couple who had shared a lifetime was that

they rarely shared death. One of them was destined to end up alone, and that had been enough to push her dad over the edge. What would happen to Andrew when Scarlet went? Last Christmas he'd had only two cards on display. One of them was from Hannah.

The window air-conditioning unit rattled as Hannah squatted down to where Scarlet was curled up in a nest of towels rank with cat pee. Her right knee crunched, and not for the first time, Hannah wondered if knee replacements were in her future. See? She should be contemplating aging gracefully, not daydreaming about a younger guy.

"When was the last time she ate?" Hannah said.

"Yesterday."

"How much?"

"Half a can."

Scarlet purred.

"She's still drinking?"

Andrew nodded and rubbed one of his watery eyes.

Hannah eased herself back to standing. "You're giving her the immune support?"

"Yes." His right hand began to tremble.

"Let's keep taking it day by day. It's not her time yet, but when it is, I can help her along."

Hannah stared at one of the cat pictures. "You know, I have a friend who's an artist. Would you like her to come with me tomorrow and sketch Scarlet?"

"Thank you kindly." Finally, Andrew smiled. "I used to draw, back in my younger days. That charcoal of the Siamese? I did that for the wife."

*Perfect.* In the middle of darkness, there was always hope.

Hannah did something she hadn't done in years—drove at seventy miles per hour on Redbud Road with no thought for deer or for the sheriff's car that often tucked behind the trailer park mailboxes. She ignored the rattling under the hood and sped down the driveway, bouncing in her seat as the old Ford thumped in and out of potholes.

Yet again Will was pacing, and the large sweat stain on the chest of his snugly fitting T-shirt suggested he'd been at it for a while.

Blazing sunlight reflected off his golden hair and washed out his skin, making it ethereal. He was caught in the daily half hour when the sun reached the space between the house and the cottage, but as he swung around, his body entered solid shadow. The shade was near-perfect for picture taking; the expression and beauty of the subject *were* perfect. This should have been his author photo. If she had her camera, she would light his face with her flash and snap his portrait. Capture this moment on film and store it in her keepsake box with her wedding ring and the handmade Mother's Day cards.

He took off, running toward the truck, and certainty punched her. Unequivocal certainty. She had always hoped to fall in love again, but not like this. Not now. Not while Galen was struggling to crawl through each day. Not while she had to help an eighty-year-old who may or may not be in danger.

*No.*

An invisible force clutched her heart, grabbed and squeezed. Stole her breath.

*No.*

She gasped. Will's head had thrust through her open window.

"Sorry. Didn't mean to make you jump. Are you sure I shouldn't have called 9-1-1?"

*Don't look at his eyes, don't look at his eyes.*

Hannah took small, quiet breaths and stared at her clogs.

She did this every day—set aside personal feelings to do her job. Will was no different than a client who needed her expertise, her ability to take charge. He needed her to be the person in control. *She* needed to be the person in control. She took a bigger, slower breath. Filled her lungs with warm air so she could breathe again, so she could be the person they both needed her to be.

"How long has he been missing?" she said.

"I don't know. I overslept."

Hannah kicked off her clogs, then retrieved her hiking boots and shook out the socks stuffed inside. She waved Will back so she could open her door.

The dogs whined a welcome, but they needed to stay in the house with Galen. Hannah tightened the laces on her boots and slowly created two perfect, knotted bows. She centered her thoughts and released a quick prayer.

*Let Jacob be safe.*

As she eased herself out of the truck, the back of her neck prickled with sweat. The mercury would hit eighty before noon. Once again, Saponi Mountain was imprisoned under brilliant blue skies and a blistering sun.

Will flicked his hair back from his face. "Ready?"

"Do you have your phone?"

He nodded.

"Good. That way we can split up if we need to. Once we find him—"

"*If.*"

"Trust me, we'll find him."

His eyes settled into a look she couldn't decipher, then he turned to watch a pair of black vultures circling over the dead rat snake in Miss Prissy's pasture.

"I don't trust," Will said. "It's what keeps me alive as a rock climber."

"Since you're not dangling off a rock, now might be a good time to start trusting. No one knows that forest better than I do."

"Sorry." He drummed his fingers on his cheek. "I'm amped up and losing it."

"I can tell," she said. "But I need you calm so we can focus on practicalities. Can you manage that?" She nearly added, *For me.*

He breathed heavily. "Calm I can do. I'm an expert on calm. Lead the way. I'm right behind you."

She blocked the image of spooning with Will. "Follow me," she said.

And he did.

Dodging a large cobweb, they entered the forest through a clearing behind the concrete well cover. Years earlier, Hannah had considered carving out a path from this spot down to the creek, but enough generations had crisscrossed Saponi Mountain with trails. Besides, she loved her daily game of never repeating a route into the forest, of knowing her destination but allowing the journey to be a surprise. If this were her first time in the forest, she would head straight, aim for the crest of the hill and the old trading path. Jacob had likely done the same. But if he didn't want to be found, he wouldn't be. An experienced woodsman knew how to lose himself, but that was not a thought worth sharing.

She stopped and waited for Will to catch up. "You might want to consider this free service the local sheriff offers for tracking seniors with electronic bracelets. A couple of my clients use it with great success."

He shot her another look, but this time the meaning was clear.

"Yeah, like he's going to agree to that," Will said.

"You know, it's not the information that matters so much as the presentation."

They started walking again.

A pileated woodpecker with a crown of red feathers scooted up a dead pine and began hammering. How long before the drought weakened the more vulnerable trees and brought them down? As if they hadn't lost enough trees, thanks to the planned McMansions on the ridge. All spring she'd listened to logging trucks rumble up the private road leading to the land-for-sale sign, polluting with noise and fumes, aiding in the rape of the forest.

Hannah stepped onto a rotting log and paused, watching for copperheads. Will did the same.

"With a transmitter, he can have more freedom," she said. "And we can have less worry."

"You mean *I* can have less worry."

"Why do you find it so hard to accept that Poppy and I like your dad?" she said.

"Frankly? He's not that likable."

"Oh, come on. He's a sweet old guy. Surely he's earned the right to live the remainder of his life with dignity?"

"You don't think I treat him with dignity?" Will's voice betrayed nothing.

"No. I'm saying Hawk's Ridge didn't. The second time around, you'll get it right."

"You're an optimist, aren't you?"

A branch snapped under his khaki-colored Converse.

"I'm a realist who assumes someone as smart as you is unlikely to repeat his mistakes."

"How do you know I'm smart?"

"You wrote an international bestseller when you were, what—twenty-five?"

"Twenty-four. But that doesn't mean squat."

Was he insecure or fishing for compliments? Either way, she wasn't arguing the point. "How's the search for a retirement home coming?"

"Frustrating. I've found a decent place called Azalea Court, but I'm on the wait list. Basically I'm hoping some poor bastard croaks so an apartment opens up. In the meantime, I'm back to checking out facilities in New York."

"Without visiting them?"

Will kicked at a small, mossy-covered outcrop that rose through the leaves. Another week and none of the stones on the path would be noticeable. Maybe he wasn't smart enough to avoid repeating mistakes. Yes, Azalea Court was a decent retirement home. Flashy, but well kept. It was also close to the Durham county line, which, for Jacob, was as alien as New York.

They passed a huge root ball from Hurricane Fran and trudged onto the old trading path. The undergrowth rustled, and Hannah raised her face into a rain of falling leaves.

"I suppose," Will said, "that now might be a good time to talk about Poppy's plan."

"What plan?"

"You don't know?"

"Know what?" Hannah fanned her T-shirt against her chest. If not for the drought, she would consider it a two-shower day.

"Poppy and my dad want me to buy the cottage."

"But it's not for sale," Hannah said. Although, for less than a second, the idea of Will staying…

"Don't worry, the plan sucks balls."

*How eloquent.*

"Poppy has no medical training and my dad needs to be in assisted living with the option to upgrade to hospice care."

"Upgrade?"

"You know what I mean." He scratched through his hair. Clearly he hadn't combed it since he got up, but he wore the disheveled-writer look well. The phrase *morning-after bed head* slotted into Hannah's mind, and she picked up her pace, marching toward the carpet of periwinkle up ahead. At some point there must have been a garden here, a woodland garden. Showy perennials that flashed fat, garish petals in the sun did nothing for her. Flowering shade plants, however, spoke of magic.

She grabbed a spindly dogwood tree and hauled herself up a bank.

"Just like Occoneechee Mountain, this is another big hill with a grandiose name," Will muttered behind her.

"I figured it was once part of something more majestic, probably the ancient Sauratown Mountains to the west. The view from the ridge is stunning. Sadly they're opening it up for development. One house is already finished and occupied. This time next year, there could be ten families living on Saponi Mountain." She sighed. "I'll have a community of neighbors."

Their footsteps crunched through crispy yellow and brown leaves, his echoing hers.

"The forest is surprisingly open here," Will said.

"It changes dramatically once you're over the ridge and descending into the wetlands." Talking about nature with Will was safe. She could almost pretend he was just another stray wandering through her life. "The creek's dry, of course, but there are ferns and wildflowers everywhere on the other side. And each spring a wave of daffodils marks out a long-forgotten homestead. I like to picture an old woman with threadbare gardening gloves planting the bulbs, never imagining that they will endure and outlive both her and her house."

Will gave a soft *huh*. "There's a writer in you."

"Hardly, but I do like to create stories that bring the past to life." She stopped and turned. "I like to believe that people who die never really leave us."

The forest had sunk its claws in once again. Dragged him back as if he were easy prey. And where was Hannah heading with this conversation? Could they not just find the old man and get out?

Will bent down to brush aside the leaves, to touch the hard, compacted dirt under his feet. *Dirt never lies,* his dad always said. Young Will couldn't figure out whether that was Occaneechi lore or Jacob lore. The lines were fuzzy because his dad was good at making stuff up—almost as good as his mom had been. Except she'd been flat-out delusional.

"There must be graves near here." Even though he couldn't see any markers. The forest was keeping its secrets, which was fine. He wasn't that interested. Really.

"There's an old burial plot up ahead. The boys found it when they were younger and frightened themselves silly. I told them it spoke of peaceful death in old age."

"Did they believe you?"

"Until Galen realized one of the nameless markers was considerably smaller and undoubtedly belonged to a child." Hannah sighed. "How did you know, about the graves?"

"Periwinkle." He pointed. "Planted on graves to suppress weeds. My dad taught me to read the land. He also encouraged me to play wherever I saw vinca growing, since it doesn't provide enough cover for snakes. Come to think of it, I spent most of my childhood playing on graves. Which makes it totally impressive that I didn't end up as a serial killer."

She gave a laugh.

Her hair was gripped back today, but a blond curl had escaped to frame her jawline. How would it feel to grab that hair and pull her lips to his, to feel her mouth yield? Despite the faded jeans and tatty T-shirt, she was a babe. He'd never dug an older woman before, although she wasn't that much older. Just a decade. Hard to decide whether her ass or her legs were more distracting. She had great legs. Long legs. Did she ever wear skirts and heels? Of course, heels would make her taller than he was. *No, please no.* He was getting a boner.

*So not the time, Will.*

She had a great figure for the mother of two grown sons, but maybe that's what happened when you popped out babies while you were still one yourself. Were you ever ready to be a parent, though? And once you'd discovered that elation and terror, were you ever ready to stop? You didn't just walk away from parenthood because your son was dead—or because he wanted to be.

"Your plant knowledge is so like your dad's," Hannah said.

"I'm nothing like him."

"Your mother, then?"

"No."

She shrugged, and he looked at the ground. There she was again, making things easy. He called and she came; she asked questions but didn't push for answers. Hannah pointed to an area that looked as if a giant had taken a bite out of the land.

"This was the site of an old grist mill," she said. "That's the headrace, and on the other side is where the wheel would have been. The dam was destroyed in the yellow fever epidemic."

"To kill off mosquitoes?"

"Exactly. There are so many memories on this piece of land, piled up top of one another. So many lives." She exhaled. "So many deaths."

Will followed her gaze and could have sworn he glimpsed someone watching them from down near the headrace. He nearly called out, *Dad!* But no one was there. The forest grew still.

"This is a beautiful spot." Suddenly chilled, he rubbed his arms. "Peaceful, but the air feels heavy."

"You feel it, too, the sadness?" Her voice rose.

"I wouldn't go that far."

"Do you believe in ghosts?" she said.

"Not really." He was not going to talk about the dead, the spirit world, any of it....

"I do." She smiled. "My mother taught me to believe in them."

"Yeah, well, lucky you. Mine taught me to believe in human monsters." He glanced back at the headrace. Again, the feeling of being watched. "Your mother liked a good ghost story?"

"She was psychic."

"No shit."

"Your mother liked a good horror story?"

"She was insane."

"No shit," Hannah said.

Will laughed and was surprised how good it felt, as good as mountain air on naked limbs. But then he saw Freddie curled up beside him during a June thunderstorm. Remembered the smell of his shampoo, the heat his little body generated in sleep, the softness of his Buzz Lightyear pj's.

The laughter died in Will's throat. His breath burned; his heart was on fire. He wanted to sink into the leaves, let the forest devour him, but no. He did what he always did: he kept functioning, kept moving, his legs and his brain on autopilot.

Leaves snapped and crackled to their left, and Will jumped. Hannah seemed not to notice.

"What happened to your dad?"

Hannah stared. "Why do you ask?"

"We've covered my trust issues, the scenery, my dad and our dead mothers. I've heard a couple of things about your father from Galen. I guess I'm curious to know more." And it had been months since he'd taken an interest in anything or anyone.

"So that's what you guys talk about in your nightly therapy sessions."

"What happens at the cottage after midnight," he said, "stays at the cottage."

Hannah watched him. "Okay, then, I'll tell you about my father." She unclipped her hair, brushed it with her fingers and reclipped it. "They were close, Galen and Dad. And so alike. Both quiet, easy to be with, sensitive. Eager to hide from the world."

"It's an unusual diagnosis—death by broken heart. Is it true?"

"In a sense, yes. My mother's death broke him." Hannah paused. "My father killed himself. Here, in the forest."

*Jesus.* Will's spine tingled. Through the trees, the cottage was hidden, but if he went straight, he could make a run for it.

"Few people know. Poppy, my brothers…and now you." Hannah spoke as if she were placing a takeout order for pizza: *Thin crust, extra cheese. Ready in fifteen minutes? Yes, that's fine. Thank you.*

"Why me?" His voice squeaked. Didn't he have enough secrets of his own?

"Galen's already curious about the genetics of depression. I was trying to figure out how to tell him when you and your dad showed up. My mother taught me that everything happens for a reason. And here we are—you and I, standing on the spot where my father died.

"I didn't want my sons growing up under the specter of damaged DNA, but I always planned to tell them after Liam turned twenty-one. The past month just sped everything up. There's quite a story to tell, though—my grandfather had holes drilled into his skull, and my father struggled against bouts of depression his whole life. He hid them, of course, as his generation did, but I often saw him huddled in the garage in the evening, crying. After my mother died, he fell apart. I thought if I brought him here and smothered him with love, everything would be fine. But love isn't always enough. You can love someone, but that doesn't mean you can keep him safe."

*Amen.* You could plant yourself in every corner of your kid's life, research the heck out of every piece of kid equipment on Consumer Reports before you bought it, and still not make a difference.

"As a doctor, he knew how to kill himself," Hannah continued. "He took pills."

"And I thought I had family baggage."

"It's good to know there's someone worse off, isn't it? But please don't feel sorry for me. I'm not someone who peddles regret. I'm someone who believes the present exists because of the past. It's a symbiotic relationship."

He loved the word *symbiotic,* loved the way it sounded in his head.

"Do I wish my father were still alive? Of course I do. I miss both my parents every day. I talk to them all the time." Hannah smiled her easy smile.

If he could talk to Freddie, what would he say? *I'm sorry, I love you, I miss you?* Or would there be no words—just one last hug?

"My father didn't commit suicide to hurt me," Hannah continued. "He killed himself because it was the only path he could take. I like to believe he found the peace in death that he couldn't find in life. But I also need to believe a part of him stayed behind—" she stared at the headrace again "—as my guardian angel. As Galen's savior. I'm not a kook, but I like to believe my father's spirit lives on. I know that's selfish, and I know my mother would say I'm holding him here on earth, preventing his soul from moving into the light, but I do feel him sometimes. In the forest."

No one knew what happened once a family retreated inside a house, pulled the curtains and locked the front door, and life rarely made sense. But standing among the hardwood trees, surrounded by squirrels that were noisier than a bunch of preschoolers in Central Park, Will understood. Despite the talk of angels and light and crap he didn't believe, he understood this woman who, like him, had lied to protect her broken family. Maybe he wasn't the only person who needed to bury the truth in a story.

Had he known Hannah before, things might be different. She might be a confidante, someone who wouldn't abuse his secrets. But in the trajectory of secret keeping, he'd passed the point of no return. For the first time, he hadn't shared with Ally or consulted with his overpaid, pit bull publicist. No, this was his mess and his alone.

"I'm not sure what to say," he said.

"You don't have to say anything. But I do want to ask a question." She sucked on her lips. "How do you think he's going to react?"

"Hannah, he's your son. You know him better than I do."

"I'm not sure I do these days."

*Please don't lay this on me.*

Her phone rang and she turned her back on him, shutting him out. *Thank God.*

Will followed the path onto a rickety old bridge over the dry creek bed and jiggled the railing, testing it. A fall from this height could bust an ankle, and then he and his dad would be even more dependent on Hannah. The last thing she needed.

On the other side of the creek, the ground rose sharply. Would they make it up to the ridge? He wanted to experience the view she'd mentioned; he wanted to be up high looking down on the world.

"That was Galen. I asked him to let us know if your dad showed up at the house. He hasn't." Hannah joined him on the bridge, and they walked across side by side.

Will glimpsed an abandoned squirrel's dray hanging from a huge white oak. It looked like Spanish moss attacked with a flamethrower.

"Have you read any of Galen's poems?" she said.

"I've offered, but he seems reluctant to share."

"He has a gift. First published at eight, and in high school he won a national competition that's been going since the twenties. Sylvia Plath was a previous winner. How's that for irony?"

"The Scholastic Art and Writing Awards? Did he win a senior writing portfolio?"

"Yes. How did you know?"

"Past recipient. Why are you smiling?" His dad was really, really right about that smile.

"I finally get why you and Galen are friends. You're so similar," Hannah said. "Both self-contained, both writers, both kindhearted."

"I'm not sure anyone's described me as kindhearted before."

"You dropped everything for your dad. That says something."

"It's not like I had a choice," he said.

"Actually, you did. Poppy tells me you were the one who pulled him out of Hawk's Ridge. If you'd agreed to play by the director's rules, Jacob could have stayed."

"Yeah. I guess the ultimate screw-up was mine. Thanks to me, Dad's close to being homeless."

"Maybe we should consider Poppy's plan," she said.

"No. It's not fair on anyone. Least of all, you."

"See? You do have a big heart."

Could she not cool it with the compliments? A hawk screeched overhead, its usually assertive cry weak, scared, desperate. Lonely.

"What if we struck a deal?" Hannah said.

Deals were to be avoided. There was always a catch.

"You come straight to me if Galen tells you anything that you feel I should know, and I'll do the same for you with your dad."

"You want me to break a confidence?" he said.

She began twisting her silver ring around and around her index finger.

Realization came slowly, but then he normally bailed before the conversation got this intense. And she was recruiting him for the front lines. Or was it more of a press gang maneuver? "You mean that I should come to you if I think it's a matter of life or death."

She took a deep breath. "Yes."

"Jesus, Hannah. I'm way out of my depth here."

"So am I."

He rubbed sweat from the back of his neck. There wasn't a wisp of a breeze in the forest. If he were alone, he would strip off his T-shirt. Although, the thought of being half-naked and near Hannah was enough to make him reconsider.

"I haven't thanked you," she said, "for not judging Galen."

"I haven't thanked you for not judging my dad." *Or me.* People were always making assumptions, thinking they knew him. But no one did, except for Ally.

Maybe Hannah was right. Maybe things did happen for

a reason. An experienced climber knew when to shake out and conserve strength. When to rest so he could make it to the top and back down. Maybe being at the cottage was like reaching a solid hold on a difficult route and pausing to rest. Maybe he needed to be here while he gained strength to move forward with his life. A life without Freddie.

"We need to find the old wagon trails," he said. "My dad will be following them."

"You do know that your dad would be miserable in New York."

"Of course I do. But I might not have a choice. If I can't find a local facility, he'll have to come north with me. And maybe that would be better. At least I could see him regularly. I can't just abandon him when he's the only family I have left."

"Aren't you forgetting your son?"

"Freddie's with me always. I didn't mean that."

But she didn't look as if she was buying it.

"How do you know about the trails?" Once again, she was letting him off the hook.

"Not hard to figure out. Lots of people were trying to scratch out a living around here, and they settled near the fords so they could stay connected—establish communication and trade routes. Every group had its own road—wagoners, people with pack horses. There were even black roads."

"Black roads?"

"African-Americans had their own roads just as Native Americans did."

"I don't understand." She shook her head slowly. More curls bounced free of the barrette. God, she was adorable.

"What don't you understand?"

"You belong here just as much as your dad, but you walked away to live in New York."

"I didn't walk, I ran. *Shhh*." Will held up his hand. "Did you hear that? Dad? Dad, is that you? It's me, Willie!"

"Willie?" she whispered, but her voice had turned playful.

"Family nickname." Just another squirrel, not the old man. "Didn't you have one?"

"No. My family was excruciatingly serious about everything. There were no shortcuts, even with names. I guess that's why I was so wild as a teenager."

Hannah, a wild teenager? How improbable. Although she did have her own quiet way of approaching life, much as he did, and he'd certainly had a few wild years—smoking at twelve, drinking at fourteen, sneaking around with Ally. By junior high, though, nothing mattered beyond safeguarding his ticket out of Orange County: his GPA.

"Did your parents ever call you William?"

"No."

"It's such a beautiful name. Can I call you William?"

He whirred around, pushing aside the memory of Cass's voice: *I shall always call you William*. "No."

"Another off-limits?"

"Yeah." Was she keeping a running tally?

"Wait." Hannah grabbed his arm and he felt it again, an exchange of energy passing between them. Although this time it was definitely lust, since it landed squarely in his groin.

His dad materialized about twenty yards ahead of them, like a deer appearing by the edge of the forest on a foggy morning. And he was smiling. *Smiling?* Will ground his teeth together.

"What you two young'uns doin' up here?" Jacob said.

Will wanted to speak, but his jaw refused to unclamp. Hannah, however, didn't miss a beat.

"I came to invite you and Will for lunch," she said. "I made pumpkin soup for my son last night and have enough to feed half the county. I was hoping you guys would help eat it."

The old man held up a Ziploc bag with a limp sandwich inside. *Un-friggin'-believable.* He'd packed lunch?

"Brought along some PBJ, but I reckon homemade soup sounds a whole lot better." His dad grinned.

Will rolled his head back to look up at the crows. How much longer could he play nanny to a grown man while his life collapsed around him?

"Why don't we all go back to the house and have a little feast." Hannah moved toward his dad, and they linked arms. "I've been out since six this morning, and I'm starving. Did you find anything of interest up here?"

Will wasn't sure what to say or do, since he'd clearly become irrelevant to the conversation. He kicked a dead branch across the forest floor as if it were a soccer ball. Okay, so that was just childish.

"Found me a coyote den."

"Yes, we avoid that," Hannah said. "The coyote bit Daisy's bottom last time she sniffed around there."

"It were probably the male coyote, bein' all protective. Found a small cemetery, too. And my mind's been seein' all manner of ghostly figures in them trees."

Great. Hannah and his dad were going to exchange ghost stories now. It was a mystery that people didn't find real life frightening enough.

"Did I ever tell you I were a grave digger, Hey You?"

"You certainly did, Jacob. Do you have any stories to share?"

And the moment turned almost as quickly as if Will had snapped his fingers.

His dad glanced at him, his forehead furrowed. "You young'uns been out on the mountain again? How's your mama, Ally?"

"This isn't Ally, Dad." Too late he blushed and realized

Hannah was staring. He wanted to explain, to shout, *No, it's not what you think.* Why? Why should he care?

"Best thing you two did, Willie, bring me back to the woods. Had me a fine ol' time."

"Dad, you can't wander off by yourself and get lost. We were worried."

"Lost? I ain't lost. I reckon you're the one who's lost, son. You been livin' in the city too long if you think your daddy could get hisself lost in the forest. Me, lost in the forest," Jacob mumbled. "I was fixin' to come home before sundown."

"I get lost up here all the time," Hannah said.

This whole conversation was about as fun as squatting in a tick nest. Will needed a drink—a good stiff one. He might have to dip into his dad's Wild Turkey, set some bad examples for his aging father. Maybe just a single, anesthetizing down-in-one shot. Except he could hardly turn up at the afternoon's retirement home appointment stinking of liquor.

"Since you don't have a cell phone," Hannah continued, "Will might have to get you a small electronic bracelet to wear. So we know where you are when lunch is ready."

"You buying this, too, Angel? About me being lost?"

"No. But you want the freedom to wander the forest by yourself, right?"

"I sure do, Angel."

"Well, this will allow you to do that without Will calling out the National Guard when he can't find you. Right, Will?"

Ever the peacemaker, ever the force of calm and reason.

"Yeah, right." Then Will fell silent and concentrated on finding his own calm, his own quiet place between anger and desire.

# TWENTY-TWO

Galen watched from his bathroom window. Mom and Jacob were arm in arm, smiling, and Will trailed behind, head bowed, hands in his pockets. Will had looked a lot happier when they'd entered the forest, and he'd been checking out Mom's ass.

Shouldn't he feel indignation that Will had been eyeing up Mom? Relief that a guy was interested? Sadness that she was oblivious? Emotions were reverberations from a life Galen no longer remembered. Nothing touched him; nothing spoke to him; nothing enabled him to interpret experience. Poetry was the medium through which he translated the world. Without it, he was blind, deaf and dumb. Zombie Galen.

The other night, Will had described returning to North Carolina as being trapped in a crack between the present and the past. It was an idea worth exploring in a poem. Or it would have been. How odd—to consider stealing from a commercial writer.

The handful of pills disintegrated silently in the bottom of the toilet bowl. Bubbles the size of pinpricks rose to the top of the water level. The pills blanched his life. They made him numb, lethargic, and he wanted to feel in Technicolor. Even desire had deserted him. His libido? Gone. Erections? Gone. The psychiatrist had warned about sexual side effects but hadn't given options. *Take this pill, it'll make you impotent but you'll be too apathetic to care.*

Everyone insisted he take the pills as if they were some miracle cure. But he was ingesting chemicals. Being an alcoholic was different. Alcohol offered a window to oblivion, not a lobotomy. He had never been a pill taker—not one Motrin for a headache—but for over a month he'd been pumping his body full of toxins.

Nausea came and went. Even though he was standing still, it was as if he were spinning. He grabbed the shower curtain and steadied himself through another wave of dizziness. Tapering off the medication would, no doubt, be wise. Just stopping was, no doubt, a mistake. But the sooner he flushed the poison from his system, the better. He'd quit alcohol cold turkey. How much worse could this be? Short-term hell, long-term gain.

He picked up the pill bottle, dropped in some aspirin, screwed the top back on. An empty pill bottle would only alarm his mother. Not that she would monitor him. Mom had always given him privacy. In high school he could have dumped his used condoms on top of the kitchen trash and she would have said nothing. Still, he'd buried them at the bottom.

Down in the yard, Poppy appeared and shouted, "Everything okay?" Unlike Mom, Poppy had noticed their good-looking writer-in-residence. It was easy to see why Poppy had the hots for Will. If he were gay, *he'd* have the hots for Will.

Women had probably always fallen for Will. Every woman except the one he loved, poor bastard. *And Mom.* They would make a handsome couple, Will and his mother. She looked good for her age. Everyone said so. And he'd seen guys other than Will give her the once-over. He'd never understood her refusal to date. Was she protecting herself or her sons? Back in high school, he and Liam had tried to set her up with their English teacher, a sweet divorced guy with two kids. She'd refused.

Mom was hard to read. Like the two-headed Roman god, Janus, she had a second face that she rarely showed even to her family. Where did this insecurity come from, this need to make other people happy, to fix them? And what did she do for herself, other than go to the occasional sweat ceremony? On her last birthday, he'd given her a gift certificate for a massage. She'd regifted it to one of her clients with back problems. "He needed it more" had been her explanation.

When Galen was sixteen, he wrote a poem about her called, "Inside I Weep." Mom had assumed it was his reaction to the divorce, and Galen hadn't disillusioned her. So many times he'd heard her crying when she thought she was alone—crying either for her marriage or for his grandparents. Both of them gone within six months of each other. He didn't really understand how Papa had died. *Grief killed him,* Mom always said. But when they were studying DNA in eighth grade, his bio teacher said it was romantic myth that people died of broken hearts.

Galen flushed the toilet, and the detritus of pills was sucked into a whirlpool, into the septic system. Into the water table.

He opened the door and ambled downstairs to see what was going on. A smile tugged at his lips. It felt good.

"Galen?" Mom frowned up at him. "Are you okay?"

"Wonderful," he replied. He flexed his fingers and stared at the fine black hairs and the bloodied, chewed skin around his nails. "Wonderful, just wonderful."

"That's great, sweetheart."

It was that easy? All he had to do was lie? She was so trusting. He flipped his right hand over and grabbed his wrist, his thumb finding his pulse. And yet, everything was wonderful, because finally, he knew what to do with his life.

Galen's smile was a little disconcerting. Yes, of course she wanted to see him happy again, but this smile was beatific. While she was out rounding up a stray senior, had her depressed son found God? Hannah glanced at Will, but he was in the living room, examining the framed photograph of her blowing out candles on her twenty-first birthday.

"Great picture of Mom, isn't it?" Galen said to Will.

"Yeah." Will turned with the photo in his hand.

"I had youth on my side," Hannah said.

A false memory flashed. She was meeting Will when she was his age, before the lines, before the stomach sag. Before. Hannah unclipped her hair and ruffled it forward to hide the blush. Normally Poppy would have noticed, commented— teased—but she was too busy ogling Will.

"You haven't changed at all." Will replaced the photo.

It was a generous comment and a lie. No one could compare that picture favorably with the face that greeted her every morning in the bathroom mirror. Will lied well, almost as well as she had done for the past twelve years. But no more; no more. Everything had changed in that one, brief decision to trust Will, and the relief was as comforting as one of her father's hugs.

Life was about choices. Her father had chosen to die; she had chosen to keep the circumstances of his death secret. Now she had chosen to tell Will. Choices allowed you to control the present but they also set the future in motion—for good or for bad. And now the time had come for another choice.

The short-term repercussions would likely be recriminations, but Galen needed the knowledge that she had withheld. She wasn't looking for snake oil and miracles, but maybe the truth about his grandfather could help Galen feel less alienated on his journey to recovery.

Clearly, he was looking for answers and had already considered—at least once—seeking them in alcohol. They hadn't talked about the incident with the wine, because she'd been too afraid. Of all the thoughts that had raced through her mind when she'd seen Will with that bottle, the most terrifying was the realization that her son was still so close to the edge. But right now, he didn't look like a person who was floundering. He was smiling, really smiling. Looking strong enough to handle the news.

Closing her eyes briefly, Hannah sorted her thoughts. She could wait until the house was empty, until she and Galen were alone, but she'd chickened out before. And Galen might need someone to turn to. He might need Will.

"Galen," she said, "can I talk to you in private, in the den?"

Will looked at her, eyebrows raised. Barely moving her head, she gave a nod, and he responded with a small smile. Offered understanding without language.

"Poppy," Hannah said, trying to sound cheerful. "There's pumpkin soup in the fridge and a fresh baguette in the bread bin. Can I leave you in charge?"

"Sure thing, girl. Come on, boys, time to eat."

Galen followed her into the den and flopped into his dad's ancient armchair, the one Inigo had left behind with his family.

Her son draped one long leg over the arm and waited for her to close the pocket door.

"You seem to be feeling better," she said.

"Yeah, how about that."

"I guess the pills are finally working."

He shifted. "I guess."

A thought floated through her mind but didn't take root: *Is he lying?*

"I need to tell you something," she said.

Galen rested his head on the chair back. His black hair fanned out and for a moment she was distracted by his casual good looks, so like his father's—despite the now-hollowed-out cheeks. "I'm listening."

"Your grandfather—"

Galen rolled his head to one side. "Suffered from depression, right?"

"You knew?"

"I started wondering if there was a genetic component." He stared up at the ceiling. "And Dad's family may be mean for treating him like a deviant and us like lepers, but they're not mentally ill."

"Depression isn't—"

"Mental illness? Yes, Mom. At the level I have, it is."

He was right, of course, but hearing him bite down on the words *mental illness* slapped her across the face. All those years she had kept him safe, and yet she had failed to protect him from the greatest threat of all: himself.

"I've been remembering things," Galen said. "Things I didn't understand when I was ten."

"But now you do."

If he were a client, she could answer his questions with nothing but fact. Her mother, who'd spent most of her life shutting out other people's emotions, had taught Hannah the skill of detachment. Except she didn't feel very detached right now. She wove her fingers together and waited for the first question.

"Was it bad?" Galen said. "Did they lock him up? Shock him? Drill holes into his skull?"

"No, that was your great-grandfather."

Galen sat up. "Fuck."

She swallowed her reprimand. If he was being loose with words, he was being punished enough. "What do you remember about the day your grandfather died?"

"I remember Dad telling us but in a backward way. He said you wouldn't be having dinner with us, then he said we were getting pizza, then he tacked on that Papa had died."

"Your father doesn't like emotional mess."

"Unless it's his."

Hannah didn't respond. She'd never dissed Inigo in front of the boys; she wouldn't start now. In the months after he left, she used to shut herself inside her closet and scream into her sweaters so the boys wouldn't hear, but within a year she'd forgiven him. She always forgave. It was stitched into her psyche. Could she blame that on serotonin levels, too?

"You were the last person Papa spoke to," she said.

"I know. He told me he was going for a walk and that I couldn't come. I was angry and wouldn't let him kiss me. For months I thought I was the one who broke his heart."

God, she needed a cigarette, even though she hadn't smoked since Inigo's wannabe punk rocker phase. "I'm sorry. I tried hard to convince you that wasn't true."

"I know you did, Mom. And I understood that he'd wandered off like a wounded animal, that he chose not to die in front of me and Liam, but—"

"You didn't buy it," Hannah said.

He chewed the skin around his fingernails, gnawing on himself. A habit from childhood, it was astonishing that he hadn't permanently disfigured his fingers. Galen stood. "If

I promise not to be mad, will you tell me what you're keeping inside?"

Hannah smiled. He was quoting her standard phrase from when the boys were little.

Galen wrapped his arms around her. Hugging him used to feel solid and secure, but now he was little more than skin sagging over bones. Sorting out his eating habits needed to move up her list of priorities.

"I won't make you promise," she said. "Because you have every right to be angry."

Galen's arms slid from her, and she counted to ten silently. *Count to ten and it'll all be over,* her dad used to say before he dug out a splinter or ripped off a Band-Aid. So much could happen in ten seconds: your husband could tell you he was leaving; your father could say goodbye without you realizing that this one was forever; your son could decide not to forgive you.

"Your grandfather killed himself."

Galen stared at her. "How?"

"Effexor mixed with sleeping pills. He'd been stockpiling his medications."

"I always said prescription drugs were bad for your health." Galen sounded calm, but like her, he did anger quietly, with introspection. And then, he did exactly what she would have done: he left.

On the other side of the hall, Poppy laughed and a chair dragged across the kitchen floor. For a brief moment, Hannah was the little girl who got lost at JFK Airport while her family was on its way to Europe. Travelers had rushed past, ignoring the silent child in the red patent shoes. It was the first time she had understood that family couldn't protect you, that each family member was a separate entity. She had looked up into a world of chaos and realized she was alone. It was the first time she had understood fear.

Will hovered in the hallway, curiosity too strong to ignore. How did it feel to let go of pretense and surround yourself with truth? There was no sound coming from the den. No raised voices, no smashing of furniture, no kicking of the walls. Nothing but eerie quiet.

The door opened and Galen pushed past.

"You okay?"

Galen ignored him, flung open the front door and ran.

*No.* Will took off in pursuit. He was not heading back into the forest on another search and rescue mission for someone else with messed-up brain chemistry.

"Dude!" Will caught up effortlessly. "Slow down!"

Galen reached a huge red oak by the edge of the forest and fell against it. He made a gagging noise and spat onto the ground. *Nice.*

"Any time you want to join me on a run, you're welcome," Will said.

Galen looked at him as if he were a cockroach.

"You don't run?"

"No," Galen said.

"You should try it. Running's good for your emotional well-being. Helps boost your serotonin. Didn't any of your doctors tell you that?"

"You mean it's a natural drug for crazies like me?"

"Pretty much."

Galen gave a feeble laugh. "My mother's been keeping se-crets."

"Yeah, mothers tend to do that," Will said. "Fathers, too."

Will glanced into the forest. He was not going back in there willingly, and yet staying out here wasn't much safer.

He didn't want to care about Galen; he didn't want to care about Hannah. And yet he'd made that deal. This was why he hated deals—they slowed you down, kept you from powering on through the difficult crap. "Want to talk about it?"

"My grandfather killed himself. Swallowed a bottle of pills."

Will gave a supportive *huh*. At least he hoped it was supportive and didn't suggest that he already knew the family secret. Even though he did.

"Why did she lie to me?"

"You were a kid when he died, right?"

Galen coughed and pounded his chest. "Yeah. I was ten."

"Then she did you a favor. Consider yourself lucky. My mom was psycho but never diagnosed, and the only thing I gained from growing up with that knowledge was fear. Complete, utter terror of what she would do next. Ignorance would have been a blessing—you can trust me on that one. And I doubt the stigma of suicide is something a kid should have to shoulder. Bad enough when you get teased because your mother behaves like an extra from *One Flew Over the Cuckoo's Nest*."

"That rough?"

"One time she turned up at my middle school and tried to yank me out of class for a demon hunt. By high school, her antics were standard locker gossip. She was certifiable."

Galen grappled with the tree trunk as he hacked through a cough.

"Dude, you're seriously out of shape. We have to start you exercising," Will said.

"We?"

Will stared at Galen's natural-colored Toms—canvas shoes for the socially responsible. He owned three or four pairs in various colors himself, but Galen's were butt ugly. Screamed,

*I am a grad student with suicidal tendencies.* Very homespun, very vegan. Hard not to notice that Galen had the weirdest eating habits. Organic was one thing, but Galen took it to extremes. Even eating overwhelmed this guy.

"D'you own anything other than those burlap Toms?" Will said.

"I have a pair of old hiking boots around here somewhere. I used to hike a fair bit."

"Ever climb?"

Galen looked confused.

"Rock climbing."

Galen shook his head. "You?"

"Not as much as I'd like to."

"Figures, seems like a legit sport for a badass."

"Thanks," Will said.

"Neither of my parents would have interpreted that as a compliment."

"Different generation." He totally didn't mean to say that. Galen's dad might be an old fart—for all Will knew—but Hannah felt like a slightly more responsible contemporary.

"How long have you been climbing?"

"Most of my life. Started with scramblings and bouldering on Occoneechee Mountain. Nothing extreme. I didn't go on my first roped climb until I was fifteen. My parents couldn't afford lessons, but climbing's a family talent. Most of my dad's relatives climbed, so I learned from watching them and reading how-to books."

"You taught yourself to climb by reading books?"

"What better way is there to teach yourself anything?" Will said. "Except for overcoming my fear of heights. I did that with a self-hypnosis tape from the thrift store. I was a self-sufficient kid. Wanted to know something, taught myself."

"Why would you climb if you don't like heights?"

"It's not about heights. When the slightest shift in the position of one finger can make a difference, it's about skill—balance, agility and precision."

"You're an adrenaline junkie?"

"Total opposite." Will flicked back his hair. "Climbing takes me to some stripped-down spiritual place. Stress, worry—both disappear. When I'm climbing, my mind empties of everything but the purity of the moment. The world shrinks to what's directly in front of me. I find this laser focus I don't possess even when I write. Nothing matters beyond my movements on the rock. Nothing exists beyond what I can reach. I concentrate on my breath and the placement of my feet. It's almost like choreography. I guess you could say climbing's a controlled dance."

"So it's a control thing?"

Will liked this guy. Saw straight through his bull. "Yeah."

"What if you fall?"

When he went soloing in the Gunks, Will hadn't permitted that thought to enter his mind. He'd been focused on one thing only—himself. He would never have considered doing that climb unroped while Freddie was alive, and he would never consider it now. Once again, his actions had consequences for other people. But was he thinking about the effect they could have on his dad...or on Hannah?

"Falling's a given—if you're roped," Will said. "You can fall multiple times before figuring out the entire sequence, especially if you're pushing the limit of your ability. But if you do it right, you fall safely. You check out the hazards ahead of time, you follow the path of least resistance, you trust nothing but your partner. You double-check every piece of gear, the placement of every piece of hardware, and you use only bombproof anchors. Even your backups have backups. You prepare, prepare, prepare, and leave nothing to chance.

In fact, I was thinking about doing a climb this weekend." Actually, he hadn't been, but his rack was still in his trunk from the trip to the Gunks. It might be good to take a day to check his rope, his harness, his hardware, clean off his shoes. "Want to join me?"

"You're asking a depressive who may or may not be suicidal if he wants to participate in a deadly sport?"

"It's only deadly if you screw up."

"You trust me enough to believe I won't?"

"I'd take you to a small crag, do a controlled climb, set up a top rope. First sign you're not following protocols or listening to me, I'd call it off. I won't climb with a madman."

"That's reassuring. I guess."

"And you'd have to make nice with your mom, see if she and Poppy could dad-sit for me."

"I don't feel like talking to Mom right now. Would you do it?"

"Galen, don't ask me to play piggy-in-the-middle. I have enough of my own problems."

"Sorry, that wasn't fair."

"Listen. If you deal with your mom, I'll take care of the equipment and find someone to belay for us. I'll even buy you a brain bucket."

"Brain bucket?"

"Helmet," Will said. "Come on, man. Didn't you ever want to leave the world behind and experience nature from a perspective intended for birds?"

"What does it feel like? To be up high, above everything?"

"Like speaking to God."

Galen straightened up. He looked older, more confident, more like a cocky young grad student who could pour contempt on genre fiction writers. A pair of hawks cried back and forth on Saponi Mountain, and Will shivered. Far as he knew, there were only two reasons for speaking with God: to make a confession, or to find peace. Hopefully Galen wasn't thinking about everlasting peace.

"You're not contemplating hurling yourself off a rock, are you? Because no way am I taking you if you're going to risk both our lives."

"I find nothing appealing about dying with an audience. If I were going to kill myself, I'd do it behind a locked bathroom door. Lie in a warm bath with a glass of vodka and a sharp razor, then open my veins."

So, Galen had strategized his own death scenario. That couldn't be a good thing.

"How would you do it?" Galen said. "Jump off a mountain?"

Now they were comparing suicide techniques? Yes, if Will were going to kill himself, he'd totally want to die doing something he loved. But only if he could do it with no one else around. "No. I couldn't screw with climbers who might be watching. You don't mess with people's spirituality."

"Like my mom and sweat lodges?"

Will inspected his fingernails and tried to ignore images of Hannah surrounded by steam, her naked body glistening. "Your mom goes to sweat ceremonies?"

"Yeah. She didn't tell you?"

Will shook his head.

"Careful or she'll invite you along."

And a ripple in his mind, less than an afterthought, said, *I wish*.

# TWENTY-THREE

Thrashing through a tangle of nightmares and erotic fantasies had left Hannah's mind raw and her eyes rheumy.

She paused by the hall mirror, squinting at the latticework of crow's-feet under her left eye and the gray hairs that had begun infesting her scalp. She flattened her palms across her cheeks and lifted, raising her skin upward by ten years. It made no difference. This tired, aging woman was not someone Will Shepard would find attractive.

And yet he had invaded her sleep unremittingly. She hadn't recognized him until he'd turned to appraise her with those eyes—cold, distant, familiar. Eyes she remembered but could not recognize. Then he was behind her, his hands sliding up her ribs to tease her breasts, his voice on her neck, whispering, "Make love to me."

Such dreams didn't belong juxtaposed against those of Galen stumbling through a black forest, Galen being chased by a pack of baying hell hounds, Galen sinking to the bottom of an icy lake.

At one point in the night, camisole and boxers soaked

through from sweat, she'd roamed the house, turning on lights, trying to ground herself in the mundane. Even awake, fear had pelted her.

Then she woke at 3:00 a.m., the hour of hauntings, with her heart pounding like a jackhammer. Pure evil had sauntered out of her subconscious to hover in her bedroom doorway, watching, waiting, barring her escape. For a moment, she had thought Galen was screaming—a distorted scream like a manufactured Hollywood sound shot through a wind tunnel. But when she'd tiptoed upstairs to check on him, he was lost in peaceful slumber.

Why was her mind torturing her now, when Galen was beginning to heal? Even though he had been unwilling to engage in a conversation about his grandfather, Galen had repeated, several times, that he felt wonderful, the surprise on his face suggesting he believed his words to be true.

Hannah walked out into the afternoon heat. On the porch, her pumpkin had begun to rot. She'd carved it too early, hoping Galen might find his festive spirit and join in. He hadn't. And now the pumpkin was turning black and collapsing in on itself. Its shrunken, toothless mouth sneered.

The October sun burned the back of her neck, hitting the spot Will had kissed in her dreams. Crispy leaves sprinkled to the dead grass where he was sitting, cross-legged, watching a box turtle lumber toward the shade of her redbud tree. He was surrounded by what appeared to be climbing gear: a thick, coiled rope, an assortment of metal clips and pulleys and something that had to be a harness but looked more like a huge, nylon diaper. Safety equipment, in other words, for a life-threatening activity.

Hannah approached him and stopped, arms folded. "You are not, I repeat *not,* taking my son rock climbing."

Will tilted his face to glance up at her, then glanced down at his lap. If he smiled, her resolve would unravel.

*Hold on to your anger, Hannah. He's just a guy with a sexy smile. One who's letting his youth show.*

"October is the high season for adult deer ticks," she said, hating the condescension in her voice. "You'll need to do a tick check when you're done sitting on the grass."

"Yes, ma'am."

Did he have to call her *ma'am?* "I won't give my permission."

"He's of age. You can't stop him."

"Want to see me try?"

Will picked up a pair of nylon shoes, inspected the soles and bashed them together. "Are we having our first fight?"

"Unlikely. I don't fight."

He frowned. "Neither do I."

"No? Then why are you pushing me on this?"

"I'm not. I asked Galen to come climbing—he accepted."

In the distance, a car honked repeatedly. Tires squealed and someone else honked. Road rage had finally moved into Orange County, which was hardly surprising. The heat and drought had been chipping away at tempers for months.

"But it's a dangerous sport, and he's in clinical depression and he's—"

"Suicidal?" Will said quietly.

Why did people keep throwing that word around, tattooing it across her son's chest? He'd made a mistake, one mistake, but it belonged in the past. Never to be repeated. He was doing better, and the world needed to forget.

"Are you worried he's going to be careless with his life or mine?" Will said.

"Does it matter?"

He stood, moved closer and brushed something from her arm. She went rigid.

"That was a tick," he said. "You can thank me later."

"Oh."

"Look, I'm not irresponsible, Hannah. And climbing isn't a sport for crazies. The moment Galen starts screwing around, we're done. Experienced climbers take new climbers out all the time. We consider it our responsibility—to teach good stewardship of the sport."

"Do you trust him enough to do this?" She would not cave, she would not.

"Do you trust *me* enough?"

"Yes. But that's not the issue. Give me more, more reason."

"You seem to believe that I can help your son."

She nodded.

"Then let me try this. Conquering the physical and mental challenge of climbing releases a flood of endorphins. It's empowering. What if it leads him back to his poetry?" Will put his hands on his shoulders, rolled his neck and stared up into the cloudless sky. "Look, I know you're scared. I would be, too, in your position, but this I'm good at. I won't fail him. Or you. I promise."

Not a traumatic decision, after all. In the end, it was as simple as trusting a man who promised not to betray you.

"Okay," she said. "I'm putting my son's life in your hands. Please don't make me regret this."

"No pressure, then," Will said.

"Not if you're as good as you think you are."

"I've found this guy who can belay for us—help us with the climb—on Thursday. I'll have to leave you in charge of my dad, though. I doubt we'll be back before late evening."

"Strange way to spend All Hallows' Eve—home alone worrying about the two of you."

"Halloween's a totally pointless holiday," Will said. "I prefer to forget it exists."

"Trick-or-treating with Freddie in the Big Apple must be quite something."

Will went back to sorting out his equipment. This reticence about his son made no sense, no sense at all. How could the father of a young boy not get swept up in the fun of Halloween? Although not talking about Freddie could just be Will's way of finding peace in unbearable absence. When the boys were Freddie's age, she grew restless if either of them was away from her for longer than an hour. However, when Liam was four and flooded the inside of her truck with the garden hose, she had fantasized about packing him off to kindergarten boarding school. Poor Will, he must miss his own baby so much.

"And how are *you* doing?" she said.

He glanced up through his hair. "Excuse me?"

"Caregiving's exhausting. Are you taking time to look after yourself?"

"I will—once I get out of here."

When he said things like that, it was easy to pretend that she didn't care, that she could never care. That he would return to New York, and his leaving would mean nothing.

# TWENTY-FOUR

William loaded the last bag of gear into the car. He should have been planning to take Freddie trick-or-treating, not preparing to spend Halloween climbing with a depressive who may or may not be suicidal. When they were divvying up the holidays, Cass had insisted on Easter, July Fourth and Thanksgiving. Will got Halloween. Christmas had still been up for grabs when she'd hurtled into a wall and obliterated the future.

He tried not to think about how much money he'd spent on Galen in the past two days. A great deal more than he'd spent on Freddie's last birthday. Buying top-of-the-line equipment had eased the anxiety over Galen's safety but had also been an ugly reminder of the non-revenue-generating status of corporation Will Shepard. If he never sold another manuscript, could he live off his backlist? He had at least thirty years of career ahead; at some point he had to return to work. And yet whenever he imagined himself locked away in his Manhattan office with only a screwed-up fictionalized friend for company, a hollowed-out feeling settled in his gut.

Where the hell was Galen?

Will checked the time and pushed away impatience. Negative emotions were not wanted on a climb, even if your partner was twenty minutes late. Galen did everything at half-speed, and Will had a thing about punctuality. He didn't need a psychologist to explain the reason. Spend your formative years in a house that spun with chaos, and anyone would draw comfort from the structure of a start time and an end time—the start time being flexible within five minutes max.

As the week had progressed, Galen had seemed if not excited about the climb, then at least energized, and that fact gnawed at Will. Misgivings? Yeah, he had a few. Was Galen feeling better, or was this a last hurrah? Either way, from the moment they parked the car, Will was not taking his eyes off his young friend.

The chickadees squabbled over the half-empty bird feeder, and Hannah smiled. Doubt about the climb had vanished, replaced by the certainty that Galen would be safe on Will's watch. Even though she'd have to look after Jacob, it was as if Will had given her a day off. Whenever Galen was in the house, anxiety sucked at her attention span. Chores were abandoned incomplete. Worst of all, she hovered. Galen didn't need her reminding him constantly to eat, to shower, to sit up straight, but like a parent with poor impulse control, she seemed unable to stop. Maybe he needed a break, too. He had certainly seemed content, or rather relieved, in the days since Will had proposed the climb.

*Right, chores.* After she fed Jacob and helped him trawl the web for pictures of places Freddie had visited, she would wash out the hummingbird feeders. Then she would store them for the winter, pack them away with the knowledge that next time she used them, this phase of her life would be over. Galen would, hopefully, be back in grad school, with a new girlfriend. She and Inigo might even be able to get to-gether and say, "Remember when…" And Will would be back in New York, probably dating some young babe. Would she ever see him again? Unlikely. But she and Poppy would visit Jacob wherever he ended up. They might even spring him for holidays.

Thank God Inigo wouldn't know about today until Galen was home. The ex would have lectured her on trusting strang-ers, even though their son had spent weeks in the care of people they'd known nothing of beyond name tags and job descriptions. Will, however, had the most important tag of all: parent.

And maybe, on this quiet Sunday, she might glimpse him again in that role. Such tales Jacob had of Will! Except, of course, for those that included Ally. Those Hannah preferred to not hear. But only the day before, Jacob had talked about the last time Freddie had visited. About how his grandson was such a happy boy—full of noise and energy and curios-ity. About how Will had such patience—the kind of daddy who never raised his voice.

The dogs followed her up the steps to the cottage. She knocked, then stuck her head inside. "Jacob? I'm coming in to make breakfast! A huge breakfast with eggs, pancakes, the works!"

The dogs clearly understood the word *breakfast*. As she opened the front door wide, they shot into the main room, tails wagging.

Delicious cooking smells wafted from the cottage every evening around six, but Will was, no doubt, a premade-meals guy. He probably had his own chef in New York, or dined nightly on expensive takeout. She would check the contents of the fridge and then run back to the house for supplies.

A half-full French press and a clean coffee mug sat on the

kitchen counter with a note that read, "Dad—zap your coffee cup in the microwave for one minute. NO LONGER." *No longer* was underlined twice. Will's handwriting was surprisingly ordinary, his letters medium-size and undistinguished. Nothing that demanded attention.

Hannah touched the side of the glass container. *Still warm.*

She tugged open the fridge door and scanned the shelves. Apart from the generic orange soda and a large bottle of ketchup, everything was stamped with the 365 Whole Foods insignia. She picked up a carton of eggs—cage-free—and set them down on the table, and then eased open the deli drawer. Some aged Gruyère and a wedge of Lincolnshire Poacher— her favorite cheddar but difficult to find and very expensive. No bacon—in fact, no cold cuts. Meat lovers' feast was definitely off the menu.

Curious, she eased open one produce bin, then the other. Everything was fresh and hand-chosen. No bags of salad, no ready-to-nuke veggies. Instead, there were two heads of lettuce, baby carrots, a hothouse cucumber, grape tomatoes, blueberries, strawberries and apricots. She picked out a fat onion and an even fatter green pepper. Omelets were a definite option. What else did Will have?

She shut the fridge and randomly opened cupboards and drawers. She found the griddle, the whisk and a packet of pancake mix, but nothing was where she expected it to be. How intriguing. A man who was passing through had taken the time to reorganize the kitchen.

According to Poppy, food at Hawk's Ridge was low-fat, salt-free, tasteless and served in minute portions. Hannah grinned, picturing a smorgasbord of breakfast delights. She was going to feed Jacob until he groaned, *No more.* First things first: find out what he wanted.

"Stay," she said to the dogs, pointing at the ground. Daisy and Rosie flopped to the floor; the other dogs followed.

She walked to the bottom of the stairs and called for Jacob. Nothing.

"Jacob?" she repeated. "This is Hey You. I was wondering if I should start breakfast. Would you like blueberry pancakes or an omelet?"

Still no answer. Goodness, had he wandered off again?

She ran up the stairs. "Jacob." She didn't mean to say his name as a reprimand, but fear emboldened her.

The door to the smaller bedroom stood wide-open. Flung open. Will's imprint was everywhere: in the lingering smell of his soap, in the pillow dent, in the rumpled bottom sheet, in the twisted heap of bedding half kicked off the end of the bed, in clothes left wherever they were tossed, in the towel puddled in the middle of the floor. She was inside, picking up the damp towel before she pictured Will standing where she was standing, naked. As if scalded, she dropped the towel and ran back into the hallway.

"Jacob?" She knocked on the main bedroom door. "You okay in there?"

A moment of quiet was followed by a sob.

"Jacob, honey?" Turning the knob slowly, she entered.

He was sprawled on the floor.

He were dreamin' about Freddie. Real bad dream. He got up, needed the bathroom. Next thing he knew…he were on the floor.

"Angeline?"

No, weren't his Angeline. An angel, then? Had he crossed over? She looked like an angel—blonde, smiling. Prettiest smile he'd ever seen, except for Angeline's.

He'd always been partial to wakin' up to see two things:

the forest and Angeline's face on the pillow next to his. Demons didn't take her when she slept. If a man could open his eyes every mornin' and see the woman he loved and the forest, then sweet Jesus had blessed him indeed.

He should sit up, act like a man, but he felt mighty wobbly. And his groin were warm and damp. Sweet Jesus, no. He hadn't pissed himself, had he? Willie would shove him in a nuthouse faster than you could say, could say...

Why were his pajama pants wet? Why the fuck was he on the floor?

"Jacob," the angel said, "it's me, Hey You. I think you lost your balance and fell. Does anything hurt? Can you sit up?"

'Course. He knew it were Hey You, not an angel. His worthless, crippled mind were playin' tricks again.

"Had me a real bad dream. Hard to shake off them bad thoughts when I wake. I get confused sometimes. C.R.S. Can't remember stuff."

He grabbed at her. Must get up, must get up off the floor. What would she think, Hey You? He couldn't be lyin' on the floor like some wounded animal. Why could he smell urine?

"Do you want to talk about the nightmare?" Hey You said. She had a pretty smile, almost as pretty as his Angeline's. Had Willie noticed her smile? She tucked her arm under his and that little lady, she were stronger than she looked, 'cause next thing he knew, he were up and leanin' against the bed frame, with his useless legs stuck out in front of him.

"Can't talk about it. Real bad dream. Why would a mind do somethin' so awful?"

Hey You sat beside him on the floor. "I have bad dreams, too, about Galen."

"Who's Galen?"

"My son." Hey You gave a real big sigh, plum full of things she didn't want to say. "The crazy one."

"Crazy One. That's a good nickname. My wife were a little crazy sometimes. But she were my angel."

"And Galen's mine. He just has some problems to work through." Hey You looked real thoughtful. "You and I need to figure out how to dump our bad dreams."

"What say you to makin' some dream catchers, little lady? Haven't made one in a while, but I reckon I still remember how."

"I'd like that."

"First, we got to find us some willow branches, to make the loops. I have leather and beads in one of them boxes in the corner, but we also need feathers from the all-seein' night owl."

"That shouldn't be a problem if you like scavenger hunts. There's an owl living on the edge of the forest. I've even seen him during the day."

"Yup, I've heard him, too. That old rascal's got plenty to say." His heart were racin'. Reckon he'd just sit for a while, get his breath back. Let his mind settle a bit. "You know the most important thing about makin' a dream catcher?"

The angel shook her head.

"Got to leave a hole in the center. Now that hole's the starting point and the ending point. All dreams come into the web, but only the good dreams know how to get through the hole. And them good dreams, they filter down the feather of the all-seein' night owl to reach the sleeper. Them bad dreams? They don't know how to get through. They get caught up in the web and perish in the sunlight. That's why the womenfolk hang them outside in the mornin'."

What was that smell? Had he pissed himself? Had Hey You noticed the smell?

"Well, I think we both need dream catchers. But first, Jacob, we need to get you cleaned up."

"Angel?"

"Yes, honey?"

"I think I pissed myself." And then a big ol' tear escaped. "Don't tell Willie. You tell Willie and he's goin' to pack me off to one of them nuthouses. He always wanted me to do that with his mama. He never understood, never realized I couldn't do that to her. I tried to keep them both safe. That's what you do, right? A man, he has to protect his family. Couldn't always, though. Couldn't always.

"I know in his heart Willie thought he were doin' right by his mama, but she wouldna managed without us. She were a free spirit, his mama. Couldn't bear to see her drugged and confined. And I knew Willie would be okay. Were tough for him, real tough, but he had this gal. They looked after each other. What a pair—always findin' trouble. 'Course he wanted to grow up to marry her, but that weren't never gonna happen. She loved him, but not that way." He paused. Hey You hadn't said anything in a while. Mind you, his mouth were runnin' on like a freight train clickety-clackin' all the way to Mebane. "Not like me and his mama. She were so fragile, his mama. She needed a whole lot of lookin' after. She couldn't manage without us. I loved her always. Love her still."

"I know, honey. I feel the same about Galen."

"Who's Galen?"

Hey You smiled. "Crazy One. Will's taken him rock climbing today."

"You think that's a good idea?"

"Yes, I do. He needs to reconnect with nature. He needs to find joy again."

"We talkin' about your son or mine?"

Hey You smiled. "Can you get up?"

"Sure can." He sniffed. Couldn't believe he'd cried in front of a gal. Real pretty one, too.

"I'm going to help you into the bathroom, turn on the shower, then leave you in peace. But I'm going to wait in here, okay? When you feel like you can get dressed, you shout through the door, 'Go away!' and I'll go down and make the best breakfast you've ever had. Do you like blueberry pancakes?"

She were an angel, all right—knew that kin should share Sundays, should sit around a table with a big ol' stack of hot blueberry pancakes and Aunt Jemima's best. Tried to do that with Willie and his mama on a Sunday mornin'. A family needed traditions, needed to come together to share food, needed to be thankful. It might not be Sunday—hell, he didn't rightfully know what day it were. But he were feelin' mighty thankful.

"I sure do, little lady."

She heaved him up, and they staggered into the bathroom. Embarrassin' to be in the bathroom with a pretty gal, but Angel, she just kept smilin' at him, like they did this every day. He put his hands on the sink for extra balance while she turned on the shower.

"Thank you," he said.

She kissed his cheek. "You're welcome. If you can convince me by the end of the day that you're not hurt, this can stay our little secret. And after you've gotten dressed, leave your pajamas on the floor and I'll wash and dry the evidence before Will comes home. Does that sound like a plan?"

"Sure does, Angel."

Hannah sat on the bed and listened. The shower door opened and closed and water continued to run. So far so good, other than the fact that she had broken her promise to Will. Did that mean he, too, was capable of violating their trust?

It was the tears. She'd never been able to deal with a man's tears. Always they reminded her of her dad sobbing quietly at her mother's funeral, searching for dignity in grief. An eighty-year-old man was crying and she had the power to make the hurt go away. How could she not keep Jacob's secret? But she would be vigilant in the extreme for the remainder of the day. If Jacob showed even the slightest sign of disorientation, she would tell Will the moment he returned.

Jacob began to hum, or rather warm up his voice. She'd only heard him sing once before—a smoky, guttural voice that held unexpected power. When his melody boomed through the door, goose bumps rose on her forearms. How tragic that he'd packed away his music along with his memories. Did he still have his banjo? She looked around the room but saw only the stack of taped cardboard boxes in the corner and a small framed photograph on the nightstand.

Hannah picked up the picture and gasped. The beautiful older woman in the photo could only be Will's mother, but she was no stranger. This was the woman who had found Rosie scavenging in the Occoneechee Mountain parking lot. And she had the same eyes as her son.

# TWENTY-FIVE

A muscle in his neck cramped into a spasm, and Will kneaded it with his fingertips.

"You okay?" Galen asked.

"*Hmm.*" Will sat up and swallowed. Aged sawdust contained more moisture than his mouth. "How long have I been out?"

"Since we left the parking lot."

"All those manly pursuits and fresh air. Damn. Used to be the only thing on my mind after a climb was cocktail hour. Now I sleep like the poster child for those Old Guys Rule T-shirts. Tell me I wasn't drooling."

"Only for the first hour." Galen gave a muted smile, but a good one. Genuine.

Will cleared his throat. "What time is it?"

Galen turned the power off. "Around midnight."

No moon, no stars, just a blanket of darkness. Ahead, a fortress of trees rose like a battalion of undead guards. Two coyotes howled; Saponi Mountain was alive with the kill.

"Once you closed your mouth, you looked peaceful." Galen

picked up the smart key and tossed it to Will. "And the unlit country roads were so tranquil. I decided to drive in circles. Let both of us zone out."

"Hey, it's cool. I haven't slept like that in weeks."

"Will?"

The kneading of his fingers sent strokes of warmth down his shoulder. "Yeah?"

"Thank you for giving me a second chance—after I was such a dick when we met. Today was a good day. I'm glad I spent it with you."

The porch light from the cottage shone into the driver's side, illuminating Galen's face with a ghostly glow. The guy really should put on some weight, puff out those cheeks, but at least the gray pallor had gone.

"You're not going to suggest a man hug next, are you?" Will said.

"Not your thing?"

Will shook his head. "I'm a non-discriminating non-hugger."

A quiet laugh. "Did I stress you out today?"

"Only when you dyno'd over that ledge and out of view. Next time, don't make me wait until I see your head at the top of the climb. Answer me when I call."

"Really, you'd take me climbing again?"

"Sure. Anytime."

Galen turned to stare out into the night. "I imagine you're already planning your first father/son climb with Freddie."

Will snapped wide-awake. "I haven't thought about it." An honest answer, because it had always been a given: *One day, I'll teach my son to climb.*

Another dream lost, but today he'd also won a small, surprising victory over grief. Today he had focused on the physical and emotional well-being of another person out of choice.

Dealing with the old man was not about free will, and soloing in the Gunks had been nothing more than a self-test, the desire to prove he was still alive. Today hadn't been about proving anything, and while he wasn't paying attention, Will found himself caring—about Galen's safety and Hannah's trust. It went deeper, too. He'd wanted Galen to enjoy the experience.

"It was a good day for me, too, Galen."

"Like talking to God?"

"Yeah." Will smiled. "I think so. How about you?"

Galen nodded. "There's a poem circulating in my head."

"Seriously? That's fantastic, man."

"I'm going to try and write it down before I go to bed."

"And share it with me tomorrow?"

Galen nodded.

Maybe the climb had been a step forward for both of them. And maybe the incident with the ledge was as meaningless as the moment Galen decided to jump before clipping a bolt.

Will tumbled out of the passenger seat and stretched. Galen closed the driver's-side door and then leaned onto the car.

"Tired?" Will asked.

"No. Just pensive."

"I told your mom we'd be back by ten. Think she's worried?"

"She didn't text, so I guess not. She's never been the type to wait up."

"At least you don't think she has."

Hannah's bedroom was sealed in blackness, as Will expected it to be. Even so, he pictured her sitting in the dark, waiting for her teenage sons to come home. Not wanting to fuss, but not being able to sleep until she heard the dead bolt on the front door click into place. He would have been that way if…just *if*.

"You want me to unload the gear?" Galen said.

"No, we're good. Let's deal with it tomorrow." Tonight, Will just wanted to sleep.

The dogs waddled across the yard, tails wagging.

"Hey, ladies." Will crouched down, and Rosie and Daisy headed straight for him.

"I guess Mom stayed up, after all."

"Oh?" That sounded casual enough, right? Nothing lustful, nothing that announced, *In my dreams, your mother's naked.*

"Yeah, she probably felt she should in case your dad needed something. She's like that. Mom can sit up all night with a sick animal or a sick kid."

"Or an aging dad?"

"That, too. Besides, if Rosie's around, so's Mom. Rosie's her protector."

Rosie licked Will's hand; it tickled.

"One time a friend of mine was drunk and accidently fell into Mom's bedroom. Rosie pinned him against the wall. Probably would've attacked if he hadn't been too terrified to move." Galen paused. "Mom?"

"Think she's okay?" Will stood and rubbed at his stubble.

"Mom?" Galen called louder.

Will spotted her first, curled up on the cottage porch swing in a white toweling dressing gown, a pair of pink velvet slippers abandoned on the boards beneath her. Never in a millennium would he have pegged her for a woman who liked pink velvet.

He pulled ahead of Galen, which wasn't hard—the guy moved like a turtle—and reached the cottage steps. The dogs brushed past, but Will paused to lean into the railing. She looked as young as she did in the photograph from her twenty-first birthday. Not that they needed to, but the years had slipped away. As had her dressing gown, which revealed a bare thigh and the hint of pink-and-white-striped boxer shorts. What else did she own that was pink?

"Mom?" Galen stood next to him.

Will was about to say, *Let her sleep,* but Hannah sat up—revealing a white lacy camisole that hinted at the outline of her breasts. The breasts he'd imagined jiggling while he moved rhythmically inside her. God help him, he gave a low moan, and before he could cover it up with a cough, an owl answered.

"What time is it?" Hannah dragged her hands through her hair and looked sexy as hell. Despite the huge brown stain over her right boob. She grabbed the collar of her dressing gown and tugged it up to her neck, and he felt like a kid caught with his hand in the bowl of Halloween candy. Had he been staring?

"I spilled coffee down myself," Hannah said. "Waiting up for you guys."

"It's my fault, Mom. We would have been back hours ago, but Will fell asleep and the roads were so quiet and mesmerizing. I just kept driving. Sorry."

"No, no need to apologize," Hannah said quickly.

So, Will wasn't the only one exhausted by the endless need for atonement. Although, now that he thought about it, Galen hadn't apologized once today.

"How was the climb?" she asked Galen.

"Energizing," Galen replied. "I'm going to head back to the house. Make some coffee and work on a poem. 'Night, guys." Galen kissed his mother's cheek, and Will felt something he probably shouldn't have.

"Thank you, Will." Her voice was husky with sleep.

She held his gaze and frowned.

"Something bothering you?" The question had slipped out

unintentionally, but her stare was intense. Uncomfortably so. He shoved his hands into his pockets.

"No." She shook her head, as if fighting off the remnants of a dream. "It's fine."

"My dad okay?"

"Fine." Hannah stood and yawned.

Great. They'd established everything was fine. Except for the fact that Hannah was only partially dressed, and he was trying not to imagine her straddling him. Deep in his pockets, Will screwed up both hands into fists.

As if sharing his thought, she tightened the belt on her dressing gown. "I exhausted Jacob with a hike. He went to bed around nine, and last time I checked, he was sleeping like a baby. Or maybe not, given what appalling sleepers my two were. Especially Galen."

"Colic?" Will said.

"Yes. Your son, too?"

"I don't know. I didn't meet him till he was nine months old."

"Goodness. That's rough."

"Yeah. Nine months of memories I don't have."

Head cocked to one side, Hannah stared at him again. No way could she have figured out his secret, but she'd clearly caught a whiff of cover-up. From now on, he would say nothing about Freddie. Not one single comment would escape his lips. He would have to be even more guarded.

# TWENTY-SIX

Overnight the energy in the house settled into a calm ebb and the constriction in Hannah's chest unwound. Galen rose early, cooked her breakfast and ran out to pick up dog food. Finally, he left the house for something other than A.A. And rather than sleep all afternoon, he had spent the past two hours in the front of the old PlayStation blowing up zombies.

Everything felt different; everything had shifted. Thanks to Will, Galen had turned a corner. He had come back to her.

Hannah smiled. *Imagine*—she was actually grateful that her gifted poet was frying his brain, goofing off like a normal student. The living room shuddered through another video-generated explosion, but the dogs, collapsed around Galen, slept on. Only Rosie stirred.

"Popping over to the cottage," Hannah said.

Galen grunted an acknowledgment, and Rosie pushed her muzzle into Hannah's palm, handing her a still-warm memory of Will's mother darting in and out of her life. Her own mother would have loved that fleeting connection, would have taken that brief moment in her daughter's life and constructed grand meaning. Hannah, however, wanted only to ignore yet another gravitational pull back to Will.

But suppose someone could offer her a new story about one of her parents? What a gift! The map of life redrew itself constantly; the borders never stopped shifting. How wonderful, though, to rediscover that part labeled *daughter*.

Her parents had been ripped away too soon, and without motherhood to give her purpose, she would have been adrift as a grown-up orphan. There had been no time for final words or final moments. No time to presort memories and select ones worth keeping. But this was a good memory, and it belonged to Will.

"Coming with me, baby?"

Rosie's tail thumped against the floor.

As they crossed the gravel, a thrush—nature's flautist—announced the gloaming. Another thirty minutes and darkness would fall, but right now the house and the cottage were suspended between day and night, caught in that moment when nothing was defined and everything seemed possible. Galen had written several poems about the gloaming, and she often found herself out in the woods with her camera at this time. The French called it the blue hour; photographers called it the golden hour; Hannah called it the in-between hour. It spoke of endings and beginnings. And today, it spoke of promise for a better tomorrow.

Orange sunlight entered the forest from the west, skimming through the treetops and casting tendrils of shadows. Hannah smiled, imagining her father, her guardian angel, waving from the tree line.

*Thank you, Dad, for keeping Galen safe.*

Rosie mounted the cottage steps ahead of her and went straight to Will, who was pushing back and forth on the porch swing.

"Do you have a minute?" Hannah asked.

"Sure." Will shot up and looked at her with his mother's eyes. The swing continued to rattle behind him. "How about a glass of wine? It's nearly six o'clock on a Friday, and I have a cabernet that comes well recommended."

Life could change in five minutes, in one minute, in thirty seconds, but there was harmony to drinking that bottle of wine, this evening, with this person, with this dog at their feet. If she could choose to be anywhere in the world, with anyone, it would be here, right now, with Will.

"Wine would be lovely. Thanks."

He disappeared into the cottage and Rosie lay down. Hannah placed her palm on the swing cushion—still warm, still molded to Will's body—and sat as far away from his indentation as possible. A squirrel barked, and crows called one another home. Hannah tugged off her sweatshirt. Once again, the heat of the early evening had caught her off guard. Once again, she'd dressed for fall, as if pretense had the power to influence seasonal change.

When Will elbowed open the screen door, she leaped up to help, claiming the glasses in a clumsy handoff. He sat next to her, close but not too close, and she had the most ridiculous thought: *Which bra am I wearing?*

She twisted her legs together and angled them away from him, then folded her left arm across her stomach and tucked in both elbows. With her right arm braced across her chest, she held up the wineglass that had been part of a wedding gift. As Will poured, she stared at an object that had once represented the happiest day of her life, and felt nothing. Then she watched Will set the bottle down on the porch, and silently acknowledged the desire coiling in her gut.

"Cheers." She chinked her glass against his. "And thanks again, for yesterday. I assume there were no problems?"

"Galen totally nailed it. Awesome focus for a beginner."

"But?"

"A couple of things niggled. Nothing big." Will sipped his wine. "I'm sure they were nothing."

"Will." She uncrossed her legs. "You can't say that and not elaborate."

"He was a little careless."

"Beginner's mistakes?"

"Possibly." Will paused. "How honest do you want me to be?"

"As honest as if he were your son."

Will sucked in a deep breath. "I was concerned—at one point—that the thought of slipping to his death might not be a problem for him."

The porch swing creaked as it swung like a pendulum.

"Are you going to freak out now?" he said.

"No, because you're wrong. Galen's in a good place. I can't explain how I know, I just do."

Will nodded, but kept the frown. "Did he write that poem?"

"Working on it, apparently."

"How was Dad yesterday?"

She swirled her glass and wine sloshed against the side. If she didn't talk about the morning, she wasn't lying. "He reminisced."

"About?" Will's tone suggested caution.

"His musical career. Have you ever considered writing down some of his memories?"

"No, for the simple reason he didn't have a musical career."

"Only because he did what he thought was right for his family."

"No. He did what he thought was right for Mom. Always." Will's voice hardened. "I just filled in the cracks."

"It didn't sound that way to me."

Will glanced sideways at her. "What exactly did he tell you?"

"That he was in a band with your uncle and they were offered a recording contract, which meant traveling. Jacob refused the deal because he couldn't leave you alone with your mom, and your uncle was furious."

Will drained his glass. Then he leaned down to retrieve the bottle. He topped up her glass, even though she'd drunk only two sips, and filled his to the top. Was she allowing her son to hang out with a closet drinker?

"So. Now Dad's rewriting the family history." Will took a slug of wine. "Whatever he's told you, this is the truth—my dad was a grave digger with a talent for the banjo, my mom was a storyteller who was batshit insane. There were so many overlapping realities, it was hard to know where madness ended and illusion began in our house. Mom could create whole worlds in which good battled evil. When I was a kid, her stories and her manic energy were the best. The embarrassment and shame came later, as her behavior grew more erratic. One day I was living a fairy tale, the next I was on the set of a disaster movie. I never had friends over. Couldn't risk it, not when the house throbbed with her moods. Hiding our lives became a time-consuming lie. She refused to seek help and Dad refused to force her hand. They made their decisions, and our lives revolved around her craziness. Maybe it rubbed off on him."

Will stomped on the decking boards and the swing stopped moving. "Recording deal, my ass."

They resumed their rocking.

"I used to do this every night," Hannah said, "sit on the porch with a drink and star gaze."

"Why did you stop?"

"After my father died, my thoughts turned maudlin, especially at night. Time alone wasn't wise. I took a step back, grieved for both my parents and then forced myself to start life over. I changed some of my old habits and started new ones. It seemed an important part of my healing process to establish a before and an after line."

"And did that work?"

"For me, yes. I stopped looking to the past for answers."

"Have you always been this nauseatingly wise?"

She gave a laugh. "You know, you still have a chance to reach your dad, to forgive him for whatever happened with your mom. He might have made decisions you didn't support, but that doesn't make him a bad parent."

Will leaned back and rested his arm along the porch swing. A trace smell of his soap—or maybe it was his shampoo—drifted into her space. Remembering the damp towel on his bedroom floor, Hannah edged away.

"I knew the band members had a falling-out, and I assumed Mom was the cause. She was the cause of everything bad. But it didn't have to be that hard, you know? If she had just admitted she needed help. You really think Dad did that, for me?"

"Why don't you ask him?"

Will said nothing.

"What do you have to lose?"

"The glimmer of hope you just gave me?"

"What if I could give you another one?" She reached over and placed her hand on his knee. Without thinking, she had slipped into vet mode. Sharing important news—good or bad—was always easier if you were physically connected to the other person, like an emotional lightning rod. But they jerked apart in unison, and the porch swing vibrated violently. For a moment, the world seemed to tilt and Will drifted out of focus. Was she drinking too quickly?

Hannah shook her head clear and pressed on as if nothing had happened. "Was your mom petite with thick white hair down to her waist? Eyes the mirror of yours?"

"Yeah," he mumbled, those familiar eyes narrowing with question.

"I met her," Hannah said. "I met your mom. She found Rosie in the Occoneechee Mountain parking lot, loaded her in the car and drove her straight to me. I never figured out why. She must have seen one of my flyers in the library, or maybe one of her friends recommended me."

"My mom didn't have friends." He put his glass down on the porch floor and raked his hands through his hair. He had workman's hands, not the hands of an artist. "Jesus, is there anything else you want to throw at me?"

"I only met her that once."

"How long ago?" he said.

"Four years."

"Which month?"

"March? I'd just come back from a hike in the botanical gardens and the trout lilies were blooming. I love trout lilies."

Will didn't move. "Mom died that March, of a heart attack. I hadn't seen her in over a year. Did you look at her and think, *Omigod, total whacko?*"

"No. She was sweet."

"For real?"

"She talked fast," Hannah said. "It was a little hard to follow her thread. She wanted to pay me to give Rosie a checkup and stitch a wound, but I told her she could make a donation to the local shelter instead. She said she wanted a dog for when her grandson came to visit."

Will slumped into himself. "She never met Freddie. I wouldn't allow it. I couldn't." He sighed. "I was waiting until he was bigger, so she couldn't pull some of the shit she had with me. Once, she dragged me by my hair. Please don't repeat that—especially not to my dad."

Hannah had witnessed so much cruelty, so much abuse inflicted on animals, but a mother with her own child...? She pushed her palm against her breast and tried not to imagine what Will must be seeing, feeling, remembering.

"What else did she say?"

Hannah swallowed and looked down at Rosie. Her Rosie-girl, the dog that had brought such happiness into her life. "Rosie was in bad shape, so I asked to keep her for a few days." She sighed. "Your mom said she'd return the following week. She never did. To be honest, I was relieved. It was love at first sight for old Rosie and me."

"Yeah, Mom had a limited attention span for anything or anyone."

"I'm guessing she died before she could come back."

"Possibly," he said. "Did she look rough, like a hobo? Is that why you didn't charge her?"

"No, it's a judgment I make sometimes. Her car was beaten-up and, despite the cold, she wasn't wearing a jacket. I see a lot of older people who would rather go without groceries than neglect their pets. I'm in this business because it's my calling, not to get rich. I won't take money that needs to go to food."

"I sent them money all the time. But Mom was so impetuous. She'd buy this crap they didn't need. And my dad never said no to her. Not once. Why didn't he ever say *no?*"

"Love complicates," she said quietly.

"I always wanted one good memory of her, but I could never find it."

"Take mine. After all, your mother brought me Rosie. There've been many stray dogs in my life, but never one as special as Rosie. She's my animal soul mate."

Hannah slipped off her clog and ran her foot through Rosie's baby-soft fur.

"Weird, that you of all people should have met my mom," Will said. "Talk about a plot twist. Put this in a novel and no one would believe it."

"I told you—things happen for a reason."

"Yeah? But that doesn't explain what's happened in my life."

"Right. You being a bestselling author and all that."

"Talking to you is so easy. You make everything so…"

"Easy?"

A smile danced at the corner of his lips. "Are you teasing me?"

"I don't like drama. My guess is you don't, either."

"Legacy of my childhood. And having a kid with a woman who was, I mean, is—" the smile disappeared and he flapped his words away "—just as crazy as my mom doesn't help. What's your excuse?"

"I bottomed out on melodrama. My mother died in a violent accident, my father committed suicide, my husband decided he was gay. And now I have Galen's depression. Family life is never about the picket fence and the home-baked dinner rolls. It's about surviving crises. You get through one, there's always another one waiting in the wings."

Will reclaimed his glass. "Why hasn't your ex-husband visited since Galen came home?"

"I asked him to stay away. Inigo understands bad behavior, the kind of stunts our younger son used to pull, but he doesn't get depression. He thinks Galen should snap out of it. I hope you have a good relationship with your ex, because parenting gets different, not easier. And there comes a point when you have to ignore your instinct to tighten the reins. By the time your son gets to high school, parental micromanaging will add pounds of stress to your life without impacting his."

The rusted chains on the porch swing squeaked.

"I didn't choose to be a parent," Will said. "I knew by the time I was sixteen I didn't want kids."

"But fate had other plans."

He jumped up, more restless than a male dog around a bitch in heat.

Hannah stood, too. "I'm sorry. You've made it clear you don't want to talk about Freddie. But you know where I am, if you change your mind."

"Don't go," he said. "We have half a bottle of wine left."

"We don't have to drink it all in one night." She tried to ignore the burden of duplicity, the irrational sense of being involved in activity she should hide from her son. Now that Galen had hallmarked Will as his friend—his only friend at this point—the net binding them became more entangled.

Will grazed her shoulder. Less than a pat, but her skin tingled; her muscles tightened. Even as she tried to put her mind elsewhere—anywhere—her body whispered, *Touch me again.* Holding his gaze, she stayed still. Thankfully, only the whites of his eyes showed in the dusky light.

"I'd really like you to stay. It's, well, it's been a while since I've—" His hands flew in front of his face, and he suddenly seemed shy. "I haven't hung out with someone normal in a while. No offense to Galen."

"What about Poppy?"

"It's a little awkward between us, since the shower episode. I mean, she's smart and funny—"

"And sexy."

"I guess, but she's not—" Music burst from his pocket, a song Hannah didn't recognize. Will pulled out his iPhone. "Ally!" he said, and mouthed at Hannah, *Back in five.*

He sauntered down the steps and disappeared into the evening, but she could hear his voice murmuring. Hannah finished Will's sentence in her mind: *She's not Ally.*

*And neither am I.*

Hannah inhaled wood smoke and prayed the newbies in their big mansion up on the ridge weren't stupid enough to burn leaves in a drought. And yet, smart people made terrible decisions every day. And intelligent women could say the most ridiculous things when distracted by flukes of fate and handsome younger guys. Why had she tested him, goaded him about Poppy? Like a dream catcher without a hole, there was no escape route for her thoughts. But she had to find a way out, because these feelings for Will? She needed them gone. If her connection to his mother was a sign, then it was a sign of one thing only: Will was here, in their lives, for her son, not for her. Nothing mattered beyond her son's recovery. And please God, Will would stay long enough for her to be sure this shift in Galen's behavior was not an aberration.

She leaned over the railing and dumped her leftover wine in the dirt, and then she went into the cottage to find a pen and a piece of paper.

"I'm not going to ask if you're okay, but I'm sending you a telepathic hug," Ally said.

So, she hadn't forgotten today was the four-month anniversary of Freddie's death.

"The day's nearly over. That's the best I can say." And then he could start the countdown to the next marker. Five months.

He considered walking into the black forest, away from the lights of both houses. Walking until he collapsed and curled up in a bed of leaves like a wild animal. He did that once to escape his mom. Worked, too, until his dad had found him and carried him home.

"Listen, Ally. I can't talk."

"Meeting a hot babe?"

Will cleared his throat.

"Omigod, you *are* meeting someone. You dark horse." Ally laughed.

Years ago, he had believed her laugh to be the sweetest sound in the world. Part of him wished he still did. Loving Ally had dragged him through adolescence; her rejection had given him the determination to get the hell out of Orange County—to prove to her that he was not destined to be the next county grave digger. The first three Agent Dodds novels were written for Ally. Maybe the fourth, too.

"Come on, you. Spill the details to Auntie Ally."

Will tried to think of a comeback. Technically he wasn't meeting anyone, since Hannah was already on his porch. Well, her porch, and yes, she was hot, and yes, he felt shots of electrical currents when they touched. Of course, that could just be ramped-up lust, since he hadn't gotten laid in at least eight months. A big, fat, pregnant eight months. Maybe that explained the dreams about Hannah. Maybe he was just horny as hell, but thinking about sex when his son's ashes were sitting in an urn in his apartment—that was beyond heinous.

"Let me guess." Ally caved first, but then, she always did. "It's complicated."

"You have no idea," Will said. Was Hannah the reason he had extended his search to retirement homes on the Virginia border? Was he engineering excuses to stay? "Listen, I'm planning to be back in New York next week. Can you handle everything till then?"

"What do you think?"

"Sorry. Silly question."

"Is it strange, being home?"

"Yeah. Like plummeting into a time warp. Everything's

the same, except for the people. And the fact that my dad is, you know, losing it."

"I thought you might decide to stay," Ally said.

"Nope. Way too much crap waiting for me every day I wake up here."

"Gotta resume the role of New York author?"

"Yeah, I guess. Listen. Did you ever hear anything about Dad and a recording deal?"

"Nope. He still picking that banjo?"

"Not really. The only time he's played since Mom died was to piss off the director of Hawk's Ridge."

"You should get him back into it."

"I tried, darling. I tried." Admittedly, not very hard.

"Okay, fuck off, then. Call me before you leave. And, Williekins? Do us both a favor and get laid."

"Hate you. Love Seth, hate you."

"Hate you, too. So does Seth."

Will hit End Call and smiled. Ally could always make him smile—even today. But she wasn't the only one. Hannah had made him smile, too.

He stared up at Venus, the evening star. So bright, so full of dreams. As a boy, he used to wish on Venus: wish for his mom to get better; wish to be part of a normal family; wish to grow up and marry Ally and live on Occoneechee Mountain. What a load of sap. Not one of his wishes had come true. Not one of them had even held the possibility of coming true.

He turned back to the cottage. With any luck, Hannah would stay for another glass of wine and he could pretend, for half an hour, that he was a regular guy sharing a drink with a beautiful woman. He could pretend today was just another day; he could pretend Hannah would kiss him good-night.

But when he got back to the porch, Hannah was gone, and the bottle of wine and two wineglasses had been placed on the wrought-iron table next to the porch swing. Propped up was a note written on the back of a Trader Joe's receipt. Will held it under the porch light.

*"Please put this away before Galen comes over. H."*

Her neat writing—round and fat and friendly—told him nothing.

He flipped the note over looking for...what? A kiss? A snappy "Same time tomorrow"? He had no right to expect anything, but still, he'd hoped. Hope wasn't always a good thing, and neither was wishing on stars.

Will kicked off his Converse, which was easy, since he hadn't bothered to lace them. He wasn't sure why he'd gone back outside. Maybe to spy on Hannah. Her bedroom light was on and so were all the lights upstairs. They must have finished supper and gone their separate ways. Maybe Galen was working on that poem.

*Good writing vibes, man. Write for two.*

Will tracked a path across the living room, turned and repeated. The wood floor was too warm under his bare feet. He wanted sharp, biting ice.

He paused, swallowed and glanced at his Rolex. An embarrassing status symbol, he liked to joke it was a knockoff purchased on a trip to Hong Kong. Only he knew it was real.

Ten minutes, he'd managed to waste ten minutes. The longest ten minutes ever.

His hand was shaking, his palm sweating, his breathing shallow. A thousand imaginary termites wriggled through his intestines. He huffed out a breath.

8:15 p.m.

He just had to make it to eight-thirty—the time the first bystander had called 9-1-1 to report the crash—and then to nine, when the medics had pronounced Freddie dead.

Those were the only two facts to survive. Masquerading as the brother of the poor loser who'd died in the wreck, Will had tracked down every person at the scene. Finally, those research skills had proved useful. But despite all the rescuers milling around, all those professionals who dealt with carnage every day, no one could answer the one question Will asked: Did the people in the car suffer?

Had the lack of negation been affirmation?

Will grabbed his hair and tugged. Couldn't go there.

If only Hannah had stayed, maybe he would have been too distracted to notice time. No—he held up the thought with his right hand—no. He didn't want to forget. Ever. A solitary vigil was best.

*Inhale, exhale. Inhale, exhale.*

He stared at the stupid map that now resembled a preschool art project. Had it all been a mistake, a selfish mistake? He didn't know; he just didn't know anymore.

At least Galen wouldn't shuffle over in his worn I-am-a-grad-student Toms for another two and a half hours, and the old man was tucked up in bed, knocked out by not one but two after-dinner temazepam. Drugging his dad was pretty low, but necessary. Worse, Will had planned it. Cut the old man's afternoon nap short to keep him tired.

8:17 p.m.

Will had glided through the day, coasting on the fumes of memory. He needed the calendar to roll over into the second of November; he needed to get back to New York where he could reconstruct the work habits that had kept his life running smoothly for ten years. A tough boss, Will demanded people on his payroll—he hated the word *employees*—answer texts and emails at odd hours. He expected absolute loyalty and absolute secrecy and used Ally as his enforcer. He'd constructed a Will Shepard universe with its own twenty-four-hour clock and everyone in his orbit had to comply. Everyone, that is, except for Freddie.

And now?

Climbing had taught him the importance of control, but his life had become a free-for-all. It wasn't working for him— or Team Shepard—and it sure as hell wasn't working for his dad. He needed to get back on track.

8:18 p.m.

The wine bottle was still on the counter where Will had half-hidden it after Hannah left. He grabbed it and headed upstairs to bury it at the back of his closet. Once again, he was concealing stuff from his dad. Finishing the bottle wasn't an option, not today. This was one anniversary Will didn't want to spend drunk.

He mounted the stairs as slowly as he could. One more minute ticked past.

He hid the bottle. Another minute.

What the hell had Cass been doing, driving—drunk— through New York with Freddie at 8:30 p.m.? Why wasn't Freddie tucked up in his red racing-car bed with the co-ordinating sheets and comforter? Why hadn't Cass hired a babysitter or called Will? She knew he would take Freddie anytime. She *knew*. All she had to do was ask, but instead she'd taken Freddie out for a late-night dinner with some guy. What was his name, the poor bastard who'd died with Freddie? Couldn't remember. Was this how his dad felt every day—battling to find the missing piece of information that was just out of reach?

They hadn't even been coming home. They were head-ing to a 9:00 p.m. reservation. What else had she and this guy been doing in her apartment before the crash? Having sex while they got plastered? With Freddie in the next room?

8:21 p.m.

Will threw himself onto his bed, missing his laptop by less than an inch. Maybe he should spend a few minutes clearing out messages on Facebook. Follow some of the psychobabble he'd thrown at Galen about fighting self-absorption. Of course, when your main reason for using Facebook was to promote your author persona, you couldn't pretend you were doing it to take an interest in other people's lives.

Pushing up with his knees, he crawled backward to lean against the mound of pillows. Legs bent, feet rooted in the comforter, he pulled his MacBook Air onto his lap and typed in his password—the name of Freddie's favorite Build-A-Bear. Freddie's face grinned back at him. Spreading his fingers wide, Will touched the screen. Hannah had talked about before and after rituals. This was definitely a habit borne of grief. Four months ago, he would never have done something as irresponsible as put his hands on his laptop screen.

*Daddy loves you, Munchkin.*

Will logged on to Facebook. He rarely checked his author page before eleven every night, but even so, fans responded to his posts within minutes, as if they were just hanging out in cyberspace, waiting. Jeez, there was some form of fan blitz. No way could he find the energy to deal with so many messages. He clicked onto his personal page, opened "friend requests" and accepted all of them without checking. Ally would be pissed. The message icon was red and somewhere in the double digits. With a sigh, he clicked. Some website share from his agent. Why hadn't she called to berate his lazy ass?

A message from Ally. Call me, you doofus. Followed by a smiley face.

A message from Galen, or rather a poem, a poem called

"To See the Face of God." And one sentence underneath that read: Don't let Mom clean it up.

"No...no... Ohmyfuckinggod, no."

Will threw his laptop aside and ran.

# TWENTY-SEVEN

The screaming inside Galen's head had stopped. He was ready to step outside the awful responsibility of being, ready to accept his inheritance.

The gift of genetics. Depression flowed in his blood.

The plan was memorized. He knew it by heart.

No more failure, no more.

Trepidation fluttered. Pain, there would be pain, but death was the anesthesia. And at the end—salvation. And Papa waiting? Not that it mattered if he wasn't. Thoughts had no consequences. Only one thought still mattered: tomorrow didn't exist.

Galen unzipped his old camping duffel, pulled out the scalpel taken from his mother's supplies, touched the edge. Yes, it was sharp enough. He placed it on the side of the bath, then dug back inside the bag and found the two gray towels. Mom kept these for the dogs; they could be tossed afterward. He flattened the towels alongside the tub. A preventative measure. Less cleanup.

The bathwater rose slowly. Lousy water pressure, as always.

Mom would forgive him. She had tried to understand, but depression was his nemesis. No amount of parenting could change that fact. Eventually Dad would forgive *her*. Liam would have to manage his anger before he could find forgiveness. Anger was the prism through which Liam saw the world—his first emotion and Galen's last.

He swept his hand through the water. The temperature was perfect. Hot enough to dilate the blood vessels and make it easier for the tainted blood to pump out. Not so hot that he couldn't relax. Relax—he breathed—he must relax. Forget the pain of slicing into his flesh, of cutting deep to find the artery.

Warmth traveled up his fingers, into his chest. Reached his heart. The future and the past no longer existed. Life had gone full circle, back to the womb. The end had become the beginning.

*Cut with weakest hand first.*

*No crying out.*

*Physical pain has purpose.*

*Water will stop the blood from coagulating so keep arms in the bath.*

A lot to hold in his mind.

He stood and dried his hands, and pulled a Ziploc of pills from his jean pocket: his benzodiazepine, some leftover Lunesta and his mother's Tylenol. A cocktail of oblivion.

If he chickened out of cutting, he would leave the world drunk and stoned. Pills—the worst kind of déjà vu for Mom. He held up the plastic bag and counted. Then he counted again. Order was vital. He placed the Ziploc by the scalpel.

Returning to the duffel, he tugged out the bottle of vodka he'd picked up while buying dog food. He unscrewed the top and swigged. The taste exploded in his throat like a star going supernova. Swallowed, licked his lips, took another gulp—enough to help numb the pain, not enough to make him sloppy.

A.A., something else he'd bombed.

He lined up the bottle next to the pills and the scalpel, and started removing clothing. Folded his T-shirt—refolded, didn't fold evenly—then his jeans, then his boxers. *Yes, that would do: a neat stack on top of the toilet seat.* Would Mom keep his clothes or donate them to the thrift store? She never gave up on anything that held the possibility of being recycled.

*Sorry I wasn't strong enough, Mom.*

He slid into the bath and sank under the warm water. Holding his breath, he opened his eyes and stared up at the white ceiling—a mosaic through the ripples. Then he imagined his depression-ridden blood seeping out of his veins and hauled himself up through the surface like a sea monster waking from hibernation.

It was time to begin the process of ending his life.

Sitting cross-legged in the middle of her bed with her iPod, Hannah unplugged the world by plugging in her Chrissie Hynde mix. "Hymn to Her" started playing, and the dogs went crazy.

She tugged out her earbuds and jumped. Will was weaving around in the threshold of her bedroom, barefoot and looking unhinged. Or rather terrified.

"Did something happen to Jacob?" She leaped off her bed and tripped over Daisy.

"No." Will panted. "Where's Galen?"

"Working on his poem, he asked for peace and quiet, he…"

Will shook his head vigorously, and Hannah shuddered. *Someone just walked over your grave,* her mother would say.

"Shut the dogs in my room," Hannah said.

She sprang up the stairs, two at a time, calling Galen's name. Blood hammered in her throat. The bathroom door at the end of the hall was closed.

Hannah rattled it. Locked. "Galen?" She pounded with her fist. "Open this door."

"Go *a-wwway.*"

He was drunk! Thank God, he was just drunk! Flunking out of A.A. was a setback but not insurmountable. She would put him under house arrest—twenty-four-hour surveillance, sleep on his beanbag as she'd done when he was a boy crippled by night terrors. "Sweetheart, I know you're drinking. You need to let me in so I can help."

No response. *Keep him talking.* "What are you doing in there?"

"I'm having. A. Bath." Galen's voice grew quieter.

"You haven't had a bath since you were a kindergartener, sweetheart."

Will appeared and moved her aside. "What did you say, dude?"

Galen swore and then there was a thud as something hit the bathroom floor.

"We have to get inside, Hannah," Will said. "Now."

A frenzy of splashing came from the bathroom—the sounds of desperation. Was Galen trying to drown himself? She looked at the locked door separating her from her son.

"Break it down," she said to Will, and stepped back.

Will threw his shoulder against the door. He aimed a kick, then another one. Strong, methodical kicks delivered with calm, well-harnessed force.

The door buckled and Will jettisoned himself into the bathroom. Hannah followed and stumbled over a bottle of Grey Goose lying on the ceramic tile floor. Galen had taken the time to buy the good stuff?

He was frantically searching for something in the bathwater.

The *pink* bathwater.

Hannah screamed, but Galen ignored her. He grabbed a Ziploc of pills from the side of the bath, opened it and shoved a handful into his mouth as if he were eating a fistful of Skittles. Blood from the three-inch gouge that ran down his forearm to his wrist smeared over his face. For an instant, he looked like a vampire.

There was nothing halfhearted about the slash.

Galen reached for the vodka, even though the bottle was nearly empty, but Will was faster and sober. He kicked the bottle backward, snatched the plastic bag from Galen and threw it into the hallway. Pills scattered.

Galen slumped into the water and slurped like a wild beast drinking from a stream. Then he tossed back his head and swallowed. Hannah tasted vomit and breathed hard.

She grabbed Galen's right arm, but her fingers slipped through the blood. A spatter hit her across the chest.

*Clean cut, fresh wound. Blood hasn't had time to coagulate.*

"Go. Away." Galen's words were heavy.

She lunged for his left forearm, held on and flipped it over. Not even a scratch. They'd interrupted him, but one severed radial artery could still prove fatal. He could exsanguinate, bleed to death. She must raise his arm.

Galen teetered to standing, sloshing water over her.

*Please God, please Dad, help me, please help me.*

Will sprung at Galen, half catching, half restraining him. Galen moaned, clearly from pain, but Hannah wanted screams. She wanted a battle cry that shouted, *I will fight to live.*

"It's over, buddy." Will's voice was almost melodic. There was no judgment, no anger, no horror. "I'm going to help you get out of the bath."

Galen went limp in Will's arms.

Will tugged his iPhone out of his back pocket and handed

it to her. She couldn't take it, couldn't send her son back to the psych ward. She'd promised....

"Tourniquet." She wiped blood down her leg and took the phone. Her son had slit his wrist and she was worrying about cleaning off her fingers before using Will's phone?

"On it," Will replied. He unbuckled his belt with one hand and whipped it out through the belt loops.

*Belt, good.* She wouldn't have thought of that.

Will wrapped his belt around and around Galen's bicep. He pulled tight, and the blood flow slowed to a trickle.

"Please. Don't." Galen rested his head on Will's shoulder and stared at the phone in her right hand. "Can't go back." He closed his eyes.

Hannah started hitting bumps on the side of the phone. All that Apple technology yet nothing said on. A round button, at the bottom of the screen. She pushed, and the screen lit up with the face of a giggling brown-haired boy. Will's son, unlike hers, was full of life. Slide to unlock, the screen said. She did.

"You. Promised." Galen's voice faded; his arm had begun to turn purple.

Hannah turned her back on her son and hit 9-1-1 on the keypad. Galen was an adult, but he had relinquished the ability to look after himself. As his mother, she was claiming that right. She was picking up what he had tossed away. One day, he would forgive her. And if he didn't? She would know that she had saved his life.

Hannah's right hand began to convulse.

"Nine-one-one. What's your emergency?" The woman sounded nice. Was she a mother, too?

More splashing. Hannah glanced over her shoulder as Will hauled her naked son out of the bath. Galen had a superficial wound on his calf. Had he cut himself while fumbling in the water for the blade? Will took a step back and lost his footing in a spill of fresh blood. He and Galen landed in a heap.

She needed to find the pills, give them to the EMS as evidence. How much blood had he lost? Enough to bleed out? How many pills had he swallowed? Enough to prove fatal? How much vodka had he drunk? Enough to poison himself?

"Hello?" the operator said.

"My son tried to kill himself," Hannah said. The words came from someone else—another mother talking about another son.

Will yanked off his T-shirt and held it over Galen's wound. Will's torso was muscular, toned; Galen's was skeletal. She could count his ribs. Two bare-chested men huddled on a once-white bathmat. An embrace in blood spatters.

She answered the operator's questions, but her eyes moved up to Will's face and stayed there. He stared back until she finished the call.

"Why?" she said to Galen. "Why did you do it?"

"Why did you stop me?"

"I'm your mother. It's my job to protect your life."

"You succeeded." Galen sniffed. "Panicked. Dropped the scalpel."

"Scalpel?"

"Yours. How about that?"

Hannah stared into murky bathwater and there, on the floor of the tub, was a familiar, shiny object. "No," she whispered, then swallowed. "I need the number for your therapist. Right now, Galen."

"Don't have one."

"You lied?"

"Lot of that going around."

"But I trusted you."

"Yeah. Well. Trusted you, too." Galen began to shiver. "Cold."

Hannah yanked one of the white bath sheets from the hook on the back of the bathroom door and, squatting down, wrapped the towel around Galen and Will. Will gave her hand a quick squeeze. She leaned forward to touch Galen, but he retreated into Will.

"Stay. Away."

Had she saved her son's life but lost him, anyway?

There was a large puddle on the floor—a soup of water, vodka and blood that needed cleaning up before it leaked through to the kitchen ceiling. And why was there a neatly folded stack of clothes on the commode? Galen would never fold his clothes.

Galen crumpled and Hannah gasped. Will eased him to the floor, keeping the slashed right arm raised above his head.

"I need you to go down to the kitchen and find a wooden spoon," Will said. "Something I can use as a dowel to tighten the tourniquet."

She didn't move. The bathroom was quiet, but outside the open window the night was alive with the sounds of crickets and frogs. The owl hooted four times.

"Now, Hannah. You understand?"

She nodded.

"Then I want you to wait on the porch for the first responders. One of us needs to tell them where to come," Will said. "Okay?"

*Okay?* Her breath came in short, angry bursts.

"Don't worry. He'll be fine."

"How do you know, Will?" All her medical knowledge, and she was seeking advice from a novelist. "How do you know?"

"I think we found him in time. I'm going to position him on his side, in case he vomits."

*Right, good.*

She tried to move but her body refused. This wasn't meant to happen, not to her baby. She had pictured death as an old friend, welcomed it with peace, built her career around that belief. But there was nothing peaceful about the scene in the bathroom. Hell, they were in hell.

"Go now." Will's voice was stronger.

His face was unreadable. Had he done this before, with his mother—held her through some uncontrollable fit of madness? Because this, surely, was madness.

"Keep talking to him." Hannah swiped the back of her hand under her nose. "Tell him to fight. Tell him I love him."

She ran down the stairs, Will's phone still in her hand. Call Inigo, she must call Inigo. Have him meet her at the hospital. Call Poppy, have her call Liam. Someone had to call Liam. Find out which hospital. Could they deny her entry if Galen refused to see her? She had no legal rights; Galen was over twenty-one. Would she ever hug her son again? Would he ever *choose* to hug her?

She raced into the kitchen and tugged open the large drawer next to the oven. A wooden spoon, she needed a wooden spoon. Tongs, spatulas and pasta servers clattered to the floor as she discarded them. No spoon.

"Fuck!" she screamed, and dumped out the contents of the drawer. "Fuck!"

The cat shot from the window seat with an indignant *meow*.

She stood still and stared at the mess. Game over. She was exhausted, exhausted from the effort of tiptoeing through Galen's life, exhausted from breathing through the tension that pressed on her chest day after day, exhausted from worrying about her own mental state as well as her son's. She was exhausted, and she needed help.

She punched numbers into the keypad.

"Well, well, well." Poppy answered straightaway. "And why is Will Shepard calling me at nine o'clock at night? Want company in the outside shower?"

"I need—" Hannah sobbed "—help."

"Han? Are those sirens in the background?"

"Galen tried to…tried to… I have to call Inigo—"

"No. I'll deal with Inigo. Be there in five."

"Thank you," Hannah whispered, but Poppy had hung up.

The sirens were getting closer. Hannah ran back into the hallway and out through the front door. The night heaved with humidity, and heat lightning flashed over Miss Prissy's pasture.

Red lights appeared and disappeared and then the first vehicle pulled in front of her house. It belonged to the volunteer fire department.

Wailin'. Someone were wailin'. Jacob sat up and looked around. This weren't his shack and it weren't Hawk's Ridge. Not too sure where he was…. Didn't do to panic when he woke. If he took a few minutes, he could figure out where he was just fine. No moonlight comin' through them big windows. Crack of light under the door, though. Lights left on at night was such a waste, but Willie insisted.

Been havin' another of them bad dreams about Freddie. So bad it must've woke him up, despite that pill Willie made him take. The boy tried to slip him an extra one, but weren't no way he were takin' two. Spat the second one out when Willie weren't lookin'. Didn't need more drugs scramblin' his busted brain.

That dream catcher weren't workin' too good. Had to push

back them bad thoughts hisself. Couldn't tell Willie about the nightmares. Imagine how upset the boy would be. Freddie were the only reason his Willie smiled these days.

Colored lights flashed. Outside, all manner of noise—doors slammin', people talkin' real loud, but the cottage were quiet as a cemetery. He should know. Spent half his life alone with dead people. Death were his business. He should go check on Will, make sure that boy weren't frettin' on the porch again. Always been a creature of the night, his son, but when nighttime hit these days, Will grew more restless than a caged owl with clipped wings. Worryin' about his daddy, no doubt. And missin' Freddie, him being so far away.

Took a while to get out of bed and into the hall. Goddamn useless body.

"Willie," he called down the stairs. Nothing. Must be Fourth of July with all them flashes of colored lights. Didn't smell no gunpowder, though. Didn't hear no bangs.

He walked down the stairs real slow. Used the rail. Didn't want to fall and give Will more to worry about. His Will sure acted like a man with a lot to worry about.

Jacob shuffled across the main room to the door. The lights were brighter downstairs. And red. Red flashin' lights. He tried to yell, *Will!* but the word caught in his throat. With each pulse of red light, he saw Angeline, his dear, sweet Angeline. Angeline on the floor, arm flung out, reachin' for him. She weren't breathin'.

Where was his dear, sweet Angeline? He must get to her. She needed him.

He opened the door, but his legs wouldn't work. Willie were there! Didn't have a shirt on. Vehicles. Lots of emergency vehicles. Rescue vehicles. Thank you, Jesus. Come for his Angeline, his dear sweet Angeline. But they needed to come in, they needed to help her. She were on the floor, not breathin'.

"Will!" He held up his hand. "Willie! Your mama needs help. She's inside."

What were takin' him so long? His mama needed help *now!*

"Willie!"

"Dad!" Will looked exhausted. Didn't get enough sleep, his boy. Up all hours workin' on some story, no doubt. Been that way since he could hold a pencil.

Why was they both outside? And him in his pajamas, too.

"Everything's fine. Stay there, Dad. I'm coming." Will tapped the medic on the arm, then jogged across the yard. Such a good runner, his Will. Ran with the grace and speed of a wild stallion, but where was his shoes?

"Your mama okay, son?"

Will gave him a funny look. Did he say somethin' wrong? He turned his head from the flashin' lights. Too bright. And sirens now. He couldn't smell fire, but there were a fire truck. And Willie, he had red paint on him. What were that boy up to now? Such a wild one, his son.

He grabbed Will's arm. "Where's the fire, son?"

"It's okay, no fire."

"You're wet, son. You need to come inside, get some dry clothes and a bowl of soup. Why you half-naked?"

"Galen had an accident, and I gave him my T-shirt. But he's fine. Everything's fine."

Willie didn't look fine. He were all pale. He shouldn't be half-naked with ladies around, neither.

"Who's Galen?"

"Hannah's son." Will hesitated. "Hey You's son."

"Ah. Crazy One."

Willie looked real upset. "You can't call him that."

"Hey You does. She chose that nickname. Where's Hey You?"

Will nodded at the ambulance.

"Crazy One gonna be okay?"

"I don't know, Dad. I think that's up to him."

A painted car screeched up to the cottage, and, well, he never. There were Poppy, the brightest comet blazin' across the sky. She were frownin', though, and dressed real funny. In pajamas? 'Course, young women wore the strangest clothes nowadays.

Grabbing her phone, Poppy flung open the driver's door and flew at Will. She gagged, covered her mouth, tried not to barf. Blood, he had blood smeared on his abs and sprayed on his jeans. Like a pinup for the Spartan army.

"Galen?" she whispered through her fingers.

"Unconscious but alive. Only had time to slit one wrist."

Her heart raced like a runaway truck on a mountain pass. Until she died, Han would have to live with the knowledge that one of her sons had planned his own death. "Han?" She swallowed. "Where's Hannah?"

"Went in the ambulance with Galen."

Will eased her aside. He leaned into the Civic, turned off the engine and handed her the keys. Thunder rumbled in the distance. If she knew how, she would pray.

Since the beginning of the summer, when Galen had confessed there was nothing to live for, she should have known this day would come. She should have known to break confidence and tell Hannah. She just should have known. Instead, she'd made a catastrophic error that had nearly cost Galen his life. And yet, she could make amends, tug on her big-girl boots, step up for Hannah.

"I need to call Inigo." Poppy waved her cell around. "Which hospital?"

Will massaged his forehead. "UNC."

"You okay?"

"Fine," he said.

Poppy didn't believe him. Not for one blink.

"Poppy!" Jacob shuffled over, smiling. "Bit late for a paintin' lesson, ain't it?"

Will moved quickly to grasp his dad's elbow. "Come on, old man, let's get you inside."

"Don't let your mama hear you callin' me old."

"No, sir." Will gave a tired smile, glanced her way. "Come with us, Poppy. You and I have to talk."

She trailed behind Will. Speaking quietly, he helped Jacob inside and upstairs. She couldn't make out words, just the tone—gentle, supportive. Such patience Will had—with his dad, with Miss Prissy. Yes, she'd seen him cooing at her horse when he thought no one was watching. Galen did the same thing. Her dear, sweet Galen.

*Focus, girl, focus.*

She threw her keys into one of the armchairs, blinked back a stray tear, dialed Inigo's home phone. Matt picked up. A devoted ex-student of Inigo's, Matt was a sweet guy who adored Galen and Liam, and could be a total man-bitch on the subject of Hannah.

"Matt? It's Poppy. Can you talk privately?"

"Sure thing, babe. What's up?"

"You need to get Inigo to the UNC E.R. Galen's fine, but he tried to kill himself."

A shriek and a thump as something fell. "W-what happened?"

"Slit wrist—only one. Hannah got to him before he…did the other one."

"But we thought he was doing better. Hannah told us—"

"No. You're not going there, Matt. None of us are playing the blame game. You hear me?"

Matt blew into the phone.

"You hear me?" Oh, yeah, she could do righteous indignation. She was ending this shit before it began. "Galen had us all fooled, and Inigo should understand that better than anyone." She paused. Matt said nothing. "You need to tell Inigo that Galen's okay, but his condition is likely serious. You also need to give Inigo this message from me: if he goes after Hannah, I'll castrate him with a hoof pick. *Capisce,* babe?"

She hung up and started to shake. She needed to get to the hospital before Inigo. Protect Han all the way.

"I swear, Inigo, if you…" she muttered.

*Hurry up, Will, hurry up.*

In her mind, Poppy saw the tousled-headed toddler waddling around with a book saying, "Read to me, *Poppeeee. Puhleeze.*" Apart from an unhealthy bank account and a string of disastrous love affairs caused by her for-shit taste in men, she'd led an enchanted life. No family crises, no death except for grandparents when she was too young to care. *But Galen…*

On the coffee table, a bottle of Wild Turkey with a glass. She poured a shot, tossed it back and poured a second. Two wouldn't impair her driving. Not really.

"You think that's a good idea?"

She spun around like a kid caught stealing five dollars from her mother's purse, which, admittedly, she'd only done once, but she'd never forgotten the look on her mama's face. Will had that look now. She hadn't realized before how serious he was, how responsible. Kinda like Hannah.

Oh, he'd put on a sweatshirt. Changed his jeans, too.

Poppy tipped back her drink and swallowed. "Talk to me so I can get out of here."

Will threw himself into an armchair. "She was awesome. Totally awesome."

Curious start. "What happened?"

"Slit one wrist, dropped the scalpel in the bath before he could do the second. Took vodka and pills, too, but we have no idea how many or what."

Something about the way he said *we* got under her skin.

"Clearly he planned it." Will pulled forward and collapsed around the waist. His arms hung between his knees.

"How do you know?"

"Writers trade in details. The details tell me it was well orchestrated."

Poppy eased herself down onto the arm of his chair.

"Yesterday, when we went climbing, Galen was too calm for a first-timer," Will said. "He listened, followed my instructions, but he had no fear, and that made me nervous. A guy only has one reason to not be afraid on a cliff face—he doesn't care. I should have paid more attention."

"Me, too." Poppy sagged. "The rock climbing didn't feel right. Galen hates sports. For twenty-two years he's been Mr. Cautious, choosing to live through words, not risk." She stared at the world map, at all the colored stars she'd stuck on, at all the colored lines she'd drawn to show Freddie's route. Poor Will. He must want to hug his own kid so bad right now.

"You know, when Galen was Freddie's age, I lived in an apartment complex with a pool. Galen swam like a shark, but nothing I said could coax him into the deep end." Poppy hesitated. "On some level, I knew he was suicidal months ago. Should've told Han. Didn't."

Will glanced up. Pillow talk she could do, but the way he looked at her felt way too honest. And they were sitting way too close.

"Please don't share that fact with Hannah," Will said. "She's going to need you like she's never needed you before."

How could she have been such a dimwit? How could she have missed the obvious? Will didn't act like a cornered animal around her because he'd seen her shake her booty. It was because he'd seen the wrong woman naked. Even someone with her track record in commitment—two words, *married men*—could see Will was a keeper, a stud-muffin with a heart. And she'd thought—well, fantasized—that maybe, maybe if she moved in with Jacob, Will would visit more and more frequently until he realized...

"Can I could fix you something?" Poppy jumped up. "A hot toddy? A hot chocolate?"

"I'm worried about Hannah."

Right. They were going to forge ahead, have the conversation.

"I'll call you from the hospital." Poppy kept her voice bright.

"What if I went and you stayed here, with my dad."

"Hannah's my best friend, Galen's my godson. I have to go."

"But can you drive?" He nodded at her glass. "I can't let you go if you've been drinking."

Normally she would rip into a guy for a comment like that, but from Will it was sweet. Why did he have to be sweet? Bastards were more of her territory. "I'm a big girl, really. I know my limits."

"Man, she was incredible tonight. So strong."

"That's Han. Shit together all the way, but don't be fooled. Inside she's a mess. Galen wrote a poem about it once."

"I know. She doesn't look after herself." He gave a shadow of a smile. "Galen calls her a people pleaser with shitty boundaries."

Poppy screwed the top onto the bottle of Wild Turkey. *Damn it to hell and back.* He didn't just have the hots for her best friend, he'd gone and fallen in love, hadn't he? Well, he'd better be there for Hannah every step; he'd better treat her like the best woman in the world, because she was. And after that shit Inigo, Han deserved…she deserved someone like Will. "On second thought—" Poppy turned. "I don't think I'm safe to drive. Would you go in my place?"

Will leaped up.

"But you've got to promise you'll take care of her and promise you'll deal with Inigo. He's beyond a prima donna. Class A drama queen. I don't want him dicking her around, making things worse. Promise?"

"Promise." Will gave her a dry kiss on the cheek. "You can sleep in my room."

Lie in sheets that had touched his body? *Nuh-uh.* "Nah. I don't sleep much. Prefer the sofa and movies-on-demand. Don't worry about a thing. And I won't drink, I swear. But text me when you get there. Let me…let me know my baby's okay."

"Poppy?"

"Yeah?"

"Thank you."

"*De nada.* Go!" She flicked him away and walked into the powder room to cry alone.

# TWENTY-EIGHT

Anger built. Anger at Galen, for being selfish, for being careless with his life. For having choices Freddie never had. For wanting to die and managing to live.

Hitting the gas, Will tore along a deserted Highway 54 with his windows open. The night whipped around him, heavy with ozone and silent but for a distant rumble of thunder. An apartment complex with a space-for-rent sign shot by and his speedometer wavered around sixty-five. Let the cops pull him over, what did he care? Seventy, he was driving seventy in a forty-five-miles-per-hour zone.

Inigo was probably there by now, offering comfort. Will gripped the wheel tighter. It should be him; he wanted Hannah to need *him*.

A kaleidoscope of sound filled his ears—the roar of pumping blood, the alarm bells of a body feeding off adrenaline. His lungs tightened under some invisible clamp, and his arms started to shake. Was this panic, delayed grief or love?

*Let it be anything but love.*

Love didn't belong in this uproar of death and devastation. How could he be so heartless, so disloyal to Freddie?

Will braked hard. *No.* He would not behave like his mother, behave like Cass. He would not be this out-of-control loser, driving with disregard for the safety of other people. An accident could be only seconds away. He knew better than anyone.

Turning onto Manning Drive, Will followed signs to the emergency department, hurtling into another parent's tragedy while he was slowly choking on his own. He shouldn't be here; he should have gone back to the city weeks ago, not dragged his sorry ass through Teflon-coated procrastination. No matter how many excuses he fed himself about wait lists, there was only one reason he was still here: Hannah.

The unlit road dipped and curved. Tenements of student housing rose into the darkness, each window a square box of orange light. On either side of him, black trees. He turned right. Ahead was a monstrous building with a huge red sign that spelled out Emergency. Will swallowed. He would not think about ambulances, flashing lights and crash scenes. He would not.

He pulled into the parking lot and stopped at the barrier. Tokens? For real? He swung around in his seat and watched two cars drive past him to stop under the concrete overhang. A valet! Thank God. He threw the car into Reverse, squealed toward the hospital entrance and abandoned his car—door open, engine running—by the valet station.

"Sir, wait!" The valet ran after him waving a ticket. "You need this, sir!"

Will took the parking stub and slid it deep in his back pocket. Not that he gave a rat's ass about the Prius—a car was merely a means of travel—but without it, how could he drive Hannah home?

Back toward Highway 54, more thunder rumbled. If it rained he could tell Hannah; she might even be happy. So now he was delusional, thinking a woman could care about the drought while her son lay unconscious in the E.R. Four months out from his own son's death he still didn't care about anything. Except—Will slowed to walk through the glass doors of the emergency department—that was no longer true.

Fluorescent lights buzzed and the intercom called for doctor so and so to go to room whatever. One of the security guys acknowledged him with a nod, not rapid-fire Q and A. Where was the chaos and carnage he'd expected? And where was Hannah?

He moved to the windows that reminded him of bank teller stations. On his left, a large waiting area with a smaller glass antechamber labeled Triage Waiting Room. Hannah was alone in the far corner, curled up in a plastic hospital chair like a teenage girl: legs tucked into her chest, sweatshirt tugged down over her knees.

"Hannah?"

She didn't look up.

He turned back to security, dumped his iPhone and wallet in the gray plastic container and passed through the metal detector. Behind him, a woman started screaming in Spanish. The intercom called for a translator.

Will reclaimed his possessions, then ran into the triage waiting room.

Blood, blood was smeared on her face. Why had no one told her? How could no one see that she needed help?

"Hannah," he said, and rushed forward.

She stood slowly, her eyes red and her cheeks blotched. The intercom announced another page and there was a rhythmic wave of electronic beeps; the Hispanic woman became hysterical.

Yanking up his sweatshirt, he used it to wipe Hannah's cheek. "You have a speck of bl—"

"Is it gone?" Her head fell to his shoulder as Galen's had done an hour earlier. "Tell me it's gone."

"Gone, darling." *Didn't mean to call her that. Really, really didn't mean to call her that.*

Hugging had never come naturally, but he began rocking her the way he'd rocked Freddie after a nightmare. Hannah clutched at him, moving so quickly he almost lost his balance. She said something, but it was muffled.

"I didn't hear you, darling." There it was again—that word.

She raised her head and stared at him. Eye-to-eye, exactly his height. Holding her felt so comfortable, so warm. So easy.

"Your dad?" she said.

Always she thought of other people.

"Poppy's with him. She wanted to come, but I persuaded her to stay. I...I had to see you."

Hannah laid her head back on Will's shoulder. He pulled her into his body and wanted her closer.

"They asked so many questions," she said. "And I couldn't answer them. I don't know what he took, how much. I don't know anything. The most important thing is to figure out the combination of what he took, and I don't know. I don't know. The bag had so few, so few... And they asked about his medical history, and—" she gulped "—they asked about family history."

"Shh," he said softly.

"His vitals are good, they don't have to intubate him, but they need to empty his stomach. Give him charcoal to absorb the drugs. If they're worried about cardiovascular function, he'll go to intensive care." She was talking fast, dumping information. "Psychiatry will do a consultation when he sobers up, when he can talk, but since it was a serious attempt, it's likely he'll be transferred to the psych ward. Voluntarily or— Hospitalization isn't really optional." She clung to him. "He's going back, Will. He's going back."

"Who are you?" said a deep voice.

Will turned, his arms locked around Hannah. Two men stood in front of them, but only one was glowering at him with hard, dark eyes—a broad-shouldered guy who was seriously ripped. Everything about Inigo was crafted with care: the citrus cologne, the graying hair trimmed to perfection like a presidential wannabe, the knit shirt he wore like a second skin, the faded jeans that fit a little too snugly around the groin. Christ, he was looking at another man's package.

Still fastening Hannah to his chest, Will extended a hand. "Will Shepard. I rent your wife's cottage. Sorry, man. I mean, your ex-wife."

"Matt." The other guy, the younger—much younger—one with small, frightened eyes, preempted Inigo and shook Will's hand.

Inigo glared. "You're the one who took Galen rock climbing."

"Will saved our son's life," Hannah said.

An older African-American woman cradling a sleeping child blinked up at Will, then turned to stare at the Tar Heels game on the flat-screen TV in the main waiting room.

"Let's all sit down." Matt touched Inigo's arm, but Inigo shrugged him off.

"Our son could have died, Han. Died. What were you thinking?"

"The rock climbing was my suggestion," Will said.

Inigo ignored him. "You allow Galen out on some testosterone adventure with a stranger and yet you wouldn't let me, his own father, anywhere near the house? You let our son go off on an adventure with this...this person, and twenty-four hours later Galen tries to end his life? You told me you could handle this." He jabbed a finger toward Hannah's face. "You told me you had everything under control." Another jab. "You told me I would make things worse."

*One inch closer with that manicured fingernail, dickhead, and my fist will be crunching into the bridge of your nose.*

"Well, it doesn't get much worse than this," Inigo said.

"Wow, time out." Will raised his hand between Hannah's face and Inigo's finger.

Matt flinched; his glance jumped from Will to Inigo and back again.

"I wasn't aware I asked for your opinion," Inigo said to Will. "In fact, I don't know why you're here. This has nothing to do with you. I want you to go. Leave."

"He's here," Hannah said, "because I want him to be. And that's enough, Inigo. We need to concentrate on helping Galen. Come and sit down, please."

Without warning, Inigo disintegrated into a flood of wails. Heads in both waiting areas turned and Will had a flashback to his mother at the powwow, to that awful feeling of being exposed under a spotlight, front and center stage. Will wanted to pity Inigo, wanted to say, *I know, I understand the terror,* but he was swallowing the urge to scream, *You have no idea how lucky you are. No idea. Your son's been alive for twenty-two years, that's seventeen more than my son. My son will never play on a Little League team, have a first kiss, build the unopened Lego set in his bedroom.*

*And today is the four-month anniversary of his death.*

Hannah stepped away, but it was as if she'd been snatched from him. Without the warmth of her breath on his neck, it was cold, so cold. He rubbed his arms and watched Matt and Hannah settle Inigo into a chair. Then Will claimed the empty chair on Hannah's left side. Reaching for her free hand, he folded his fingers around hers and squeezed. She squeezed back.

Poppy had been right that day at Hawk's Ridge—he made crap decisions. And that simple physical gesture was proof. Both he and Hannah knew he was leaving, and yet by holding her hand, he was blasting open whatever it was that hung in the air between them. Like they both needed an extra layer of emotion right now.

Even on the phone that first night, her voice had triggered a strange high as if someone had spiked his senses with a stimulant. When they met it was that plus the opposite: a sense of calm and well-being. Until the powwow tossed him into the downward spin of lust. Until half an hour earlier when he sat at a traffic light, paralyzed by the pain of love.

He was in the middle of Armageddon, and he was in love.

An old instinct was calling out to be heard, one that had served him well in the past, one that he was trying to ignore.

*Run, Will, run.*

Manhattan had killed Will's night vision. After they left Chapel Hill, the traffic disappeared and the roads retreated into black stillness. The engine hummed; thunder clapped intermittently.

The evening had tethered him and Hannah in a never-to-be-forgotten string of events, and yet they were caught in silence. Silence that stung like razor burn. They had so much to talk about. Or maybe not. How many ways could he say, *I'm sorry?*

Inigo had nailed him with accusations about the climb. The guy was just lashing out, being the overprotective father, but suppose he was on to something? After all, one kid had died on Will's watch. And the whole time he'd been holding Galen in the bathroom—*the whole time*—he'd imagined himself holding Freddie.

Watching for deer, Will glanced into the blockade of trees looming on either side of the car. A buck running out could do serious damage to the biggest big-ass pickup truck. Who knew what it could do to the hood of a Prius? He slowed down and squinted, pulling forward to search for the Nascar bar on the corner of Hannah's road. His seat belt locked, cutting into his chest, pinning him in place.

"Bit farther," Hannah said, her face angled away from him.

It was the first time she'd spoken since leaving the hospital. Galen had been smart enough to take the path of least resistance and go to the psych ward voluntarily. The doc had explained they were lucky to get a bed, since people often had to wait in the E.R. for days, or be transferred to another facility. Hannah had remarked, her voice cold, that there was nothing lucky about knowing your son was returning to a locked ward. She had remained calm, poised and distant, while Inigo had bawled into Matt's chest. If only Hannah would do that now—lose her shit. Hysterics and tantrums Will could handle. Withdrawal was an unknown monster.

A streak of lightning lit up the road ahead.

"Man, that was close," Will said

The last few fronts had rolled in blind, without rain, and recent pop-up thunderstorms had split around Saponi Mountain as if they were skirting the edge of a black hole. If it rained, would Hannah talk?

The wind picked up and low-growing branches snapped back and forth under the power lines. As he clicked on the turn signal, pellets of rain fired at the windshield with the force of hail.

"How about that? It's raining." Could he sound any more

stupid? He half expected Hannah to reply with, *Well, duh,* but she didn't even move.

"We're home," he said. More five-star inanity.

They bumped along the driveway and rain lashed the car. No rain for months and then a monsoon. Will shivered. If his mom were still alive, she'd be dancing barefoot in the mud, doing the escaped lunatic pirouette.

He parked as close as he could to Hannah's porch. "I've got an umbrella in the trunk—"

But Hannah was out of the car and walking away. Too beat to protest, Will flopped over the steering wheel. He would check on his dad and then grab a few hours' sleep before taking Hannah back to the hospital, as promised. After that? Pack up and return to New York with his dad.

Watching Hannah and Inigo ground themselves in happier memories had led to this decision. Recriminations vanished the moment they began to guide each other through their living, breathing family album with remember-when-Galen-did-this moments. The same had been true of him and his dad with Freddie's trip.

Hannah and Inigo faced a long recovery with Galen. They needed to come together, and so did he and his dad. It was time to retreat into the family shell, to think small and close ranks. It was time to salvage happy memories before there were none left, before his dad forgot his grandson's life as well as his death.

Since leaving New York, Will had repeatedly questioned his behavior, his lie. Not anymore. Lying to his dad had been the right decision, and so was taking him back to the city. Who knew how they would manage, but family was family, and the old man was not ending up in some shithole wearing Depends and being spoon-fed. His dad had once taken care of Will, and now the situation would reverse. Surely that was the natural order in normal families.

And his feelings for Hannah? Irrelevant. He'd left love behind before and survived. He could do so again. Decision made—New York or bust.

Hannah knocked on his car window and Will was out in the downpour before he could draw breath. Pathetic, but she held his strings. Needed to cut those, too.

"Come in?" she said.

He nodded and they ran for the porch.

The dogs welcomed them inside; Rosie went straight to Hannah and shadowed her as she slipped off her clogs. Will unlaced his Converse and lined them up nearby. Then he stood, playing with his watchband. Hannah began flicking off switches one by one, throwing the living room into darkness. He should have noticed, should have turned them all off before he went to the hospital. Should have done that one small thing for her, just as now he should talk, set the tone, do something guy-ish. If he suggested changing out of her wet clothes, would she think he was taking advantage?

"I'll ask Poppy if she can stay with Dad while I drive you back to the hospital." Will shook rain from his hair. "Any idea what time you want to go?"

"Visiting hours are flexible on the ward, but I can drive myself. You concentrate on your dad. I'm sure all the disruption has unsettled him."

If he didn't drive her to the hospital, they could be gone by the time she came home. No explanations necessary.

"Do you think you'll be able to sleep?" he said.

"No. I'm exhausted but wide-awake. You?"

"The same."

Hannah started walking toward her bedroom and stopped. "I can't be alone. Stay with me?"

Did she mean stay with me in my bed? Or stay on the floor by my bed? Maybe she meant stay and talk with me. Climbing was so much easier than getting a foothold with a woman. What did an older, more experienced woman expect when she invited a man to "stay with me"?

She didn't feel like an older woman, but she had a way of processing the world that made her seem so in control. They were both dealing with tragedy, but she was doing so as a full-fledged grown-up; he was doing it as a full-fledged screw-up.

Back to basics: *stay with me* didn't mean standing in the living room like a moron.

She opened a closet door in the hallway, pulled out two white towels and offered one to Will. He declined.

"Would you like me to sleep on the sofa? Stay until I know you're asleep?" *Inspired, Will.*

She had started toweling her hair but paused to throw him a puzzled look. Okay, so clearly he'd missed some clues. Older women—whole new game with separate ground rules.

"No. I meant stay with me in my bedroom."

"Right," he mumbled, and followed her. Did she just make a pass?

"Please don't think I'm some desperate middle-aged woman making a pass."

"Never crossed my mind."

"Yes, it did," she said. "You're a crap liar."

Crap decision maker, crap liar, crap friend to Galen, crap everything right now.

"You don't have to explain," he said. "I'm not sure I could be alone, either." *Although for reasons you can't possibly guess.*

Before he could stop himself, Will glanced up the staircase. Suicide cleanup was one task a parent shouldn't have to face. Something else Galen had thought through. When

Hannah was asleep, Will would find her cleaning supplies and take care of it.

The dogs lay down on the floor surrounding the bed, but he hovered in the doorway. Hannah closed the window, then disappeared into the adjacent bathroom.

A dark stain on the natural-colored carpet suggested she hadn't shut the window in time. Sleeping on the ground floor with her window open was so dangerous. Almost as dangerous as him joining her in the room with the large, unmade bed.

Strange, he would have pegged her for an early-morning bed-maker, not a woman who left domestic tasks undone. Or was she in bed when he'd barged in hours earlier? He barely remembered the first part of the evening. Blood gushing out of a gaping wound was an effective mind-wipe. He'd researched and written worse, but witnessing the gore in real time, with someone he cared about...

The room was white and sparsely decorated, with a pine rocking chair in the corner. A turquoise see-through bra was draped over the back.

Definitely not leaving the safety of the door frame, then.

A strip of small spotlights illuminated a gallery of black-and-white photographs on the far wall. The still lifes of sassafras, sweetgum, tulip poplars and red oak drew him in. When he glanced down, he was standing over the stain in the middle of the carpet. He was inside her bedroom.

Will moved closer to peer at a panorama. It was taken from the tower on Occoneechee Mountain.

"Who's the photographer?" he called toward the bathroom door.

"Me."

Every time he thought he had her figured out, she surprised him. Finding the real Hannah was like exploring an exotic locale without a AAA guide. He stared at another stunning print, this one of a cloudless sky through the spiky needles of a loblolly pine.

"You're really good."

"Thanks."

He turned to see Hannah sitting on the bed in her white dressing gown.

"My clothes were soaked. Your jeans?"

"Fine," he answered quickly. God help him, she'd better be wearing something under that robe. He pictured the tattoo weaving toward her right breast and gulped.

Thunder boomed and rain rattled against the window. His heart was galloping all over the place. Did she expect him to sit on the bed next to her or in the rocker with the lacy bra?

"You could sell these," he said, gesturing to the photographs.

"Why? I take them for me. Only me."

*Admirable.*

"This one—" he pointed at the panorama "—reminds me of quiet moments soloing."

"Soloing?"

"Climbing unroped and alone. It's how I gain control when my life feels as if it's being dragged off by a herd of wild horses." He was jabbering, but the image had just popped up like spam.

"You don't have a cigarette, do you?" Hannah said.

Will shook his head. "I would never have pegged you for a smoker."

"I haven't been for twenty-five years."

"Really?"

"Is that so hard to believe?"

Was there a wrong answer to that question? "You just don't seem the type. I can't imagine you doing anything unhealthy."

"That's because of what I do, not because of who I am."

She fell back on the bed and spread out her arms. One hand was balled up in a tight fist.

He had a flash-thought about getting laid, which was beyond sick. Maybe he should just leave.

"I don't really have my act together," she said. "I make everything up as I go along."

"Hey, that's my line."

"I don't think I can go through this again." She raised the heel of her clenched hand to her forehead. "I lost my mother, I lost my father. I can't lose my son. I can't…"

He was across the room in two strides and then sitting next to her. Two damaged parents, just trying to drag themselves into another day. Lightning flashed in the space between them.

"You'd be surprised," he said, "what you can get through when you have to."

"Are you speaking as a parent?" She lowered her arm and stared at him, dry-eyed.

Tonight of all nights, he couldn't talk about Freddie. An explosion of rain pounded against the window like the rat-a-tat of automatic gunfire. Thunder crashed overhead, and two of the dogs scrambled to get under the bed. Will fell back into her white comforter, letting it swallow him.

"Your father talks about Freddie nonstop, and yet you never mention him. Why is that, Will?" she said.

Will closed his eyes. *Tell her.* It would be so easy to tell her the truth, but he couldn't, not after everything she'd been through tonight. Besides, he had made the decision, minutes earlier, to keep the lie alive, to keep Freddie alive. To do what he believed was best for his dad.

He rolled his head toward her and opened his eyes. She had propped herself up onto her elbows. She was so close. Close enough that he could feel her body next to his: thigh-to-thigh, chest-to-chest, heart-to-heart. Close enough that he could kiss her. A light kiss on the lips, as chaste as the kiss he'd given Ally in kindergarten, right before she'd bitten him and left the tiny scar on his bicep—the wound of his first, and until now only, love.

"I'm sorry." Hannah stared out into the room. "I don't know why I asked that. I understand that you don't like to talk about your son, and God knows I don't want to talk about mine."

"We don't have to talk," he said.

She opened her palm and revealed a familiar orange capsule. "Matt gave it to me, to help me sleep. But I don't want to be drugged—in case Galen needs me."

"My dad takes those," Will said. "They're pretty innocuous. They just relax you. I gave him two earlier in the evening, and he still woke up when the ambulance came."

She stared at the pill.

"Take it, get some sleep. I'll listen for the phone, and I promise to wake you if there's any news."

She raised her hand to her mouth, tossed back her head and swallowed.

He sat up.

"Wait, where are you going?" She grabbed his arm and her fingernails dug deep.

"Just to the sofa, so you can sleep in peace."

"No! No!" She burst into tears. "Please don't leave me. Please don't leave me alone."

He reached out and wiped under her eyes. "Hey. It's okay. What if we just lie here, together? And pretend nothing exists outside this room."

"I'd like that," she said.

*I'll hold you while you sleep,* he used to tell Freddie.

"I'll hold you while you sleep."

★ ★ ★

The storm rumbled through, but the rain continued for another hour. Soft rain that seeped into the soil and fed the roots. Already it was the day after. The day after the four-month anniversary of Freddie's death, the day after Galen's attempted suicide. This dark morning should feel like a beginning, but it felt like a hole in time. A gap.

*Mind the gap* was the warning he'd heard over the intercom the last time he'd traveled on the London Underground. *Mind the gap.*

Hannah was breathing in a soft rhythm. His right arm, wrapped around her body, was numb, but he couldn't move. He wouldn't get up and clean the bathroom before dawn. That way if she woke up, she wouldn't be scared and alone in the dark.

He planned out his day—or rather, his escape. His stuff would take twenty minutes to pull together, his dad's not much longer. And all the boxes from Hawk's Ridge were stacked and ready to go. He would talk to his dad, then pack up the car, then call a cleaning service. They could be on the road before midafternoon.

He made mental lists and thought about everything and anything except for the woman curled up asleep in his arms.

Hannah shifted and he buried his face in her hair. Lavender, she smelled of lavender. Maybe some things weren't meant to have a future. Maybe they could just lie here, together, and never move. Maybe this was enough. Raised on tales of heroic acts committed in the name of devotion, he'd always believed in love that endured, love that never died. After Ally spurned him, he'd convinced himself he would never—could never—love again. And then he'd stumbled into someone else's family crisis and reverted to that little boy who believed in the curse of happily-ever-after.

He kissed the top of her head. A stolen kiss. She would never know. He wasn't taking advantage, being a douche bag. He just wanted one memento to carry with him after he left.

Hannah's head moved up into the crook of his neck, and then kept moving. Her lips brushed his with a sweet, warm kiss, a sleepy statement of reassurance. Nothing that screamed sex, but his body hummed like a tuning fork.

Her hand fumbled with his zipper, and he reached down to stop her. She didn't want this. She was drugged, half-asleep, seeking escape. And he wasn't taking advantage of—

She kissed him again. Nothing chaste about the second kiss. It felt like hunger, like raw need. A primal yell stuck in his throat, and in that fragment of distraction, she tore at his sweatshirt, yanking it over his head.

Will grabbed at her robe, tugged it open and pulled her back against his chest until her heart beat into his. The perfect echo. He should slow down, create a golden moment, one that would last forever. But as his mouth found hers, his mind ripped into a thousand sparks. He was light-headed, dizzy, smashed on desire, and then he was spinning outside his body, no longer human. Drunken sex had always been his preference, but this? High on dopamine, he couldn't figure out where he ended and she began. Didn't want this; didn't want to need another person this much. And then, he had no thought at all.

Gently repositioning her, Will slipped out of the bed and watched Hannah sleep. How could he walk away from this woman?

He had given in to mind-numbing sex without speaking a word, without saying *I love you*, without even stopping to ask, "Contraception?" And yet, he had no regret. Months of blackness had retreated into the corner. Soon enough he would, once again, be alone with his grief. But right now, it was just him and Hannah.

Raindrops from the night's storm were splattered on the screen beyond her window, and the first streaks of dawn filtered across Saponi Mountain. He closed her curtains, shutting out the day.

He grabbed his boxers and, stepping over Hannah's dressing gown, tiptoed out of the room and into the kitchen. It didn't take him long to find what he needed. When it came to cleaning supplies, Hannah was unsurprisingly logical. Balancing his load—a mop, a bucket, bleach, rubber gloves and a roll of paper towels—he crept up the stairs and headed for the bathroom.

The door was wide-open, as he'd left it. A sour, rancid odor kicked him in the stomach. In his writing, he described the smell of blood as metallic, but this was more like rotting flesh. And urine, he could smell urine. Had Galen pissed himself?

Entering the bathroom, Will kept his eyes on the window as he squatted down, dropped his arm into cold, bloody water and pulled the plug. A few hours earlier, he had looked out of that window and seen flashing lights down below. An image sprung, of emergency vehicles surrounding a crash scene in New York. Had Freddie peed into his car seat in those final moments? *Jesus.* He ran to the toilet, flipped up the seat and puked.

Sinking to his knees, Will clung to the toilet bowl. How had he conned himself into thinking he could help Hannah when he could barely help himself? Pushing up to standing, Will looked at the blood pooled on the floor and splattered across the mirror. He would scrub until nothing remained but the scent of bleach, and then he would shower off the stink of attempted suicide and return to Hannah's bed. For just a little while longer.

# TWENTY-NINE

Hannah rested her head against the door. Walking back into her bedroom could be as devastating as waking up earlier and facing two crushing memories: her son wanted to die, and she had forced herself on his friend.

Her son wanted to die. And in the past hour, she had discovered that the only person with the power to save him was the guy lying naked in her bed.

She breathed through the impulse to retch. The stench of bleach permeated the house, but it could never erase the memory burned into her mind.

*My son wanted to die.*

She turned the doorknob.

Will sat up, and the sheet fell to his groin. Images besieged her, images of stripping off his clothes and pinning him to her bed. Using him the same way she'd used the temazepam. To forget that her son wanted to *die*.

Shame settled: cold, heavy, suffocating.

"Hey."

"Hey."

Will looked younger than ever, whereas she'd aged overnight. For the first time, she was aware life was half-over, not half-begun.

Keeping hold of the doorknob, she eased the door closed behind her and leaned into it. "Thank you. For cleaning the bathroom."

"You're welcome."

"Last night—I'm…I'm just so sorry."

He twisted the sheet, then untwisted it. "You regret sleeping with me?"

"No, just the sex part."

"Oh."

"I mean, it wasn't…that wasn't me."

"Demonic possession?"

"A break with reality."

"It was pretty intense." He blushed. "We didn't even stop to talk contraception."

"Tubes tied. After Liam was born."

She broke eye contact first. "What kind of a mother has sex while her son—"

"Hannah," he said softly. "There's nothing wrong with what happened between us."

"How can you say that?" She glanced up. "There's a world of wrong with what happened! I'll *never* forgive myself for being so irresponsible, so selfish, so amoral."

"I share the blame. I didn't exactly stop you."

"I wish you had. I wish life had stopped twenty-four hours ago. I wish today was yesterday and the future was still unlived."

"Come here." He started to reach for her, but she couldn't risk moving. Couldn't risk a repeat performance of the night before. She could fix this, if they could just forget what had happened in her bed.

His hands jiggled in the air. "Not to…you know…just to cuddle. Last night—you and me—we were good. Together, I mean. Wow." He smiled. "Stellar communication from someone who's spent ten years on the *New York Times* bestseller list."

"Nothing good can come from last night, Will. Nothing."

He dug his hands into his hair, combing it back from his forehead. "All I know is that last night we needed each other. You told me things happen for a reason. What if you and me—*us*—was one of those things that was meant to happen?"

*Was,* not *is.* Already she was his past.

"How can it be, Will? You're a celebrity author who lives in a skyscraper and dates gorgeous young things twenty years my junior. I have two grown sons and a quiet life in the middle of nowhere. You go to charity galas. I stay home and read."

"I love to stay home and read, too, and I've only been to one charity gala, with my ex."

"It's irrelevant, Will. We're on different tracks, heading in different directions. We need to forget last night, concentrate on the only thing that matters right now—saving my son." She paused. "My suicidal son."

She had finally branded her son. But this wasn't labeling, this was staring down truth. This was marching up to the enemy and saying, *I've seen your face, I know who you are and you will not win. You will not claim my son as well as my father.* She was going to fight for her son, fight for his life, and right now the only thing that mattered was convincing Will to help.

He squinted at her alarm clock. "Eleven o'clock? Why didn't you wake me?"

"I thought you should sleep. Poppy said she could stay with your dad as long as you needed."

"What time are you going to the hospital?"

"I'm not. Galen refused to see me. He doesn't want to see

Inigo, either. The only person he wants to see—" she stared at Will "—is you."

"Me? Why would he want to see me?"

"Because you're his friend. And right now, I'm the enemy." She opened the door. "I'm fixing breakfast, so why don't you get dressed and join us. Then I'll pack a bag of clothes for you to take to Galen. He's going to call your cell phone with the password for the day. You can't speak to him without it."

Will was wasting time. He needed to get moving; he needed to get to the hospital; he needed to show Galen he was not alone. That he was loved.

"Don't ask me to do this, please," Will said.

"I'm not asking you. My suicidal son is."

"That's even worse." He swung his legs around and, jumping out of bed, stood before her, naked.

She kept her eyes on his face. "You're the only person who's reached my son since he came home. Please, Will. I need you to do this for Galen's sake."

"I can't," he whispered.

"So Galen has to suffer because I made a terrible mistake?"

"Do you honestly believe that's what's going on here?"

"I don't know. You tell me."

"This isn't about us, Hannah. Can we just leave it at that?"

"No!" She threw up her hands. There was no time for anger; she had to stay calm. "Okay, okay. Let's be adults here and forget that I forced myself on you while my son was fighting for his life. Forget that we—" she shielded her eyes "—forget everything but this. Galen needs you."

"I'll do anything else for you, Hannah. Anything."

"I'm not asking for anything else."

"Please. You have to trust me when I tell you I cannot help your son."

"Why?" She folded her arms and waited, but Will stayed

silent. "Let me guess, because you have to get back to your life in the city?"

"Yes, no, I mean—"

Hannah turned and left, because what could she say? The only words that filled her mind spoke of humiliation for screwing—quite literally—with the one thing that mattered to Galen: his friendship with Will. But it was irrelevant, because if he wasn't going to help Galen, then she was done with Will Shepard.

Will grabbed the edge of the sheet and tugged it off the bed. Tucking in the ends, he hopped after her like some comic-strip mummy. "Come back, let me explain! Darling, please."

He stumbled, stubbing his toe. "Damn it, Hannah—"

The sheet began to unravel. *What the hell.* He ditched it and jogged down the hallway.

However she phrased it, she was offering him the parental reins. He'd never wanted to be a parent and yet, for a while, he'd allowed himself to believe fatherhood would be his greatest achievement. But history had a nasty habit of repeating itself. And like his mom, he had proved to be incapable of looking after his son. No way could he fail someone else's son; no way could he stick around to see if Galen finished the job.

"Hannah—" He rushed into the kitchen. "Come back and—"

"Willie!" His dad pushed up from one of Hannah's pine chairs. "No sleepin' naked with the womenfolk around. Cover yourself, son." He handed Will an oven mitt. Poppy, over by the sink, was holding a dish towel that would have covered more of his groin area, but she seemed reluctant to share. She winked, then craned her neck for a better view.

Hannah turned her back on Will, picked up a metal whisk

and began beating a bowl of raw eggs. Up Saponi Mountain, a hawk screeched. Another hawk answered, and for a moment, a soulful duet resonated around the kitchen.

Will shuffled toward his dad in a parody of a straight dance—the warrior dance that was slow and graceful with no fancy moves—and felt stupid as shit. He grabbed the oven mitt.

"Thanks." Great, now his dad was looking after him.

Hannah cranked and cranked the pepper mill. "I'm fixing everyone breakfast," she said. "If you want to join us, Will, I suggest you take your father's advice and get dressed."

The look she threw over her shoulder shriveled his dick to nothing. He swallowed back a *Yes, ma'am.*

"Ah, c'mon, Han," Poppy said. "Us girls gotta get our kicks wherever we can."

Spontaneous evaporation would have been a blessing.

"Hannah, I—" *I what? I love you, but I can't be there for your son?*

"Yes?" She flipped around with the whisk in her hand, and for one brief moment, he wondered if she might hit him with it.

The phone rang and Hannah snatched it up. "Andrew? It's okay, take a deep breath and start again." She paused. "Scarlet hasn't eaten in how long? Okay. Keep her comfortable, and I'll be there within an hour."

"Really?" He didn't like his tone, but now he was ticked off on Galen's behalf. This was the kind of stunt she'd pulled on his first night home. Had she learned nothing? "Your son's in the hospital, and you're going to look after a cat?"

"I'm going to do my job, since my son refuses to see me." Hannah placed the phone back on the cradle and avoided eye contact. "He does, however, want to see *you.*"

Will tossed the oven mitt onto the counter and ignored

Poppy's comment of, "Nice bod. Got yourself a keeper there, Han."

"Galen's right," Will said. "You're a people pleaser with shitty boundaries."

"Now, son. None of that language around the ladies."

"Yeah? Tell someone who gives a fuck. I'm going to the hospital."

Something clattered to the counter, but Will didn't turn to find out what. He stormed into the hallway and slammed Hannah's bedroom door. That, without a doubt, was the harshest morning-after scenario ever. Yes, he'd woken up in the wrong bed before and summoned charm he didn't know he possessed to extricate himself, but this was different. He didn't want to be the one leaving; he didn't want Hannah to wish him gone. Clearly, she did. In her eyes, he was little more than a *terrible mistake*.

A sound came from her bedroom floor—a voice message alert on his phone. He snatched up his jeans and pulled his phone out of the back pocket. One voice mail.

"Call the ward," Galen said, and rattled off a number. "They'll ask for the code word. Flower. Don't tell Mom."

Another secret to keep from Hannah.

Will sat on the edge of her unmade bed and stared at his iPhone, at the blank screen, at his reflection in the black mirror.

If he didn't go, if he bailed on a friend in need without even saying goodbye, what did that make him? He could still head back to New York—that part of his plan didn't have to change—but he didn't have to go today. He could sit with Galen, be there for him—since Hannah wasn't going to fight for the right. If that were his son, he would be banging on the locked doors, demanding entry. Demanding Freddie not be alone....

Will glanced up at the framed photos. Beautiful pictures without people. Studies in loneliness. He would go, but not as Hannah's substitute, not as a parental figure. He would go as a friend.

And tomorrow he would head back to New York where he was known yet unknown. Where those who crossed his life—the woman at Starbucks, the building doorman—smiled and asked how he was doing without caring that he answered by rote.

Twelve years ago he'd gone to New York to lose himself in crowds, to find anonymity, not to expand his social network. And it had worked. Ask him to identify any of his neighbors in a lineup, and Will would flunk. These days, people knew the name, the face, the P.R. propaganda—everything but the darkness of his true story. In New York, he could be whomever the hell he wanted. And Hannah would never have to see him again.

Will threw the phone onto the bed. *On my way, dude.*

# THIRTY

"Will Shepard here for Galen Jones," Will shouted at the intercom. And tried not to imagine a phalanx of hidden cameras staring back. For reasons unknown, he also saw infrared lasers.

"I know the code word."

*Lame.* He was trying to prove he was worthy of entry just because he could say *flower,* the word that acted like an unlimited calling card for the mental hospital. Galen once told him everything you said on a locked ward made you sound insane. Did that apply to visitors, too?

The door buzzed open. Ten feet ahead of him—another set of doors.

His chest tightened, and his right hand began to tremble like he had the DTs—*delirium tremens* aka *withdrawal shakes. Research, novel eight.* He would never survive confinement, never function as a shut-in. Every ounce of control you had was ripped away the moment someone put you in a room and turned the key in the lock. How could you breathe if you couldn't see the sky? How could you breathe if you couldn't feel sunlight on your skin? But this wasn't about his psycho-baggage, about his crazy childhood, about his claustrophobia—Will rubbed his hands down his thighs to erase the evidence of sweat—this was about Galen.

The second set of doors buzzed open and a young woman welcomed him. Pretty. Normal-looking. Will walked forward, and the tightness in his chest loosened.

"I'm the ward clerk." She offered a smile and a clipboard. "I need you to sign in, Mr. Shepard. And ask if you have any contraband items."

Contraband items? Did he look like a criminal? "Car key, wallet, iPhone." He reached into his pockets and pulled out the offending items.

Another smile.

"And clothes from his mom." He handed over the bag, then signed his name.

*Think of this as research, Will.*

"Galen's in the day room," she said. "I'll take you to him."

"He's not in a padded cell?"

"This isn't *One Flew Over the Cuckoo's Nest,* you know. We encourage patients to get up, move about, engage with others."

The young woman turned and headed down the hallway. Will fell into line behind her, trying not to feel as if he were attempting to navigate a straight line on a listing boat. A door slammed, and he jumped.

"I gather you're representing the family?" she said.

"Yeah." *No.*

"It's good that he has someone—not just for now but for when he gets out. So many people have to go through this alone."

*Way too much information. I'm here to say goodbye, not to be his recovery guide.*

They passed a group of people in a side room. All in street clothes, not a straitjacket in sight. *Interesting.*

The day room—thirty-by-thirty?—was airy, quiet and comfortable-looking with a microwave and an ice machine. Outside, two guys in jeans were playing Ping-Pong on the porch. A stunning view of the town lay beyond the shatter-proof glass.

Galen was slumped on a modular sofa, asleep and wearing his purple hospital gown. *Research, novel six, E.R. patients who are a danger to themselves or others—or in danger of wandering off, like Dad—get the purple gowns.*

Despite everything, Hannah had thought ahead, had known to send in clothes. Even in the worst trauma, she kept moving, kept thinking and acting as a parent. If he had anyone left to parent, Hannah would be Will's role model. Except for the whole putting-work-first thing. He needed to remember that so he could stay angry. Anger would make it easier to leave.

A nurse walked by. "Hi, just checking on Galen." Another smile.

Will wasn't sure how to respond, so he jerked his chin in greeting.

He grabbed a chair and tried to pull it across the floor, but it refused to move. Seriously? The furniture was bolted down? Easing himself onto the sofa, he sat next to Galen. Should he touch him, take his hand? Christ, he looked like a plague victim. So pale and his hair all matted. Maybe it was good that his mother couldn't see him. A lifetime of conversations un-lived with Freddie raced through his mind: the first shaving lesson, the first girl talk, the first conversation about college.

"Galen?" Was this like a coma case, when you should talk to the patient, tell him about the minutiae of your stupid day? "Hey, dude. It's Will. I got your message, decided to drop by."

Outside the Ping-Pong ball bounced—*pop, pop, pop*—then stopped.

"I read some of your poems. Loved them. You've got to start writing again, when you...you know."

Another patient got up and shuffled out of the space; someone at the nurses' station coughed. They were alone except for a family grouping near the far wall. The mother figure was in tears.

"Your mom—" Will gulped back the image of Hannah sleeping, her hair fanning out on the pillow next to him. How would it feel to wake to that scene every morning? "I know she won't come and visit until you ask for her, but she's desperate to see you. You're lucky, to have a mom like Hannah. She loves you more than anything."

Still nothing.

"I, um, I have to say goodbye, Galen. I'm going back to the city. I walked out on everything up there. Got to get back. Taking Dad with me. But when you leave here, I hope you'll come visit." He meant it, too.

He reached out to stroke Galen's head, then snatched his hand back. Suppose Galen thought he was being patronizing, or worse, parental? And what of the emotional connection between caring for this young man and caring for his mother? Nothing happened in isolation. The butterfly effect of falling in love in your thirties. Making love with Hannah had been an oasis of peace in the middle of chaos, but his feelings for her were also an integral part of that chaos, woven through everything. He had fallen in love because of—not despite— the suicidal son and the senescent dad.

"I don't want to leave you. Or your mom." And yet he was planning to do just that. "But I'm...I'm in bad shape right now. It's not fair to anyone if I stay. There's personal stuff no one knows about. Stuff I need to figure out, you know? And your mom—" Will sighed. "I think I'm in love with your mom. Does that freak you out? Or maybe you guessed. Maybe not. I'm a pro at hiding my shit. And you, I never meant to let you in. But I did."

Will remembered the fear that had punched him when he'd lost sight of Galen on the rock, the fear that had stopped his breath the moment he'd catapulted through the bathroom door and seen blood. There was nothing tenuous about his feelings for this young man. "What you think matters. Don't assume the worst of me, when you find out I've gone, buddy. Okay?"

Galen licked his lips, then stretched his neck to force down a swallow. "Water?"

"Sure." Will sprang into action, pouring water from a plastic jug on the nearby table.

"Here." He slipped his arm under Galen, helping him forward. The pillow wedged behind Galen felt scratchy—polyester, not cotton.

Galen swallowed slowly, and Will eased his head back down.

"I didn't plan to be here today."

"I know, dude. And I'm sorry, but can you blame me, not your mom? She just wanted to protect you. Keep you safe. That stuff she said last night, about being a parent—all true."

Galen said nothing.

"You going to try and kill yourself again?" Might as well ask.

"That's the big question of the day," Galen said. "They want to know, too—keep asking about my suicide ideation."

"And?"

"Undecided." Galen paused. "Your son's young, right?"

"Five." Will stared up at the ceiling. *Five for all eternity.*

"Be a while, then, before you have to…" Galen closed his eyes.

"Deal with this kind of crap?"

"Yeah."

Will fingered the Band-Aid covering the cut on his right palm, the mark of his first clumsy grab for the scalpel as he'd cleaned out the bath. Cold air rattled through the overhead vent and the world shrank to two guys sitting in a waiting room. Blood brothers who had visited hell and created a sacred bond of bare honesty. The only authentic relationship he had right now, and it was with a double suicide survivor.

"I'm not a parent anymore. I haven't been for four months and sixteen hours. My son is five, was five, will always be five. He'll never see six."

Galen blinked slowly, clearly fighting the haze of meds. "He's autistic?"

"I wish."

"You mean—worse?"

"Yeah."

"Like dead worse?"

"Yeah."

He couldn't say the words out loud. Hearing someone else speak them was surreal enough. In the past month, Ally and his publicist were the only people he'd interacted with who knew Freddie was dead, but it hadn't been discussed. And in that month, he'd allowed himself to believe the fairy dust, to think, *What if?*

"That's why you understood how I felt." Galen's eyelids flickered. "But your dad, he doesn't know."

"Knew but forgot, and I couldn't find the strength to repeat the news. I'd like to pretend I did it for some altruistic reason, but I played along because it was easier. Do you know how hard it is to tell a grandparent that he's outlived his grandson, to then watch as your six-foot-tall father falls to his knees and sobs, to watch as he's restrained and sedated? Nobody would want to relive that."

"Pretending your son's alive…that's depraved, even by my standards."

Galen had a point. "I never expected my dad to get so caught up in the whole thing, and then it was too late to tell him the truth. But in some strange way, it's been good. Given us both a reason to live."

"You're not planning on disillusioning him, are you?"

"Can't."

"And I thought I was messed up…."

"Guess we're a club of two." Will smiled. "The messed-up writer and the suicidal poet. You'll keep my secret, right?"

Galen nodded slowly, but it wasn't enough. Will needed more of an endorsement, even if his confidant was sedated.

"I'm living in this gray area where the rules of truth are irrelevant. Last night Dad thought the ambulances had come for my mom. She's been dead for four years. A month from now he might not remember she ever existed. Why take the time he has left and force him to relive the bad stuff? With a handful of false memories, I can erase the horror. I can replace it with joy. I realize that makes me sound as if I have a God complex, but I'm just trying to get both of us through. You do understand, don't you?"

"Yes."

"And you understand why I have to leave?"

Galen nodded.

"You need your parents, Galen, and they need you. They're terrified. You've got to let them in. You've got to deal with this as a family."

"Mom promised I wouldn't have to come back to a locked ward."

"And you promised you were in contact with your therapist. That makes you guys even." Will paused. "Can I tell your mom she can visit tomorrow?"

"I guess."

The Ping-Pong players came back inside and shuffled past.

"How're you feeling?"

"Like my head's stuffed with cotton balls. Like all I want to do is sleep. Like I was ready to die and failed. Again."

"Want me to leave?"

"No. Stay." Galen closed his eyes. "I've got to warn you, though, they check on me constantly. They'll probably try and drag you in. They want me *engaged*. Keep talking about all these groups I have to go to. They keep you busy in here." He gave an ugly laugh. "Will?"

"Yeah?"

"I'm sorry—about your son. I bet you were a good dad."

"I tried to be."

"I tried to be a good son. Didn't work out too well for me, either." Galen rolled his head toward the window. "You should tell Mom. About your son."

"She's not talking to me right now."

"Give her a hug. She likes hugs."

*Been there, done that, plus a whole lot more.*

"Tell me a story." Galen's voice had grown sluggish.

Will held the words inside for a moment. *Tell me a story, Daddy.*

"Fiction's a dry well for me these days," Will said. "But I'll tell you a real story. About growing up poor. About growing up surrounded by whispers of identity. The Occaneechi tribe didn't earn state recognition until 2002, but we all knew we had native ancestry. My dad told me when I was a little kid, just as my granddaddy told him. A family secret passed down through the generations. 'Shhh, don't tell anyone. You're an

Indian.'" Indan, if he were being honest. No *i*. Or Yesah, the people. But genealogy was for guys who cared. "My life started with a secret, and the secrets grew.

"I was a half-caste kid who always felt like an outsider—part white trash, part Native American, smaller and smarter than I wanted to be. Only time I felt like me was when I was running wild on Occoneechee Mountain or losing myself in the world of make-believe, like my mom. There was a time when that horrified me, when I thought I was crazy, too. So much of this crap is genetic, you know? Dad and I covered up her madness, and the three of us lived in shadows, pretending. Making excuses. Living empty lives of denial. I'm a thirty-four-year-old guy who doesn't know how to love. How's that for a sick cycle of dysfunction?

"At some point, I told myself I no longer cared about my mom, about her craziness. That was a lie, too. I left home, planned to never come back, but every day I circled her crap in my writing. I've spent the past ten years hanging out with fictional psychos."

"And now you're hanging out in a locked psych ward."

"Yeah, how about that?"

Galen slipped into sleep, and Will decided to stay. He would watch over Galen for the rest of the day and report to Hannah that her son was safe. This time tomorrow she would be sitting here and he would be on his way back to his apartment in the sky. Not home, never home, because he didn't have a home. But back to the world he'd constructed to keep him sane.

# THIRTY-ONE

While Will had been cocooned in the world of mental patients, clouds had rolled in, lowering the sky, threatening to obliterate dusk. Barely five o'clock, but already it felt like night. The distant *whop-whop-whop* of a helicopter drew closer. Rotating blades thumped and sliced through the air, creeping toward the dogwood parking deck. Medevac for an accident victim or transportation for a donor organ. Was the helicopter carrying death or a second chance at life? There was a time when the sound of every emergency vehicle triggered his imagination. Now it just opened the sinkhole of grief.

The pain started in his chest and radiated up into his jaw, into his teeth, filling his mouth with a silent shriek. The helicopter whirred overhead, each *whop* rattling through his body and shaking his brain inside his skull. Will closed his eyes and covered his ears. How could he keep moving forward when the clock on his desk had stopped at 8:30 p.m. on July 1?

He ate, he showered, he pretended to write, he pretended to sleep. The only thing that had brought meaning in the past four months was an interlude of sex that had, apparently, caused nothing but shame and regret. *A terrible mistake.*

The drone of the helicopter faded, replaced by the hum of five-o'clock traffic. Husbands and wives returning home to their lives after a day of work. Home where they would reconnect with their kids, walk the dog, open the mail. Eat dinner with people they loved or pretended to love. Home—the place normal people retreated to at the end of a day.

In his pocket, his phone rang. Someone found him, no matter where he hid. He was always connected to others through text messages, email, social media.… With a long, slow breath, he answered the call.

"Mr. Shepard?" Female, voice unknown.

"This is Will."

"Thelma Pickering from Azalea Court. I'm delighted to tell you an apartment just opened up." She didn't sound delighted. "And since your father is at the top of our waiting list, we can move him in at your earliest convenience."

"You mean someone died."

Ms. Pickering cleared her throat with a fussy little *ahem.* "That's typically the way this happens, Mr. Shepard."

"Sorry. That's great, just great. I mean, great for my dad, not for the poor bastard who… Can I get back to you?"

"If you're no longer interested, we do have other families—"

"No, no. I'm interested, very interested. It's just that I'm in the middle of a family crisis. Nothing related to my dad." *Nothing related to me, either.* "Can you give me twenty-four hours?"

"Of course, Mr. Shepard."

Will hung up and walked back to the husk of his life.

He crossed the road without looking and passed a clump of perfectly shaped burning bushes glowing scarlet against the concrete of the parking deck. A gust of wind brought the crisp sound of dead leaves tumbling across the sidewalk.

Hannah believed things happened for a reason. He believed life was all about the math of timing: meeting the right woman at the wrong moment. What category did this latest development fall into?

If the call had come a month earlier, he would have been relieved, maybe even glad. Azalea Court was the best retirement community in Orange County, with three levels of care that included assisted living and hospice. No views of Occoneechee Mountain, or the forest, but a big garden with mature trees. And the staff seemed pleasant enough. His dad could move in with no history of a reaction to the news of a dead grandson, and the Great European Adventure could live on undisturbed and unthreatened. Jacob could stay in his beloved Orange County; Will could return to his rooftop garden in New York. Everything would click together the way it was ordained, and the past month would be expunged.

So why did this feel like defeat? If he took this option, was he being a realist or was he, once again, turning his back on his parents—despite everything he'd just told Galen?

Will tugged open the car door, jumped in, flicked on his high beams and headed for Occoneechee Mountain.

Clouds darkened, promising a doozy of a storm, and within seconds a deluge battered the Prius. Only a fool would attempt to walk the trails in this weather with this level of light. But no way could he go back to the cottage. No way could he face Hannah or his dad.

The tires swooshed over a sliding sheet of water, and Will rolled into Hillsborough.

He passed the Occaneechi sign and glanced right. A pair of vultures—peace eagles—soared above the old ghost field.

Underdogs labeled dirty scavengers, vultures were really nature's cleansers, cleaning up carrion. People, not nature, had given them the bum rap.

He ducked to look through the passenger window, but the dying foliage kept the living village hidden. How strange that the powwows had been moved from here to the ancestral lands. Maybe the tribal council was focusing all its efforts on promoting the Homeland Preservation Project up at Pleasant Grove. Maybe the living village had become more of a tourist destination. Maybe the town had, once again, kicked out the Occaneechi Band of the Saponi Nation.

Rain punched the roof of his car like the fist of some divine being reaching down to beat the crap out of him, and the vultures continued to circle. *Guiding you home in bad weather,* according to his dad, the hopeless romantic. "You got bad weather, that old vulture, he's the only bird in the air," his dad used to say. "You get lost, he'll guide you."

*What the hell.* Will turned right and parked behind the courthouse. He didn't want to revisit memories that shouldn't be unearthed, but curiosity had always been his downfall. Thanks to his mom, he'd never seen the evolution of the Occaneechi village.

The lot was empty; nothing surrounded him but the past.

Even as a cornfield, this had been a place for ghosts. Before they discovered the burial site, he and his dad used to dawdle through after an evening spent fishing on the oxbow, and Will would imagine the whispering of spirits.

The excavation of the pre-European settlement on the banks of the Eno River began the year before he started kindergarten, but the first powwow wasn't held until the end of his high school sophomore year. The buzz of celebration that summer had splashed his world with color and meaning. During the ceremonial blessing of the land two years later, Will had made the commitment to return the following summer and help with the reconstruction of the village. And he had. He'd even brought friends. Lots of new friends who knew nothing about his old life—until his mom's public humiliation. He hadn't been back since.

Will slammed the car door and dashed for the trees, arching his arms over his head. Rivulets of water slid over the clay path still baked solid from months of drought. He skidded and slowed to a walk. Keeping his head lowered, he inhaled the musk of wet earth.

The unwanted memory flooded back: his dad cajoling his mom into the truck. The drums, the dancers' sweat, the shock and pity on his new friends' faces. All those years of struggling to safeguard his mom's secrets—cover up some of the crazy-ass exploits that had caused so much gossip in high school—and in half an hour she'd blasted to the world that she was certifiable. Left no doubt in anyone's mind. His dad severed contact with the tribe after that, and Will escaped his mother's shadow for good. In the remaining college summers, he came home only briefly—to see his dad. After graduation he moved to New York, landed a job in the ad agency and hung out with Agent Dodds every night.

Will stepped into a huge puddle and swore. Cold water had seeped into his Converse.

He glanced up at the sign—Mecou Witahese! Welcome Friends!

Welcome to what? This wasn't a reconstruction, this wasn't a tourist hotspot; this was abandonment. A handful of cedar poles that should have marked the perimeter of the village leaned like drunks. Weeds choked the fire pit, and the matted sides of two small huts had begun to peel off like burned skin. The living village was an empty coffin. It represented nothing—no past, no present, no future. Nothing.

Will sank to his knees. Rain drummed on his shoulders, and he tipped back his head, allowing it to sting his face. Each droplet hit like a tiny spear.

If he were an animal, he'd howl.

By the time he'd parked outside the cottage, the rain had stopped and night had fallen. He was also caked with mud. Mud had even wormed its way into his hair. Of course, prostrating himself on the ground like a comatose mud wrestler would do that.

As he leaned down to grab his sodden shoes, Will glimpsed the outside shower. He should wash off so he didn't trail Carolina clay across the cottage's pale floors. Bad enough that he was bailing on Hannah. He didn't need to burden her with extra housekeeping. That reminded him: he needed to hire a cleaning service.

Walking across the gravel was surprisingly painless. Then again—he tossed his shoes onto the porch—the soles of his feet were hardened from years of scrambling over rocks barefoot. He stripped off his sweatshirt, flipped up the top of the trash can and dumped it inside. The sweatshirt belonged to his night with Hannah; he would never wear it again. Maybe he'd chuck out everything in New York, too. Downsize and buy a one-bedroom loft.

He stepped into Hannah's huge galvanized tub and yanked the cord for the outside shower. Cold water battered his chest as he spread his arms wide and closed his eyes. In his mind, he was standing naked under a mountain waterfall as a veil of water cascaded over the cliff above, separating him from the world, muffling his grief with its roar.

A branch snapped and Will jumped. He turned around to find an audience: Hannah and her pack of strays.

"I was worried about you," she said.

He turned off the water and let her wrap a huge, white towel around his shoulders.

"Why don't you take off your jeans, and I'll put them in the dryer," she said.

Removing his jeans was easy now that he'd donated his belt to saving Galen's life. Hannah disappeared with them but returned moments later, empty-handed. If he abandoned the jeans as well as his sweatshirt, he'd have one less thing to sort out before leaving tomorrow. Will stepped out of the huge tub onto the teak slated shower mat and began to dry his body: left leg, right leg.

"How's Scarlet?" Not that he gave a shit about some cat, but they had to start somewhere.

*Left arm, right arm.*

"She passed. I handed her off to another vet, so I could be available if you called. You didn't."

There was no malice in her voice, just quiet acceptance, as if he'd performed within expected parameters. He slid the towel down his torso, secured it around his waist and slipped off his boxers. Less than twenty-four hours since she'd stripped him of his clothes, and she didn't flinch, didn't even glance at his bare chest. Not once. Was this some sort of preternatural control, or did she really not care that he was naked under her towel? He wanted her to care.

"How's my son?" Hannah said.

"Sedated. Mostly he dozed while people came by to check on him. It's a busy place, the locked ward. You'll discover for yourself tomorrow. He says you can visit."

She crossed her hands over her chest and seemed to deflate with joy, relief, gratitude…who knew. They had shared bodies, not minds.

"Thank you," she whispered. "Will, thank you."

He wanted to hold on to his anger from the morning, but

he felt only emptiness. "I'm sorry about being MIA all day. This is just…hard for me."

"I understand."

No, she didn't.

"I'm sorry, too," Hannah said. "Sorry for dragging you into my family drama, sorry for throwing myself at you last night, sorry for handling this morning badly. I was so scared, so angry, so embarrassed." She sighed. "But what you did for us last night, what you did for me today—"

"It's fine, Hannah. Let's just move on. Where's Dad?"

"In the house."

"And Poppy?"

"She's been helping Andrew bury Scarlet. They turned it into a little ceremony."

Will picked at a loose thread on the towel. "I got a phone call from Azalea Court a few hours ago. A spot just opened up. I've decided to move Dad in tomorrow. Then drive home to New York."

Sleep deprivation was forcing him to use words badly. He had never before referred to New York as home. Rosie waddled over and nudged his leg, and a small herd of white-tailed deer glided in and out of his sight line.

Hannah drew in her breath. "What if you're already home?"

If she thought that, she didn't know him. At all. He'd spent most of his life scraping off the knowledge that Orange County had once been home, making sure it would never be home again. He didn't have a home; he'd never belonged anywhere with anyone. Except for last night. Briefly, he closed his eyes and remembered their silent lovemaking: the frenzy, the heat, the unspoken need. Was she asking him to stay? Did she want him to stay? But he couldn't. He had to leave; he had to run; he had to forget. No, he had to remember. He was too tired, his thoughts too incoherent.

"I've never had a home." The words felt heavy. "Did you know the Occaneechi village is gone? Abandoned."

"Yes, although I didn't realize you were interested in tribal affairs. But then again, the space between us is filled with things you don't tell me. By the way, you left your watch in my bed."

Will bowed his head, then raised it slowly. "Come to New York with me."

They stared at each other. Yet again, words had slipped out unedited. Yet again, exhaustion had spawned a sentence that contained the power to change his life. The first time he'd asked a woman to move in, and it was a meaningless request. Worse, they both knew it.

"The only place I can go tomorrow is the hospital. I could say, 'I'll come to New York in the future.' But why lie? You don't find too many country vets in the city. You, on the other hand, are a writer. You can work anywhere."

"I can't. I need silence and solitude."

"And that's why you live in one of the busiest cities in the world?"

Put like that, it sounded stupid. "Yeah."

"People rarely go to New York to find silence. I'm betting you're no exception. Perhaps you went there to lose yourself among strangers."

He'd been right all along about Hannah. She was too intuitive. Another reason to leave.

"You can find silence here." She swept her arm around in an arc and pointed to the sleeping forest behind them. Despite her father's death, she found nothing but peace in the very place that spoke to him only of unwanted memories.

"I am curious, though," Hannah continued. "Why *are* you so terrified of commitment? Is it because of your mother— or because of Ally?"

Will bent down to pick up and wring out his boxers. "I should get some dry clothes on, and we should both get some sleep."

"Want me to bring your dad over later?"

*Jesus.* He'd forgotten his dad *again.* Will scratched his forehead.

"It takes a family, doesn't it?" Her voice was soft, the sort of voice he used when Freddie woke after a nightmare.

"You've lost me."

"I mean, it's hard to look after an aging parent alone. You need the support of an inner circle."

"Or a really good care facility such as Azalea Court."

"Poppy would be cheaper."

"This isn't about money—this is about making good, solid decisions." Like he did that so well. "Azalea Court is the best possible alternative to Dad coming to New York. I can return to work, and he can stay in Orange County, be near the forest. What more could he want?"

"He wants to stay here, on Saponi Mountain. And I can make that happen. Jacob doesn't have to be as lost as my dad was after Mom died."

"The two situations aren't the same, Hannah. Yes, my dad's mind is dying, but he's not going to kill himself. I learned something today, at the Occaneechi village. Revisiting the past doesn't give you a better outcome. It doesn't give you a road map for the future. The only way to move forward is to forget."

She hugged herself, and he felt like a jerk.

"A few months from now, Dad probably won't even know who you are. He certainly won't care where he lives. You have to let this go. We both do."

"Would you consider a trial run?"

"No. Azalea Court wants an answer in the next twenty-four hours. Less than that. Look, my dad needs care 24/7."

"Poppy and I can give him that."

"You can't take him on. You have Galen to think about. And Poppy has zero medical training."

"I won't give up on your dad."

Silence had always been his weapon of choice with a woman, and staying relaxed was the key to staying alive on a rock face and in a relationship, but Hannah was way out of bounds. "You think I'm giving up on my own father?"

Dead leaves rustled in the darkness and the tree frogs croaked. They both stood still.

"No, of course not, but we can fix this together. Together we can mend our families, help them heal. Maybe your dad was right all those years ago to shut out other people." She looked up into the night. "But shutting out the rest of the world means shutting you in. Here, with us."

"I can't do this, Hannah. Don't ask me to do this."

"I've seen plenty of wounded animals, Will, and you're no different. You might think you wear your scars on the inside, but they show. How can you ask me to move halfway across the country and yet not let me in—not tell me what it is that keeps you prowling around out here at night?"

He didn't dare breathe. "Leave it alone."

"So that's it? We had sex and now you're walking away?" She turned *sex* into a hard, ugly word.

"You're the one who more or less threw me out this morning, Hannah."

"I know. How many times do I have to say I'm sorry? Please, don't go."

"I have to. It's complicated."

"No shit, Will!"

Her spike of anger was confusing, disorienting. He had

never imagined her capable of raising her voice and yet here she was, yelling. Yelling at him.

"I remember every detail of the first time I saw you—every sound, every smell, every emotion. I don't understand our connection. I can't figure out what binds us, but I feel it in here." She slapped her heart. "I've had the whole day to think. I've done nothing but think—about my mistakes with Galen, with you. Our connection through Rosie. You were right this morning. We *do* need each other. I know our families are linked. I know you're meant to be part of Galen's recovery, and I know I can help with your dad. We can do this together. I want us to do this *together*. I need you to stay for my son. And I need you to stay because, because…" Her hands shot to her mouth.

"Please don't cry." Face-to-face breakups had never been his forte.

"I'm not." She moved her hands up to cover her eyes.

He glanced toward the main house, where his dad peered out from one of the living room windows. But when Will turned back, Hannah was walking away, the dogs at her heels.

If he'd wanted to say, *I love you,* he'd missed the whole moment. But maybe that, too, was unfolding as it should.

Been a while since he'd heard a woman's voice raised in anger. Although Angeline, woo-wee, she could raise the roof with her fire. Poor Willie, he used to cower under the kitchen table when his mama started. Sometimes, he had to lock Willie in his room. Just to be safe. Never seen eye-to-eye, those two.

What could make a little lady so mad? Willie better not be the cause. Needed to go outside and check. He might be little more than the straw boss these days, but he were still the daddy.

Oh, sweet Jesus, no. Hey You and Willie were arguin'. Even a blind person could see his Willie and Hey You were in love. When a man and a woman were in love, they shouldn't make it so hard. Did he need to give them a good talkin'-to? Made a real nice couple. Handsome, too. Maybe Freddie would come live with them. Now that would be somethin', to be part of a family again. You could surround yourself with people, but if they weren't kin, it didn't make a lick of difference.

And his boy were half-naked. He couldn't be takin' off his clothes again.

And now Hey You were walkin' away and she looked real upset. Had Willie upset her? When a man and a woman were in love, they shouldn't be throwin' anger at each other. He'd brought Willie up better than that. He didn't get angry with his Angeline, not even that time she…what? What did his angel do?

"You cryin', Angel?" he asked Hey You.

"Allergies." She smiled, but it weren't a real smile. That weren't good, that weren't no good. He felt a bit like yellin' hisself. What were Willie thinkin'? He brought him up better than that. He taught him to love and cherish and protect.

He put out his arms and she stepped in. Hey You needed one of his special hugs.

"Son." He tried to sound harsh. Time to be the medicine. Medicine didn't taste good, not at all, but it were necessary, to make you better. *That's how it goes.* And Willie needed to take some medicine, because he couldn't be makin' his mama cry, not like he did at that powwow.

Only time he ever saw Willie mad. Mad weren't no good. Willie were real mad that day. Damned if he could remember why. Remembered Willie leavin', though, sayin' he weren't never comin' back, and he were as good as his word. Near broke his mama's heart. Or did he come back? C.R.S., C.R.S. But the boy didn't come back for his own mama's funeral. That much he knew.

Willie looked real sad and Hey You looked real sad. Willie had a lot to learn about women.

"Here, Angel." He pulled out a tissue from his pocket.

He'd never let Angeline out of his sight for longer than a day. Without her... His poor, beautiful Angeline. He were real tired, real tired. Needed to lie down. Didn't like to see a lady so upset. Certainly not this pretty gal with the big blue eyes.

Where was his Angeline? His mind were popping like firecrackers. Needed to go lie down. Sleep for a bit before dinner.

"Willie? I need to go lie down. Rest a bit."

"We have to talk first, Dad," Will said.

"I need to nap, son. Busy afternoon. Hey You and me, we finished them new dream catchers."

"Dream catchers?" Willie looked at Hey You, but she weren't lookin' back.

"Your father's been having nightmares about Freddie. The last dream catcher we made didn't work, so we're trying again." She smiled. Smile of an angel.

"I told him it was my bad," Hey You said. "That I didn't know what I was doing the first time around. This time, though, we're going to make sure we trap all the nightmares."

Will squirmed like he did when he were a tyke and got into trouble with that friend of his. Pretty little thing. Ran wild all over the mountain, them two. Weren't no one's fault she didn't love him right.

Had to talk to Willie about not walkin' around naked in front of the womenfolk. Will liked to walk around naked. Liked to sleep naked, too. He told him just the other day not to do that with them womenfolk around. And look at him—

half-naked again. Kids didn't always listen. Hard bein' the daddy sometimes. Real hard.

"Let's go in, Dad. We need to talk," Will said, although he sounded more like the daddy. That weren't right, though. Will weren't a daddy.

Will hauled himself downstairs, leaning heavily on the railing. One step at a time. That was the key to moving through the living, breathing nightmare of this endless day. His feet were freezing. He should've taken two minutes to sit down on the bed and pull on socks, but the bed had looked too inviting. If he lay down, he might never get up.

His dad was standing in the middle of the living room, arms behind his back, frowning at the world map lit up with colored stars and photos like a decorated Christmas tree. Would Azalea Court let them stick stuff up on the walls?

One more day and this episode of his life would be over. One more day and he would be back in his sterile apartment. With any luck, it would still be warm enough to sit out in the roof garden.

"How about I fix us hot chocolate with marshmallows?" A peace offering before he delivered the blow.

His dad turned and looked at him with the face of someone who'd given up on life. "Willie, did somethin' bad happen to Freddie?"

Will grabbed the newel post. He tried to speak, tried to spit out a simple, *Why would you ask?* His jaw was moving, he could feel it open and close, but no words fell out. Sonic booms seemed to pound through his head and vibrate down into his chest; his stomach clenched as if about to hurl its meager contents up through his throat.

"Your mama used to fix you hot chocolate with marshmallows." The old man gave a laugh and shook his head.

"Now, before you say anythin', I know it weren't very good. I saw you dump it down the sink. But she were tryin', Willie. She didn't always get it right, but she never stopped tryin' with you."

So that was it? Truth attacked and then fled? The memory lapses were coming closer and closer together—a salvo of short fuse detonation. The sooner he got his dad settled with professional help, the better. There could be no more indecision on his part, no more doubt. Maybe they should forget the milky drinks and head straight for the liquor. Sign the deal in alcohol.

Will straightened up and inhaled the subtle scent of pine that seemed to linger in every room of the cottage. Even when he was cooking, he could still smell it. "Tell me more about your nightmares."

"Not much to tell, son. Just my useless mind trickin' me into believin' bad things happened to Freddie. It's hard when the devil visits in the middle of the night. Don't know what I'd do without them stories of Freddie's great adventure."

Will glanced at the cardboard tube propped up in the corner. His dad had left it there on the day they moved in as if he'd known all along they wouldn't be staying.

"Your mama, now, she could tell a mighty fine story. You, too, son. I hope Freddie has the family gift. Wouldn't that be somethin'? Three generations of storytellers. Think Freddie'll come visit us after his trip?"

"Sit, Dad. We have to talk." Will fell into one of the big club chairs.

"Then you'll give me the Freddie update, right?"

"Yeah, Dad. I'll give you the update." Although the itinerary had disappeared from his radar, displaced by real-life drama. And for the first time, the idea of returning to his research felt like a chore, not a pleasure. Had Freddie's story stalled, too?

Groaning slowly, his dad lowered himself into the chair across from the coffee table angled between them like the world's tallest dam. Will bit down on impatience, on his desire to leap up and help. His dad was eighty—moving slowly was his entitlement. He could almost hear Hannah talking about dignity and pride.

"Dad, I'm going back to New York. Tomorrow." Will took a deep breath; his dad said nothing, just stared hard. "And you can come with me, or you can move into a place called Azalea Court. An apartment just opened up, and it's yours if you want it."

"No need for either, son." His dad had yet to blink. "Poppy's goin' to come here once you leave. Not quite sure what we're doin' with her kilns, but we'll figure that out. We expect you to visit often. You'll be back for Christmas? With Freddie?"

Poppy had kept this preposterous idea alive in his dad's mind? She was manipulative as hell, but he'd expected more of her. Will pulled forward, resting his forearms on his knees.

"Listen, Dad. You can't stay here, and Poppy shouldn't have told you otherwise. It's not fair on Hannah. Her son had a breakdown."

"Crazy One?"

"Yeah. Remember the ambulances last night? They came for him. He's in the mental hospital. And when he comes out, he's going to need his mother's full attention."

His dad nodded. "I reckon he needs that now, son. Ain't right for him to be in the nuthouse. He should be here, with his kinfolk. You spring him. Crazy One likes you."

"Dad, I'm done. I can't do this anymore. I have to get back to New York. I was hoping you'd come with me, but if you want to stay in Orange County, you'll have to move into Azalea Court. It isn't far. In fact, it's close enough that Hannah and Poppy can visit whenever they want. I'm sorry, but staying here, in the cottage, isn't an option. It would only be selfish."

Pushing off the arms of the chair, the old man wobbled up to standing. He peeled down the map, pausing to smooth out the pictures Hannah had pasted on for him. Then he rolled the map up tightly and slotted it into the cardboard tube. The kitchen clock ticked, and his dad muttered something incomprehensible. Then he pulled the roll to his chest as if protecting a swaddled newborn.

"Can I see the forest from this *place* of yours, the one you've found for me?" There was a droplet of spit on his dad's bottom lip.

"They have a nice garden. With lots of trees. And there's a library filled with history books. I checked."

"And you, son, you ever gonna come back and visit? Or you gonna be too busy with that life in New York?" His dad turned. "Think I'll go to bed now if you don't mind. Have me an early night."

"Wait, the hot chocolate—"

"Don't want no hot chocolate."

"But dinner? You have to eat."

"I'm tired, son. Real tired. Sleep's the only thing a man wants at my age."

His dad stopped on the bottom stair. "I'll leave for one reason—I won't be no trouble for Hannah. She's a good woman. She deserves better than the pair of us."

"Dad—wait, please—"

"You need to learn a lesson about parentin', son. A father, he has a responsibility to give his kids roots and wings. I failed you, Willie. I gave you wings, I never gave you roots. Don't repeat my mistake. Let Freddie follow the trail of his people. Let him come visit me and his grandmama's grave. Give him roots."

Will's head sank into his hands.

*Too late, Dad. Too late to give him anything.*

The stairs creaked one by one as his dad climbed toward bed.

Half an hour and he'd take up an omelet, fixed the way the old man liked it with green pepper and onion and Swiss cheese. And lots of black pepper.

But first… Will picked up his iPhone from the coffee table.

Found place for Dad. He typed a text to his agent. Back this weekend. Let's talk Monday.

Talk about what, though? He still hadn't figured out how to rescue Agent Dodds, and he no longer cared. He hit Send before he could reconsider. There, he'd set his plan in motion. Now all he had to do was leave.

# THIRTY-TWO

Beads of rain clung to spiderwebs strung between branches like celebratory bunting, chickadees and cardinals called to one another and Hannah's old hiking boots squelched through soggy undergrowth. A light wind rustled dying leaves that clung on and refused to let go, and sunrise streaked through the treetops on Saponi Mountain.

Thirty-three hours since her son had tried to kill himself. Thirty-three hours that felt like thirty-three years.

Hannah pulled out her phone. No service up here. What if Galen was trying to reach her with the password of the day? Ridiculous worry—it was far too early for him to call. The night staff were probably still on shift at the locked psych ward.

*Locked psych ward.* Three words that made her want to scream until she was hoarse. But this time—thanks to Will—she could see her son, something she hadn't been able to arrange after the first suicide attempt. Not one but two. Two suicide attempts forever stamped across his medical files. A repeating pattern. He might not have actually cut himself the first time, but he had been suicidal.

*Third attempt lucky,* a dark thought taunted.

Hannah huddled into her hoodie and kept walking. Yesterday's cold front had blasted the temperatures into fall. The drought and never-ending Indian summer were already forgotten. Winter would soon be tapping on her door, and she welcomed it.

Following the route of the old trading path, Hannah veered right at the conservation easement sign. With the trails hidden beneath layers of leaves, it would be easy to get lost on the mountain, but intuition guided her.

Random thoughts tumbled. When she got the call about Galen in September, it had seemed vital to find the positive, to use work as a way of regulating a life that was spiraling into anarchy. And yet today nothing mattered beyond the basics. Life had compressed into a bite-sized to-do list: exercise the dogs, eat breakfast, get to the hospital. In September and October she'd wanted to hold on to normalcy; in November she wanted to let go.

*My son wanted to die.*

Brushing aside a branch, she paused to stare at her left hand. For the first time in years, the absence of a wedding ring stung. Alone, she would be handling this alone.

*I will not cry when I see my baby.* –

*I will be strong enough for two.*

*I will not cry—*

The tears came, and Hannah kept walking. Maybe it was better to give in. To grieve for the little boy she had lost, to accept the man he had become. Life could never be the same, nor should it be. She would grieve now, with no one else around, and by the time she arrived at the hospital, she would be ready to step inside this new phase of her life. This ugly twist of motherhood that she had no choice but to embrace. There was no out, there was no reprieve; there was only forward motion, because whatever the future held, she would be Galen's mother until the day she died.

Since her father's suicide—yes, she would use that word until it no longer hacked at her heart—she'd been running from the very thing she should have been running toward: the knowledge that depression was a family disease, that she could pass on the defective gene as easily as she could pass on color blindness. If only she had been hypervigilant, watched for signs of depression. If only she had listened the way her mother had encouraged her to do.

But no, always she needed people to be happy, because if her mother had been right—that Hannah, too, could hear the thoughts of others and experience the horror of their darkness—then being psychic was also genetic. Unlike Will's mom, her mother was never labeled mad, never called a freak, but still, their family was different. Come Halloween, her mother was the parent handing out crystals, not candy.

Had the desire to be the same, to blend in, been the reason she'd turned her back on negative emotions time and time again? Was this why Inigo's betrayal had blindsided her; why she had blocked Galen's depression; why she had devoted her life to finding peace in death?

Death—the lunar halo that now surrounded her son.

How could she look Galen in the eye and not wonder about the scar that could never heal? For twelve years she'd shielded him from the stigma of suicide, but once the bandages came off, he would be forever branded a suicide survivor. The world would stare; the world would judge. And she could not protect her son.

She should never have followed Galen's lead in the past month, never have been satisfied with, "I'm in touch with my therapist and social worker in California." Why had she not snooped, monitored, intervened? And yet. *And yet.*

She'd had no power then, and she had no power now.

The doctors couldn't discuss his case with her. She would have to be satisfied with secondhand information edited from Galen's perspective. He was beyond her legal grasp; she was powerless, and the only person they both trusted to help was heading back to New York.

Black tree trunks surrounded her like mourners gathered around a grave, closing in to offer comfort. Hannah released her mood into the forest, let it reverberate off the trees and bounce back with solace.

The wind shook dew from the branches of a small sassafras with mismatched foliage the color of burnished orange. Three different-shaped leaves on the same tree and aromatic bark. Nature at its most resplendent. Hannah admired a clump of wild ginger, stooped down and ran her fingers through the fronds of a fat fern.

With a sigh, she stood and sidestepped a fallen tree limb covered in moss so bright it seemed to light her way. She filled her lungs with the scent of pine needles and raised her face to the high-pitched whistle of a tufted titmouse. Farther up the mountain, a pileated woodpecker piped. Even in the darkest moments, the birds sang. They never stopped singing.

Galen could look like hell and still she would give him a mother's kiss, stroke his hair and show him how proud she was to be his parent. Her touch would reveal that her love was nonnegotiable, that she would always see him with the wonder that said, *That's my son. My son.*

An owl swooped in front of her, warning her off its roosting spot, protecting its own little corner of the world, and the dogs startled a herd of white-tailed deer. Six deer sprung through the trees, racing away from a perceived threat, surviving as a pack, as a family.

Her family would survive. Her idiosyncratic, dysfunctional family would survive. Galen was alive and he was safe. For today, that was enough. And when he came out? Anyone could feed and love a newborn, but a young man battling depression deserved a parent who would not falter, who would not flinch. She would be that parent.

She would go to the library and check out every book on depression. She would research her way to becoming the mother of a depressive. She would open her mind to darkness. She would welcome every negative emotion her son hurled at her.

Will had carved out time for Galen every night; she would do the same. If she had any hope of earning her son's trust, she would have to prove that things could change, that she could change. She would move her work life out of her personal life, separate the two worlds that collided constantly. As Will had pointed out rather nastily—but he had been naked and humiliated—she needed to establish boundaries.

Setting up an on-site office with a separate phone line would be the first step. Treating pets and owners in their homes would still be a priority, but some appointments could be dealt with as office visits. That wouldn't be so hard. Perhaps she would establish regular office hours; perhaps Poppy could help. Whatever happened with Jacob, Poppy remained at a crossroads. She was about to get kicked out of her apartment, and her business had stalled into a time-consuming hobby. Art therapy had seemed a good solution, but there'd also been talk, a while back, of a course in horse massage. What if Hannah agreed to fund it in return for part-time hours?

The cottage could easily be turned into an office. Hannah could claim the front room and the rest could be Poppy's. With Poppy living there, it would be easier to deal with after-hour emergencies.

Rosie stopped, and Hannah stumbled over her flank.

She peered at the ground where, two feet ahead, a copperhead lay coiled and camouflaged in a nest of dead leaves.

"Good girl." She patted Rosie's rump. "Let's take a detour."

Keeping an eye on the venomous snake, Hannah swung around in an arc, stepping off the path. Up ahead was an opening, framed in early-morning light.

*Why not?*

For months she'd avoided the private road that scarred Saponi Mountain. The rumblings of logging trucks throughout the spring had been distressing enough. For fifteen years, this mountain had been hers. Would neighbors post no-trespassing signs and refuse her access to the old trails?

Hannah pushed aside a cluster of spindly sweet gum saplings, jumped over a culvert and landed on tarmac. According to the large for-sale sign, there were still two open lots—each twenty acres. Apart from the one mansion that was finished and inhabited—an angular block of steel and concrete that screamed, *I don't belong*—several of the houses on the ridge were already framed. In the winter, when the forest was bare, there would be no escaping the sight of these homes. Did the owners realize how isolated they would be? A mere dusting of snow or thin coating of ice and the road would be impassable.

But the view. Her whole life she'd dreamed of a view like this—reserved, surely, for the birds. Her mother would have talked about destiny or reincarnation, but maybe it was a simple case of belonging. To be ripped away from this land? She couldn't begin to imagine....

The sun was struggling to rise above the forest, and a red-tailed hawk drifted across the blue sky. When Galen was little, he was fascinated by birds of prey. She would bring him here when he came home—if he came home. Suppose he decided to stay with Inigo? Suppose he decided to move back to California?

For years she had fretted over his separation anxiety. Three feet tall and his favorite phrase was, *Don't leave me, Mommy.* Now she was the one who wanted to cry, *Don't leave me.*

Hannah stared down the mountain to where her house stayed concealed. Her empty home. Since her boys had learned to walk, she'd wished them independence and happiness. Especially Galen, who was always so withdrawn, so sensitive, so easily hurt. He seemed to believe he was incapable of receiving love. Undeserving. Something else he'd inherited from her.

Rosie butted her. "I know, baby. Dawdling's good for the soul, but this is avoidance, isn't it? I guess it's time to face Will."

They started walking down the road—the shortest, quickest way back. Will had been up at 4:00 a.m. loading something into the trunk of his car. Packing, no doubt, although she had chosen not to watch. Part of her hoped he had left already. But no, a bigger part of her hoped he would wait and say goodbye. Goodbyes were more important than hellos. And this one, she would get right.

From the moment Will had arrived, she'd known he would leave. Falling in love hadn't been part of the plan, but maybe it had been part of her journey. Her mother would have approved, would have told her that people crossed one another's paths for a reason. Hannah's mind meandered back to the decision she'd made in the middle of the night. Nighttime decisions rarely held up in daylight, but this one still fit. Will was a free spirit and she couldn't keep him here. Nor should she have tried. She had chosen a gift for him, a gift that would, hopefully, allow him to leave Orange County with better memories than when he'd arrived.

★ ★ ★

Will leaned back against one of the cedar posts supporting the deck, crossed his ankles and resumed his vigil. The
Prius was packed and all that remained was to wait. The air
smelled cold and fresh; the leaves were the colors of spices.

From here, he could see Hannah before she saw him. He
could watch her stride down the mountain with the dogs, her
cheeks flushed, her hair loose. Why she bound those corkscrew curls in tight ponytails, he couldn't fathom. If he could
just watch her for two minutes, he could say goodbye silently
from a distance.

Aiming away from a clump of wintergreen with scarlet
berries, Will dumped the cold contents of his coffee mug on
the ground. As soon as his dad was awake, he'd make a fresh
pot. Microwaving coffee was a new habit that needed ditch-
ing. Starting today, he was going to rediscover the things that
used to matter. First off—no more zapped coffee.

Wind rippled through the trees like babbling water, and a
chain saw revved, but there were no sounds of dogs crashing
through the undergrowth, and no flashes of a Tar Heel blue
sweatshirt, size unknown. Was Hannah a small or a medium?
Really, he knew so little about her. Would know even less
once he left. She wasn't fat, though, and she wasn't skinny.
She was just right. Practically perfect, like Mary Poppins.
He blew out a sigh. One of his jobs this week would include
boxing up the Disney DVDs. Maybe he could donate them
to a local children's hospital.

He heard the dogs before he saw them, but coming from
the direction of the road, not the forest. That was weird. The
dogs came into view—all of them, even Rosie. But no Hannah. He threw the coffee cup to the ground and ran.

Daisy barked and met him halfway, and Rosie turned her
head. If Hannah was surprised to see him running toward her

in some lame Heathcliff-Cathy moment, she didn't show it. But like him, she was good at pretense. Or maybe this wasn't an act; maybe, despite everything she'd said the night before, she didn't care. That bothered him, too.

"Something wrong?" she said, not varying her pace.

Rosie slowed to flank her mistress. Was her doggie sense warning her to protect?

Will stopped. "I saw the dogs without you. I thought, you know, something bad had happened."

"I'm fine." She pushed her hair behind her ears, and he tried to believe she'd worn it loose in some secret signal of love. Or lust. Anything other than indifference.

"Right," Will said. "Can we talk?"

"Before you leave?" Hannah glanced at the Prius.

"Yeah, something like that."

A battalion of birds—robins, pigeons and blue jays—rustled through the fallen leaves.

"Have you had breakfast?" she said.

"I'm not very hungry this morning."

"Unfortunately, I am. Would you mind if I ate while you talked?" She started walking toward the house, and he followed. Always, he followed.

"I spoke with Galen last night," Will said.

"You did?"

"I wanted to repeat an invitation to come to New York. You're invited, too."

"Thanks."

"Is that a *Yes, I'd love to,* or are you just being polite?" Will said.

"Are you that insecure?"

"Yeah, I am."

"Finally, Will Shepard. An honest answer." Hannah petted Rosie. "I've found my peace with what happened between us. No regrets." She glanced up, her eyes clear and bright. "How about you?"

"I haven't regretted it for one minute. And *that's* the most honest answer I've ever given a woman." He drew alongside Rosie—*The filling in the sandwich,* Freddie would say. "Our timing was appalling, but it was inevitable."

Hannah smiled. "We're not very good at this, are we?"

"No. But the sex—" he couldn't contain the grin "—was incredible."

"It's a bit blurry for me. I remember seeing shooting stars, though."

*A whole galaxy of them.* "Maybe next time we meet we could, you know, try it without the drugs?" He fiddled with his fingers. "I don't want this to be…"

"An end?" she said quietly.

He sighed. "Yeah."

"Me, neither. By the way, I have a gift for you."

"Really?" When was the last time someone who wasn't on his payroll gave him a gift? Obsessed female fans who sent sex toys didn't count.

Hannah opened the front door—unlocked, of course—and he closed it behind them. If only she would take more care with her personal safety. She lived in the middle of nowhere and didn't even have an alarm. When he was a kid, no one locked anything, but he'd started checking the local news. The rash of recent break-ins told him she needed a better warning system than a motley collection of mutts who rarely barked. He could offer to fund an alarm—use his dad as the excuse.

"Here." She picked up a framed photo from the storage bench in the hall, handed him the panorama of Occoneechee Mountain.

"I can't take this, Hannah."

"I insist. It has your name on it."

He flipped it over. "'For Will,'" he read aloud. "'Nothing but good memories.'"

He held the photograph flat against his chest. "I'll hang it above my desk." *Next to Freddie's picture.*

She leaned in to kiss his cheek and, for a moment, he wanted more. But Daisy passed gas and the air stank of deer scat. Could they not have one romantic moment without real life intruding?

"How serious were you," he said, "about a trial run with my dad?"

"Very."

"In that case, I have a proposal. A compromise, I guess. My dad's still on the wait list for this place at the bottom of Occoneechee Mountain. I really liked it when I visited. They have a housedog, this big, old black Lab that wanders around, slobbering on everything. Farts, too." He grinned, and so did she. "All the rooms have a view of the mountain. It's not as fancy as Azalea Court, but I think Dad could be happy there. Could take a while, though, till they have a vacancy. You guys want to dad-sit in the interim?"

"I wouldn't have suggested it if we didn't, Will."

"Okay, but here's the deal—you have to agree to a test run, and so does Dad. Azalea Court's willing to hold the apartment for a week. That gives you and Poppy time to figure out if it's working or not. We'd have to talk every night, and if you guys are struggling by the end of next week, I'll come back and move him into Azalea Court. And the four of us need to meet. I want us all in agreement."

"What changed your mind?"

"My dad—talking about roots. His roots are on that mountain, and I realized it's all he has left."

She leaned back against the white wall and gave him a hard look. "Except for you and Freddie."

"I should go finish packing." *Such a lie.*

"When are you leaving?"

"After the four of us have talked. I'm assuming you want to go to the hospital first."

She pushed off the wall. "Yes, but I'm not planning to stay long. I don't want to tire Galen. I just want to give him a hug."

A hug. He would give the world for one last hug with Freddie. "I have to go check on Dad."

"You're both welcome to join me, for breakfast."

"Thanks, but no." He walked to the front door. "I think I'll take him out for blueberry pancakes. There's this fancy diner on Main Street...."

"A last breakfast?"

"Kind of." Will paused. "And thank you, Hannah."

"For what?"

*For being you.* "For everything."

"Will?" Hannah said, but he didn't turn. "You're doing the right thing—for your dad."

The doorknob was cold and slippery. Tightening his grip, he eased the door open and stared at the giant post oak by the side of the cottage, its shriveled leaves turning brown in defeat.

*No, I'm doing the right thing for me.*

# THIRTY-THREE

As Will stroked the surface of the dining room table, Hannah tried to forget how gentle his touch could be. But the memory breathed over her shoulder, refusing to leave.

Under the table, her leg jiggled. Her thoughts raced, jumping from Will to Galen and back again. In the kitchen the ice maker clunked, spitting out a pitiful round of ice cubes for one.

By the time darkness fell, Will would be gone, and Galen would be spending his second night in the mental hospital. Was Galen finally awake? He'd slept most of the hour she'd sat with him. Only once did he open his eyes and say, "I'm sorry, Mom," and she replied, "I'm sorry, too, baby." Two short sentences in one hour, but it felt like a beginning. This strained meeting around her dining room table, however, felt like an ending.

She massaged her leg, warming her muscles.

She would have faith; she would *choose* to have faith. This new scheme of Will's would bring him back to Saponi Mountain when he was ready. Now wasn't their time.

"Beautiful table," he said.

"It belonged to my parents." Hannah smiled. "My mother's pride and joy."

"Tiger maple. Wasn't Uncle Darren's Les Paul tiger maple?" Will asked Jacob.

"I reckon so, son. That were a real nice guitar." Jacob turned to Poppy. "My brother, Darren, he were a fine guitar player. We had us a band. Long time ago."

"And you were one fine banjo picker." Poppy popped three Mentos into her mouth and offered the packet around. No one accepted.

"I told you that?" Jacob clasped the cardboard tube to his chest.

His memory was bad today. Not a good sign.

Will laid his palms flat on the table. "Dad, do you want to stay here?"

"You know I do, son."

"And you know I have to get back to New York?"

"So you keep tellin' us."

"And Hannah's son is in the hospital. So she has a lot going on right now." Will stared at her with bloodshot eyes.

"Willie." Jacob sighed. "C.R.S. Can't remember stuff, but I know where you're headin' with this. I won't go happily, but I'll go, for the womenfolk. Already told you that. No need to turn this into a council meetin'."

Will tugged on the neck of his long-sleeved T-shirt. "Hannah and Poppy have agreed that you can stay here, with them."

"Know that, too, son. You the only one who wants me in a home for old folks."

"Dad, I'm—"

"We have a little problem, Jacob. And I think you can help." Hannah reached out and touched Jacob's hand. The skin sagged over his knuckle, but it was smooth and warm, not dry and leathery. "Will's not sure you'd be happy at Aza-lea Court. He wants to hold out for somewhere with views of Occoneechee Mountain. It could take a while, though."

Jacob's head bobbed in agreement.

"In the meantime, Poppy needs to find somewhere to live and Will needs to return to New York." Hannah sat back and gave Will a reassuring smile, but he was staring at the ceiling, oblivious. "Would you be willing to share the cottage with Poppy? If so, she'd be willing to cook for you. She loves to cook."

Of course, this destroyed her new plans for the business, but she would rethink that tonight, when she was alone. It would keep her mind from the loss of Will.

"And I'm a meat lover." Poppy smirked. "Lots of juicy steaks with peppery sauces. None of this vegetarian crap your son serves."

Jacob gave Poppy a huge smile. "I need a bit of lookin' after."

"So do I, sugar."

"Here's the deal, Dad," Will said. "You get to try this for a week. So everyone can see how it works. And I'm going to pay Poppy to be your—"

"Companion," Hannah said.

Will scowled.

"You all right with this, son?"

"It seems to be what everyone wants. But it's only temporary, Dad, until a room opens up in the right retirement place."

Poppy gave Jacob a high five, and Will looked outgunned.

"This isn't permanent, guys. You are listening to me, right?"

"And won't this be a great place for Freddie to visit?"

"Yeah, sure, Dad."

"Now, Poppy, we might have to mess with the sleepin' arrangements when my grandson comes to stay. You bringin' him for Christmas, Willie?"

Will shot up. This time, there was no doubt: he was stuck in a pattern of avoidance. Or possibly denial. And she should know, being painfully familiar with both. When she'd kissed his cheek earlier—and he'd held on to that picture tight enough to crack the glass—a thought had niggled, had hinted that the bottled-up angst had something to do with his son.

Poppy and Jacob were huddled like kindergarteners plotting a messy craft project.

"When can you move in, Poppy?" Will said.

"This afternoon soon enough?"

"Fantastic," Will mumbled.

Hannah pushed back her chair. "You okay?"

But Will didn't answer, and this time, he didn't close the front door as he left.

Hannah was out of the house and on the gravel in seconds. No way could she let him drive back to New York while he was sleep deprived and distressed. He could fall asleep at the wheel; he could end up in a wreck on I-95; he could die.

"Hey." She grabbed Will's upper arm, and his muscles clenched. "It's getting late, and you're tired. Why don't you stay another day?"

"What happened to waving me off with no regrets and a goodbye present?" Will pulled his arm free and stomped over to the cottage, grabbed a green duffel from the porch and walked back toward the Prius.

"I don't think you should leave." Hannah positioned herself in front of the trunk.

"Could you move your ass please?"

"No. You shouldn't drive in this state. Do you know most car wrecks happen when people are mad?"

"I think you'll find most of them happen when people are drunk."

She didn't like his tone, but then she'd raised two teenage boys, one of them a borderline criminal. Will Shepard couldn't intimidate her if he tried. Folding her arms, she leaned back against the Prius. "The mother in me can't let you leave until you've calmed down."

"Why, Hannah? Why do you really want me to stay?"

"Why do *you* really want to leave?"

He glared.

"Okay," she said, "I'll go first."

"Because you're older and wiser?"

"Because I'm tired of people I love leaving."

Her forsythia bush was turning to plum and lemon. That shrub hadn't wilted once during the drought, and next spring, it would shine with yellow blossoms. Nothing held back a forsythia. Nothing.

"You're supposed to respond," she said quietly. "When a woman tells you she's in love."

He stared at the gravel. "Don't ask me again to stay. Please."

"Why? What's stopping you? Your glitzy New York life?"

"I don't have a glitzy New York life. I don't have a life." His head shot up. "I have nothing except a screwed-up relationship with my dad."

"That's not true, you have your writing—"

"I haven't written a word in months. Surely you've figured that out. My career is pretty close to being flushed down the toilet. This time next year I could be working at Home Depot."

"And you have your son—"

"Let it go, Hannah." His voice had hardened. He was issuing a threat, which she was going to ignore.

Hannah placed her palms on the Prius and braced herself

against the body of his car. One of the dogs barked inside the house. A single bark that suggested Poppy was handing out illicit tidbits.

Confrontations had never been Hannah's thing. In fact, she couldn't remember the last time she'd cornered anyone. She hadn't asked Galen the tough questions because she'd been scared of the answers. Will, however, was going to give her answers.

"Are you leaving because something happened to my son—" she paused "—or because something happened to yours?"

"I have feelings for you, Hannah. Strong feelings. And what happened between us will always be special. But this isn't about us. This, I can't share. Please, get out of my way."

"No. I want the truth. I want to know why you never talk about your son. I want to know why you're plagued by head-aches and insomnia. I want to know why your dad has recur-ring nightmares about—"

"Why?" Will threw the duffel to the ground. "Because the whole time I was holding your son I was wondering why I could only save the wrong kid."

Her hand flew to her mouth. It all made sense: the insom-nia, the migraines, the pacing. Will was battling grief. The giggling brown-haired boy on his iPhone…

Jacob shuffled out onto the porch, holding his cardboard tube. Poppy was behind him. Dear God, why hadn't she closed the front door?

"Will, don't—"

"You want the truth? I'll give you the truth. We both failed to keep our sons safe, Hannah. My son is dead, and your son is barely alive. My son is dead, you get it? Dead. Killed by his drunk mother. She was a crazy bitch and she killed her-self and my son. He burned to death in the backseat of her car. Strapped into his five-point-harness car seat. A car seat I bought because it was the safest car seat on the market."

Hannah glanced at Jacob, but neither of them moved.

"People heard screaming. That could have been him. Every time I close my eyes I imagine him screaming for Daddy, screaming for me to save him. But I didn't, I didn't save him. I didn't even know he was in danger. You want to know what I was doing as my son died? I was solving a plot problem. Oh, but wait. It gets better. I didn't save my son, but your son? Your son who doesn't give a flying fuck whether he lives or dies? Him I could save."

Part of her wanted to yell, *You're wrong, my son does care.* But it would be a lie. She choked back bile.

"Willie?"

Will whirled around. "Jesus," he muttered. "Dad, Dad, I—"

"Willie? Why you talkin' that way about my grandbaby?"

Will gulped for air as if he was hyperventilating.

She was trapped inside a slow-moving nightmare, her body frozen in time. Her vision blurred as the world slipped away; the thud of her heartbeat stifled every sound in the forest. Will's son was dead. A child, a five-year-old child, was dead.

"Freddie died, Dad. He's dead. Killed."

"But the Great European Adventure?" Jacob dropped the cardboard tube. Poppy picked it up and leaned it against the dining room window.

"A story I made up." Will closed his eyes. "Freddie died in a car wreck in New York, on July 1 at 8:30 p.m. He was with his mother and her new lover. Single-vehicle accident. No survivors."

"The heiress?" Poppy said. "*She* was Freddie's mother? But the press said—"

"I have a well-paid, well-oiled P.R. machine. So does her family." Will spat out his words.

Hannah clutched at her throat, and her pulse banged against her thumb.

"Them nightmares, they was real?" Jacob swayed and Poppy helped him down onto the rocker. "Why, Willie? Why did you lie to me, boy?"

"Why did you lie to me about Mom, pretend she was okay?"

"For you, son."

"I did the same, Dad. I did the same."

Hannah inhaled through her mouth, then exhaled. Breathed in, breathed out, and inched toward Will. She tried to say his name, but nothing came out. Touch him, she had to touch him. Her hand moved forward and Will grabbed it, tightening his grip until she gasped.

"I should have known better. I should have learned something from the lies. I certainly had enough time to think about it during all those hours you locked me in my room when I was a kid. I never understood why you did that, Dad. Why did you put me in my bedroom and turn the key in the lock? Why?"

"So you wouldn't see your mama when the demons took her. And sometimes I needed to go find her, bring her home."

"Didn't you realize how scared I was? How alone I felt?"

"I—I wanted you safe, son. Wanted you hidden so you'd be safe."

"But it only made me resent you and hate her."

"Don't speak about your mama that way."

"Why not? She ruined our lives because she wouldn't admit she needed help, and you enabled her."

"She were a free spirit, Willie. I let her be herself."

"She was batshit insane."

"You will not talk about your mama that way. You won't, you hear me? She loved you, son. She just…" Poppy put her arm around Jacob. "Motherin' were real hard for her, real hard. But she were so proud. She told everyone about her son."

"She told me," Hannah said.

Three pairs of eyes stared at her.

"I met her once—she brought me Rosie. She was leaving when she saw a picture of the boys. She said her son had just become a father, and she was so proud because he would be a good dad, the best."

"Why didn't you tell me?" Will released her hand, and she flexed her fingers.

"I'm sorry, it was such a brief exchange and…I didn't remember that part until now."

"She wanted to be a grandmama real bad," Jacob said. "Maybe they're together. You reckon they're together?" He turned to Poppy. "I never wanted to think of my Angeline alone under the dirt. I wanted to think of her runnin' wild in the forest, like the wind. You reckon Freddie's with her? You think they're together?"

"I think so, honey." Poppy kissed his cheek.

"So, Freddie's passed on?" Jacob said.

"You knew and then you didn't. And I…I just…couldn't. Couldn't do it. Couldn't tell you again. Tell you he was—" Will buckled and collapsed onto his knees. "I want him back, Dad. I miss him so much and I just…I just…need him back. I don't know what to do with this pain. I don't know how to be without him. It hurts so much, Dad. I can't do it. I can't." He thrust the heels of his hands into his eyes and began rocking.

Hannah sank down in front of him and eased his head onto her chest. In the distance, bottles and cans clunked into the recycling truck. Their world was imploding, and it was recycling day.

Will pulled himself up. "How do you live without Mom?"

"I have you, son. And I have her stories." Jacob patted his heart. "And I have the forest. And I have this beautiful day."

Jacob was so calm—shockingly so. Had he known all along? Had some part of him believed the nightmares but he, too, had chosen the better story? Jacob stood—strong and tall and straight. People talked about she-bears protecting their cubs but what about father bears?

"There'll be no more talk of goin' back to the city, son. You'll be stayin' here with your people, with your kin."

"I'm sorry, Dad. I'm sorry. I'm so used to looking after myself, and then Freddie blasted my world apart, and I can't, I just can't…" Finally, he spoke to Hannah. "And I wanted to tell you, but I couldn't, I couldn't—"

"Poppy," Hannah said. "Take Jacob back inside and serve some of that carrot cake you brought over earlier. Will and I are going to stay here for a while."

"Come on, Handsome," Poppy said. "We're on refreshment duty. Do you know I make the best carrot cake in the county? Cream cheese frosting to die for." And she led Jacob inside.


Exhausted. He was exhausted.

"I just want to sleep," Will said.

"I know, baby, but you can't do it on the gravel. Can you stand?"

He shook his head.

"When you're ready, I'm going to help you inside. You're going to lie down in my bed, and I'm going to bring you something to help you sleep."

Yes, that's exactly what he wanted: to lose himself in Hannah's white bed with the overstuffed pillows. To sleep and never wake up. The gravel bit into his knees, but he couldn't move. Not yet. Not till he'd told her everything.

"Galen knows, about Freddie. I had to explain why I couldn't come back. Are you hurt that I told him the truth and not you?"

"You had your reasons, Will, and rehashing what's done is pointless. Galen is a kind soul. He was a good choice."

But she needed to hear everything, to understand.

"I nearly told you so many times, but I knew if I did, I'd be asking you to lie to my dad. When I told Dad that Freddie had been—" he hesitated "—killed, it was a really bad scene. I drove down in the middle of the night to tell him in person, and it was awful. They had to sedate him. And then, when he started talking about Freddie's journey, the staff assumed he was delusional. I didn't mean to lie to him, but he was driving me crazy—drinking every night, trapped in this loop of forgetting, repeating himself over and over. Angry all the time. And one day he just forgot about the accident and I couldn't..."

"It's okay, Will. You don't have to explain."

But he did. He'd spent his life retreating, always feeling he'd said too much when he'd said nothing at all. For once, he wanted a different ending. For once, he wanted to tell the truth. Since leaving New York, he'd been struggling to hold on, refusing to let go. Every climber knew a controlled fall was the only way to avoid injury. And yet he'd hung on to the bitter end, made the worst climbing mistake. Until Hannah had pushed him.

"No, no, I do have to explain. Because I told myself I was doing it for Dad, and it worked. He was calmer, drinking less. But life became a little easier for me, too. I could think about Freddie in the present tense. Dad's memory sucked away everything I didn't want to confront, gave me the excuse I needed to rewrite my own story. I wanted so hard to forget, and then all I wanted was to remember." He blinked and took a deep breath. "In the beginning, I lied for Dad, but I kept lying for myself. My life is about me, Will Shepard. Always has been. The only person I know how to protect is me. You hate me now. Do you? Hate me?"

Crows cawed, mocking him the same way they'd done when he was a kid hiding from his mom.

"This changes nothing, Will. You've been protecting yourself since you were a kid because you've had no choice. You had to survive. I've watched you with your dad and with my son. You're kind and generous, and you don't deserve this." She paused. "I'm so sorry about Freddie. Losing a child, I can't imagine."

"But I think you're the one person who can. You've faced that fear every day since Galen came home. If I stay here, with you, will you help me figure out how to let Freddie go?"

She nodded.

He cupped her face. "Also…I think I…you know." Last time he told someone he loved her, it didn't work out so well. Why do it again now, in this moment of despair? He moved closer and kissed her. A first kiss, a last kiss, and everything in between.

She tasted of tears.

Her mouth was soft and warm, her kiss tentative, as if she knew she could crush him.

"You going to break my heart?" He rested his forehead against hers and wove his fingers into her hair.

"You going to break mine the first time a cute young babe gives you the eye?"

"You think I'm that shallow?"

"No, I'm thinking my AARP card will come in the mail eleven years before yours."

"Ten. I turn thirty-five on Christmas Eve. I want you in my life, Hannah. I want the fairy tale." He twisted one of her curls around his index finger and tugged it gently across his lips. When he was ready to climb back into life, she would be his anchor. "What's Liam like?"

"Feisty. Galen's the easy one. At least—" she hesitated "—he was."

"We need to get him writing again. Writing saved me once, it can save him, too."

"Will?"

"Yeah?"

"Tell me you love me."

"I do," he whispered. "I do love you."

"Louder."

He stood up and pulled her with him. Then he took a deep breath and inhaled wood smoke and lavender—the smells of home.

"I love you," he said. What words! What strength they gave him! His heart, his lungs, seemed to expand, to fill his chest.

"I love this woman!" he shouted into the sky.

And somewhere on Saponi Mountain, he thought he heard drums.

# THIRTY-FOUR

*Christmas Eve*

Will blew on his fingers and went back to typing. It was sixty degrees, ridiculously mild for late December, but the sun had begun its descent, and his corner of the porch was sinking into shade. Hannah was worried it was too warm for a Christmas Eve fire, but Will and Galen had spent the morning splitting logs. Even if they had to turn on the air-conditioning and wear shorts, she would have her fire.

Inside the house, his dad and Galen were decorating the Charlie Brown Christmas tree chosen by Galen for its deformity. Decorating the tree had always, apparently, been a family affair, and every day for the past week the damn thing sat outside in a bucket—a painful reminder that Will was the cause of a family rift. Liam was home for the break but refusing to visit. Sadly, this didn't prevent Hannah's youngest from huffing and puffing via phone. Will had been called many names before but never a gigolo. Pretty ironic, considering Inigo's living arrangements.

At least the old man was quietly content these days. There were moments—heart-crushing moments—when his dad called Galen Freddie, and as if by secret agreement, no one corrected him. The old man would still need full-time care but, with any luck, not before they were in the new house with the caregiver annex—plus caregiver, now that Poppy worked for Hannah.

His dad had also been teaching Galen to make primitive weaponry, and at Galen's suggestion, they were putting together a demonstration for local elementary schools. Galen had proved to be surprisingly gifted—both with his hands and in his care of the elderly. Come spring, all three of them would be helping with the tribe's Homeland Preservation Project. A future that Will could never have imagined was evolving, gaining substance. Giving hope.

*Right.*

Will cracked his knuckles and stared at the half-full page on the screen. *Make word count before dinner.* Dinner with birthday cake and candles. Hadn't had too many of those in the past thirty years.

He scratched his neck, then pummeled the lumps in the cushion behind his back, but his mind refused to budge. It was stuck on Hannah's birthday present. *A lunchtime quickie,* she'd whispered as she'd dragged him into the bathroom, pushed him against the door and used her mouth to shush his moans. They'd done it standing up. Earth-shattering sex with the woman he loved—best birthday present ever.

Two squirrels chased each other across the gravel, and guilt slunk into his gut. Some days he felt no pain at all; others, it twisted like a dagger. How could he disappear into passion when he should be lost in despair? His first birthday, first Christmas Eve, first Christmas without Freddie—each one a glass wall of grief impossible to scale.

*Happy Christmas Eve, Munchkin. Daddy loves you.*

Love and loss were learning to coexist but in a tentative balance that was easily tipped. Galen understood better than anyone. They had resumed their evening therapy of two—brought forward to 9:00 p.m., the time Freddie was pronounced dead. There would be no more anniversaries spent alone. And eleven o'clock was now reserved for Hannah. Finally, Will fell asleep holding someone instead of wrestling images of his door cracking open and Freddie saying, *Daddy, can I sleep with you?*

His cheerleading squad of two—Hannah and Galen—had also encouraged Will to walk away from Agent Dodds. No one else applauded this midcareer detour. Or death, according to his agent. Eventually he would come back to Agent Dodds, but for the first time in his life, he wanted to write nonfiction, even if it hadn't turned out as planned. After the second interview with his dad, Will had realized he wasn't excavating a family memoir about mental illness—he was uncovering a love story.

Growing up, he'd never understood why his dad didn't leave. Now that love had become his guide through grief, everything made sense. In the bedlam of his parents' marriage, his dad had held on to unconditional love. Jacob had sacrificed so much, and yet, as he'd pointed out, walking away from music had been his choice. There'd been room for only one passion in his life and that had been his Angeline. *Such music we had, Willie. Such music.*

Will had always seen his parents as trapped in empty, unfulfilled lives, but he'd been wrong. The focus of their relationship was love, not insanity. And now, with his failing mind, his dad's love for his mom was the one memory that never faltered, that cast its shadow over everything. *The Memory Shadow* was his working title.

Muffled music came through the closed window. For a second, Will was the little kid in his footed pj's who'd snuck out of bed to watch his parents dance. Sometimes his mom pushed aside all the furniture in the main room, and his parents danced into exhaustion. His dad moved elegantly with a natural sense of rhythm; his mom moved like a hummingbird. Sometimes Will joined them and visualized the music pulsing through his blood stream. Really, it had been a form of mindfulness, filling him with the same focus, the same meditative calm, as rock climbing.

*What the hell. It was close enough to quitting time.*

Will hit Save, slotted in his flash drive and backed up his work-in-progress. He hadn't written much today, but what he'd produced was damn good. Writing during daylight hours was new and unexpected, as were the challenges of working in a house crammed with noise. He'd tried writing in his old bedroom over at the cottage, but the downstairs was alive with pets, and Poppy was an impossible housemate with a penchant for Green Day. He liked "21 Guns" well enough, but not vibrating through the walls for two hours straight.

Continuing the theme of musical beds, his dad had taken over Liam's old room—another source of irritation for Liam—which meant the only place Will could write in peace was on the porch. And truthfully, working outside with a view of the forest was inspiring. As a kid, he used to run into the forest with his notebook, hide in his secret den and scribble imaginary adventures. In some strange way, he was rediscovering the joy of creating those first stories.

Will snapped his laptop shut and breathed in wood smoke. Galen and the old man must have started the fire. He should go inside and help, but the need to wait for Hannah, to have her to himself for two minutes, eclipsed everything.

On Saponi Mountain, naked branches rose to heaven like

arms held up in prayer. Tomorrow they would spread Freddie's ashes up there on the new property—bring him home to his roots with a small ceremony planned for the late afternoon. But Will had another idea, one he was eager to share with Hannah. Maybe they should keep some of Freddie's ashes to spread on his mom's grave. What a Christmas gift that would be for his dad.

A column of smoke rose from Hannah's chimney—their chimney—and drifted into the sky. A flock of Canada geese flew over, honking; four vultures circled, and the hawks called to one another on the edge of the forest. Soon, all the birds except for the owl would retreat from the night. Owls fascinated him, always had. Despite their perfect night vision, despite heads that could swivel to see anything within a two-hundred-and-seventy-degree radius, their eyes couldn't focus on what lay directly in front of them.

Well, he knew what was in front of him, and he would never, ever take her for granted. Will stood, stretched and smiled toward the cottage. Any minute now, he would see Hannah.

He turned as the front door opened, and Galen stuck his head outside.

"Did you proof 'The Space Between Emotions'?" he said.

Will pulled the poem from under his laptop. "Fantastic, man. It's ready to submit."

Galen nodded, then gave a half smile. He was still way too hard on himself, but every now and then a glimmer of self-belief escaped. The first time Will tore apart one of Galen's poems, he was worried he'd gone too far. But then Galen confided that the poem was a reject. On some level, Galen had been testing him, and he'd passed.

"Listen, can we skip tomorrow morning's run?" Will rubbed his shin. A bit overly dramatic, but some lies, little white ones, were necessary. Galen's first dry Christmas would be tough; he didn't need to know about the mimosas Will and Hannah would have in bed before anyone else was up. "I think I pulled something today."

"Sure," Galen said.

"So, while your mom's not around. What did Liam say?"

"You don't want to know."

"He's never going to agree to meet with me, is he?"

"Enjoy the peace. Writing with him in the house is impossible."

It could get *worse*? He needed to call the architect—fast-track those plans.

"Mom still working?" Galen frowned.

"She's got five more minutes, then I pull the plug. You guys started the fire already?"

"Your dad insisted. He takes Mom's wishes seriously. She only has to say, 'We're going to have a fire tonight,' and he's on a mission to make it happen. He threw on the hickory, too."

"How did he seem this afternoon?"

"Good. I introduced him to Mumford and Sons." Galen opened the door wide and sounds of folk rock—heavy on the banjo—drifted onto the porch. "And we've been reading Robert Frost. Jacob's not as uneducated as he makes out, is he?"

"Don't be fooled by the whole 'droppin' out of high school to work in the cotton mill—third shift—before I were a grave digger.' Ask him about his song lyrics."

"Your dad used to write lyrics? Wow. That's rad."

Will grinned. "Radical, indeed."

Galen went back inside, and Will watched the cottage door. The lights went off, and there was *his* angel. Wearing jeans, clogs and a UNC sweatshirt that was practically a museum piece, Hannah had never looked more beautiful. She turned to talk to Rosie and then threw him a coy smile that said, *I remember lunchtime, too.* Her smile just about undid him.

Will jumped down the porch steps and ran to her, his body buzzing. He needed to touch her, to ground himself in her kiss. Sweeping her into his arms, he twirled her around.

"First things first. The cell phone stays off for the next twenty-four hours. Hand it over."

She did and he tucked it into his back pocket, keeping his left arm firmly around her waist.

"Good." He tugged her closer. "Now kiss me like you mean it."

"That's quite a welcome, considering I haven't seen you in at least three hours."

He loved her laugh almost as much as her smile, and when she was this close, he couldn't see, couldn't smell, couldn't hear anything but Hannah. He didn't deserve to be this happy, but he couldn't help it. His hands crawled under her sweatshirt, tugged up her T-shirt and lost themselves in warm, soft skin.

"Stop. I don't want to give your father a heart attack or send my son back to the psych ward."

His hands retreated and Hannah fingered the necklace of bear claws his dad had given him for his birthday. Then she snuggled into him, filling the empty space that surrounded him on today of all days. For a while they stood still, holding each other. If he concentrated, he might hear the forest breathe. His mom had loved this part of the day, when the light of the gloaming burst golden rich through the trees.

"I love the gloaming," Hannah said. "My mother used to say it was a time of endings and beginnings. I think she stole that from her Scottish mother."

He smacked a kiss on her cheek.

"What?" Hannah looked up.

"You, reading my thoughts—you having a Scottish grand-mother, too. You, being connected to me by invisible threads. Mom always said the gloaming was magical."

"I agree. It's so fleeting, over so quickly, and yet it seems as if the clocks slow down and time can stretch to whatever you want it to be. It's not quite day, it's not quite night—it's like being caught between possibilities."

"Or between two worlds and not belonging to either."

"Are you projecting?" She chewed on the corner of her lip, one of many habits he'd come to adore.

"I'm being honest. I always want to be honest with you. No secrets, no lies. Not between us." He traced her lips with his finger. "I've spent the past thirty-five years feeling as if I didn't belong anywhere with anyone."

"And now?"

"Now I'm home." He buried his face in her hair and inhaled miracles.

"So, did you slip any last-minute gifts under the Christmas tree?"

He straightened up. "Selling my Manhattan penthouse so I could buy you twenty acres of prime real estate on Saponi Mountain and hire the best architect in Chapel Hill to design our dream house wasn't enough, woman?"

"Nuh-uh."

"How about my undying love for all eternity?"

"Perfect," she said.

"And what do I get out of this deal?"

"A trip or two to a sweat lodge. And did I mention the life-time of sex with the full-coverage, money-back guarantee?"

He grabbed her ass and squeezed. "Maybe I should switch genres, start writing erotica. Which would mean an exhaust-ing amount of hands-on research."

"You authors are so demanding."

"And one other thing."

She raised her eyebrows.

"Dance with me."

Will closed his eyes and kissed her, letting pure, unfettered passion guide his lips. But Hannah pulled back.

"What's wrong, darling?" he said.

A Jeep had parked in front of the cottage, and a young man in ripped jeans with studded black leather buckles around both wrists and a mess of dyed black hair climbed out. His earlobes were stapled with multiple hoops, and was that a nose stud glinting in his right nostril? *Gross.* If Will were casting him as a character, Liam would definitely be the bad-boy rocker. Gone to seed with a nasty coke habit.

"Not interrupting, am I?" Liam peered over the top of his sunglasses. His eyes were even deeper blue than Hannah's. And scary as shit.

Hannah rushed to Liam and hugged him. Family resemblance flashed between mother and son—their expressions identical—and Will squirmed like a teenager caught with his hand shoved into his girlfriend's bra. This was *so* not how he'd planned to meet the errant son.

"Sweetheart! Why didn't you call?" Hannah said.

"Thought I'd surprise you." Liam sneered. "Seems I did."

"Are you staying for dinner?" Hannah's voice was higher than usual.

"Undecided. Galen's been on my case to swing by, pick up some gift for Dad. I was in the neighborhood so I thought, like, why not?"

"Well, come in." Hannah linked her arm through Liam's.

Time to take the situation by the jugular. Be the authority figure, behave like a father. "Hannah, can I talk to Liam alone?"

She gave Will an uncertain smile. "Of course. I'll see you both inside."

Liam lit a cigarette, took a deep drag and exhaled. Will tried not to stare at the purple nail polish.

The front door opened and closed.

"So. You're Will."

"So. You're Liam."

"Happy thirty-fifth birthday."

"Thanks."

Liam removed his sunglasses and slotted them into the vee of his T-shirt. Black, of course. Also ripped, although the slashes looked very symmetrical, very well-designed. Very expensive. Might have to rethink the typecasting. Maybe more of a dealer than an addict?

Liam tapped ash onto the gravel. "I didn't bring a present."

"I didn't expect one."

"I hear you saved my big bro's life."

"More of a group effort."

Liam smiled as if his mouth were full of poison darts. Then he leaned toward Will. "Just so you and I are on the same *page*—you break my mom's heart and I'll snap every bone in your writing hand."

Will nearly said, *I'd like to see you try.* Liam might have the advantage of height, but he seemed more of a party animal than a gym bunny. The gray circles under his eyes bellowed hangover.

"And if I were your stepdad?" On the off-chance Liam was hanging around for Hannah's traditional Christmas Eve exchange of presents, he might as well be prepared.

"You, like, asking for my permission?" Liam took another drag, then blew a smoke ring. A guy who blew perfect smoke rings all the time, no doubt.

"You know I'm a rock climber, right?"

"My bro mentioned it. In passing."

"Well, when you're climbing, the most important part of the protection system is the anchor."

"That so?"

Will swallowed. "From the moment she entered my life, your mother has been my fail-safe anchor, the one that's strong enough to hold no matter what the climber does."

"You better not be comparing my mom to a piece of sports equipment." Liam's eyes became slits.

"No. I'm saying that for the first time in my life, I feel safe with my feet on the ground. I belong here, with your mother, and I'm not leaving. Which means you and I need to figure out how to deal with each other. I won't ask her to choose between us, and I hope you won't, either."

"Are you going to make me call you Dad?"

"As if, dude."

"Well, then." Liam gave a smile, a real one, and extended his hand. "Welcome to the family, Will."

★ ★ ★ ★ ★

# ACKNOWLEDGMENTS

*The In-Between Hour* was written during a succession of personal crises that helped me dig deep to connect with my characters… but created horrible hiccups with deadlines. Never-ending gratitude for the support of my amazing agent, Nalini Akolekar of Spencerhill Associates, and huge thanks to the team at Harlequin MIRA for enabling me to put family first.

I was blessed to work with not one but two MIRA editors on this novel. To Miranda Indrigo, thank you for believing in my beloved Will. To Emily Ohanjanians, thank you for graciously leading me toward a better story, for not letting me take shortcuts, for suggesting I put Will on the rock and for loving Jacob as much as I do. Your revisions inspired me.

Group hug with my brothers- and sisters-in-arms at Book Pregnant, especially cofounders Lydia Netzer and Sophie Perinot, and my personal heroine, Anne Clinard Barnhill. Wiley described us as a wolf pack. Oh, we are. I can't imagine being on this journey without you guys. (Besides, I get to bask in your publishing glory.)

Thanks to fellow MIRA authors Pamela Morsi and Rebecca Coleman for adopting the clueless newbie, and to Laura Drake and Laura Spinella, who never hide from emails that scream, *Help!* Special thanks—with penance—to Charmi Schroeder, whom I forgot to mention last time.

Thank you to the local booksellers who have helped make the transition to published author fun and memorable, especially the staff at Flyleaf Books in Chapel Hill and Sharon Wheeler at Purple Crow Books in Hillsborough.

Thank you to everyone who helped with research and apologies for any facts I have mangled: thank you to Jennifer Carruthers, Kelly Hammer and Loran Smith for trying to explain climbing to someone who's terrified of heights; thank you to Perrin Hammond Heartway for showing me the life of a holistic vet; thank you to Bonnie Hauser and Marilee Mctigue for all things Orange County; thank you to Steve Barrell, Lisa Brown and Steve Rogat for helping me understand what it means to be an empath. Sergeant Butch Clark, thank you for the information on Project Lifesaver; Lori Hilliard— thank you for helping with tree identification! To Dan Hill, thank you for teaching me *batshit insane* and such great phrases as *Teflon-coated procrastination.* (Where would I be without my Dan file?) Thanks to Dr. Jack Naftel and Laura Catherine Newton in the Department of Psychiatry, School of Medicine, of the University of North Carolina. And endless gratitude to Caroline Furman, Kathleen Gleiter, Harriet Ling, Della Pollock, Maureen Sherbondy, Stephen Whitney and Carolyn Wilson for helping me find—and understand—this story.

Special thanks to John Blackfeather Jeffries and his wife, Lynette Jeffries, for sharing their memories, photographs and scrapbooks. I wish I could spend all day every day listening to both of you talk. And apologies for pushing the 2013 powwow into October to fit my story!

Thank you—and thank you again—to my writing partners Elizabeth Brown and Sheryl Cornett, who helped brainstorm, read various versions of the manuscript and listened to all my freak-outs. Thank you to reader Karen Perizzolo, who picked up on so many details I had wrong and helped clarify the all-important birdsong issue. A million thanks to my beta reader, Leslie Gildersleeve, who gives brutal and brilliant feedback topped off with Friday-afternoon gin therapy. This one's for you, girl.

Bowing and scraping to Julie Smith and her one-woman mission to sell TUG one book at a time—and for providing comfort food, and for helping me research depression and bipolar disorder. A friend indeed!

As always, thanks to my transatlantic village—friends and family on both sides of the pond, and a teary farewell to the staff and teachers of Camelot Academy in Durham, North Carolina.

Love and kisses to my mother, Anne Claypole White, chief cheerleader, and to my sister, Susan Rose, a gifted artist who has been entertaining me with her storytelling since I was a child. A wave to the memory of my father, Reverend Douglas Eric Claypole White, who passed on his fascination with Native American history and culture—and his sense of humor.

Mother/son hug for my award-winning poet, lyricist and musician, Zachariah Claypole White, who provided invaluable feedback, encouraged me to believe in my "quiet story that screams" and allowed me to steal "traveling faces" and "the space between emotions." Please never ignore texts that say, Word choice emergency!

And to my husband, Lawrence Grossberg: I'm so glad you stalked me at JFK Airport twenty-seven years ago. Thank you for supporting a penniless writer and soldiering through domestic chaos so she could be a dreamer. (And for critiquing every blog post.) Without you—nothing.

# THE
# IN-BETWEEN
# HOUR

## BARBARA CLAYPOLE WHITE

## Reader's Guide

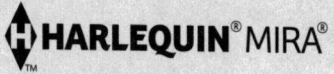

1. A label of mental illness still carries a stigma in our society. Will has spent his life running from this shadow, and it has made him intensely private. Does your family have any experience of mental illness, and if so, have you struggled to find the balance between the public and the private? Do you think we have made any progress against the stigma?

2. How do you feel about Will's relationship with his mother? Do you think he should have accepted and made allowances for her behavior in the way that his father did, or do you think Will was right to call Jacob an enabler?

3. Will pretends Freddie is traveling in a moment of exhaustion and grief, but he makes a conscious decision to keep the story—and Freddie—alive. What do you think of Will's actions?

4. Do you believe grief manifests differently in everyone and that we all find unique ways of coping? Is Will merely trying

to survive the unimaginable by leaning on the one thing he can control—storytelling?

5. Hannah believes that there is living, breathing history on Saponi Mountain. Will echoes that thought when he sees pictures of Hitler's anti-aircraft flak tower. Do you believe that places or buildings can retain an imprint of the past almost like a stored memory?

6. What do you think of Hannah's comment that family life is never about the picket fence and the dinner rolls but about surviving crises? What do you think of Will's comment that no one knows what happens once a family shuts the door and pulls the curtains?

7. What do you make of Hannah and Will's connection through Rosie? Do you believe in fate, or do you see their relationship as growing out of a chain of events orchestrated by Poppy and Jacob? What do you make of Will's comment that they fell in love because of, not despite, their respective family dramas?

8. The North Carolina forest is an important element of the story. How does the setting impact each character? Can you imagine the story working in a different setting?

9. The line between truth and lies blurs constantly in the novel. Do you agree that lying—or spinning a story—is sometimes necessary to protect loved ones? Why do you think Will and Cass worked so hard to keep Freddie's paternity secret? Do you think it was realistic to assume they could do so? Do you think Hannah was right to hide her father's suicide from her sons? What would you have done?

10. What do you think the future holds for Galen? Do you see him finding ways to cope with his depression?

11. In your opinion, what is the significance of the title, and how does it relate to each character's story?

LISTENING GUIDE

*"The Ghosts That We Knew"* - Mumford & Sons
*"Hymn to Her"* - Chrissie Hynde
*"Under Control"* - The Strokes
*"Flashing Red Light Means Go"* - The Boxer Rebellion
*"Save Me"* - Muse
*"Horseshoes and Handgrenades"* - Green Day
*"Lover of the Light"* - Mumford & Sons
*"Who's Gonna Ride Your Wild Horses"* - U2
*"Ultraviolet (Light My Way)"* - U2
*"Maps"* - Yeah Yeah Yeahs
*"Half of Something Else"* - The Airborne Toxic Event
*"Two-Headed Boy"* - Neutral Milk Hotel
*"Explorers"* - Muse
*"Shadows and Light"* - Simple Minds
*"Never Too Late"* - Three Days Grace
*"Famous Last Words"* - My Chemical Romance
*"Safe"* - The Airborne Toxic Event
*"Dear Alyssa"* - The Arcadian Project
*"Sorry For It All"* - Dead Sara
*"In Between Days"* - The Cure
*"Timeless"* - The Airborne Toxic Event
*"I Will Wait"* - Mumford & Sons

**What was the inspiration for this story?**

*As with* The Unfinished Garden, *the original story seed came from a dark what-if moment in my own life. An older family member was experiencing short-term memory loss that generated anger, confusion and a string of emotionally exhausting phone calls. In the middle of one of those phone calls, I had a terrible thought—could life get any worse? I decided, yes, it could. And my mind created Will's dilemma.*

*Memory, grief, mental illness, rural Orange County...ideas started swirling and I did what I always do—I followed my gut, my curiosity and my research. I'd been toying with a ghost story, and that idea had already unearthed threads about psychic healing, rock climbing, Native American spirituality and animal guides. All those roads led to Will and Jacob. Poppy popped out pretty much formed, and Galen evolved while several people close to me were battling depression. (Echoes of my life run through everything I write.)*

My real problem was Hannah. Finding empathy for a holistic vet was quite a challenge, since we don't even own a goldfish. I started out with false assumptions about Hannah and found her too calm and too spiritual. I agree with Galen—she's a hard person to read. But when my son relapsed into crippling obsessive-compulsive disorder (OCD), Hannah suddenly lit up for me. I realized she was just another terrified parent. I also learned that being the mother of a child struggling with mental illness is very different to being the mother of a young man in the same situation. That was something I wanted to explore further and I did, through Hannah's journey.

**What did you enjoy most about researching and writing *The In-Between Hour*?**

My research took me to places I couldn't imagine, but my favorite part was hanging out with John "Blackfeather" Jeffries, former Chief of the Occaneechi Band of the Saponi Nation. The first time we met, I turned up with a string of questions. Within minutes I abandoned the interview and just listened. John told me so many wonderful stories about his childhood, his family history and the history of the tribe that I lost track of time and almost missed school pickup. The second time I was smart enough to take a recorder! We spent hours looking through his scrapbooks from the excavation of the ghost field and the reconstruction of the living village. John's shed is the best-kept secret in Hillsborough. It's a museum of living history.

**What do you hope your readers will take away from this novel?**

The In-Between Hour is about two broken families coming together to heal. I hope readers will find it an uplifting story of redemption and community, and a story that reveals light in the darkness of grief and mental illness.

**The story is an emotional read that explores dark issues. Was it a challenge to write some of the scenes?**

*I went through a string of personal crises while writing the manuscript, and the characters became my escape and my therapy. I found it surprisingly easy to walk out of my problems and into theirs, but the trick was finding emotional distance, especially from Hannah. I didn't want to project my family's struggle with OCD onto her family's struggle with depression. The scene that was the most emotional for me was the one in which Will breaks down. It's hard to put yourself into the thoughts of a grieving parent and stay detached. On the flip side, the suicide scene was surprisingly easy to write, because Galen is at peace with his decision.*

**Do you have a favorite scene?**

*Please don't think I'm a sick person, but the post-suicide scene is my favorite. I love the interaction between Will and Hannah, and I love the way the action unfolds. I wasn't sure I could write action, but a friend helped me choreograph it, and I was thrilled with the result. We really did act out most of the scene! (Yes, alcohol was involved.)*

**How did you create the character of Angeline? Is there a reason that Will never attempts to diagnose her?**

*The character of Angeline was inspired by the idea of families keeping secrets, whether those secrets involve alcoholism or mental illness. I started by researching various diagnoses and reading a number of memoirs, but Angeline quickly became her own character—wildly creative with severe mood swings. In the end I decided she should have no label since she was never diagnosed. I also found the impact of her behavior on family life more intriguing than the source of her demons. The reality,* too, is that many people with mental illness are misdiagnosed. (That happened in our family.)

**Can you explain your fascination with mental illness?**

*My aunt, who lived with us for a while when I was growing up, was diagnosed in later life with paranoid schizophrenia. Even as a child, I struggled to understand why she led such a seemingly empty life—always treated as if she were frail and always kept apart from others. My grandmother worked tirelessly to shield her from what she perceived as the shame of mental illness. When my son was diagnosed with OCD at a young age, I wanted the opposite for him. I'm drawn to memoirs and stories that find hope in the darkness of mental illness, because I need that hope for my son. I also struggle with the stereotypes of mental illness in popular culture—especially those of OCD. So often the focus is on failure or weird behaviors and not on the incredible courage it takes to live a life framed by mental illness, to admit to that diagnosis publicly and to fight back. (For the record, my son is academically gifted, and an award-winning poet, lyricist and musician. I am incredibly proud of him.)*

**Both your debut novel, *The Unfinished Garden*, and *The In-Between Hour* touch on grief. Why do you write about loss?**

*My father died when I was in my late thirties, and my subsequent grief was a very isolating experience. No one close to me had lost a loved one, and I didn't know how to make sense of my thoughts, especially the layers of guilt. I tried to be strong for my mother, and I tried to pretend I was coping, but I'm a creature of emotion. The moment I collapsed and dumped on my husband, I began to find my way forward. I believe strength comes from admitting you're struggling and seeking help. You have to face the monsters within.*

**Woodland settings figure heavily in your writing. Do you, like your characters, have a special connection to the North Carolina forest?**

*My mother teases me that when I moved to London I said, "As long as I can see one tree from my bedroom window, I'll be fine." I don't know where my love of the forest comes from. Even though I grew up in an English village surrounded by open countryside with rolling fields, I had this fantasy of a bathroom with a huge window that looked into woods. The moment I stepped into our house—and saw the view—I felt as if I had come home. We live in the middle of the forest, at the bottom of a very steep hill that inspired Saponi Mountain. I love woodland gardening; I love watching the seasons change through the leaves; and I love the way the light of the gloaming makes the treetops shine gold. My original title for this novel was The Gloaming.*

**Why do twists of fate play an important role in your fiction?**

*In my mid-twenties, I was working in the London fashion industry and focused on my goal of becoming an assistant fashion editor. When I failed to snag the job of my dreams, I was devastated. My boss suggested going to work for her husband, and a few months later my new job took me to New York. Flying home through JFK Airport, I started talking with this guy. We discovered we were on the same flight and swapped seats to sit next to each other. Even though we chatted the entire way across the Atlantic, we never exchanged last names. (I know, really?) After we landed at Heathrow, I was stuck in customs for two hours and assumed I would never see him again. But I emerged in arrivals and there he was—desperate to pee but too terrified to move in case he missed me. He was a sweatshirt-clad professor living in a small Midwest college town; I was a London fashionista with a wardrobe of designer leather skirts. I was the daughter of an Anglican priest; he was* the grandson of a Hassidic rabbi. I grew up in rural England; he grew up in Brooklyn. He was divorced and thirty-eight; I was twenty-four and determined to stay single. Last summer we celebrated our twenty-fifth wedding anniversary. Now ask me why I believe in fate....